'Fleur McDonald has woven a captivating story set in rural Australia. Dave Burrows has become an all-time favourite with readers . . . *Rising Dust* is the perfect, gripping page-turner for a comfortable afternoon on the couch.'

Blue Wolf Reviews

'*Rising Dust* successfully moves between Dave's investigative efforts and his personal life issues. A compelling link to the past ties all the respective threads of this arc together, creating one magnetising read from the beginning right until the very end of this story . . . *Rising Dust* is another winning rural Aussie crime suspense tale and I'm looking forward to my next thrilling visit to Detective Dave's rural patch soon!'

Mrs B's Book Reviews

'McDonald is to be given kudos for capturing the essence of the Australian agricultural industry.'

The Rural

'Detective Dave Burrows is my hero!'

Reading, Writing and Riesling

'McDonald's characters are meaty and convincing and she has a skill of depicting rural life and the sense of community that is often embedded in country areas.'

Weekly Times

Fleur McDonald has lived and worked on farms for much of her life. After growing up in the small town of Orroroo in South Australia, she went jillarooing, eventually co-owning an 8000-acre property in regional Western Australia.

Fleur likes to write about strong women overcoming adversity, drawing inspiration from her own experiences in rural Australia. She has two children and an energetic kelpie.

Website: www.fleurmcdonald.com
Facebook: FleurMcDonaldAuthor
Instagram: fleurmcdonald

FLEUR
McDONALD
Rising Dust

ALLEN&UNWIN
SYDNEY · MELBOURNE · AUCKLAND · LONDON

This edition published in 2023
First published in 2022

Allen & Unwin
Cammeraygal Country
83 Alexander Street
Crows Nest NSW 2065
Australia
Phone: (61 2) 8425 0100
Email: info@allenandunwin.com
Web: www.allenandunwin.com

Allen & Unwin acknowledges the Traditional Owners of the Country on which we live and work. We pay our respects to all Aboriginal and Torres Strait Islander Elders, past and present.

A catalogue record for this book is available from the National Library of Australia

ISBN 978 1 76106 881 2

Set in Sabon LT Pro by Bookhouse, Sydney
Printed and bound in Australia by the Opus Group

10 9 8 7 6 5 4 3 2 1

*To the best tech guru I know, and who doubles
as my godson, Alex. He saved this book
from disaster, twice, so you all could read it.
Alex, I now know how to save files so much better!*

*And to those who are precious—what was, still is,
and I am grateful.*

AUTHOR'S NOTE

Detective Dave Burrows appeared in my first novel, *Red Dust*. I had no idea he was going to become such a much-loved character. Since then Dave has appeared as a secondary character in fifteen contemporary novels, and six novels (set in the early 2000s), where he stars in the lead role, including *Rising Dust*.

Fool's Gold, Without a Doubt, Red Dirt Country, Something to Hide, Rising Dust and *Into the Night* are my novels that feature Detective Dave Burrows in the lead role. Eagle-eyed readers will know Dave from previous novels and it was in response to readers' enthusiasm for Dave that I wanted to write more about him.

In these novels, set in the late 1990s and early 2000s, Dave is at the beginning of his career. In the first books, he's married to his first wife, Melinda, a paediatric nurse, and they're having trouble balancing their careers and family life. No spoilers here because if you've read my contemporary rural novels you'll know that Dave and Melinda separate, and Dave is currently very happily married to his second wife, Kim.

Dave is one of my favourite characters and I hope he will become one of yours, too.

PROLOGUE

'Kita harus menyingkirkannya.'

'We must get rid of her.'

Both languages were familiar; although her native tongue was easier to understand.

'Mengapa? Dia tidak akan berbicara.'

'Why? She will not speak.'

With her eyes shut, the woman frowned but the action hurt her.

Someone was repeating the words from the man who was speaking Indonesian.

The throbbing pain made her want to vomit. Her body was hot—not just hot, boiling. Like she was sitting in a bath of scalding water. She needed to move.

Raising her head, she opened her eyes and looked down at her body. It was bare and showing the telltale signs of sunburn across her already brown skin. How long had she been out here like this?

She looked around for a place to get away from the heat. Surely there was something close by to cover herself with? Even a thin shirt, just to give her some relief from the fiery temperature that seemed to be engulfing her; making her pant as if she were a dog. Even though it was warm and humid in her country, the ferocity of the sun was nothing like this. The heat zapped her energy and moving an inch felt too hard.

Her fingers were swollen from the warmth and hard to bend, but she tried anyway. Slowly, slowly, they responded to her will, then she managed to reach out her hand. Searching for anything to cover herself. There had to be something.

The sound of lapping water filtered through her muddied mind. Water. Cold. She could . . . Dragging herself sluggishly along the deck, trying to ignore the pain, which was only second to the heat, she moved towards the lapping noise. Gentle, tiny waves rocked the boat she was in.

The sun set the surface alight with sparkles; glittering, moving diamonds everywhere her puffy eyes looked. The turquoise sea, on which the boat bopped gently, lapped at a beach that morphed into ochre sand, then red soil, which in turn stretched into grey-green bushes. Rugged stony hills stretched up behind the beach and seemed to connect to the sky.

This was not her home country. This was not a land she knew.

The panic started, but as she let out a little moan, she realised it didn't matter where she was. The most important thing was to cool her body. Then get away, for she knew she was in danger.

Memories filled her mind and she felt fear swirl through her. She had to get away. There wasn't just one man. Or two. There were three or four—she'd lost count how many had been on the boat with her. What she hadn't lost count of was how many days she'd been subjected to their desires.

That was the throbbing between her legs. The men had forced themselves on her day after day after day. Over ten days.

She remembered because she'd counted the times the sun had gone down and come up. Although she wasn't sure how long she'd been passed out for this time.

'*Dia harus mati.*'

'She must die.'

'*Tidak*,' she whispered. 'No!' This time she found a strength that she'd never known herself to have before. She raised herself up, ignoring the shooting pain and dizziness that swept over her.

Away from the shore, the jewelled sea stretched to where the sea and sky touched. The water would be cold—it would help cool her. She must slip in. Could she swim somewhere? Away from the men who wanted to hurt her.

She couldn't form the words in her native language, but she knew what the feeling was.

Terror.

These . . . animals! These animals had pulled her from the streets where she had been babysitting her little brother, weaving fishing nets as her father had asked them to. They'd held a knife to her throat and bundled her into a small van with no windows. Inside that vehicle had been dark

3

and smelled like cigarettes, dog piss and rotten meat. She'd screamed and clawed at the doors as they'd shut, but the streets were so busy, so noisy that no one except her little brother had taken any notice.

She'd heard him crying as the van drove away. Then there was just the roar of the engine, the stench and the men in the back, leering at her. They all had thin moustaches and sullen faces. One had a cigarette hanging from his lips while another was missing his front tooth. The other two looked at her as if they could eat her right there. She'd shrunk against the wall of the van, realising it was unlikely she would ever see her family again.

~

The boat had been small and the waves large, when they had sailed. She had no idea where they were headed or why the men had even taken her.

Not many hours had passed before the first one had entered the small cubicle where they had stashed her. The light had filtered in and she'd held her hands up to block the brightness.

Unable to see anything but his silhouette, she'd whispered to him. '*Tolong bantu aku*.' Please help me.

Instead, she'd heard the tinkle of a belt buckle and a zip and she'd screamed again, trying to find a place to hide.

There was nowhere in that small room.

He had held her arms behind her back, and entered her with a force that had made her eyes roll backwards. Her scream had been swallowed up by the waves and wind that were pounding the small vessel.

That had happened time after time after time.

The men weren't far away now. She could hear their voices drifting from the shore across the water. And the tinny sound of steel on earth.

Digging.

Quietly, she moved to the back of the boat and looked over her shoulder. They weren't taking any notice of her.

She dangled her legs over the side and slipped into the water without so much as a splash.

The relief was instant; the cold water enough to make her draw in a deep, quick breath. Salt stung her lips. Treading water, her feet sought the sand beneath the waves, but there was nothing, so she used one hand to hang on to the boat. Her eyes looked for an escape route, but her brain wasn't keeping up.

'*Ayolah.*' Come on, she muttered to herself. Tears pricked her eyes. Her brother. Her family. Where was she?

Suddenly, two hands reached down and grabbed her under her arms and pulled her back into the boat.

Opening her mouth to scream, one of those hands came down heavily across her mouth. 'Shh. Don't make a sound. I'll try to keep you safe,' the man said. He draped a towel over her shoulders. The first sign of kindness in many, many days.

She wasn't sure whether to trust his gentleness or not.

'Where is she?' another voice asked and the boat rocked as someone stepped onto the deck.

'I'm going to take care of her,' the kind voice said.

For some reason, she believed the voice. Her body started to relax.

'You? You wouldn't know how to get rid of a body, let alone deal with her. I'll do it.'

Rough hands grabbed her and took her off the boat, through the water and onto the beach. The sand felt soft beneath her feet. Familiar. It gave her comfort.

'Just leave her with me.' The kind voice sounded fed up. 'I've got a plan.'

'You know what you'll do?'

She heard a fist hit a jaw and a bone crack.

'What the fu—'

Then there was silence. A few more steps and they were at the edge of the large red-coloured hills. She was having trouble understanding. There was nothing like this in Indonesia. There, it was green and rainy and the sun shone, but not with the heat she was feeling now. She licked her dry and cracked lips.

She saw a deep, long hole had been dug. She closed her eyes and conjured up an image of her grandmother sitting on the floor in their shack on the edge of the sea. Her grandmother always stroked her hair back from her face when she was upset. She tried to remember what that touch felt like.

If she had to take a memory to her death that would be it.

Then she felt a push, and she was falling.

Until she hit the bottom of the grave.

CHAPTER 1

'There's no noise.'

'What?'

'There is absolutely no sound. Anyone out here could scream, and no one would hear. Not a person for miles.'

Bob leaned back in his chair and tipped his head towards the sky. 'Give me strength.' He looked back at Dave. 'You've only just worked this out? Who made you a detective?'

Dave was lying on his back, looking at the stars. 'I'd forgotten,' he said simply. 'It's been a few months since we've been outside of the city and I'd just forgotten how peaceful the bush is.'

'Yeah.' Bob got up and pushed his foot against the log in the flames, sending sparks shooting into the air, then grabbed another log and threw it onto the fire. 'Well, I reckon your life is pretty noisy at the moment.'

Dave was quiet, his eyes searching the sky. It was weird that he couldn't see the saucepan constellation. Then he realised that it was because they were further north and the formation wasn't visible at this time of the year.

There were more stars than Dave remembered from when he'd camped out last time he was up here, high above Carnarvon. The night's silence was only broken by the crackle from the small blaze or the gentle breeze. He turned his head at the orange glow coming from the east and saw the moon making her presence felt. Murky shadows from the white gums stretched out across the spinifex and blue bush, while the water in the river was as still as a millpond, reflecting the light of Lady Luna as she rose. Dave paused. *Lady Luna*. The name Mel always called the moon. He couldn't help but think of the phrase every time he saw her rise.

Cold air crept around his ears and he pulled his beanie down a bit further. Not just cold; icy. Tomorrow morning, they'd be lucky if there wasn't condensation inside their swags.

Then he registered what Bob had said. *Reckon your life is pretty noisy at the moment.*

'Profound, mate,' he said dryly.

While pouring himself another whiskey, Bob said, 'Well, think about it, son. You've got your father-in-law throwing lawyers at you.' He waved the bottle around and the amber liquid glowed in the firelight. 'Then you've got Mel . . .' His voice trailed off and Dave knew his partner couldn't describe his soon-to-be ex-wife's behaviour.

Neither could he.

Bob cleared his throat and took a sip. 'And now we've got this new missing sheep case. Lots of noise.'

There were things that Bob hadn't mentioned, like the death of Dave's old partner, Spencer Brown. They'd worked together, stationed at Barrabine, for two years a while back. In that short time, Spencer had made a mark on Dave he'd never forget. His death had shaken Dave to the core and made him question everything he believed about policing and relationships. How long did it take to grieve someone? Dave didn't know.

What he did know was that if he could put his hand inside his chest and pull out the ache and despair, he'd do it in a heartbeat. Tear out the guilt and sadness of Spencer's death. And the rest.

He shut his eyes and breathed in deeply like his counsellor had told him to do.

In. Out. In. Out.

Jumping, glowing flames from the fire.

In. Out. In. Out.

Smell of smoke.

In. Out. In. Out.

The deep breaths lowered his heart rate and he was able to reclaim his thoughts.

'Meditation, Dave. Best thing for you,' his counsellor had said.

He'd never wanted to go to counselling, but even Bob had thought it was a good idea. 'Son, there are some things your mates can't help with. Look at me.' He'd held up his glass and toasted Dave. 'This is how I cope, and I'd rather you didn't end up like me. Just learn from the good bits, all right?' He'd grinned but Dave had known how much that would have cost Bob to say. Bob! He was the epitome of the strong, silent type, dealing with any emotion deep within himself or not at all.

The counsellor was about Bob's age, with grey hair pulled back into a ponytail. He looked like a hippy and Dave had wanted to leave the minute he'd arrived.

'What do you like doing best, Dave?' The counsellor had leaned forward, encouraging.

Dave had leaned back. Not encouraging.

'Fishing? Camping? Walking, maybe?'

'Camping.'

'Right, go out camping. Light yourself a fire and lie beside it. Look at the stars, close your eyes and breathe. Breathe deeply. Don't move. Only breathe.' He paused. 'And try not to think.'

That had been five weeks ago. Dave had been too busy to go camping. Instead of lying next to a fire, he'd lain outside on the lawn and watched the stars.

At first, he'd been restless. Not wanting to stay still for long. He had focused on the hum of the traffic and occasional honking of a horn. His mind had begun wandering, reliving that disastrous afternoon when everything had changed. The ghosts of the past had crowded in, and Dave had tried to run from them. By moving around; shifting his thoughts to a case. Getting a beer from the fridge; pacing the edge of the garden.

Sometimes he thought he could hear his mother-in-law, Ellen, calling out to him. Other times, it was Spencer. Whoever it was, they always wanted his help. Help he couldn't give.

One horrible night, as he was lying there under the inky sky, his eldest daughter, Bec, had screamed out his name, telling him Bulldust was coming for her.

Bulldust. The cattle-thieving, murderous bastard, who'd torn Dave's family apart in one fell swoop.

Dave had jumped up then ran to get his gun, searching for Bulldust, forgetting he was in a jail cell somewhere. Forgetting he couldn't hurt anyone anymore.

The heaviness of the gun in his hand had pulled him back into the present, where he could still hear Bec's voice, even though he knew she wasn't in the same house as him anymore.

The voices were all in his mind, but so real and loud they could have been next to him.

Later, after many, many attempts at meditating, he didn't hear the horn of the vehicles anymore. The voices were still there, but he found them easier to quiet now.

Now, out here under the stars, half of his body was hot from the fire Bob had just added to, and Dave needed to warm the other half. He sat up and stretched his arms above his head. 'Yeah, my life is pretty noisy,' he said. 'But the bush isn't. I'm liking what I'm hearing out here.'

They were both silent as Dave turned and lay down again, breathing deeply. Letting his body relax.

Nothing but peace and quiet and . . .

Bob let a fart rip and Dave frowned, then burst out laughing. 'Aww, god you're an animal! Fire needed help, did it?' He got up and dusted off his jeans and jumper then pulled out his chair and sank into it.

'Just checkin' you were still awake. Didn't want you sleeping on the bare ground. Might get cuddly with a snake.'

'Not in this weather.' Dave pulled his beanie down over his ears again and crossed his arms.

In the distance a high-pitched scream rose into the night. It echoed around the deep gully and bounced off the water.

A breath, then it sounded again.

They both shot to their feet, Bob's hand moving to his waist for his gun.

'What the—' Dave whipped around, trying to get a bead on where the noise was coming from. The hair stood up on the back of his neck. A high, thin wailing—loud, then fading before coming back louder than before.

'South,' Bob whispered as the night fell silent again. He took a couple of tentative steps. 'I don't think . . .'

This time a second squeal—a different, more guttural yowl. There were two people out there.

'Jesus!' Dave felt his heart thudding.

The noise rose high towards the sky, carrying on the freezing air.

Galvanised into action, Dave took off at a run towards their police-issued troop carrier. 'Sounds like someone is hurting a kid. Do you want your gun?' His hand scrambled inside the console for the keys to the gun safe, then yanked open the back door, all while his other hand was feeling for his torch.

Bob gave a loud laugh and dropped back down into his chair. 'Don't worry, son. Don't reckon you'll find those two.'

Half turning, while still searching for his torch on the back seat, Dave frowned. 'What do you mean?' He saw Bob stretching out his legs and leaning back in his chair, his pannikin of whiskey once again balanced on his ample stomach.

'Cats, son. Haven't you heard cats fight before?'

'What, wild cats?'

'Well, I don't think they're your garden variety. Sounded a bit scratchy to me.'

Dave stood still as he thought about the noise. Then the two cats started again, like two banshees yowling at each other. This time he could hear the noise for what it was. He slammed the door shut and grabbed a beer from the fridge, ignoring the adrenalin running through his system.

'Two toms probably,' Bob confirmed.

Dave popped the top of his stubby, pretending his heart wasn't beating through his chest. 'Bloody hell, I hope they're not going to carry on like that all night.' He walked off in the direction of the squalling and stood there listening. 'I didn't think there'd be cats out here,' he said. 'Still, there're cats everywhere, aren't there? Mongrel things.'

'Better than dingoes.'

'For us maybe, but not for the birds and the like.' He sat down and took a long swallow, not able to stop his eyes straying from the light the fire cast into the shadows of the night. What was out there behind the small glow of their campfire? Cattle, sheep, dogs. Cats. But what else? He was glad that he knew Bulldust was languishing in a cell.

A thump, thump, thump behind them.

'Roo,' Bob said.

'Emu,' Dave countered.

Bob paused. 'Native animal.'

Dave laughed. He'd heard plenty of both. So much for the silence. Still, they were good noises. Peaceful noises.

Except the fighting cats. They were enough to put the wind up you.

He changed the subject. 'What do you know about this Mick Miller?' No point in trying to keep his mind quiet now. They were on their way north for a new case and it was time they discussed it. 'DoubleM Station, wasn't it?'

'Yeah. Been in his family for three generations apparently. Gave me the spiel on how each generation of sons had been given the name Mick, hence the DoubleM Station name.'

'Hmm,' Dave said, not really caring about where the name of the property had come from.

'I've come across him once before, I think,' Bob continued. 'When I was up investigating banana thefts out of Carnarvon.'

'Bananas?' Dave looked at Bob disbelievingly.

'Oh, yeah! Group of fellas came in and took off with about five thousand dollars' worth of fruit overnight. Surely you know that nothing is sacred in this world, son?'

'Never heard about that.'

'Before your time. But this Mick, he's pretty big in trying to get the dogs under control up here. Has been for a long time. Often hear him on the radio talking; think he might be tied up with the Pastoralists and Graziers Association, as well.'

'Agri politics type of fella then?'

'Yeah, think so, but from what I've heard about him, he's pretty down to earth. Not like some of the other idiots that love their own voice and who're willing to subject everyone to the sound of it. When he talks, most people listen.' Bob leaned forward and looked deep into the flames of the campfire. 'Mick's stopping short of saying his sheep have been stolen, but he can't find them.'

'That's what we're usually called out for,' Dave muttered. 'What info do you have?'

'Not a lot. One neighbour is a young lad who's running the place next door.' Bob's voice was low. 'Lost his dad in a gyrocopter accident. The bloke was out checking waters when it came down. I looked up the report before we came up here. It's in the file on the back seat. Pretty nasty.'

Dave looked over at his partner. The orange flames flickered over Bob's face and the deep wrinkles of policing, trauma and alcohol were prominent. He inhaled through his nose, and when he let it out, his breath floated away on the air.

Dave hadn't noticed his mentor getting older. They'd worked together in the stock squad for the last three years, since Dave had left Barrabine. In all that time, Bob had stayed the same. Or at least Dave had never noticed a difference. Lately though, he hadn't looked closely, caught up in his own tale of woe, but what he saw tonight was that there was a stark difference from the Bob Holden who Dave had first met, and the one beside him tonight.

Bob had stayed quiet, and he sounded and looked as if the years and cases had finally beaten him down.

'What's that tone of voice for?' Dave asked.

'Just that . . . Ah, doesn't matter.' Bob threw his hand out in a 'don't worry about it' gesture.

Scratching at his two-day-old stubble, Dave considered what to say. Bob never sounded defeated. 'Don't reckon that's right,' he said. 'What's really going on?'

In the distance, the cats were back fighting, but they had moved further away; the screeching wasn't as loud or disconcerting.

'It's a shit of a gig sometimes, isn't it? We lock up crims to make the state and community safer. But as soon as we do that another freaking lowlife comes along and takes the previous one's place. We're on a merry-go-round we can't get off.' Bob paused. 'Look at what's happened to you.' He tilted his head back and let the last of the whiskey slide down his throat.

Dave got up to get him a refill.

'You know I've been in this game a long time and I've seen practically everything I thought was possible. And I still get the hit of adrenalin when I know we're about to make an arrest but . . .' Bob's voice trailed off and he held out his pannikin as Dave stood in front of him with the bottle.

'What happened to me was so far out of left field, you can't ever think that's going to happen to someone else,' Dave countered. 'Yeah, my time undercover brought Bulldust into the lives of my family, but he was after me. My family just got caught up in it.' Even as he said it, Dave felt the clench of guilt in his stomach that never seemed to go away. He hadn't seen his kids for eight months now, and it felt like an eternity.

The phone calls he had with Bec once a week were short, and he knew Mel was listening in the background, monitoring everything that was said. She probably had her hand on the disconnect button the whole time, in case he said something she deemed not appropriate. His youngest daughter, Alice, was still too young to be talking, so he didn't really have any contact with her.

His lawyer was trying his best, but was so far being stonewalled by Mel's. Or rather the lawyer who Mark had employed for his daughter, at great expense. Much more than Dave could ever afford.

'True enough, son, true enough,' Bob said now. 'But no matter how many of the buggers we lock up, there's another one coming up to take their place. We're not making headway here.'

Dave let out a bark of laughter that frightened the nearby corellas, which were roosting in one of the big gum trees nearby. They let out an annoyed squawk and flapped their wings before settling back down again.

Bob looked up. 'Shut up, you mob of bloody gossips!' His words didn't hold any heat.

'Mate, if we were making headway, we'd be out of a job!'

'Ain't that the truth, too.' Bob straightened. 'Forget I said anything. Must be getting soft in my old age.'

'Not possible,' Dave said.

Bob looked over at him. 'Dave?'

'Hmm?'

'Son, look at me.'

Glancing over, Dave realised Bob was staring at him intently. 'What?'

'Do you regret anything about your life, son?'

'Regret?' Dave felt the bittersweetness of decisions he'd made in his life flow through his gut, not for the first time wondering why campfires seemed to bring out deep and meaningful conversations.

'Yeah,' Bob said. 'Any regret at all?'

Dave's breath hissed out through half-closed lips as he wrapped his hands tighter around the beer he was holding. His heart had given a bit of an extra hard thump at Bob's question, and pinpricks were running down his arms. All sure signs of his anxiety.

How to answer that?

He remembered that day when he was outside his in-laws' house, looking into the lounge room where Bulldust had taken his family hostage, knowing that was the best way to get Dave to come to him. Bec was standing on the couch looking through the window, when suddenly she'd cried out that she'd seen her daddy. Mel had been holding Alice, and Ellen had been by Mark's side—Bulldust had given Mel's father a bit of a flogging just before Dave had arrived; he'd had blood on his face.

Bulldust's first bullet had grazed Bec's upper arm. Mel had run hysterically from the house, screaming for people to come and help her. Bec's face had been pale and there was blood everywhere. Flesh wounds always bleed a lot.

But they didn't know that at the time. Dave thought she was dead. Bob had leaned over her, telling Bec she was going to be okay.

His partner sat silently now, staring into the fire.

Dave got up and walked over to the edge of darkness where the firelight didn't reach, remembering. It had been chaos that afternoon when he had lost his family. Bulldust's bullet finding Ellen's chest. The blood, the screaming. Her death.

Mel's loathing of him, and Mark's scathing words and hatred.

If he was honest, he didn't regret Mark being hurt. The man had made it his mission in life to make Dave's world as uncomfortable and difficult as it could be. Ellen, however—well, her death was another matter. He had found an unlikely and unexpected ally in his mother-in-law among all the shit Mel and Mark had flung at him.

He turned around, searching Bob's face. The flames flickered between them, dancing eerily.

'Do you have any regrets?' he asked, his eyes falling on the burns that scarred Bob's hands and arms. Dave had heard the story behind them from another colleague—a high speed car chase and crash that he guessed Bob would like to forget.

He was equally sure that on dark nights like this, the memories plagued his partner, just as they inundated Dave and most of the other coppers he knew who had faced some kind of workplace trauma. Post-traumatic stress disorder seemed to go with the job.

A question came into Dave's mind. 'Is it regret or are the feelings guilt? Are they the same?'

He heard Bob exhale through his nose. 'Sorry, son.' Bob's words made him jump. 'I shouldn't have asked.'

Dave raised a shoulder in a half shrug, without turning around. 'I can't answer the question,' he said simply.

CHAPTER 2

The sun rose quickly, casting out pinks and golds across the landscape. Every surface was wet to touch—the dew had been heavy last night, just as Dave had suspected and he'd woken to the cold drips of condensation on his head.

Dave walked out into the low scrubby bush, the damp red dirt sticking to the soles of his boots. He felt like he was a couple of inches taller by the time he got to the water's edge, plastic cup full of water and toothbrush in hand, towel slung over his shoulder.

When he was far enough away from camp, he doused his face with cold water from the waterhole, filled the cup with the freezing water, then stuck his toothbrush in the liquid before starting to brush his teeth.

The thin grey clouds which covered part of the sky were alight, fiery red as the sun threw its rays across the dawn sky and the first tip of the sun could be seen above the horizon. Dave breathed deeply. How freaking lucky was he to see sights like this? He did have a dream job, he thought, reflecting quickly on last night's conversation. Sure, there were some shitty sides to policing, but mostly it was the best job in the world.

A plop sounded from the water and he turned to see two Australasian darters. One had just landed on the water and was slowly submerging. His Indigenous mate, Kevin, a young bloke he'd met on another case, had told him that these waterbirds kept most of their bodies under the water, leaving just their long necks above the surface. That was how they'd got their nickname of snakebird.

The other darter had landed on a dead stump in the middle of the waterhole and was stretching its wings out to catch the early morning sun.

A chorus of corellas, mulga parrots and babblers chatted and cawed, as if excited the sun was rising and a new day was here. A day where they could do the same as they did yesterday—sing, fish and fly.

Dave smiled as he slowly turned around and watched the land come to life. His connection to the country went back to when he was a little boy, and his grandfather would take him around their family farm or on camping trips during the school holidays. This area he was standing on now was their favourite place to go. His papa, as Dave had called him, would stop the ute near the native bush and walk out, showing him how to recognise wildflowers and bird calls. It had been his papa who had taught him how to track animals and read nature and, if the need arose, to stay alive out here.

When Dave had been chasing down Bulldust and his brother Scotty, the trail had taken him out into some fairly isolated country north-east of Barrabine. While investigating Spencer's death, another copper from the station had been with him. Tez had felt pretty uncomfortable out in the bush, and Dave had repeated his grandfather's words to him: 'If you watch nature, you'll never die out here.'

It was true. Birds indicated water. So did tall gum trees. The bush could be small and scrubby, the land covered with stones, but if he looked across the country and saw tall trees in the distance, there was a fair chance there was a river and therefore water close by.

Wiping his mouth with his towel, he walked back to camp just as Bob shovelled some bacon onto a plate.

'Grub's up.' He put the plate on the table and indicated for Dave to help himself to the toast that was cooking over the coals a little way away from the fire.

'Fit for a king,' Dave said appreciatively as he buttered the toast and put the eggs on top. He squeezed a bit of tomato sauce over the sausages and mushrooms and took a bite.

'Crucify that good meal I've just cooked by putting dead horse on it,' Bob said, shaking his head, reaching for the Worcestershire sauce instead.

Dave didn't bother to answer. It seemed to be a discussion they had every time they headed out on the road. He ate quickly, his mind racing over the track they had to take today.

It would be a good six-hour drive north, probably longer if the road conditions they'd already been over were anything to go by. He needed fuel at the next stop and . . .

'What do you think?'

'Sorry, wasn't listening.' Dave used the last piece of toast to wipe the egg yolk and bacon grease from his plate and stood up, still chewing. He glanced at his watch and saw it was 6.30 a.m. They could be at DoubleM Station by 1 p.m. if they got going in the next half an hour.

'Reckon we might try to stay at Corbett Station Stay,' Bob said. 'That's another hour or so on from DoubleM Station. Not too far to get to and it won't matter if we make it there after dark.'

Dave did a double take. 'Why? We usually camp out bush.'

'Yeah, I know, but they've got showers and a bar. Won't have to cook that way.'

A bar. Dave nodded his understanding, hoping Bob wasn't about to go on a bender. He quickly checked the dates in his mind. July. August was when the car chase had happened and Bob often went on a bender around the anniversary.

He knew Bob still had nightmares about the crash. A driver had run a red light and, during the police pursuit, had slammed into a family of four. The father and one child had been killed, while Bob had pulled the mother and another child out of the burning wreck. Now Bob wore the burn scars and found the anniversary almost impossible to deal with sober.

The questions last night made Dave realise he'd have to watch his partner a bit more closely than normal. He could only hope they'd get immersed in the new case and the date would come and go unnoticed.

Rinsing the plate, he stacked it in the tuckerbox and hoisted his swag onto the trailer, tying it down tightly. He double-checked the trailer plugs with a wobble, and then gave the thumbs up to Bob, who had wandered over to the troopy and was waiting for Dave's signal. He flicked on the righthand-side blinker, then the left. Both were working.

'All good,' Dave called before bending down and making sure the split pin that held the draw pin in the hitch was all secure. Last thing he needed with all the corrugations they'd be driving over was to have the trailer come loose. Or do a wheel bearing.

Casualties on these rough, potholed dirt roads weren't unexpected. Sometimes the roads had deep gouges running through them. Most had many little dips, which weren't easily seen, and an inexperienced driver could hit them with too much speed. Wouldn't take much to snap an axle. Dave had learned early on, driving on these isolated, outback roads, that speed wasn't always the way to get somewhere quickly.

Yesterday, they had passed two caravans that had been jacked up on an isolated stretch of dirt road within a couple of kilometres of each other. One had a wheel missing and the other was jacked up but with both wheels still in place. A tyre lever thrown down in the dirt. Clearly the person trying to fix the flat tyre hadn't been strong enough to undo the wheel nuts and had gone for help.

They'd pulled over to make sure everything was okay, but without cars or people there, Dave and Bob had assumed the drivers were on their way to the closest town. Not much else they could do other than keep driving and hope everyone was all right.

While Dave walked around the trailer, which was carrying their motorbikes and petrol, pulling on the straps to make sure neither were loose, Bob shovelled dirt over the fire and packed up the last of the breakfast. The billy was sitting on the edge of the trailer, steam coiling its way into the pink sky, waiting for Dave to make his last coffee to take with him.

The murky water of Rocky Pool rippled under the morning light. Dave sighed heavily. A few days here would have done him good.

He loved the white gums lining the bank; their leaves were heavy with dew, and deep welts lined the red dirt beneath the trees where drops of water had already fallen. The silence of the morning seemed so loud it could hurt his ears, and when the spinifex pigeon cooed it sounded as if there was smooth caramel flowing somewhere in the creek.

The place was peaceful and restful. Healing.

Bob turned the key, shattering the stillness, and left the troopy idling as Dave made his coffee in his travel mug. With one last look around to make sure they'd left the camping site as close as they could to the way they'd found it, Bob asked, 'Good to go?'

Without waiting for an answer, he climbed into the passenger's seat and took out the file he'd been poring over during the drive yesterday.

'Yep, good to go.'

Bob turned to Dave as he hopped in. 'This could be a needle in a haystack type of case, son,' he said.

Putting the vehicle into gear, Dave glanced in the mirrors and then over at Bob. 'Needle in a haystack?' he questioned. 'Why?' He pulled onto the two-wheel dirt track then headed towards the main drag. They'd talked about the case yesterday and Dave hadn't seen any reason to do things differently.

'You'll see,' said Bob.

CHAPTER 3

Brody pulled up at the homestead and flicked his motorbike's stand down. He sat there for a moment, arms crossed and flies clustering around his eyes.

He adjusted his hat and sunglasses and bent down to pat the two station dogs that came wandering over, sleepy in the midday sun. The lean border collie, Booster, flopped next to his front tyre after getting a pat, while the black and tan kelpie eyed him cautiously. Oreo had always been timid, but Brody loved putting her in the paddock and watching her bring the sheep to him. Any nervousness she had around people quickly disappeared when she got out into the bush.

Brody got off the bike and pulled up his jeans. The leather belt that kept them up around his waist needed another hole. The weight was dropping from him and none of his jeans fitted any longer. He'd have to make sure he got to the shed this afternoon to find the leather punch.

'Good dogs,' he said quietly. They were now sitting at his feet, tongues hanging out and their tails and ears flicking slowly to keep the flies away.

Although the sun had a piercing heat to it, the breeze had a lower chill factor so Brody was glad he had his heavy coat on as he walked over towards the camp grounds he'd set up around a year ago, after his dad's death. He'd had to find another way to make money and it seemed to him that getting on the tourism gravy train was a good option.

What he hadn't factored in was the general public. Some were nice, some weren't. Some were experienced and most weren't. Some wanted very little and were glad of the rustic showers and toilets, and others complained about everything their twenty dollars bought them for an unpowered site.

A nineteen-foot caravan pulled in and slowed as they read the signs and then drove in his direction.

Brody wanted to roll his eyes. What was it with people who went camping but took everything with them? He knew that inside the van there'd be a TV, stove and large fridge, plus a washing machine, shower and toilet. The benches would be a marble look-alike and glossy, and the leather couches plush and comfortable. It was a far cry from the swags and camp beds he and his family had used when they'd gone on camping holidays many, many years ago.

'G'day,' he said with a friendly smile as the couple pulled up next to him and wound down their window. 'Looks like you're needing a rest.'

'Absolutely we are,' said the man, hanging his hands over the steering wheel. 'These roads, I'm sure we're going to shake to pieces. I can still feel the buzzing in my hands from the vibrations!'

Brody wanted to tell them that the van they had really wasn't suitable for the road they were on—they had a touring van, not an off-road one—but far be it for him to give any advice. He had enough troubles of his own.

'You missed the grader by a couple of months,' he said. 'Roads aren't usually too bad once they've been out here, but well . . .' He looked around. 'There're more travellers than usual this year and that means the roads break down a lot quicker.' He gave a shrug.

Such is life.

'We'll grab a site then, if you've got one,' the man said.

'But we must have power,' said the woman, leaning over her husband. 'We need to run our air conditioner. God, it's so hot up here. And the flies . . .' She let her sentence hang. Brody wondered why they had even bothered to head north on a holiday if there was no enjoyment in it for them.

A movement to the side made Brody glance around. The honeymooning couple were packing up their camper trailer, getting ready to leave, and there were still five different holiday-makers in the camping area. One of them was the older couple who he'd had a run-in with last night.

That old geezer had no idea how to back a van into a camp site. He'd also been downright rude when Brody had offered to help reverse it in for him before there was a divorce!

He looked back at the newly arrived people. 'Sorry, I can't help you with the power side of things. I don't have electricity at the house, so you're not going to get it here. Can sell you an unpowered site, though.'

'No electricity at the house?' The woman looked towards the rambling homestead, where the small, green lawn and tidy verandah were situated on the bank of the creek. 'How do you survive?'

'Got a generator. Does what we need it to.'

The woman pursed her lips and got out her phone. 'I assume I can use EFTPOS to pay?'

Brody shook his head. 'No, the machines don't work out here, unfortunately. Cash only.'

'What?' Her voice rose in disbelief. 'Well, surely you have mobile range?' As she glanced at her phone, her eyes widened and she shook the device as if that was going to make a difference to the connectivity.

Brody wanted to laugh. Instead, he said, 'You obviously haven't been up here before. There's some mobile range, but not a lot. Usually closer to towns than we are here. All of our internet connections are through satellite.' He shrugged. 'Just the way it is, I'm afraid.' He paused. 'It does say on our website that we're cash only.' Brody didn't add that folding notes were a convenient way for him to siphon a bit of money into his own bank account. God knows, even as the owner, his wages weren't much for a twenty-three-year-old and he did like a night out at the pub with his mates once in a blue moon.

'Right.' The woman had become snippy now. She handed over a twenty-dollar note.

Brody smiled. 'Thanks,' he said, putting the note in his pocket. 'You can choose your site. Showers and loos are over there.' Pointing to a tin shed with a corrugated-iron roof near the abandoned cattle yards. 'And the camp kitchen is—'

'We won't need that,' the woman broke in. 'We have our own facilities.'

'Sure. Look, you can have a fire if you like. If you don't have any wood, we sell it at the homestead for ten dollars a bag. But the communal fire is always alight and right next to the camp kitchen.' Brody turned the key on his bike. 'Anything else I can help you with?'

'What are the rest of these sheds around here? Are we allowed to look?' the woman asked.

Brody wondered if she might be a modern version of Monica Hadley, Carnarvon's local gossip and busybody. She'd died a few years ago, and according to his mum, no one had taken her place in the area.

He pointed to the house which was situated at about eleven o'clock. 'Okay, this is our homestead. Mum and I live up there, so if you ever need me during the night, that's where I'll be. As you can see it's a bit of a walk from the camp, maybe takes five to seven minutes. Behind that, is our general purpose shed and that is out of bounds to visitors.' He swung his arm around to the two o'clock angle to a shed that was a couple of hundred metres away from the homestead and even further from the camp site.

'That's the hangar for the planes and, again, out of bounds to visitors. You'll find where you're not able to go is clearly marked. This track here,' Brody turned to four o'clock, 'that heads off down to the beach, which is a couple of ks away. An easy walk or you can drive. I know that everything is spread out, but you'll get your bearings soon enough. An easy way to remember where you can go is anything north of the house isn't a place you can go. All right?'

'Good to know. Thanks,' the man spoke quickly before his wife could. 'We'll head off and find a nice camp. Are there spots on the river?'

'I haven't been down there this morning, but there have been people leaving today and you're here early enough. I'd say you've got a good chance to get one.'

The man thanked him and drove off, weaving his way in and around the other campers.

If he hadn't been so annoyed, Brody would have laughed. He was sure it wouldn't be long until there would be an argument between the newly arrived couple. Backing vans in seemed to bring the worst out in everyone, especially when they were inexperienced.

Looking towards the house, he saw his sister's car parked next to his mum's van. His mood lifted a bit. It was always good when Belle came to visit.

He waved to the honeymooning couple, who were hanging out of the windows of their ute, smiling as they drove away, their camper trailer bouncing behind them.

Brody wandered back towards the homestead, his boots sounding loudly on the worn wooden porch, and he stopped to take them off, leaning against the wall of the house for balance.

He stilled as he heard Belle's voice loud and clear. 'Mum, you've got to do these exercises otherwise . . .'

Brody could hear the frustration in her voice and, this time, he did roll his eyes. The argument was a well-worn one, where Belle continued to harp on about their mother's health and their mother, Jane, continued to ignore her. He opened the door and let himself into the kitchen, before putting the kettle on the stove and walking down the hall towards his mother's day room.

The hall held photos of his mum and dad before the accidents. He'd often wondered how they could be so unlucky to have had two severe disasters in as many years.

His favourite photo of his mum hung just inside the front door. She was sitting astride Hickory, her stockhorse, saddle bags either side and her hat pulled down tightly over her ears so it wouldn't fly off when they got a gallop up. Dressed in jeans and a short-sleeved shirt, and her long hair, which was almost the same colour as Hickory's coat, was up in a ponytail. That had been taken only a year before the accident.

If you looked closely, Brody knew the lines of grief were visible around her eyes. The photo had been taken only eight months after his father's death and everyone was still feeling his absence keenly. But Jane, ever the optimist, was smiling at the start of that muster and looking forward to shearing.

He picked up a note that had been left on the sideboard, next to the phone, and looked at it. Another couple of bookings. He tucked the paper into his pocket so he would remember to put the newcomers' names on the blackboard at the front of the camping ground.

His mother's voice was strong and clear as she said, 'I know, darling, but I just don't feel like it today. You understand, don't you?'

Brody leaned against the door. Both his mum and sister were facing away from him as the sun streamed in over the desk his mother sat at to do the station books. This had always been her favourite room in the house and, most weeks, Brody would find some wildflowers or gum leaves to bring back to brighten her office. The bunch of yellow everlastings he'd picked yesterday were on the desk.

'G'day,' he said.

Belle wheeled around and threw him a frustrated smile. Her slight frame was tense and she looked as if she was about to launch herself at someone. 'Brody, can you tell Mum—'

He shook his head. 'Nope. No can do.' Belle knew better than to ask him to convince their mum to do something.

His sister turned back to their mum, who looked at her expectantly, even though Brody knew she knew what Belle was going to say. 'Mum, the human body is made to move. And if you do the exercises the physio gave you, it's only going to be of benefit. See, because you're sitting in a wheelchair constantly, your shoulders will tighten up and your arms will too, because you're using them to push you around. You don't want that. You've been in the chair long enough to know all of what I'm telling you.'

'Yes, darling, you're right.' Flicking her long hair back and smiling at Belle, Jane rolled her chair forward and put her hand on her daughter's arm. 'I *do* know all of this. It's me who's been in this situation for three years now. Just relax. Everything is fine. I did the exercises yesterday and perhaps the day before.' She gave Belle a mischievous smile. 'I can't quite remember.'

Belle let out a loud and irritated groan.

'I know you can't help but put your nurse's hat on, darling, but just let me do this my way. Okay?'

'Cuppa anyone?' Brody asked, hoping to break Belle's tension. His mother looked like she was doing her best to hold in her laughter. He marvelled at her positivity and insistence on seeing the world full of possibilities. 'I've got the kettle on.'

'Sounds divine,' his mum said, moving past Belle. Brody moved from the doorway so his mother could get through and then watched as she expertly manoeuvred herself down the hall and into the kitchen.

'Why?' Belle asked, flouncing past Brody. He caught her arm and gave her a quick hug. She returned it fleetingly and pulled away, looking at him puzzled.

'Because Mum does what she wants. She always has. And she's the one living like this. We can't take the small part of control she has over her life away from her.' Brody patted her shoulder and indicated for her to head to the kitchen.

'I'm paralysed not deaf,' Jane called from the kitchen.

Belle snorted and led the way.

'Sorry,' she said when she got to the doorway. 'I just worry. There're so many things that can go wrong when you're in a chair and I don't want . . .' Her voice broke. 'I don't want to lose you, too.'

Brody stood alongside her and watched his mother wheel herself around the kitchen, getting out the cups and putting tea bags into them.

It had taken a little while after the accident, but with the help of his neighbours he'd managed to modify all the benches so they were lower and wider so that his mum could fit her chair in and around them and access everything she needed. That was the thing about rural communities, everyone pulled together when things went wrong.

'Neither of us do,' Brody said.

'That's all right, loves,' Jane said sunnily. 'I know you've only got my best interests at heart, but I'm going okay. I get lots of exercise. I'm always doing something in the house. And you know I try to get outside as often as I can. I don't like being inside even if it's harder getting around out there.' She looked through the kitchen window with longing, then back at them. 'There's always lots to do. People to talk to.'

Belle opened her mouth to say something else, but wisely, Brody thought, decided to close it again. This conversation wasn't going anywhere, he could tell, so he pulled out two chairs and sat down, while Belle still hovered in the doorway. 'Can I—'

'No, you can't,' Jane answered mildly, deftly grabbing the kettle from the stove and pouring the cups of tea. 'I'm capable.' She picked up one cup and, wheeling the chair around with one hand, she put it in front of Brody then repeated the action another two times, before parking her chair under the table and smiling at Belle. 'Coming to sit?' she asked.

Brody could see Belle wanted to harrumph, but she didn't say a word, sitting down instead.

Jane smiled at them both. 'How're the camp sites looking, Brodes?' she asked.

'Not full, but it's only early. Everything's looking tidy and I've got the copper lit, so the water's hot. Few more little jobs to do—take the rubbish away and that, but here's hoping today will go without a problem. I've already had my first discussion of "no power and mobile range" for the day.' He grinned. 'The woman was going to shake her phone to pieces trying to get range!'

'An eye-opener for sure,' his mum agreed. 'I know you've copped some flak from Mick over the station stay and some of the people are difficult, but it's been worth it. And the campers certainly help cover costs.'

Brody took a sip of his tea. 'Went out to One Tree Hill paddock this morning to check the sheep. Time to try to organise a contract shearer, I think. It's a pain that old Billy Marshall retired last year. He had us as part of his regular run. We're probably going to have to find someone from down south to get up here now. I haven't heard of anyone buying or taking over his business.'

Jane shook her head. 'No, his wife tried to sell it, but didn't get any takers. There was some talk Mick was going to ring around and find a contractor, like you say, probably from down south. Haven't heard how he's got on with that. How badly do they need to be shorn?'

'Well, we're at eleven months' worth of wool, so pretty soon. Some of them are getting wool-blind and if we get a rain, there'll be flies into them pretty quickly.'

Jane dragged a notepad towards her and opened it. 'I'll see what I can do,' she said. 'I'll give Mick a ring. We're going to miss Billy Marshall. Didn't think we'd ever have to find a new shearing team. Still, there's nothing more constant than change.' She gestured to the chair.

Belle sat up. 'You'd better get a count of the sheep,' she said.

They both looked at her. 'What do you mean?' Brody asked. 'We always count them.'

'Harry and I had dinner at the pub last night and I saw Mick Miller and Sandy Jackson in there. They'd just come out of their wild dog meeting, and we were having a yarn.'

'Ah, how's Sandy?' Jane broke in. 'I haven't seen Anna or him for ages. We must get them over for dinner soon.'

'He's good. Anna wasn't with him. Anyway, Mick made mention there might have been dog attacks over at DoubleM Station as he's missing some sheep, and Sandy thought he'd seen a wild dog on the road into town last week.'

Brody nodded. 'Yeah, I'd heard that. It's concerning, for sure. Especially if the dog fence has been compromised in some way. On the upside, I haven't seen any evidence of dog attacks here, though, and there's a bit of distance between us. A hundred ks or so.

'Dogs can travel a lot of distance in a night,' Jane said.

Playing with her cup of tea, Belle looked down. 'Neither of them are sure if it is actually dogs taking the sheep,' she said quietly.

'Oh, there's no doubt with a dog attack,' Jane said with certainty. 'The mongrels often attack from behind. You can see wounds on the hind legs, so you can tell from the carcass. Then there'll be blood around the throat. Depending on how hungry they are, they'll play with the sheep first, then kill. If they're playing, they often just maul the side and go in for the kidney fat.' Jane's face was set hard. 'They're cruel bastards.' She put her teacup down. 'It's been a while since there've been any attacks here. Mick, Sandy and their team did a great job of getting the dog fence up and protecting our areas.' She paused then said softly, 'Your father had a lot to do with that, too.'

'Yeah.' Brody looked at the table and fiddled with his cup as he thought about his father clomping over the verandah in his good clothes, heading off to the dog fence meetings in town. He'd always be smiling with Jane alongside him. The only time Jane went into town now was to doctors' appointments. Belle was speaking again and he wrenched himself from his thoughts.

'That's the problem,' Belle said. 'They're missing sheep.' She paused. 'And the amount of sheep they're missing doesn't add up to the carcasses they've seen on the ground.'

Jane frowned. 'Ah. So, there're carcasses? That changes things slightly; there must be a dog around then. Brodes, you might need to put some baits out. Get on top of them before they take hold.'

Belle nodded at her mother's words. 'Yeah, there are. Mick said he's tried to call you, but the phone's been engaged, or something, every time he called.'

Jane nodded. 'I didn't hang the phone up properly for a couple of days last week.'

Belle looked at her mother without saying anything.

Jane gave her another smile. 'Easy mistake to make, Belle. What were they trying to get hold of us for?'

'They asked me to pass on the message; like I said Mick and Sandy are saying the dogs aren't accounting for the numbers they're missing. They think someone is stealing sheep.'

CHAPTER 4

'Boggy,' Dave said as he pulled the troopy to a halt at the crest of the river.

The Gascoyne River was flowing strongly in some parts and in others it was down to a trickle. But what Dave and Bob were looking at here was deep red creek sand, gouged-out tracks and water that might come up as far as the axles.

The dirty-looking water was still and the shadows of the trees danced across the top, making it look like there were creatures hiding under the surface. The sandbars further down the river stood up like little islands in the middle and were covered with birdlife.

'Should walk it,' Bob said, opening his door and hitching up his shorts. 'Don't want to risk sinking to the chassis.'

Dave followed, agreeing with him. They both stood on the edge of the river, their arms crossed. The ever-present white gums lined the banks, and protruding rocks created isolated pools of water.

Hearing a splash, Dave glanced to his right and saw the telltale signs of round ripples spreading out across the water. A few moments later a waterbird popped up. He wasn't sure what type it was, but he smiled at the joy it seemed to have as it ducked and dove, swimming quickly across the blanket of water to where there were a stack of sticks and leaves built up in what could have been a nest.

'Go on, then.' Bob nodded to Dave. 'We won't get much further unless you walk it.'

'Me?' Dave replied. 'What about you?'

'As the senior officer, I'm delegating.' Bob leaned against the bull bar. 'I'll be here to throw you a line if you need it. But you won't. The water's not flowing. Just need a depth measure.'

Dave threw Bob a look as he bent down and hauled his boots and socks off, looking for his thongs in the back of the troopy. He wasn't walking out there in bare feet. 'It's not hot enough for this,' he muttered.

'Look at it this way, cold water always evokes shrinkage. You were banging on about needing to lose a bit of beef. This is the way to do it.' Bob nodded as if he was convinced his argument was sound. 'And you won't have to worry about any bedroom duties.'

'Like that's happening,' Dave said grumpily.

One foot in the water and he curled up his toes. 'It's freaking freezing,' he yelped.

'Go on, son. This is for the greater good, you know.'

'Shut up.' The second step wasn't any easier but by the time he was mid-calf, he had started to breathe again. The heavy mud clung to his feet as he walked; it was sticky, but not soft. And further under, the ground was hard.

He made it out into the middle and it was only knee deep. 'Reckon we're good,' he called out. His voice seemed to bounce off the walls of the riverbed as the midday sun shone high above him and the wind gently rustled the leaves on the gums.

'Good, let's get a move on. We're only a few ks away from the homestead.'

Dave walked back to the edge and Bob tossed him a towel. 'Here you go, Tarzan.'

He shook his thongs off, then ran the towel over his legs and pulled his socks and boots back on, before slipping behind the steering wheel. 'Right-oh,' he said, putting the vehicle into gear. Making sure four-wheel drive was engaged, he moved the troopy forward slowly. Dave felt the trailer pull a little as they hit a boggy spot. A bit more grunt and the steering wheel moved under his hands by itself. He let the troopy track to the wheel marks that were already there under the surface and eased into deeper water, until they were through and up the other side.

Stopping the car, he shifted out of four-wheel drive and started off again.

'Talk about an amazing season,' Bob said, looking out the window. 'I can't remember the last time I've seen this country look so good. Check them out.' He pointed to some glossy Brahman cattle who were camped not far from the river's edge, the tall grasses almost hiding their bodies.

Dave slowed the troopy, looking at the cows' shiny red coats and the grasses waving in front of their noses and eyes as he and Bob sat watching, the cows' ears twitching. 'Bloody beautiful,' Dave said, satisfaction in his voice. 'Look there.' He pointed to the other side of the road, where a mob of recently shorn wethers were grazing. Their backs had a vivid gold line down them, which Dave knew was lice treatment. 'Won't be too long and they'll be on the boat, I reckon.'

Carpets of white, yellow and pink wildflowers stretched out under the cattle and in among the spinifex and grasses.

Dave knew that the country wasn't as soft as it looked now. Underneath there were rocks that covered almost every inch of the ground; not just small stones, but fist-sized rocks, some would be even larger. During a normal season, they'd be visible and the cassia and mulga trees would stand stark against the iron-coloured ground. This year, the grasses and ground-cover hid them, taking the desolate feel away.

He heard Bob talking and refocused. 'What's that?'

'Weather coming in by the looks,' Bob repeated, nodding towards the high cloud on the horizon.

'These mid-level disturbances seem to be coming through pretty regularly, don't they?'

'Reckon I'd better ring Corbett Station Stay and book for tonight,' Bob said. 'See if we can borrow the phone at

Mick's place, once we've finished up there. Or use the sat phone when we get going again.'

Dave followed the road, which swung around and headed west towards the coast, passing a stone tank and windmill. He slowed as he realised the trough alongside it was made of stone, too. 'Resourceful,' he said.

'Yeah,' Bob said. 'Always wondered why the blokes that turned up here thought it would be a good place to graze cattle and sheep. I mean, look at the joint.' He swept his arms out. 'Rocks and mulga trees and . . . God, mustering in these types of places would be just bloody hard. Hard on the horses, the humans and the machinery.'

'They must've turned up in a good season like this and seen the feed.' The troopy shook under Dave's hands but he kept the speed steady. One thing about corrugations was there wasn't any point in slowing down too much. You were better to skid along the top and take the small bumps than have the tyres going down into every groove and then up again. Did more damage to a vehicle that way.

'Or sheer determination to make a life for themselves.' Bob turned to Dave. 'Now, a little bit of info. I spoke to Mick Miller before we left Perth to get a bit of an idea about what's going on. He's been shearing and thinks he's about a thousand down on his last off-shears count. Still got the shearers there so we need to talk to them before we go.'

Dave nodded, committing the numbers to memory.

'He's rung a few of the neighbours and they haven't started shearing yet, so no one else is sure whether they're missing any. I understand he hasn't been able to get a hold of one neighbour and that's the Corbetts.'

They passed a sign—Dave saw that it was part of the fan of an old windmill. The hand-painted words 'DoubleM Station' with an arrow pointed them in a westerly direction.

'We can't be too far off the coast here,' he said.

'DoubleM Station backs onto Corbett Station Stay as such, but it's got a few thousand acres of crown land in between them. Corbett's is the one which goes all the way to the sea. They've got their own private beaches and the river runs through. Anyhow,' Bob scratched his chin, 'the stock are gone and he assures me the boundary fences are all in good nick.'

'They always say that.'

'It's usually true.'

'Any dogs up here?'

'Can be. But the fence is out and around most of the places.' He paused. 'Although it's sounding like the fence has been compromised somehow. There've been sightings.'

'Hmm.' Another windmill fan sign telling them to slow down. Dave rounded the corner, drove through a dry, narrow winding creek bed and up the other side. A large shearing shed with a house off to the side came into view. There was a minibus parked next to the shed and there were sheep in the yards. A lone man in a singlet, hat and shearing dungarees was perched on the railings of the yard. He lifted his hand in greeting as they drove by.

Closer to the house, parts of cars and old windmills, engines and machinery were lying on the ground and spilling out of sheds. It looked like someone was planning to hold a clearing sale.

The overgrown shed area was in need of a mow. Dave judged the grass—not lawn—to be about ankle high. *Snakes would love it here*, he thought.

'Obviously not into tourism,' Bob observed.

'No. Pretty untidy. Unusual.'

A round of barking went up and four dogs—two black, one tan and one brindle—launched themselves off the verandah and out the gate, which was swinging on one hinge, towards the car.

The staffies stood their ground, snarling and barking, saliva hanging from their jaws.

'Welcoming committee,' Bob said, reaching for his notebook and tucking it into his top pocket, as Dave turned off the troopy.

'Do we get out?'

'Wait a sec.' Bob paused, his hand on the latch just as the wooden screen door on the house flew open and a woman in jeans, jumper and boots came flying out. 'There we go.' Bob pushed open the door and got out.

The dogs were still guarding the entrance, but at the woman's sharp command they'd stopped barking.

'What can I do you for?' she called out.

'Mrs Miller? We're Detectives Holden and Burrows. We're wanting to see your husband.'

Dave watched the woman draw herself up to her full height and take a minute step backwards.

'Marly, Jackson, Casper, Molly, come behind!'

The dogs didn't move, only continued their growling and protection of the homestead.

The woman walked over and clapped her hands then pointed to the shed. 'Inside! Get on your beds,' she instructed. The dogs gave her a baleful look before they all turned and walked into the shed, the brindle one giving one final bark as she eyed Dave.

Dave stayed still, not wanting to antagonise them. Dogs could be the bane of any copper's life.

'Good dogs. Good dogs,' she said. Turning to Bob and Dave the woman smiled. 'Sorry. I've trained them to guard. Never know who's going to turn up out here. I'm Sally Miller.' She held out her hand to them in turn. 'Mick's expecting you but had to whip down and check one of the mills. He won't be long.'

'No worries.' Bob looked around. 'Good season.'

'One of the best we've had.' Sally relaxed into a smile and leaned against the verandah post. 'It's nice seeing all the feed and the stock content for a change.'

'And they look great,' Dave said. 'Saw the shearing shed on the way in, must've been in use recently, going by the shorn wethers we passed.'

'She's a beauty, isn't she?' Sally replied. 'Lots of history. Shearers are there if you want to go and talk to them, or you could come in and have a cup of tea first and wait for Mick, then he can take you there when he gets back.'

'Sure, sounds like a plan,' Bob said, hitching his shorts up again and taking a step towards the house.

Dave followed, checking the house and surrounds. On the roof was a satellite dish and a tall aerial. Internet and radio signals. The fence was wire netting on a wooden frame—half was pulled away, leaving gaping holes that wouldn't keep anything in or out.

The sound of a motorbike engine reached them, and Dave turned to look in the direction of the noise. A plume of red dust was rising against the sky, which only moments ago had held patches of blue. Now thin, grey clouds were stretched across it in all directions.

'Here he comes,' Sally said as she held the door open. 'Come in. Kitchen is to the left.'

Bob and Dave found themselves sitting at the kitchen table, wildflowers in a vase in the centre and a pile of paperwork at one end.

Even though the kitchen was clean and tidy, and completely unlike the outside of the house, it was old, with sash windows in one wall and a light covering of red dust over everything. It seemed to Dave that everything in the area—people, clothes, stock—seemed stained with the iron-red colours of the land.

On the wall was a faded photo of Sally, sitting on a horse, a sash was over her chest and she was holding a buckle. In the frame next to it was a man, also astride a horse, but he had a baby sitting in front of him.

Bob stepped up to it and read the writing on the sash. 'Rodeo champion?' he asked, sounding impressed.

'Oh, that was a while ago now,' Sally said. 'That's Mick and his niece Courtney at the same rodeo.'

'You have kids?'

Sally shook her head. 'No, we don't.'

Dave heard the pain in her voice.

She cleared her throat and spoke again. 'Mick said you needed this?' She pushed the pile of paperwork towards them. 'Sales figures, natural increases, shearing figures. Oh, and some waybills. I also pulled out the invoices of lice treatment and shearing gear we've used in previous years to now. You'll see that we've ordered the same amount as normal, but if you go to the shed, you'll also notice we've got a lot left over. So, it hasn't been used on the stock. We've never bought more than we need.'

Dave picked up one of the folders and started leafing through it. 'Normally, it would all be gone?'

'Yes, close enough. I mean you can't judge it down to the last dosage, because there're always losses of sheep, but very rarely do we have two twenty-litre kegs left over. And the wool packs, there's a good one hundred plus left over. Now I've budgeted on the wethers cutting about eight kilos of wool each and if you divide that into the one-eighty kilos a wool pack can hold, we're also down about one hundred bales of wool. That's a hell of a lot of sheep missing.'

The door slammed and a few seconds later they heard the sound of boots clattering on the lino floor.

A tall man stood in the doorway, a large smile on his face. 'G'day. I'm Mick Miller. Glad to meet you both.'

Bob and Dave stood, introducing themselves and shaking his hand. He was dressed in the uniform of the north: jeans and a block-coloured shirt. His face, and all the way down his neck to where his shirt opened into a V, was red from the sun. His grey hair was almost white. Mick looked older than Dave had thought he'd be. Maybe in his late seventies, but the energy radiating from him was that of a younger man.

Sneaking a look at Sally, he realised she was probably ten or fifteen years younger than her husband. He wondered what their story was.

'Bad business,' Mick said, sitting down with a rush.

Dave had to give it to Mick, he had presence. His voice was perfect for radio but his face was made for TV.

'Very bad business. Hope you'll be able to help us out.' Mick tapped the table with his fingers. 'You obviously got here all right. That river crossing can be a bit boggy.'

'Yeah, no problems at all,' Dave said.

Sally set cups of tea in front of them and then pulled out a cake in a plastic Tupperware container. Without a word, Mick cut himself a slice and indicated for the others to do the same.

'So, how can I help you get to the bottom of my missing ewes?' he asked.

'Right,' Bob said, taking the lead. 'I'd like to understand everything a bit more. How about you start at the beginning and tell us what is concerning you?'

As Mick started to talk, Sally sat at the other end of the table and flicked through the waybill book, leaving it open at a page, then she rested her chin on her hand, watching her husband as he spoke.

'Well, now, we started shearing two weeks ago. Should take three weeks, give or take a few days. We usually run seven and a half thousand ewes here, so working that out for shearing—four shearers doing about one hundred and twenty head per day over fifteen working days gives us seven thousand two hundred to be shorn in that time. There might be a day here or there over or under, just depends on what shearer is doing what amount per day.'

Bob and Dave nodded their understanding, while Dave kept notes of the figures.

'How many days shearing have you ended up with?' Bob asked.

Mick took a long sip of his tea, drawing out the suspense. 'Ten.'

'Ten days shearing instead of fifteen? That's why you're finishing up today. You've only had two weeks' worth of sheep shorn.'

'Yep.'

Dave did the figures in his head. Approximately two thousand four hundred sheep missing. That was not enough for four neat road trains. Full wool ewes would fill a truck with about eighty sheep per deck and on a road train that would mean about five hundred and sixty ewes.

'Right. You think you've got a shortfall of about two thousand and then some?'

'Yeah. I've done a couple of counts off-shears, just to check. You know, run the gate over them. Going on the figures I had at 30 June last year, plus the natural increase, I'd say I'm missing exactly two thousand four hundred.'

'Good way to get an accurate count,' Dave said.

'And you mentioned dog attacks?' Bob continued. 'Does this mean the dog fence isn't doing what it should?'

'I've seen eight or nine carcasses which could be attributed to dog attacks, and, yes, there has been one sighted along the road but . . .' Mick frowned and got his notebook from his pocket. 'Look, I'm just not convinced about that. I've been along the fence in the last few weeks and can't find any areas where the fence is cut, or a hole underneath, or any reason a dingo or wild dog could get through.' He flicked through the pages. 'The last dog attack around here was four years ago. We tracked it and baited. Ended up getting the bastard a couple of weeks later.' He inclined his head to one side. 'I haven't seen any dog tracks since then, and now suddenly we've got some attacks. I'm not convinced it's a dingo or some type of wild dog. Maybe it's a station dog that's wandering at night.' His deep voice held concern. 'If it is a station dog, then we need to find it. This type of attack can't go on.'

He cleared his throat and shifted in his chair, before taking a long sip of his tea. 'So, the first carcass I came across was three weeks ago, then about one every two or three days since. Our Wild Dog Advisory Board members haven't reported seeing any dingoes. Sandy, whose station is to the east of here, would probably be the first one to have them if they were coming from the national parks.'

'And are the carcasses in the same area?'

'Within a ten-kilometre radius, which as I'm sure you know is nothing for a dog.'

'Close to the boundary fence? Or a long way inside your station?'

'The furthest inside is about five ks. Rest are closer to the boundary with Corbett's. Maybe twenty thousand acres of crown land in between us all. I guess there could be a dog holed up in there. Or maybe someone has dumped one there. Could be that, too, I guess.'

Dave glanced at Sally to see what she was thinking, but her face was impassive.

'Sure,' Bob said. 'So, how much were these ewes worth?'

'On today's market? Maybe eighty bucks a head. Thirty-eight grand. Not a huge amount, I realise, but not that small either. At the same time, up here . . .' He spread his hands out, indicating the land outside. 'This country doesn't run high numbers to the hectares. Losses are a bit hard to stomach.'

'Doesn't matter the amount,' Dave said. 'If they're not here, we need to look into it. And it's sounding like they're not here.'

CHAPTER 5

A dark shadow crossed the house, casting a dim light through the kitchen as Dave's words faded. A loud, strong gust of wind, then a horrible, sudden tearing noise startled them and all four jumped. It passed as quickly as it had arrived and the kitchen was light again.

Sally got up and moved to the window.

'Oh,' she said, sounding relieved. 'It's just a loose sheet of tin. I can see it flapping on the shed. But there's a storm coming in quickly.'

A growl sounded and the land fell into darkness again, as the wind pushed the clouds across the sky, hiding the sun as they went. The thunder became louder.

Dave got up and stood alongside Sally. The change in the weather was almost instant. The high, grey cloud when they had first arrived was now replaced with heavy, leaden clouds, heaving with moisture and lightning.

The windmill creaked and groaned and the head spun faster and faster—Dave felt sure it could just spin off and go flying through the air.

'Amazing,' he muttered.

'The old girl always gets a bit of rev up,' Sally said with a smile, her face turned towards the sky. 'Never come to any harm yet.'

As quickly as it started, the wind dropped to nothing, leaving the land still and unmoving.

'Here it comes,' she said.

The stillness made it feel as if the land was waiting. Waiting for what, Dave wasn't sure, but when the wind blew itself out, the whole of nature stopped. The birds were silent, and the windmill's creaking had ceased as the head slowed to a lazy movement and finally stilled. The heaviness of the cloud was ominous.

Another loud grumble and lightning split the sky.

Bob and Mick were now at the window, too.

'Love a good storm,' Bob said.

'The high rainfall this year has been such a blessing,' Sally said. 'This will only add to it.'

A loud plop sounded on the roof, then another and another, and soon they had to raise their voices to talk to each other.

They stood for a long moment, watching the raindrops cluster into puddles, covering the cement outside. The red dirt darkened to a chocolate black and the earthy smell of rain on dirt rose to meet them.

'The power of nature,' Bob muttered, before turning back to the table. Outside the rain teemed down in a heavy curtain of water.

Mick ran his hand over his stubble. 'Hope they got all the sheep in the shed, otherwise that will put an end to shearing for today.'

'Can't shear wet sheep,' Dave agreed.

'There would have been room for them all under cover. Would be good if they didn't have to stop now,' Mick said.

Sally switched on the light as they all sat down.

'Back to the sheep,' Bob said, turning back to his notes. 'Correct me if I'm wrong, but you didn't notice anything untoward until you got them in for shearing?'

Both Sally and Mick shook their heads.

'Nope,' Mick said. 'Nothing. We went down south for a few doctors' appointments and so forth during May, but we were only gone a week. Never noticed anything out of place when I came back.'

'Do you lock the front gate?'

Sally shook her head. 'We think that only attracts people,' she said and Mick nodded.

'A locked gate seems to be a magnet to all the bloody tourists. Makes them think they should be able to go through it. I've come back to a cut chain or gates slammed in because someone has driven through them.' Mick gave a disgusted grunt. 'Nah, we leave them open, but we lock the house and fuel bowser. All the keys are taken out of the machinery and locked in the gun cabinet, too.'

'Good thinking. And how often do you go over the whole property?'

'See, that's the problem. Until we muster, we don't. Two whole property musters a year. One for shearing, one at weaning time. The ewes we've shorn are back out in the furthest parts of the station now, because we don't need to do anything with them for a while. But the wethers, they'll stay in a little closer and in a few weeks, when they've got over all the shearing cuts and so on, and the boats are in, we'll do a smaller muster and bring them back in to sell.

'So, in theory, I guess the ewes we're missing could have been taken while we were away, but there's only one road in, and I'm sure I would've noticed if there had been truck tracks. Marks in this type of ground look like they're fresh a lot longer than you'd expect.' He paused. 'Come down and have a look at the map in the office,' he said and indicated for them to follow him down the narrow, dark hall.

Dave glanced into a room off the passageway and saw three large freezers and fridges and a wall of shelves and tinned foods. Stores in case they were rained in.

The rest of the house was void of any photos or anything that would normally make a house a home. No knick-knacks, books, anything.

Dave glanced around curiously and saw the opening into the office.

The only thing that showed the couple's personality were four dog beds next to the office desk, which was a cheap wooden desk plonked in the middle of the room.

Mick ushered them into the room and strode across the floor, pointing to a large map—the only thing close to a photo on the wall. 'As you can see, there's only one track in here. It leads to the house, which is in the middle of the property, and everything else branches out from here. There wouldn't be any other areas that you could get a truck out from.' His finger followed the boundary. 'See, the creeks run along most of it and a truck won't get through those creek crossings.'

The men crowded around the map and Bob ran his hand over his chin as he thought. 'And the dog attacks were about here?' He put his fingers over the spots where he thought they would have been from Mick's earlier descriptions.

'That's right.'

'Now, you mentioned your neighbour. Ah,' Bob pretended to check his notes, when Dave knew he had memorised every word in the file. 'A Brody . . .'

'Corbett,' Sally supplied from the doorway.

'Yeah, Brody Corbett. What can you tell me about him?'

Mick went to a filing cabinet and took out a smaller map, handing it to Bob before indicating they should head back to the kitchen.

Once there, they all sat back down and Mick cut himself another slice of cake. 'Feel free,' he said once again, indicating they should do the same.

When he spoke next, it was in a low tone. 'Sad story that one. Mal and Jane Corbett took over from Mal's father when he died. That station has been in Mal's family for generations, and they were doing great things over there.

Mal had a lot of foresight and Jane, she worked her arse off. She's from station stock, too. They'd increased their sheep holdings by pasture renovations; have to say, a lot of people laughed at Mal's trial. Didn't think it could work out here. Too harsh. Not enough rain. But it did.' Mick nodded with a wry smile on his face. 'Too right it did. They increased their carrying capacity by a good thousand. And trust me, that's a huge amount up here. Things were going from strength to strength when Mal was killed.' He got up and walked to the window, his hands in his pockets as he cleared his throat. There was a brief silence until he spoke again.

'He was out checking waters in a gyrocopter and he crashed . . .' His voice trailed off. 'Mal, well, he was a good mate of mine and I tried to tell him how dangerous those bloody machines were. No better than going for a fly in a tin can. But he didn't listen. Always liked to do things his own way. He was a bit of a maverick.'

Sally went and stood behind her husband, laying a gentle hand on his shoulder. He brought his own hand up to cover hers.

'Then Jane, his wife. Horse-riding accident. Out mustering. Only a couple of years ago. Maybe three now. Time passes so quickly.' He stopped as if he couldn't make the words come out.

Sally took up the commentary. 'She fell at full gallop.'

Dave felt his heart give an extra thud. What an awful thing to happen to a family. 'She died, too?'

'Oh no, she's in a wheelchair. A paraplegic.' Sally gave a small laugh. 'Jane isn't someone you can hold down and, although she's not as active outside as she was, she still gets in among it as much as she can!

'Her motorbike is her main mode of transport outside— they had it made specially for her. A four-wheeler that's quite wide and solid. Doesn't mean she can go far from the house, but she's still out and about. Isn't she, love?'

'Yeah. Her tenacity is quite amazing.'

'And, uh, Brody?'

'Hmm. Brody.' Mick paused as if to organise his thoughts.

The rain continued to fall, the noise on the tin roof loud and insistent. Dave wondered about the river they came through and if they'd be able to get out tonight. Part of him wanted to leave now, so they could find a place to sleep and get a feed, but there was too much information they still needed to get.

'Brody is a good lad. Young and naive, but a hard worker. He was right at the end of his high school years when Mal was killed. I've tried to mentor him since then. If I'd had kids I would have liked someone to do that too, if they were in that situation, so I made an effort. Went over there once every couple of weeks after Mal's death. Gave advice when he asked for it, listened when he was upset. You know, that sort of thing.' He paused. 'There's a sister, Belle. She lives in town. Nurse. Helpful to her mother, if not somewhat overbearing. Saw her a couple of nights ago in town and asked her to tell Brody and Jane about what was going on out here. I think I mentioned before I couldn't raise them on the phone.'

Bob raised his eyebrows and leaned forward as Dave took notes. 'And the neighbours on your other side?'

'Uh, yeah, Aggie and Graham Dorrell. Again, been there a long time. Good solid station people. They run about the same size operation as we do.'

'Employees?'

'Only the contract shearers they get in and maybe a casual during the busiest times.'

'Don't forget they have a govvie,' Sally put in.

'Yeah, true. A governess for the kids.'

'Do the Corbetts have any employees?' Dave asked, scribbling quickly.

'Ah, well—' annoyance passed through Mick's tone '—Brody hires backpackers on a casual basis because he has a station stay, so there are people in and out of that place all the time. Who knows who's coming and going? Could be anyone! And this is all against my advice, mind you, but Brody thought it would help with the finances.'

'You don't agree with it?'

'No, I don't. I'm not saying anything out of school here because I've been quite vocal about this before. All this country up here is being taken over by eco-tourism. People bloody everywhere. Can't take a shit without someone turning up. We're pastoralists. We deal in livestock, dirt and rain. Not tourists.'

'You feel the same way, Sally?'

Sally sat down again and toyed with the book in front of her. 'Look, I understand why Brody has done what he's done. Jane told me when he first started it that they were short of money. Mal's death was unexpected, and he didn't leave a will so their joint bank accounts were frozen, and Jane couldn't access money. It was a right proper balls-up. Creating the station stay, well, it let them have a bit of cash flow.' She paused. 'Got them out of trouble. As for whether I agree with tourist accommodation on stations . . .' She gave a little shrug. 'It's nice to be able to share our part of the north with others, as long as they don't interfere with our business. And occasionally that's what seems to happen.'

'That's why we get the dogs we do,' Mick added. 'People lose them or they run off. Turn wild because they're hungry, then they mate with a wild dog or dingoes. Causes us no end of grief when we're trying to eradicate the bloody things from up here.'

'We have people call in looking for fuel or food,' Sally continued. 'Sometimes they even want us to do repairs for them.' She shook her head. 'That's the stuff I don't like. We've got people we don't know from Adam coming into our home. They could be honest, decent people. Or not.'

'And last time I looked,' Mick said, 'we're not mechanics or a corner store.'

'Yeah, I could see how that could be tricky,' Dave agreed, making a note about Mick's and Sally's thoughts on tourism.

Mick paced the floor. 'We deal in livestock; you can't go forward unless you work hard. But young people these days just want things easy and this station-stay trend is part of it. It's a lot easier to greet people and clean some cabins than getting on a motorbike or a horse and mustering; spending weeks at a time out in the stock camp. Young Brody just wants to make money quickly and simply. But that's not how life is; nothing comes easy.' Mick shook his head. 'That young lad . . . he tries, but he's not a patch on his old man.' He stopped and put his hands on the kitchen table and looked at Dave and Bob. 'I'd love to get into Corbett Station and give it a good shake-up. Let someone who knows what they're doing run it.'

CHAPTER 6

The silence that settled in the kitchen after that comment was heavy, and Dave made a note of what Mick had said.

Friends losing friends up here in the north was hard. They were tough men and women and often the accidents were tragic. Just as the two they had heard about today had been.

'Wouldn't mind having a chat to the shearers,' Bob said.

'Sure,' Mick said, getting up from the table. 'I'll take you over there.'

Bob held up his hand. 'No, that's okay. We can find our own way.' He glanced at his watch. 'If it's all right, though, we might camp here for the night. You won't need to worry about us, we're fully self-sufficient. I'm not sure if we'll make it to Corbett's tonight.'

Sally checked the time. 'Depends on how long you're going to be with the shearers. I think you'd get there okay before dark. The sun isn't setting until six thirty or so. And this rain won't stop you yet.'

Mick gave his TV grin. 'Just no detecting tonight, boys. You'll have to park up and have a drink.'

'Easy enough to do,' Bob said. 'What's the road like across to Corbett's? How long will it take?'

'Not long by standards up here. Maybe an hour. Hour and a half if you're unlucky. You could roll in, just in time for dinner, I'd reckon. Did you want me to ring and book a cabin for you? Forecast is looking a bit dodgy.'

'Actually, that would be great,' Dave said, checking with Bob as he spoke, even though they'd already talked about it.

'No worries. If there's any trouble, I'll let you know. Their phone didn't seem to be working last time I tried to call.'

'Fine,' Bob said and put his hand in his pocket, before pulling out a business card. 'You think of anything else or need to get in contact, here are our numbers. Satellite phone number there, too.'

'Great, thanks.' Mick took a magnet and pinned the card to the fridge, before showing them out. 'I'll have to come across and check they got all the sheep in the shed in a while. That be okay?'

'Give us half an hour,' Bob said.

'Sure.'

They all shook hands then Bob and Dave made for the troopy, the rain now gone, but the constant drip, drip, drip from the trees and the water running from the gutters was loud. The sun now shone through, and the humidity had increased.

Dave took a breath of the heavy air. It smelled and tasted perfect to him. Starting the car, he looked over at Bob. 'Thoughts?'

Bob gave a shrug. 'We'll see.'

They splashed their way through the puddles for the short distance until they reached the shearing shed. From inside they could hear laughter and the whirring of the handpieces.

On the outside, the generator ran loudly from somewhere in the distance and the yards were empty.

'Must all be in the shed,' Dave said, opening his door. 'Mick'll be pleased.'

They went up the ten wooden steps that led into an eight-stand shearing shed, with only four stands being used by the shearers.

Another sign it was hard to find shearers, Dave thought. In the station's heyday, he had no doubt that the whole eight stands would have been filled and there would have been four roust-abouts instead of two. There may have even been two classers, assessing the fleeces and putting them into the right lines.

Instead there was only one classer, who had his glasses perched on the end of his nose, checking the crimp on the wool, before putting it into the wool press and dragging the lever down to squash the wool into the bale.

One rousie, an older woman, was waiting for the shearer to finish his sheep, before she swooped down and gathered the wool into her arms and threw it on the classing table.

As they stepped into the shed, everyone looked up, was silent for a second and then went back to work. The shearer closest to the door glanced up again, a rollie cigarette hanging from the corner of his mouth, his grey hair dripping with sweat.

'G'day,' he said.

'How's it going?' Bob asked as he walked over to the classer and introduced himself.

'John Sawyer,' he answered.

Dave saw the old man still and throw them both a curious glance, before concentrating on the wool again. John's face was dirty, lined with streaks of sweat and the whole shed smelled of body odour, lanoline and sheep shit. But it was the classer's hands which drew Dave's gaze. They reminded him of his grandfather's; with dirt deeply engrained in the wrinkles and lines but soft from handling wool all day. Not many people these days knew that wool had lanoline in the fibres and acted as a moisturiser.

'How are you getting on here?' Dave asked the classer, leaning against the wool table and reaching over to pluck a strand from the fleece. He judged the micron to be medium to strong and put it back. 'Looks like a consistent line of wool. What is it? About twenty-two micron?'

John looked up and nodded. He wiped his brow with his forearm. 'Know your way around a shed?' he asked as Bob grabbed a fleece and expertly threw it onto the table.

'Worked in a few in my younger years,' Dave said, nodding.

Bob helped skirt the fleece, taking off the extra greasy and burr-matted edge, while Dave wandered over to the pens and scrutinised the sheep. He checked their ear marks and tags, making sure they were the same as what was registered to DoubleM Station, while listening to the conversation between Bob and John.

'Where were you before here?' Bob asked, continuing to help, while the roust-abouts flitted between the shearers and wool table.

'Out on the Nullarbor. Got up here about three weeks ago. Had a week bumming around in Carnarvon, getting ready to come out here. Had to find a shearers' cook and stock up with supplies.'

'Pretty used to being isolated then?'

'Much rather be out here than anywhere near the rat race, no matter how small the town. Only thing good about them towns are the pubs on the corner.'

Dave bit back a smile. A pub on every corner of every country town.

'Any talk of missing sheep?'

'Bit. Nothing concrete. Seems to be only this place where they've been proved to be gone. Haven't got out anywhere else to ask.' John turned and spat some chewy into the rubbish bin then wiped his forehead again, before digging out a tin of Port Royal and a paper. He rested his hip against the wool press and rolled a cigarette. One for him and one for the shearer near the door. Lit them both then handed it over.

The whole shed came to a standstill as Dave realised it was the top of the hour. That meant a five-minute smoko break, and smoko break up here still meant just that. A smoke.

'What about any wild dogs? Seen any evidence in your travels?' Dave addressed the question to the whole team.

'Nope. Seen nothing but red dirt and blue skies. Few cattle and goats on the side of the roads, but even the sheep seem to be staying off the roadways. There's feed and water everywhere.'

'Where you headed next?'

'Waiting to get back to Carnarvon and see what messages are at the pub for me. Left a message there to see if anyone wanted shearers now we were here.'

John drew in deeply and Dave heard the crackle of the tobacco burning. He loved the smell of Port Royal but wouldn't go near a ciggie with a ten-foot pole.

'Does Mick reckon you might get a bit of work up here?' Bob asked.

John nodded slowly. 'Yeah. Seems to think we'll be right.'

Dave went around and asked each person their name and address, giving them his card. 'If you see anything suspicious, then let us know. You can stay anonymous if you want.'

'Mate,' the roust-about called Polly stood up, holding her paddle, 'dunno what's classified as suspicious, but there's been a few ewes come through here with different ear tags.' She turned to the rest of them. 'You fellas noticed?'

Bob leaned forward. 'Is that right?'

'Yeah, there was a run of about fifty, I reckon.'

One shearer nodded. 'Yer right, Pol, there was. But that don't mean old Mick here hasn't bought 'em. Have to be careful saying things like that.'

'I know. Just thought it was strange.'

'Do you know the ear mark?'

Polly shook her head.

'Okay.' They heard heavy footsteps on the steps and turned as Mick entered with a large smile.

'How you getting on?' he asked. 'I see you got all the sheep in the shed. Thanks for that.'

'Be finished in about three hours,' John said, sucking hard on his cigarette before crushing it under foot, picking it up and tossing it in the bin. He nodded for everyone to get back to work.

'Good-oh,' Mick said. He turned to Bob. 'Sally spoke to Jane and she's got two units for you. If you're not there by dark, she'll leave the keys in the door. Bar is open tonight so you can get a feed.'

'Great, thanks. Well, we've finished here, so we'll get out of your way and be in touch when we've got any news. Thanks for all the documents.'

Bob and Dave left the shed and were getting in the troopy when a bloke they hadn't seen before materialised at the driver's side window.

Dave wound it down and smiled. 'G'day. I'm Detective Dave Burrows. You penning up out the back?'

The short wiry man, with a shock of red hair nodded quickly, glancing over his shoulder.

'Ivan Pyke. Local from around here. Picked up work when John was asking around at the hotel. Worked on a lot of the stations around here.' His sentences were short and sharp and Dave felt like there were small bullets being fired every time Ivan spoke.

Bob leaned across Dave. 'Glad to meet you, Ivan. Got something for us?'

Ivan nodded towards the shed. 'Mick's not everything he's cracked up to be. So you know, all right?'

Dave held the steering wheel steady as he directed the troopy through the swollen creek.

Normally, he would have relished the gentle sound of running water and the foam building up at the side of the creek. It would have been relaxing. But not now. Only fifteen minutes after they'd left DoubleM Station, they'd hit more rain.

The windscreen wipers were on full tilt and the rain was still pelting down. The roar of the river was loud above the noise of the engine.

Red dust had smeared across the windscreen at first, making it hard to see, but it hadn't taken long to clear the smudges, leaving only the large drops on the glass.

The jingle for the ABC radio news came on and Bob reached over to turn it up. 'Be nice to hear a weather report,' he said.

'I think they'll say it's raining,' Dave said.

Bob smirked at his partner's deadpan statement. 'You could be right. But for how long? It's only four o'clock. You'd think it was later with the heaviness of cloud making it so dark. That and rain always seem to make it feel like it's later in the day than it actually is.'

Bob balanced a folder on his lap as he tapped his fingers in time to the radio announcer's voice, telling of traffic delays and the latest news from parliament house. 'Good thing we left so early this morning. We've got a great start with the info that everyone's given us.' He thought for a minute. 'Ivan's comment was strange. Wish he could've elaborated a bit.'

'Uh-huh. Store it away in the old grey matter,' Dave said. 'Could be a previous employee with a grudge.'

Bob glanced at the large silver watch on his wrist. 'Exactly. Now how far away from Corbett's are we? 'Bout half an hour?'

'No, I think about another hour. The road's pretty slippery.'

'I'm glad Sally got those units for us.' He glanced behind him at the trailer they were towing. 'Wet swags and canvas doesn't excite me.'

'Me either.' Changing the subject, he nodded his head towards the papers sitting on Bob's lap. 'What did you do with the copy of the map of the station?'

'Here in the file.' He reached down into the footwell and grabbed the manila file, which was beginning to show signs of wear—dust smeared across the front and dog-eared corners. It looked to Dave like Bob had put his foot on it, too, because there was half a footprint on the cover. On the dash, an atlas was open to the page showing the area where they were driving. He traced his finger until he found DoubleM Station and compared the station map to the atlas. 'Okay, here's Corbett Station Stay. And here,' he said slowly, 'is Aggie and Graham Dorrell. I can see what Mick's saying about there being only one entrance. See, the boundary might as well be the river.' Dave glanced over and watched Bob's finger trace along the blue line.

'Fair bit of bush in between Corbett's and DoubleM,' Dave observed as he worked out where they were on the road in comparison to what he could see on the open page.

Moving the map to the dash, Bob flicked open the Millers' tax statement for last year and went straight to the births, deaths and natural increases. 'These figures hold steady for—' he grabbed the next one and checked '—at least two years, so to have a shortfall like he's got now does indicate that something's amiss.'

'It's a pity the other neighbours haven't shorn yet,' Dave said. 'It would be good to know if anyone else is missing any stock. Still, that won't be too far away, I don't think.'

'We won't have any idea if he's been targeted or if someone has got a bit of a fetish for ewes that aren't theirs.' Bob paused. 'Or if something else is going on.'

'I guess that's the first thing to find out: everyone else's stock numbers. Make sure no one has an increase that can't be accounted for.'

Bob nodded. 'I'll put an alert out to the abattoirs, but as I've said, this is going to be one of those "needle in a haystack" type investigations. We've got no idea when the sheep went missing, or where to start looking. Let's hope this pile of documents give up something worth learning.'

'And the neighbours . . .' Dave glanced over. 'Should we do a muster on their places?'

'Let's see what we find in talking to everyone first,' Bob said as the rain hurled down against the windows.

The mud gripped the wheels of the troopy and Dave felt it slide towards the edge of the road. He lightly applied the brake and held the steering wheel steady, knowing there was nothing he could do to get it out of a slide.

'Whoopee,' Bob said, as his hand flew above him, finding the Jesus bar.

'Sorry, Bob.' Dave felt the wheels gain traction. 'There we go.' He peered through the windscreen. 'Be bloody hard to do any type of muster with this amount of rain anyway.' As he spoke, the rain stopped as if a tap had been turned off; a loud silence replacing the deafening sound.

Dave managed to slow the wipers to intermittent. There was a smudge of blue appearing on the western horizon.

'Clouds might be lifting,' Bob said. 'Let's hope.'

CHAPTER 7

Driving into Corbett Station Stay took Dave back to the first case he'd worked on in the north, back to Spinifex Downs. An Indigenous station from where cattle had been stolen.

As on Spinifex Downs, Corbett Station Stay's homestead was a fibro construction, with a high roof for air flow and no gutters on the edge of the roof. When a cyclone came through, the gutters would never have kept the water away, so it was easier not to put them on, Bob had told Dave on his first trip up north.

The lawn was neat and the sign, once again made out of a windmill blade, said *Reception*, with an arrow pointing towards the house.

Puddles lay on the surface of the ground and the birds were flitting from one to the next, chirping and singing as they bathed themselves in the fresh water.

The sun was beginning to sink and Dave felt the relief that his driving day was almost done. He could almost taste the beer at the bar.

A young man came outside, smiling. 'G'day, you're looking like you need a camp.'

Bob held out his hand. 'Sure do. Sally Miller called to let you know we were on our way. Detectives Holden and Burrows.'

Recognition flashed across his face. 'Right. Yeah, Mum told me. We don't have anything flash, but basic, clean and dry. There're five demountable huts near the camp kitchen. Eighty bucks a night.'

Dave looked towards the camping grounds and saw a line of transportable units near a large building. The units were like the ones used as sleeping quarters on mining sites or some farms that couldn't afford to put in a house.

Bob grinned and got out the credit card. 'Sounds like just what we're after.'

'Great, come on in and I'll get the key for you.'

'Can we get two, please, mate?' He handed over the credit card.

'Sure. No worries.' The young man glanced down at the police force card. 'Cops, huh?' he added with curiosity. 'What are you doing up here?'

'We're with the stock squad, just checking out a few goings-on.'

A flicker in the corner of the young man's eye caught Dave's attention.

'Stock squad?'

'We're investigating some missing sheep from DoubleM Station. You're Brody Corbett, right?'

The young man nodded. 'That's right.'

'We're going to need to talk to you as the neighbour.'

'Sure, no problem. Follow me.' He walked across the porch, pulling open the wooden screen door and holding it for them both. 'Mum?' he called.

'Yeah, darling?' A female voice sounded from down the hallway.

'Two units, please. You'd better come and meet these blokes.'

Dave looked at the photos on the wall. A solid-built man was standing beside a slim, wiry, short woman whose long black hair was tied back in a messy bun. She wore jeans and a brightly coloured checked shirt. Her belt had a large buckle on it and the silver glinted in the sunlight. Beside her stood Brody and a young woman, slightly smaller than the other woman. He assumed this was a family photo taken a long time ago and the young woman was Belle, the sister who Mick had spoken about.

'Hello.' A soft voice came from the other end of the hall and the woman from the photo smiled at them. Except instead of standing she was in a wheelchair. The black hair, pretty smile and clothes were still the same. 'I'm Jane Corbett.'

'Mum, these guys are from the stock squad. They're here to talk about Mick losing stock over at DoubleM.'

'Ah, I did wonder if you might turn up. My daughter told me about this when she was visiting. What a shame you

79

missed her, she could have told you a lot more than what we know. Not good news for the pastoralists around here.' She put out her hand and Bob introduced themselves again.

Jane handed over two keys. 'Will you be staying long?'

'Look, we'll need to talk to you and some of the other neighbours. We're just starting our inquiries so I can't really tell you much at this point.'

'Anything we can do to help. Right, Brody?'

'Yeah, absolutely. Nothing to hide around here.' He gave them a big smile. 'Got too many people coming and going to be able to do anything wrong. What do you need from us?'

'We'll come and have a yarn tomorrow. I see you've got a bar, do you do meals, too?'

Jane moved her chair forward. 'Kelsey and Hannah are cooking tonight. You just have to put an order in before five thirty so we know what we have to do. The bar opens at four thirty, so that's already going.'

'Great, sounds very comfortable. Appreciate your hospitality. Kelsey and Hannah are . . . ?' Dave let the sentence hang.

'Backpackers,' Brody said. 'They help out around here, cleaning and cooking. Pump fuel when the tourists need it. I get a bit busy with taking the rubbish away and making sure everything is okay with the stock. So, we need a couple of extra hands. Mum—'

'Can do some things,' Jane put in before anyone else said anything, 'but not as much as I did before.'

Dave nodded, itching to write down some notes but instead committing the conversation to memory.

'Have the backpackers been here long?'

'Twelve months or so.'

'And where are they now?'

'At the bar running everything, You can introduce yourselves when you head over.'

'We will. Thanks very much for your help. You don't know how pleased we are not to be sleeping on the ground tonight,' Bob said, raising his key at Jane.

⁓

The bar had only about five people in it when Bob and Dave walked in. The fan was turning lazily overhead and the walls were covered in maps with things-to-do and places-to-see-type brochures.

Behind the bar were two similar looking women. Both tall, with long blonde hair, pulled back in ponytails. The skimpy shirts they were wearing showed their tanned arms as they pulled beers and smiled and talked with the travellers.

Dave got out his wallet and cocked his head at Bob.

'Beer, thanks, son.' Bob pulled out a chair and sat down, while Dave went to the bar.

'What can I get you,' one of the girls asked, wiping a damp cloth in front of Dave as he leaned on the bar.

'Couple of mid stubbies, thanks.' He watched her pull the beers out of the fridge and put them in front of him. 'Are you Hannah or Kelsey?' he asked, giving her a smile.

'Kelsey,' she answered.

'Nice to meet you Kelsey. I'm Dave. My mate over there is Bob. Can we put an order in for a couple of burgers, please?'

'Sure. I'll get Hannah to do them up for you.' She nodded, moving on to the next customer and Dave realised she probably had men crack on to her all the time. Not that that was what he was trying to do, but it probably sounded like it.

He took the beers back to the table and held his up in a cheers action.

'Here's to it.'

'Yeah, mate.' Bob held his stubby up too and they clicked bottles.

Laughter from two older couples rose. 'I think we ran into them when we were camped at Kununurra,' one of them said. 'Bloody character, hey? His missus could nearly drink him under the table and the way he got around in bare feet. Don't know how he did it with all those cane toads up there.'

Someone else took up the commentary.

'Their dog used to come across to our camp and nick anything we left out on the table. We learned pretty quickly to pack everything up.'

'Ah, you've got to. Ants get stuck in if you leave even a crumb on the table.'

'Did you come across that group who were camped out of Newman? Those motorbikers. Adventure riders they called themselves. They'd had a bad run. Some of their group had broken a couple of ankles and one of the bikes had the fuel tank shaken loose.'

'Not for the faint-hearted out here,' a man agreed.

Dave got up and went over to them. 'G'day people,' he said. 'Can't help but overhear. You've been on the road for a while?'

'Pull up a pew,' the younger man said. 'Yeah, we're not travelling together but seem to keep running across these rascals here.' He put out his hand and introduced himself as Darren Potts. 'This is my wife, Colleen, and these two are Colin and Sandra.'

They exchanged pleasantries. 'I'm wondering if you can help us? We're with the stock squad and investigating a case up this way. Have you seen many wild dogs? Or heard them?'

'Oh, do you know,' Colleen said leaning towards Dave, 'it's been on my wish list to see one and there's just been no sign of them at all.'

'Even camped out in the bush?'

'More trouble with ants than anything else,' Darren said.

Colin looked at Dave then across to Bob, curiously. 'What are you investigating?'

'Nothing worrying for you. Some sheep are missing.'

'Oh,' Sandra said, her eyes lighting up. 'Stock theft. What Australia is known for. Captain Moonlight and all of that. Did they pinch them . . .'

'Sandra!' Colin snapped at her.

'Sorry. But I mean, how exciting! Gosh, your job must be thrilling. Can you tell us any stories?'

Dave gave a laugh. 'Yep, as thrilling as trawling through information, witness statements and paperwork. And, nope, no stories here.'

'What type of information are you looking for?'

'Anything that will help us. Have you seen or heard trucks at strange times of the night or small trucks that don't look like they should carry stock with animals on them.'

'Actually, now you mention it,' Darren turned to Colleen, 'what about when we were camped out on the road from Meekatharra to Mount Augustus?' he continued. 'Those trucks that went past about two in the morning.'

'Yeah, I won't forget that in a hurry. Scared the living daylights out of me. Truck after truck after truck. I actually got up to have a look, but they weren't stock trucks, were they, Daz?' she asked. 'I thought they were carrying other things.'

'Yeah. Actually, you're right, they were.' He turned back to Dave. 'There were about eight or ten trucks that went past in the middle of the night. Made a hell of a noise, but Col's right. They didn't have any sheep. More machinery.'

'Even so, that's good to know.'

Hannah arrived at the table with the two burgers and put them down near Bob.

Dave smiled at her again, getting out his card. 'That's my cue, but here's my details if you see anything out of the ordinary.'

'We can be sleuths,' Sandra said snatching up the card. 'This could be very good fun!'

Dave gave them a salute with his forefinger and headed back to his table, via the bar. Bob's beer was empty and his wasn't far behind.

Biting into his burger he mumbled around the sweet, juicy meat, 'Trucks in the middle of the night on a deserted road?'

'Might be drillers for the mine,' Bob said. 'When they finish a job, it doesn't matter what time it is, they get going to the next one. Anyway, that road to Mount Augustus is a fair way away from here. Outside of the search range at this point, unless proved otherwise.'

Dave nodded and his gaze flicked back to the two backpackers. 'Wonder if they would realise if they'd seen anything odd? I mean they're from another country so they wouldn't know what was strange and what was not.'

Bob leaned back in his chair. 'You'd be right there,' he said. 'Tell you what, though. That Jane, getting around in a chair like that and still smiling.' He shook his head. 'An accident like that? I reckon I'd rather be dead, wouldn't you?'

Dave thought about his daughters. 'Hard question. I guess you can still be with people when you're paralysed, but you can't be if you're six foot under.' He paused, and with the remaining bit of his bun, wiped up the egg yolk that had dripped onto the plate. 'I think I'd still want to see my kids.'

'Yeah, I guess you would.' Drawing his hand across his mouth to get rid of the barbecue sauce, Bob said, 'That was bloody beautiful. Another beer, I think.'

Dave heard the squawk of galahs and rolled over in bed, trying to work out where he was.

One of the hardest things about his job was he slept in so many different places, in that place between sleep and wakefulness he wasn't always sure of what case he was on.

His need for coffee was great, so he went outside and opened up the troopy, looking for the twelve-volt kettle he could use to boil water from the vehicle's cigarette lighter.

All around people were beginning to emerge from their camps. Sleepily stoking fires and boiling their billy or kettle. A baby was crying in the distance and a couple of young kids wandered by with their mothers holding toothbrushes and towels.

Making two coffees he knocked on Bob's door and said, 'Coffee,' before leaving it at the door and going back to his room.

The verandah was always a good place to start the day, but he was worried if he sat still for too long, he'd think about his kids and he didn't want those horrible emotions of loss flowing through him today. He needed to focus on the case.

Instead, he took a few sips of coffee and opened the file that had been sitting on the table. He tried to commit the map of the three stations to memory. The distances and what was in between, where the creeks and rivers ran and, more importantly, what numbers of sheep each station ran normally.

Taking a sip of his coffee he traced the roads with his finger.

'Thanks for the coffee, son.' Bob stood at his doorway, dressed, his hair slicked back and tidy.

Dave's eyebrows hit his hair line. 'You're looking schmick. Any reason?'

'No.' There was a hint of laughter in Bob's tone. 'Trying to set a good example for you.' He nodded towards Dave's hair. 'You should have had a haircut before we left.'

'Mmm. Like the sheep and cattle care about that.'

'Come on, let's get going. Brody is down there stoking the fire and talking to some of the campers. I want to have a chat.'

'Be right there,' Dave said, draining his coffee and putting the empty cup on the table.

~

Bob stood next to the fire, his hands outstretched towards the flames, deep in conversation with Brody.

As Dave walked over, he took stock of what he saw. Brody was tall and thin. No, not even thin. Scrawny would have been a word Mel might have used for the young lad. But Dave could see he was strong; his arms were defined and he seemed sure of himself, by his stance.

Brody nodded to Dave as he approached. 'Hope you slept okay.'

'Like a baby,' Dave said.

'Brody here was just telling me a bit of history of the station. There's over thirty kilometres of coastline on the boundary here.' He turned to Brody. 'Thirty, you said?'

'Yep, that's right and about twenty kilometres of the Murchison River, too.'

'Ah, lots of soaks and springs then?'

Brody nodded. 'Makes for lots of wildlife and therefore lots of visitors. Sometimes I run a few small tours out to the ranges, if there's enough interest, but I don't always have time, being just me here.'

'The girls don't help?'

'They've got their hands full cleaning and cooking. Pumping fuel sometimes.'

'Where are they at the moment?' Bob asked.

Brody looked at his watch. 'They'll be at the beach. I know it's been pouring with rain, but as you can feel it's not that cold. Coming from England, they love running down the beach every day.'

'Must be great to have help. How many clients do you get through here?'

'It's always busy during the dry. In summer it's too hot for people so there's never as many then, but we've been pretty much fully booked for the last nine weeks straight. But school holidays have finished now, and it's beginning to get warm. Not that you'd know it by the weather, and that's when the customers start to die down.' As Brody talked he pointed to the camp site map on the wall. 'We've got lots of sites for caravans and campers, as you can see here. They stretch all the way to the river. But only these five units. I'd like to put more in, but that all costs money.'

'Where's the beach from here?' Dave asked, thinking he wouldn't mind dipping his toes in. Not that he would have time today.

'Look out for the signs from here.' He tapped the map again. 'You should be able to follow your nose from there.'

The sound of a motorbike reached them and they turned to see Jane riding slowly down the well-maintained, gravel track.

'Mum was keen to know how you got on last night,' Brody said. 'Making sure the burgers were up to standard.'

With a large smile, Jane pulled up and Dave could see her wasted legs inside the modified motor bike—it looked more like a golf buggy with hand controls.

'Get on all right last night, boys?' she asked. 'Is Brodes here looking after you?'

'Very comfortable thanks, Jane,' Bob said. 'Just getting the lay of the land now.'

'Good to hear.' She nodded and clicked the buggy into gear. 'Let me know if you need anything.' To Brody she said, 'I'm heading back up to feed and water the chooks.' Flashing a rueful look, she said, 'Got to account for my every movement these days unfortunately. Seems that people get concerned.'

'Rightly so,' Dave said.

'Catch you later.' Jane let out the clutch and drove slowly away.

Bob brushed the friendly flies away from his face and looked up at the sky. 'Different day from yesterday,' he said.

'I can't believe that weather has buggered off already,' Dave said, knowing that shooing the flies away from his face was futile, but he did it anyway, too. He hoped he'd remembered to pack his fly net.

'Thought it had set in, I've got to admit,' Bob agreed.

'Changeable up here,' Brody said, glancing over his shoulder. 'Anyway, I'd better get on. Gotta collect the rubbish from last night. Always heaps of beer cans and wine bottles to get rid of in the morning.'

'Sure thing,' Bob said. 'If we could catch up with you when you've done your chores, that would be great.'

Brody nodded and went to leave. A frown crossed his face as he looked towards the beach. 'What the—?'

Dave caught a movement from near the shed and turned. The two young pretty girls, from last night, ran towards them. They were wearing shorts and singlets, their hair was plastered around their faces and Dave smiled. A long time ago, Mel had run every morning and he'd loved it when she'd come back hot and sweaty. Well, not so much the hot and sweaty but how she'd looked in her leggings.

He realised it had been a few hours since he'd last thought about his ex-wife. A few hours was a step forward. She was usually at the forefront of his mind, no matter what he was doing.

Slowly, Dave realised there was a noise . . . screaming. He spun around and looked towards the girls again. Their arms were flailing around, trying to attract attention.

'Help!' one of them called.

Brody stood stock still before kicking into a run towards the girls.

Dave was closer and also took off towards them, knowing he had to calm them down enough to get them to say what was frightening them. He stopped the first one and put his hands on her upper arms. 'It's okay, I'm the police. Take some deep breaths. What's wrong? Why do you—'

The other girl stopped and put her hands over her ears and screamed long and loudly.

'Jesus,' said Bob, who had appeared at Dave's side. He bent over and talked quietly to the girl, while Dave spoke to the one he was holding.

'You're safe,' Dave said in a calm voice. 'But you need to tell us what's wrong, so we can help.'

'What the hell, Hannah?' Brody asked, his voice high with fear. He stood close to her, not touching, even though his hand had gone out to do just that, but he'd snatched it back before he'd reached her body. 'What's happened?'

'There's a—' Hannah couldn't get the words out. Dave wasn't sure if it was because of tears or because she was breathing too hard. He glanced at Kelsey. She was curled up in the foetal position, with Bob bending over her.

Other campers were coming out of their vans and looking over towards them now. A couple of people had begun to run across the lawn to help.

'Hey! You need to leave those girls alone,' someone called. 'What are you doing?'

Dave dug in his pocket for his ID and held it up. Not that they'd be able to see it from where they were, but he hoped it would be enough to stop them coming any closer.

'It's all right. We're the police. Thanks for your help, but if you could all go back inside, we'll deal with this. Thank you very much.'

He turned to Brody. 'Where can we take them that's quiet?'

'Into the house.' Brody's eyes were wild and his chest was heaving as much as the girls' were. 'What's on the beach, Hannah?' he asked again.

Hannah screwed up her eyes and shook her head, unable to make any words come out.

Dave took her arm. 'Come, let's get you somewhere quiet.'

Bob was trying to help Kelsey to her feet. She hadn't moved, except to moan loudly.

Hannah finally spoke and the words came like bullets. 'A body.'

Dave felt the kick of adrenalin, and he took a breath. Glancing over at Bob, he saw he'd heard what Hannah had said, too. His body was tense and he tried to get Kelsey off the ground again.

'We think it's a body,' Hannah said, appearing to pull herself together enough to speak properly now. She swallowed and hugged herself. 'But we're not sure. It doesn't look right.'

'What do you mean?' Confusion crossed Brody's face. 'A body? You mean like a tourist?' His tone went up a notch.

'Mate, if you could . . .' Dave inclined his head towards the camp. More people were coming out of their vans for a look and he didn't want them near the girls. 'Deal with them, thanks. We'll sort this.'

Hannah took a couple of breaths and seemed to calm herself as Brody put his hand on her arm.

'Down there . . . Near the dunes.' She took another breath and looked at Brody. 'A dead body.'

CHAPTER 8

The body, Dave was about eighty per cent sure, was male. Dave was also pretty sure he was an Anglo-Saxon.

The body—if you could call it that—was rolled up and it could have been mistaken for a large ball of seaweed. It was floppy, as bodies are when they've been in the water a while, as though every part of them is double-jointed. It had rolled and moved with the swell and tides, which had taken all the rigor mortis away.

In their quick introduction to Turquoise Bay, they had driven the couple of kilometres to the entry of the beach, then dropped down onto the sand. Hannah had told them the body was about another kilometre on from the entrance and now, as he looked across the smooth surface of the water, Dave wondered how a peaceful, beautiful place like this could be tarnished with death. The sea stretched out wide, the shallows where the water was turquoise met a line of deep blue, showing where the depth of the water changed.

The sand was so soft that Dave had sunk to his ankles as he stood observing the body. Red dunes melted into the sand making it a light orange colour, and small scrubby bushes behind showed the harshness of the landscape. They would have to stand up to the sea breezes that no doubt whipped around in the afternoons and the cyclones that came through with full force.

So much beauty and rawness. From what Brody had said earlier, there was thirty-odd kilometres of this stunning coastline that was owned by Corbett Station Stay.

And here was a body exposed to all these elements, the waves still lapping around it gently. It had to be luck that he had washed ashore here. If it had been five kilometres down the coast, this unfortunate person might not have been found. At least this way he could be returned to his family when he was IDed.

The skin had been bleached opaque by the waves and friction of the water rolling the body over and over. The hair was all gone, and the man wasn't wearing clothes. Dave knew the sea would have stripped them from him.

To his forensically untrained eye, it looked as if crabs and sea lice had also had an impact on the body. It was missing both eyes and other parts of the man's face.

'I've called it in,' Bob said from behind him. Dave glanced up and saw Bob putting the satellite phone back into the cradle and getting out some evidence bags.

'Right.' Dave squatted down, keeping his hands tucked away, and inspected the body closely. With the damage done by the sea life, it would be hard to see if there was a wound that could have killed the man.

'Poor bastard.' Bob squatted next to him and observed the body as well. 'Takes between six and eight days for a body to rise in the water. I've seen bodies look like this before. I'm guessing he's been in for all of those eight.'

Dave stood up and felt his knees crack. 'What do you reckon happened?'

'Hard to tell with the damage, son, but at first glance I can't see anything sinister. Might've fallen overboard and drowned in an earlier storm. Or had a few too many and accidentally fallen in. That's my best guess. Still, the autopsy will tell us more. You got any thoughts?'

'Yeah, well, a storm could've caused some havoc. The winds got fairly strong when we were at DoubleM Station yesterday, didn't they? So, if the same thing had happened, yep, that's a possibility. Storms up here are so sudden and fierce, one could have whipped up a swell for sure. Guess we should check the weather reports for the last two weeks and with Border Force, see what was in the area at the time. Wonder if a boat or anyone's been reported missing.'

'I know the body looks a bit untidy, but see here.' Bob pointed to a spot on the body's fingers. 'Nothing but crabs and sea lice and any other creature that's wanted to have a nibble. We're not going to have any fingerprints to work with for ID, but that's going to be Shannon's problem, not ours. There're no grazes or bruises—well, let me rephrase that. No cuts or grazes that make me think they've happened before death. Plenty of injuries for sure, but it all looks like sea damage. Anyway,' Bob got up, 'Shannon will be able to tell us more. There was a reason I never became a pathologist. That smell when they open up the guts in a post-mortem.' Bob shivered, but Dave knew what he meant. It was a smell that only someone who had been there would understand; it wasn't pleasant.

But he glossed over the last few sentences, because the word 'Shannon' was reverberating around in his head.

'Shannon's going to be handling this?' The detectives never knew which forensic pathologist was going to handle a death. How did Bob know now?

Bob looked over. 'She is, son.' He paused and looked at Dave over the top of his sunglasses. 'Problem?'

He had to answer straightaway. Any hesitancy would make Bob suspicious. 'Nope. Not to me.' Dave paused, his brain ticking over. 'Why aren't the locals handling the case? How come we're going to be stuck with it?' An image came to him: Shannon walking towards him in the corridor of the police station in Barrabine. Tall and slim and her smile wide and welcoming, even though she had been down a narrow mine shaft with a week-old body. Her long, black glossy hair was always tied back in an untidy plait or ponytail and, even when kitted up, behind the mask and protective eyewear her green eyes sparkled. Her graceful walk that day had stuck in his mind.

Dave had known before then that he liked Shannon. He'd always kept an eye out for her in the corridors of the courthouse or in the brightly lit halls of the morgue. And he'd sensed she felt the same.

Shannon understood the job. They'd known each other for years, since Dave had first joined the force. He'd been in her autopsy suite many, many times, working under other detectives.

But it had been when Dave had been stationed at Barrabine and was investigating that body down a mine shaft that they'd worked together for the first time and he'd realised how important it was to have someone who understood what being in the force was like.

Shannon had arrived in Barrabine at the height of Dave's marital problems, offering the exact understanding he needed.

Unlike Mel.

Shannon listened to him talk and then suggested they get together for a drink.

As much as he'd wanted to have a drink with her, Dave had reminded her he was married, and nothing more had been said until a few months ago when he'd run into her again. This time it had been him who had suggested they catch up for a drink. That hadn't eventuated because they hadn't managed to be in the same area at the same time. Yet.

'Locals can't deal with it, I'm told,' Bob said, bringing Dave out of his reverie. 'Under-resourced, like that's a bloody newsflash.'

'That bit makes sense, but how do you know it's Shannon who's coming?' he persisted.

Bob gave a grunt. 'This is called divine alignment. She's been up in Hedland giving evidence at a trial. PolAir has got her onboard so they're diverting to pick the body up.

Bit over the top, if you ask me. Like I said, I can't see anything that suggests a violent death.' He shrugged. 'Still, the bigwigs have decided and the body has to get to the morgue somehow, so they can check it out.'

Dave glanced up at the clear sky as an engine sound came faintly from the distance, before getting louder and stopping.

'Oi!'

Both men turned at the shouting from further down the beach.

'Oi. Hello!'

Bob nodded to Dave. 'You go. He can't come here. I'll see what I can do to secure this as much as I can.' He stared down at the quivering flesh. 'Reckon we might need some type of net to carry this up a bit. Not sure we can leave it until Shannon gets here, can we?'

Brody was getting closer and Dave took a few steps towards him and held up his hand in a stop signal.

'Wait there, please, Brody.' To Bob he said, 'Tide's going out. How far away is she?'

'Hour to an hour and a half, depending on how long it takes for them to get here from the strip. They got an early start.'

'What do you mean, stop?' Brody blustered. 'This is my land. If something's gone wrong, I think I should be able to have a look.'

'Brody,' Dave's voice held no argument. 'Stop there. I will be with you in a minute.' He turned his attention back to his partner. 'Where's the strip?'

'Right here on Corbett's.'

'I'd leave him there. Let her deal with the situation. She might have a better way to get him into a body bag. If there was any evidence to be found, it's probably washed out to sea, so let's preserve the body as best we can, don't you reckon? We can put a tarp over him, though. Stop the seagulls.'

Bob didn't answer, but squatted back down, his face angled downwards.

Dave walked towards Brody, who was pacing up and down, leaving a trail of deep footprints wherever he stepped.

'Brody, I'm sorry, but you can't be here. We've got some work to do and once that's completed, we'll be up to have a chat.'

'This is my place!' The words burst from the young man in a barrage of spittle and fear. 'How do I know that it's not a tourist who's been camped up here? I could get into a shitload of trouble or . . . or . . .' He looked around wildly as if the words he was searching for would appear over the top of the rugged hills.

'Has anyone been reported missing?' Dave asked calmly.

Brody shook his head.

'Do you know if anyone is missing from the camp sites? Do you have a site that still looks occupied but nobody's there?'

Running his fingers through his hair, Brody seemed to think about that. The fight went out of him. 'Nah, I don't think so. I've seen the younger couple in the Eagle

Eye site and that bloke by himself in the Babbler site . . .' He stopped. 'I saw him yesterday. Everyone else is accounted for, I think.'

'Fine. This death happened a while ago.'

'How long?' The words snapped out of Brody.

'I can't tell you that, but if you've seen those people in the last couple of days then what we have here is nothing for you to worry about.'

Brody poked his toe deep into the sand and kept digging it in and out. 'Sorry.' The fight seemed to go out of him. 'Bit of a concern something like this happening. Scary.' He looked at Dave. 'It'll be bad for business if this gets out and god knows we need the campers.'

'Of course. One more question: have there been any fights or arguments at the camp sites, that you've heard?'

'As in domestics?' Brody's eyes narrowed.

Dave shrugged. 'As in any disagreements between anyone.'

'No,' he said slowly. 'Not that I remember. There's always the occasional argument between a couple when they're trying to back their vans in, but nothing serious. I don't remember anyone arguing badly . . .' His voice trailed off.

'Right-oh. Well, you just leave the rest to us now. Head home. But I'll need to come and have a look at your guest register sometime soon.'

Brody took another glance at the bundle. It was stranded away from the water now. A large 'thing' on an otherwise empty beach. No wonder the girls had seen it so easily.

'I'll get Mum to get the register out for you. There's not a lot of information in it, though.'

'Great, anything is better than nothing at this stage. We'll have a PolAir plane landing here in the next hour or so, with a couple more coppers. Can we get another two units for them, please?'

Brody looked at Dave for a long moment and, when he answered, his voice was low. 'No problems.'

'Is your strip up to scratch? No potholes or anything? Do we need to do a run up and down to scare the roos or stock away from it?'

'It's an RFDS strip, so she's pretty sweet. I can head out there and check as a precaution, but there shouldn't be any stock in that paddock.'

'If you wouldn't mind. I'll be there to meet the plane when it lands.' Dave turned away and started to head back to Bob, when Brody began to speak again.

'Can we still have people coming into camp?' he asked. 'I mean, once word gets out about this, they probably won't want to, but . . .'

'Why wouldn't they?' Dave asked.

'Tourists are fickle creatures. They want the best for as little as possible. To come to a place where there's been a murder.'

The hair rose on the back of Dave's neck.

'Murder?' he echoed quietly. 'Why do you say it's murder?'

A look of confusion crossed Brody's face. 'What?'

'Why do you say it's murder?'

'Well, I just assumed. I mean, you don't usually get a body . . .' He spread his hands out in uncertainty. 'Sorry, I just . . . Forget I said anything.'

'Brody, if you know something about this, you need to tell us now,' Dave said in a low, warning tone. 'This is someone who has a family and loved ones and they deserve to know what happened to him or her.'

'No! No, I don't know anything.'

Dave heard the fear and panic in the young man's voice.

'Truly, I don't know anything. I assumed. Not many people just turn up dead.'

'I hope you're telling me the truth, Brody, because if you're not, I will find out.' He fixed the young man with an icy blue stare.

Brody seemed to shrink under Dave's gaze.

CHAPTER 9

The plane banked and circled above the strip as the pilot got a bead on the runway, then straightened up to come in to land.

Dave watched from inside the troopy, his elbow resting on the ledge of the window. He'd left Bob at the beach protecting the body.

'You make sure you give a warm welcome, eh, son,' Bob had said as Dave had got into the vehicle, and then given him a wink.

Dave had flicked him the bird but driven away with a fizz in his stomach. He wasn't sure if it was nerves, guilt or the thought of seeing Shannon again. Or the heat of today.

The Beechcraft Bonanza six-seater plane taxied over to the gravelled parking area, where they could tie it down, safe from the forecasted winds. As the propellor came to a stop, Dave could see Shannon sitting in the front passenger's seat, her face turned away from him. He wondered if she knew he was here, or if she was going to get a big surprise.

Dave watched as the pilot leaned across Shannon to unlatch the door and she uncurled her long form and stepped onto the wing.

Slipping her sunglasses on, she looked around, got her bearings and clambered down the walkway of the wing and onto the ground. She put her arms in the air and stretched from side to side, then moved one hand to one side of her head and pulled downwards trying to loosen up her neck. All with graceful and elegant movements.

Dave felt something inside him stir. A feeling he hadn't had for a long time. A longing. A desire. A need to feel another human's touch.

He wrenched open the car door and got out as the pilot followed Shannon down and opened the back door to get out her forensic bag and their luggage. He said something to her over his shoulder as he leaned inside the plane, and a large smile split Shannon's face.

Dave heard the peal of her laughter. He couldn't wait any longer. 'G'day,' he called, striding across the space in between them.

Shannon turned and a look of surprise crossed her face, then she relaxed into a small laugh. 'Well, well, Dave Burrows.' She cocked her head to one side and looked at him. 'I should have expected to see you out here. After all, this is your natural habitat, isn't it? Somewhere deep in the outback! I don't know why I didn't make that connection, especially since it was Bob Holden who called it in.' She took a step towards him and Dave thought she was going to shake his hand, so he held out his, but she bypassed it and kissed him on the cheek. 'How are you keeping?'

He gave a laugh at the natural habitat comment. 'Fine,' he answered. 'Good. How about you? Flight okay?'

'Beautiful. Do you know Mac? The eagle of the skies!' She gave another laugh as she threw a smile in Mac's direction. The pilot put down a couple of bags and got the ropes out of the back to tie the aircraft down.

'Can't say I do,' Dave said. 'Nice to meet you.'

'Heard about you, Dave. It's good to meet a legend in person.' The young man, who couldn't be more than twenty-five, with a boyish face and hair cropped close to his skull, looked in awe of Dave as they shook hands.

Dave frowned. 'Don't believe everything you've heard. Probably a crock of shit! What can I carry? Shannon, you'll be wanting to get down to the beach right away? Mac, do you need a hand?'

Mac had moved off, ropes in hand. 'Nah, mate, I'll get this baby secured, myself. She's like my own.'

Shannon flicked her hair back and picked up her bag. 'Yep, I'll come down there with you straightaway. Mac, you'll come?'

The pilot shook his head as he finished securing the plane and came over to join them. 'If we're going to be out of here tomorrow, I need to get access to a phone so I can check the weather and put in a flight plan.'

'Jump in then.' Dave nodded towards the troopy. 'I'll get you back to the units we've booked and you can take it from there. The house has a phone. Jane, the owner, will be able to help you.'

'Great, I'll see what I can get organised. You got any idea how long this recovery is gonna take, boss?'

Shannon, who had climbed into the front passenger's seat, shrugged. 'I haven't seen the body yet, Mac, so I'm not sure. Why?'

'Working out an estimated time of departure.'

'Can't help you there until I've seen what I've got to work with. What's your take on it, Dave?'

They bounced down the two-wheel track towards the homestead and camp grounds. Dave thought about the question. 'I don't know,' he said finally. 'The body is in pretty bad condition. Bob reckons it's been under for at least six to eight days.'

Shannon nodded. 'Look, it'll have slippage and will be difficult to get into a body bag, but we should be done by tonight.' She looked out of the window to where the white everlastings were flowering against the scrub. 'Stunning scenery. Oh, look,' she pointed out the window, as Dave slammed his foot on the brake.

'What?' he asked quickly.

'Sturt's desert peas. Over there under the tree. I haven't seen any of them since I was visiting the Flinders Ranges with my family. Such a beautiful flower.'

'I thought something was wrong,' Dave said.

'One body and you get all jumpy! How beautiful is this place?' She continued to look out of the window as Dave's eyes found Mac's through the rear-view mirror. He gave a slight shake of his head as if to say 'Women!' and Mac rolled his eyes.

Pulling up at the camp site, Dave handed over a key to Mac. 'House is there,' he pointed. 'Put an order in for dinner while you're up there in case we're held up today and the body takes longer to recover. All orders need to be in by five thirty, I think Jane said.' He paused while Mac opened his door. 'Just get the burgers. They're good.'

'Sure.' Mac grabbed his flying bag and overnight bag and hauled himself out. 'I'll get all of this sorted. See you then.' Slamming the door, he touched his finger to his forehead in a salute gesture, then tapped the back of the troopy in a farewell, as they drove away.

Dave glanced at Shannon out of the corner of his eye, but she was still staring out of the window, transfixed by the beauty of the landscape.

'How've you been, Shannon?' he asked quietly.

She turned to face him with a slight smile. Cocking her head to one side, she regarded him as a parent would a child when they'd done something intriguing.

'I think the question is how are you?' she replied softly. 'Nothing's changed too much for me. But you? You must've been through hell. I heard how it played out with Bulldust.'

Dave gave a one-shoulder shrug. 'It's been tough for sure, but—' he took his hands off the steering wheel and held them palm up '—what can I do but get on with things?'

'Do you see your kids?'

Dave swallowed and thought about his last conversation with his lawyer.

'Not much. Mel's lawyer has indicated that they think I'm a risk—or rather my life and job is a risk—to the girls. Apparently I could put them in danger and so they don't think it's a good idea that I see them at all.' Dave wanted to bang his hands on the steering wheel and yell. He'd do anything to protect them, not hurt them! 'I played into Mark's hands with that, didn't I?'

'That's not true, Dave. I hope you know that.' Futile words, because everyone knew that's exactly what had happened. His actions had brought a violent offender into his family's house.

'But it is,' he said quietly. 'That's already been proved.' A shudder passed through him as he heard the gunshot and screams again. The gurgling from Ellen's chest as blood bubbled out and filled her lungs, which had been torn open by the bullet.

The silence stretched out between them and finally Shannon turned back to the window.

Dave followed the well-graded track down to the beach. Brody had told Dave that this was the closest and most popular beach with the tourists. Two kilometres from the camp site was still close enough to walk or drive down. There was a large parking area set back from the beach, and the walkway was wide enough for people to use. Parts of the fragile sand dunes were fenced off, indicating that no one should walk or disturb the soil, until it was revegetated.

'Sometimes at sunset you need a bloody set of traffic lights down there,' Brody had told them.

Dave had been able to see why. The sea stretched out to the horizon with nothing blocking the view. He could imagine the red glow on the water as the sun set and the gentle lap of waves at the beach. It would have been the sort of place that he would have taken Mel to ask her to marry him.

Instead, he was here without her and the overwhelming feeling of loss and grief made him want to scratch the emotions threatening to overtake him. He'd never thought that Mel could become a stranger the way she had. That she would be living a life he knew nothing of. Sometimes his suffering felt akin to when his grandfather had died. A death. No divorcee mentioned that awful heartache. And rarely was what you were feeling recognised as that. Even if the marriage wasn't happy and it was best for both parties that it ended, there was still a mourning period.

Dave turned off to another less-used two-wheel track that wound its way over the first low, sandy hill and down onto the beach. Normally, it had a chain over the trail, discouraging people from using it, but Brody had removed that so Dave could get Shannon down with all her gear. Before long, there would be a body bag in the back of his troopy to take to the homestead. Bob had instructed Brody to make sure their coolroom was on and set to freeze, because that was where the remains would be stored until the plane took off in the morning.

To say Brody hadn't liked the idea would be an understatement.

'What? That's where we keep all the food for everyone! You can't go putting it in there!'

'We don't have a choice,' Bob had told him. 'We have to preserve the body the best we can and we don't have a morgue close by.'

In the end, Bob's negotiation skills and promise that the remains would be double-wrapped had won out, and Brody grudgingly went to do what they'd asked.

'Look at the colour of that water. Next time I have a holiday, I'm coming up north.' Shannon's voice was low with awe.

'Yeah, it's a nice area.' He inhaled and exhaled deeply three or four times, breathing out the feelings, then looked over at her. 'So, what were you doing up this way?'

'Evidence in a murder trial. Couple of prospectors had a disagreement and one came off second best.'

Dave nodded. 'Oh, that was the one where the bloke was found in an old, ruined humpy out of Meekatharra?'

'Yeah, that's the one.'

'Nasty.'

'Was fairly decomposed by the time I got to it, for sure.'

They bumped along the track in silence for a little while, then Dave pointed across the beach. 'See Bob over there? That's where we're at.'

'At least the tide's out,' Shannon said, reaching behind her head and undoing her ponytail. She deftly split her hair into three strands and braided it, before winding it into a knot and securing it with another hair band. 'Hopefully, this won't be too difficult.'

Just her simple movements made Dave's heart thunder in his chest and he blurted out, 'Should we have that drink tonight?'

Shannon stilled, then reached across and put her hand on his arm, just as they pulled up next to Bob. 'I thought you'd never ask.'

CHAPTER 10

'The body is very damaged by the water, that's for sure,' Shannon said as she pulled off her gloves and wiped the sweat away from her eyes.

The sun had become steadily hotter as it had made its journey across the sky. There was a bank of cloud out to sea, but it hadn't come any closer, and the humidity from the rain earlier in the day was rising, too.

Dave and Bob had lifted the body bag into the back of their troopy under Shannon's clear instructions and they had finished checking around the site to see if there was any trace of evidence.

There had been nothing of interest.

'But I don't see anything that's looking like a murder yet. Of course, I'll get him back and run toxicology checks and X-ray the body. There could be internal damage that shows up—broken bones and the like—but I'm not expecting anything.'

'You'll get results from the tox tests?' Dave asked as he fished out his hankie from his pocket and wiped his face.

'Yep, we'll get something. The accuracy drops with time and they might not be conclusive but that's no reason not to run them. We might get gold, too!'

'Right, well, I'll leave him in your capable hands,' Bob said. 'Let's transport him back to the coolroom and get that drink we've all earned today. Gotta say I didn't think the day was going to play out like this when we got up this morning. Bloody hell, it's humid.'

The sun slid behind the single cloud bank, casting the land into a dimness that made it feel like night would be closing in soon.

'I'm with you on that,' Shannon said with a sigh. She threw her bag in the passenger's seat before climbing in. 'Stunning scenery but the heat is a bit yuck. Wouldn't want to have to be up here when it's summer.' She shimmied across the bench seat and let Bob get in next to her, while Dave climbed into the driver's seat.

Immediately, he felt Shannon's warm leg pressed against his, although she tried to shuffle closer to Bob, so he could move the gear stick.

'I like heat,' Dave said.

'Oh no, not me. Anything over thirty and I'm uncomfortable. Always said I should move to Tasmania,' she said.

'Tasmania? You grew up in Perth! You know what heat is.' He tried to move the gear stick and accidentally touched her knee as he did. Her skin was smooth, and damp with sweat.

'Oops, close quarters,' she said with a small laugh and wiggled her leg as Dave tried to get into second. He couldn't, so he sped up a bit more and then changed from first straight into third.

'Yeah, I know, but I've always liked the cold better. Sorry, Bob.' Shannon pulled her hands up towards her chest, trying to keep them from touching either of the men.

'Nothing like getting to know each other better,' Bob quipped. 'Tell me, Shannon, how many years have you been in the job now? Doesn't seem that long ago you were a fresh-faced young forensic pathologist and now you're . . .' He stopped, and Dave glanced over at him as he reached forward to turn the air conditioner up a notch.

'Asking for trouble there,' Dave muttered.

'What were you going to say, Bob? No longer young and fresh-faced?' There was laughter in Shannon's tone as she reached forward to hold on to the dash while the troopy bumped up and over the lip that took them from the beach onto the hardened earth.

'Ah, no, only that it seems like you've been around for a while now. Everyone is young when you get to my age.' He ran his fingers through his thinning grey hair and pointed at it. 'See, old.'

'No,' Shannon said, drawing the word out. 'Not old, wise.'

Dave snorted. 'Wise? He's a know-it-all old bastard, that's what he is!'

'Now, son, don't be like that. I've taught you all you know.'

Grunting, Dave raised his eyebrows but stayed quiet. He could feel Shannon's arm now pressed against his side. He didn't trust himself to say anything. If he had his way, he'd turf Bob out and take Shannon back to the beach, where they could have a swim to cool off.

'Good to know you two like to pull the piss,' Shannon said. She turned to Bob. 'You know that your partnership with Dave is talked about by the new detectives, don't you?'

'What?' Bob's voice rose in surprise and then jarred as Dave hit a pothole.

All three of them lurched off the seat and into the air, before landing heavily, bumping into each other.

'Steady there, son.'

'Sorry,' he said. 'Didn't see it.' He'd been looking at the outline of Shannon's face as she'd been talking and he'd taken the pothole at full speed.

'Yeah,' Shannon said, ignoring the bump. 'How well you both get on and communicate. That sort of thing. They're always wanting a partnership like yours.' She lowered her voice and spoke in an awed tone. 'The stuff legends are made of.' Then she laughed.

'Don't be bloody stupid,' Bob said. 'We've just got each other's backs, that's all. Isn't that right, Dave?'

'Hmm, something like that,' he answered as they reached the homestead.

The signs indicated for him to slow down, so he lifted his foot from the accelerator and let the troopy slow itself. 'I'll find out where the coolroom is,' he said, as they came to

a stop. 'Or do you want me to drop you off at the room?'
He looked at Shannon.

'Nope, I'll get this body into the freezer first. Thanks
anyway.'

The door of the house opened, and Brody walked up to
the driver's-side door and stood there, a worried look on
his face. 'How did you get on?' he asked.

Dave looked over Brody's shoulder and saw Jane wheeling
herself onto the verandah, her face lined with worry.

'No problems at all. If you could just point us in the
direction of the coolroom,' Dave said.

There were two caravans coming in and another pulled
up at the entrance of the camp grounds. He wanted to avoid
anyone getting too close to them. Gossip always seemed to
spread around caravan parks, the same way it did through
small country towns: quickly.

'That shed over there.' Brody pointed to the opposite
side of the house.

Over the steep roof, Dave could see the side of a rusty
shed with a few bits of tin peeling away from the side and
a tall aerial on the roof.

'Cheers,' Dave said and went to drive off.

Brody put his hand on the steering wheel. 'What can I
tell everyone?' he asked.

'Nothing,' Bob said in a stern tone, from the passenger's
side. He got out of the troopy. Shannon wiggled over and
slammed the door shut. 'Just say nothing at this stage, son.
I know people in the camp grounds saw the girls come
back today, and there will be questions, but Dave and I

will make an announcement a bit later when we're done here, all right?'

Brody gave a slight nod. 'People are already asking. The ones who have been here a few days know Hannah and Kelsey. They want to know if they're okay.'

'Sure, they do. Just let us get this sorted and we'll be back over. Where are the girls now?'

'In the house with Mum, like you suggested.'

'Good, good. We won't be much longer. Stay here.' Bob indicated for him to step away from the vehicle and for Dave to drive off.

Reversing into the shed, Dave checked the rear-vision mirrors to make sure he was in line, while Shannon got out and opened up the coolroom. He'd noticed that Bob had stopped to talk to Jane for a couple of minutes, patting her hand before he came over to help.

Hitching up his shorts, Bob said, 'Well, here we go.'

Together, under Shannon's instruction, they placed the body bag gently on the floor and shut the door, before Dave placed crime-scene tape around the edge to discourage people from opening it and to ensure they knew if someone did.

'Done,' Bob said. 'Better interview these girls now.'

'I'll run Shannon to her room,' Dave said, but she shook her head.

'That's fine, I need the walk,' she said. 'Have you got the key?'

'Mac should have it, I reckon. The units are down the road to the left,' he said. 'Bathrooms are near the camp kitchen.'

She took it and gave her sunny smile. 'See you both soon.' She turned and walked out of the shed and into the light. The sun was beginning to set and deep reds and pinks were lining the sky.

'Interesting girl, that one,' Bob said as he watched her go.

'Why do you say that?'

'Never understood why she didn't have a bloke.'

Dave nodded. 'I've thought the same thing.'

'Guess there's an opening.' Bob cocked one eyebrow and glanced across at Dave, who refused to meet his gaze.

~

'Okay, so let me get this straight,' Bob said gently. 'You'd run from the house to the car park, then to the beach, where you went for a swim.'

Both Hannah and Kelsey nodded. They were sitting so close to each other, their shoulders were touching. Kelsey was calm now, but her eyes were red from the crying and her face, blotchy. Hannah was pale, but Dave thought she seemed stoic and in control of her emotions.

'Yeah, and then we always run two hundred metres in wet sand, so we started to do that. We ran past the . . . the body the first time, but on the way back I stopped to see what it was, because there was nothing else on the beach. It looked out of place.' Hannah's voice shuddered and Kelsey took up the story.

'I saw her bent over, looking, then out of nowhere she just screamed! I didn't know what had happened, thought something must have bitten her or . . .' Kelsey rubbed her thumb along her other hand in distress as she looked at Hannah. 'I don't know what I thought, to be honest. Anyway, I ran over. By then Hannah was saying, "It's a person. They're dead."' Tears pricked her eyes and she swiped at them.

Hannah broke in. 'Then we ran back up to the house to get help.'

Jane came into the room with a jug of water and glasses on the tray of her wheelchair. She set them out on the table and then left.

'And you didn't recognise the person?' Dave asked knowing it was a silly question; the face was barely recognisable as human.

They both shook their heads. 'No, it was hard enough to realise it was a person in the first place,' Hannah said, her voice breaking a little. 'Why does the sea make them look like that?'

'The water,' Bob said, but didn't elaborate on the continual friction of the water against skin.

'Is there anything else you can tell us?'

The girls looked at each other and Kelsey reached over and held Hannah's hand tightly in hers. 'Don't think so.'

'Okay, well, I think we're done here,' Bob said as Dave finished making notes. 'We'll type up a statement and get you both to sign it.' He fixed each girl with a gaze. 'This is a traumatic thing to have happened to you both. If you need to talk about it, make sure you do. Dave and I will be here to listen for the next few days while we're here, but if you start to have nightmares, or can't stop thinking about it, you must get some help, okay? The professional type.'

The girls looked at each other and then back to Bob and Dave, before nodding.

'I keep seeing it there,' Kelsey said, in a small voice.

'That's okay and very normal. It's only just happened and you've got to have time to process what you've seen. Those types of images will be with you for a while,' Dave said quietly, leaning forward. 'The memories should go in time, but Bob's right, any nightmares or if you're not able to sleep, please go and get some help.'

Bob got up from the couch and Dave heard him walk down the hall and into the kitchen, his baritone voice echoing through the rooms.

'Jane, I need to look at the register, please.'

Jane's answer was softer, and Dave couldn't hear what her response was.

He turned back to the girls. 'Have you heard any arguments between any of the campers in the last, say, three weeks?'

The girls frowned, not understanding the question, then Hannah's eyes widened. 'Do you think this is a murder?' She gasped. 'Someone we knew?'

Kelsey got up from the couch with a little moan and started to pace the perimeter of the room.

'No, that's not what we're saying, but this is very early on in the investigation so we can't rule anything in or out. We have to explore all angles.'

Hannah shook her head. 'I haven't heard anything out of the ordinary. Sometimes late at night, when everyone has had a few, it can get a bit rowdy, but I don't remember any yelling or loud arguments.'

'And you haven't seen a site that has camping gear still in it but no one around?'

Kelsey came and sat back down, shaking her head. 'No. Definitely not. We have to do a walk around every morning and night. If someone wasn't there we would've known.'

Jane and Bob came back in holding a tattered exercise book. Jane rolled her chair to the girls and put out her arms. 'Are you okay?' she asked.

The two girls returned the hug and stayed like that for a few moments, until Bob cleared his throat.

'Now, I want to ask, in the last three weeks has there been anyone staying here who really stuck out? You know, someone strange or obnoxious or overly friendly? Someone who's been wanting to know the ins and outs of the place—routines, where everything is situated. That type of thing.'

Jane turned to look at him and nodded towards the book he was holding. 'I've been back through the register, to jog my memory, but I don't think so. I asked Brody as well, and he couldn't think of anyone either. It's been school holidays, so lots of kids and their parents. But, look, I don't get down to the camp sites that often and sometimes Brody takes the bookings and brings the info back to the house, so I don't see everyone who stays here.'

'What about you girls?' Dave turned to them. 'You would see and get to know most people, wouldn't you?'

'Yeah, we go from cleaning the rooms and camp kitchen and so on, to the bar most nights. There are some who keep to themselves, or have cooking equipment and don't need to come to the kitchen or bar, but we see the majority. I can't think of anyone unusual.' Hannah looked to Kelsey. 'What about you?'

'I don't think so,' she said quietly.

Dave noticed her hands had a tremor in them. She was still in shock.

'Is there anyone who can take your shift tonight?' he asked.

'I can see if Belle could work behind the bar,' Jane said, looking at her watch. 'I think we've got time to get her back out from town tonight.'

Kelsey spoke over the top of her. 'No! I want to work. I want to forget about today.' Her voice dropped and she looked pleadingly at her boss. 'I think I need to be busy.'

Nodding slowly, Jane looked at Dave and Bob for guidance.

'I don't have a problem with that if you don't,' Bob said. 'But I'd ask you not to say anything about what you've seen today. Dave and I will have a yarn to everyone tonight. Let's not upset the whole camp.'

The girls nodded and then they stood up.

Dave put his notepad in his top pocket. 'Right, well, we'll head off. Get ready for tea. See you down there.'

As they walked out, Jane took Bob aside and Dave waited in the doorway, listening to their conversation.

'Will they be okay to work? Kelsey seems very shaken up.'

'Sometimes it helps,' Bob said quietly. 'You'll just have to keep an eye on them. And we will, too, while we're here. What about you? Are you okay?'

'Well, it's . . . it's a terrible thing to happen. And a horrible shock,' Jane's voice trembled slightly. 'But you know, Bob, worse things can happen, so as we say out here, we've got to keep going. I'll need to make sure the girls are okay. They were the ones who discovered it, not me. I'll be fine.'

'You know where I am if you need to talk.'

'Thanks.' There was a silence. 'I wonder who the person was?'

'I don't know. Hopefully, the pathologist will be able to help there. We'll get the body back to Perth tomorrow and she'll be able to start figuring that out.'

'This is all so sad. Surely someone is missing them.'

'We'll do our best to find out what's gone on here,' Bob reassured her. He gave her shoulder a gentle squeeze and smile, before walking out.

In the troopy, Bob sighed. 'Not quite how I imagined the day going,' he said heavily. They were silent on the short drive back to their units.

'What now?' Dave asked. 'It's nearly dark, so I guess we can't do anything on the sheep investigation now.'

Bob slapped his knee. 'Bugger it, I meant to ask Jane for all of their paperwork, too. I know they haven't shorn and compiled up-to-date stock figures yet, but if I have an idea of what the last few years have been, we should be able to get a handle on things pretty quickly when we do a muster or count.'

'Do you want me to go and get them?'

'I'll go. But I'm having a shower first. I'll grab a drink when I get back. What are you doing?'

'The same, except going back to the homestead.'

Bob glanced over. 'More's the pity.'

Dave knew he meant he should be doing something with Shannon tonight.

That drink they'd talked about.

Even in his mixed-up state he knew he should be, too.

CHAPTER 11

It seemed to Dave as if there were a million more stars in the sky than what he would normally see from his house in a hilly suburb above Perth. He'd moved into a smaller two-bedroom house after he and Mel had separated, and as much as he loved the area, the trees and space, there was still an emptiness about the house that couldn't be filled unless it was with Bec's and Alice's laughter.

Tonight, the air had come in cold and he could see his breath as he blew gently on his fingers, trying to warm them up. Having dropped by the bar on his way back to the tiny unit, which held nothing but a double bed and a sad-looking bench off to one side, he made his way to the porch and leaned against the thick wooden pillars. The little verandah, if it could be called that, attached to his unit had two chairs, a wobbly wooden table and a dirt floor. On the ground was a mozzie repellent candle, flickering bravely against the gentle breeze that had come up on dark.

He knew he needed to get over to the camp kitchen and then to the bar so he could talk to people to find out any information that someone could have, but he needed to clear his head first.

Bob had already been up to the homestead and collected the paperwork he needed, and then knocked on his door saying he was heading over to the camp kitchen.

Dave had told him he'd be there shortly. He should go rather than being lost in memories and thoughts, which seemed to happen when he was alone.

Mel had crowded in this afternoon, while Shannon had been working on the scene. His ex-wife's sharp voice, reverberating around his head, reminding him of how useless he was, how his actions had caused the death of her mother and nearly had their daughter killed.

The message from his lawyer also rang in his ears. 'They're saying you're a risk to the kids.'

The turmoil inside his mind didn't show on the outside. His body was relaxed as he took another sip of his beer and looked up into the sky. He thought about Spencer, his old partner who Bulldust had murdered, and how Bulldust was serving more than one life sentence in jail now.

Oh, how he missed Spencer's voice on the other end of the phone.

Spencer had often told him that he wouldn't be able to change Mel's thoughts. It would never have mattered whether Dave had left policing or not, Mel would have still been dissatisfied. These words of Spencer's bounced around in the silence.

They had again today as Shannon had worked profession-
ally alongside him and Bob. Sometimes he thought that
Bulldust had given him a gift, and at other times he felt as
if his whole world had been ripped away from him. Now
Bulldust was in jail and Spencer, his mentor and friend, was
dead. And Mel and he were on their way to getting a divorce.

The satisfaction Dave had thought he'd feel once he
heard about Bulldust's double life sentence had been
overshadowed by the sadness and guilt he continued to
feel, no matter how much counselling or drinking or talking
to his colleagues he did. Not one of his copper mates had
had their families involved in a case like him. It was hard
for them to understand that part of it, but not the marriage
break-up. Coppers had one of the highest divorce rates in
the country.

From the camp kitchen he could hear the drum of music
and then the laughter of children rose into the air. The smell
of wood-fire smoke and onions cooking made his stomach
rumble, but he still wasn't ready to go over.

He took another sip of his beer and gazed upwards.

'Hey,' a low voice came from his right.

Without looking over, he knew it was Shannon.
Nervousness trickled through his gut, but he turned his
head and smiled.

'Hi.'

'Penny for them,' she said, coming to stand next to him.

He caught a whiff of her shampoo and soap and noticed
she was wearing shorts and a long-sleeved shirt. For once
her hair was down and untamed. The way the breeze lifted

it around her neck and ears made him want to reach out and hold it back from her face.

'My thoughts?' he asked, not moving. 'Hasn't anyone told you yet? Don't have many of them!' He tapped his head. 'Not too much up here to create thoughts.'

'Oh, come now, I think you're being a little hard on yourself,' she said, with a small smile.

She raised a glass to her lips and Dave realised she was holding a wine. 'Off duty now?' he asked.

'You know we're never off duty, but unless someone dies, I can't see me being needed tonight.'

'What's your ETD?'

'Mac wants to get going early. Says there's rain coming and he's worried about getting off the strip. Since it's dirt, it looks like it could get slippery. He's keen to leave before there's any chance of the rain starting.'

Dave looked up again. 'Looks pretty clear at the moment, but the weather is so changeable up here, I'm not surprised.'

Shannon didn't answer. Instead, she pulled up a chair to the edge of the verandah where she could still see the stars and sat down next to where he was standing.

A loud burst of laughter rose from the communal fire and Dave heard the thump of wood, then saw sparks flying into the air. He thought again that he should help Bob. Shannon's body radiated heat. The pull of her company was too strong to go and help his partner.

Bob would be talking to people and committing everything he heard to memory, so he could relate it to Dave in the morning.

Dave reached out for the other chair and pulled it next to Shannon's, then sat down as well. He tried to think of something to say, but for once he was tongue-tied.

'When did you leave Perth?' Shannon asked after a small silence.

'Only a couple of days ago. Got the call and we took off. Finding stolen stock always needs to be done quickly—it's hard to track them once the fresh evidence has gone. I'm getting the impression we're already far too late for this one, but you've got to try, don't you?'

'Like any crime.'

'Hmm, yes and no. Once the stock have been killed through an abattoir, we've got no way of telling who owned them; you know, the ear tag, guts, ear mark all gone. Just a carcass with no ownership details. It's much easier to prove if we have live animals.'

Shannon nodded. 'Yeah, I understand that. Brands and all of that sort of thing aren't attached underneath the skin.'

'That's right.' Dave took a sip and looked over at her. 'So, how are things at the morgue?'

'Always busy there. Suicides, unexplained deaths, then the odd murder. Not that they come through that often, we're a reasonably law-abiding state, but there's the odd one. Adds a bit of spice to things.' She gave a laugh. 'Last week someone brought some bones in because they thought they were human remains. Took me about three seconds to work out they were a kangaroo's.' Rolling her eyes, she said, 'You wouldn't believe how often that happens. It takes

130

up time when I've got bodies lined up behind. Families waiting for answers, or to be able to organise funerals.'

'Still, I guess if they had been human remains, another family would have been glad to know the body had been found.'

'Absolutely. And I'm not whingeing. I'm glad they brought them in.' Shannon ran her finger around the rim of her wine glass, and Dave sensed she was looking at him.

A fiery orange glow started spreading across the horizon, outlining the ridges of hills. He watched, only for a second, and then saw the tip of the moon rising.

'Check that out.' He nodded towards the light being cast across the land.

Shannon let out a gentle breath but didn't say anything as the moon continued its super-fast rise into the sky, blocking out the light of the smaller stars.

'That's impressive,' Shannon whispered after the moon was two fingers away from the edge of the Earth.

'Nothing like watching it out here,' Dave said, still staring at the sky. 'There's something really freeing and, ah, shit, I don't know, it's just good to see.' He stood up and leaned against the upright again, annoyed that he couldn't find the right words.

'Hey, let's do something crazy,' Shannon said, mischief in her voice.

Dave looked at her warily. 'Oh yeah, like what?'

'An after-dark swim.' She got up and pulled at his hand. 'Come on, it'll be beautiful down there—the moon on the water and everything. Bring a beer.'

Dave looked at her, the moonlight was reflecting off her hair and her eyes were bright with recklessness. He took a breath. It was cool, but he guessed the water would be warm.

'All right then. Get your bathers.'

'Who needs them! It's dark.' She tugged at his hand again and he let himself follow her out past the caravans and campers. Some had people sitting around their own fire, cooking tea, others were inside their vans watching TV.

What a waste of a glorious night, Dave thought as he saw people sitting at their kitchen tables, staring at the TV, not speaking to each other. His heart beat faster as he and Shannon silently followed the road down to the beach.

The sand was soft beneath his feet, and he heard Shannon slipping off her shorts. Averting his eyes, he looked out to sea—it was just as she'd said it would be, the moonlight glistening on the top of the water and the quiet lapping of the waves on the sand.

'It's going to be cold,' he muttered, his toes beginning to feel the chill of the sand.

'Invigorating,' Shannon countered.

'Is that what you call it?' He looked around, suddenly feeling awkward. It had been a long time since anyone other than Mel had seen him in just his jocks.

As if knowing he was self-conscious, Shannon turned and ran into the surf, her long white legs flashing in the moonlight. He heard the splash of her diving under, then a short shriek.

'Oh my god, this is perfect! Freezing, but perfect.' Her laugh echoed across the beach to the hills where it bounced back towards him.

Taking a breath, Dave took off his shirt and shorts and left them piled in a heap next to Shannon's clothes and then followed her in.

The cold hit hard; as if it was trying to take his breath away, but after the initial shock, the water seemed warm and all encompassing. He rolled on his back and floated, looking at the stars and hearing the water lap into his ears, blocking the night's sounds to an underwater garble.

A laugh bubbled out from him. Who would have thought he would have ever been nearly skinny-dipping with a pretty girl in the dead of night? Mel wouldn't have ever entertained the idea; she was too prim and proper to even think about being spontaneous and fun loving.

His laughter died away as his ex-wife forced herself into his mind again. He saw her in front of him, her arms crossed and anger flashing across her face. Guilt seared through him and he put his feet on the bottom and stood up. A small splash to his right and he saw Shannon standing, too.

The need to feel her under his hands, to remind him he was still alive, still desirable and not a huge fucking great waste of space, was intense. He reached out to her and pulled her to him.

She let out a small gasp as she touched his chest, but her head was thrown back, looking up at him.

Dave saw the light reflected in her eyes as he bent down and put his lips onto hers, tasting the salt and passion on her mouth. Deepening the kiss, he wrapped his arms around her waist and let his hands run over the curve of her arse. Finding her hands he finally broke the kiss and pulled her towards the shore.

Picking up the towel he'd managed to grab before they left, he pulled her towards the low-range shrubby bushes on the edge of the beach. Giving her another kiss as he tried to spread the towel out with one hand, he finally gave up and manoeuvred her towards the ground. He felt her hands around his back and her legs around his waist, the sand roughly touching his toes and knees.

Tangled up in skin, he had only thoughts of this woman beneath him, how good she felt to him. His mouth kissed his way down her body, finding her nipple.

Her moans were soft, as was her touch, and her body responded to his tongue.

Dave entwined his fingers in her hair and let out a groan as her body arched towards his, meeting his need for her.

CHAPTER 12

Bob banged on the cabin door. Dave lifted his head, knowing it was his partner by the loud, strong rap, before grunting his acknowledgement. Shannon's warm legs were wrapped around his and her hair spread out across his chest.

'Come on, we've got shit to do,' Bob called as Dave flopped his head back down on the pillow and tightened his arms around Shannon.

She propped herself up on her elbow and smiled at him. 'Morning.'

'Morning,' Dave answered, running his hand up and down her spine. 'How are you feeling?'

'Pretty bloody good.' She smiled again, before letting her fingers run over his body, letting him know of her intentions.

Dave gave a low laugh. 'I think the boss is calling me. As much as I'd like to, I don't think I've got time.'

He threw the covers back and sat up, as Shannon threw him a good-natured pout.

'Always the way. Job comes first,' she said.

'And you know it.' He leaned down and gave her a kiss, before looking at her closely. 'I guess you're leaving today?' he asked.

'I would imagine so. Mac will be chafing at the bit to get back to Perth and I'll have work piled up. Not forgetting we've got our sailor to get into the morgue.' She plumped up a pillow and leaned it against the wall, before sinking back into it, watching Dave. He wanted to push her back into the bed and cover her body with his.

Instead, he sat on the edge of the bed, wrapping her hair around his fingers. 'So . . .' No more words came. He wanted to ask what was going to happen now, but he wasn't sure if that was okay. He'd been out of the game for too long. Considering their paths hadn't crossed much in the last twelve months or so, the morning after wasn't proving to be too uncomfortable.

'So,' she answered, 'give me a call when you get back to Perth.'

Dave nodded and opened his mouth to speak, but there was another bang on the door.

'Come on, son. Get your shit together. What's going on in there? You giving yourself an early morning workout?'

Dave grinned at Shannon, his eyes never leaving hers. 'You're jealous because yours doesn't work anymore,' he called back. 'Be right out.' To Shannon, he lowered his voice and said, 'You okay to get out of here? Bob will be watching.'

Leaning back and stretching out across the bed, she gave a slow smile. 'I haven't got any problems if you don't.'

Feeling himself start to harden as he watched her sensuous movements, he had to hold himself back from finding her nipple with his tongue again. Instead, he got off the bed, found a pair of jocks from his bag and began to get dressed.

Shannon got up and started to do the same. 'What have you got on today?'

'Haven't got too far with the investigation we came up here for yet, because we found your body. Guess we'll start looking into that today. What about you?'

'Oh, you know, bodies to cut up and reports to write. I haven't checked my emails since yesterday so who knows what's waiting for me when I get back into the office. Let alone the faxes which might have come through while I've been away.'

'Do you get sick of the admin stuff you have to do?' Dave sat on the side of the bed and pulled his socks on, while Shannon hooked up her bra and pulled her shirt over her head.

'Nah, it's all part of it. I love being able to give families answers by piecing information together.' She paused as she fastened her shorts. 'I would've liked to have been a detective, but I enjoyed science too much for that. This way I get to do both.'

Dave straightened and walked to her, putting his arm around her waist and pulling her to him. 'Well, Ms Scientific Detective, just the way you're talking is turning me on. You're very hot, you know that?'

She ran her fingers up and down his arms before looking up at him. 'Detective Burrows, I've been interested in you for a long time. I don't know where you're at; you've been through hell and I'm sure you're not ready for a relationship just yet, but I'd like to be on the top of your list when you decide you are.' She glanced down as her face flamed red, then tried to move out of his grasp. 'God, I can't believe I just said that. Sorry. I'd better go.'

Dave tightened his grip, before he leaned forward and kissed her. 'You're right about a few things. What I can tell you is you've always fascinated me.' He paused, knowing he had to speak his truth, but not sure if it would hurt her. 'Let's just see where it ends up without any pressure. Is that okay? I've still got a few things to work through.'

'That's more than okay,' she said quietly and smiled against his mouth when he leaned in to kiss her.

⁓

Dave walked into the camp kitchen and did a double take as he saw Bob, unshaven, sitting and eating bacon and eggs.

Shit, he probably shouldn't have left Bob alone last night.

Sliding into the seat opposite, he said, 'Big night?'

'Lots of people to talk to and you've got to be sociable, you know.' He wiped his mouth and took a slug of the black coffee in front of him. 'How'd you go?'

Dave shrugged.

'Ah, kissing but no telling,' Bob said with a grin. 'Good to know you're a gentleman, son.'

'Fuck off, Bob,' Dave said good-naturedly. Still, he wasn't feeling good-natured. When he'd left the cabin to find Bob, guilt had slammed Dave hard and all of the contentment and happiness he'd felt had dissipated as quickly as it had arrived.

Realistically, he knew he was perfectly able to have a relationship with another woman. Mel was long gone, but that didn't mean his feelings for her were. He knew he couldn't just turn off two years of dating, four of being married and two children. Erasing those emotions of loss and guilt was going to take time.

And anger. He couldn't forget the anger. Anger that his children had been snatched away without so much as a conversation or any consultation.

Shannon was beautiful, sexy and intelligent. He loved talking to her. She understood the job and that was such a pull for Dave, but Mel was still hovering in the background. Was that fair on Shannon?

No.

Was it fair on him?

Probably not.

'Don't feel guilty.' Bob stared at him across the table with bloodshot eyes.

'What?'

'You heard me, don't feel guilty. You haven't done anything wrong.'

'I know,' Dave said, frowning, annoyed Bob had read him so easily.

'Good. Now, I've had a thought.' He wiped some toast around his plate soaking up the last of the egg yolk. 'While Mac is here with the plane, we should get him to take us for a quick flight across the two stations so we can get a look from the air. See if we can see anything that stands out. You know, a mob of sheep wandering across the breakaway country or something obvious.'

'Good idea.' Dave looked longingly at the coffee that was in Bob's cup. He wanted to ask if Bob had looked through the information he'd got from Jane the night before, but by his partner's bloodshot eyes, he was certain any time he'd spent out of bed last night was around the fire with a beer or whiskey in his hand. Before he could ask where to get a coffee, too, other words cut in between them.

'Did I hear my name being used in vain?'

Mac slid into the seat next to Dave, holding a steaming coffee.

'Mate, where did you get that?' Dave asked, almost salivating at the sight of the liquid in the mug.

'Jane was nice enough to make me one at the house,' Mac said. 'You can get one over there.' He pointed towards the bench in the kitchen and Dave realised there was an urn steaming away with tea, coffee and sugar close by. He got up and went to pour himself a cup, while listening to the chatter around him.

Hannah appeared with a plate piled high with bacon, eggs, tomato and toast. She held it out to Dave. 'Jane thought you'd need a decent breakfast.' She didn't smile, and was still a little pale.

He guessed she didn't sleep that well.

Keeping upbeat, he grinned. 'You're a legend,' he said. 'That's just what I feel like! Can you thank her for me?'

'Yup.'

'How are you feeling today?'

Hannah shrugged. 'Okay.'

'Sleep well?'

'Probably woke up a few more times than normal, but I'll be fine.'

'And Kelsey?'

'I think she was the same.'

Dave nodded. 'Don't forget to come and have a yarn if you need to.'

Hannah frowned. 'Yarn?' she asked, in her English accent. 'Why do I need to have some wool?'

Dave laughed. 'No, a chat. Talk. A problem shared by talking is a problem halved.'

'Oh, yeah. I think I've heard that before.'

Dave held the plate up in a thanks gesture and moved back towards the tables, still listening to the conversation surrounding him.

A few campers were finishing off their breakfast while others were coming and going from the showers and toilets.

In the distance, Shannon was walking to the showers, a towel hung over her shoulder. She was wearing short shorts and a singlet, her hair still tousled from last night. Bed hair. He felt a warm fizz of an emotion he couldn't name wash over him. He wondered if he could picture a future with her, or did he have too many demons to ever be able to love fully again?

He caught himself. *Mate, it's far too early to be thinking along those lines. Just because the sex was amazing . . .*

It was more than that, he already knew. There was something about Shannon that had captivated him from the moment they'd met.

'Jesus, where is your brain at today, son?' Bob sounded exasperated and Dave spun around.

'Sorry?'

'I said,' Bob bit out the words, 'how long do you think we'd need in the air?'

Dave walked back to the table, carrying his food and coffee, and sat down, trying to remember what the distances were between the stations and what he'd seen on the map.

'Not sure.' He looked at Mac. 'What's your thinking?' He took a sip of coffee, then started on the soft poached eggs with a mouthful of bacon.

'Bit worried about fuel, mate, that's all. If I can get a bit more, happy to take you for a spin. But someone is gonna have to cough up for the cost of it. You know what these government departments are like. I'm really only supposed to be getting Shannon from Perth to the trial and back again. Got special authorisation to call in here. I don't want to be taking off without full tanks either.'

Dave listened without contributing, as he ate.

'That's easy enough, I've got the credit card,' Bob said, tapping his back pocket, where his wallet bulged.

'If old mate has some here, then no troubles,' Mac said, slipping his sunglasses down. 'Geez, that sun's got some sting in it.'

'I'll find Brody if you like and see what they've got on offer,' Dave said.

'Most stations seem to have a stockpile of everything, fuel included.'

'Avgas, mate.'

Dave nodded. 'No worries.' He quickly finished his meal and, taking his cup with him, he walked up towards the house, nodding at a few of the campers packing up.

The 'Champagne Charlie' caravans—the long, large vans with satellite TVs and every mod con it was possible to have—were clustered into one corner of the camping ground. They were pulled by LandCruisers or jeeps, and the women still wore makeup and pearls, even in the middle of nowhere. The blokes were dressed in branded shirts and shorts and some had heavy gold chains, or rings.

Even when these people go bush, they take their lifestyle with them, Dave thought.

He heard the sound of a motorbike and turned in the direction it was coming from. Brody was hurtling across the paddock with a trough broom tucked into the rack at the back, sticking out to the side. One hand holding on his tattered hat. Dave raised his arm and waved, trying to attract his attention, and when Brody saw him, he swung the bike in his direction.

'Morning,' Brody said, adjusting his hat as he pulled up. 'Have you found out who that person is in my coolroom?'

Dave shook his head. 'We won't know anything until we get him back to Perth. Sorry, I know you want answers, but I don't have any to give you at this point. Won't for a while. But you'll be the first to know when we do know something.'

Brody thought on that, then changed tack. 'Beautiful day.'

'It is,' Dave agreed. 'Most people on the move? Looks like it.'

'Yeah, reckon we'll be close to empty by tomorrow. Rodeo on at Onslow. Often see it empty out quickly when there's an event on close by. More outback experiences, you know.' He didn't mention it could have been the body that caused the exodus, like he had been worried about yesterday.

'That would explain it. Listen, I know you sell a bit of fuel—do you have any Avgas we could purchase for the plane?'

Brody nodded. 'Always got some on hand for emergencies. Had the RFDS out too often not to keep it in stock. How much do you need?'

'Let's do a refill. Reckon Mac will feel more comfortable with full tanks.'

Brody nodded. 'No problem, I'll get it out. It's just in a forty-four gallon drum with a pump on it.'

'Guess that'll be fine. I'll let Mac know.'

'What are you going to look at?' Brody asked, standing up on the pegs of the bike. Both men watched as a caravan nearly sideswiped a tree on the way out. The couple in the front of the wagon waved cheerily at them both, oblivious to the fact they'd almost wiped out the side of their van. Brody waved back. 'Look at these buggers. Some of them have no idea how to drive these vans. You know I had to reverse another one in last night?'

'Inexperienced?'

'Yeah, exactly. If I had a dollar for every time someone asked me if I have drive-through camp sites, I wouldn't be running this joint. I'd be holidaying in Darwin.'

Dave laughed. 'Nice thought. Anyway, we'll just finish breakfast and head out to the strip.' He skilfully avoided answering Brody's question.

'No worries.' He went to start the bike then stopped. 'So,' he sounded hesitant, 'what are you actually looking for?'

Dave paused. 'Getting a lay of the land, mate. That's all. See what everything looks like from the air. We came up here to investigate some stolen stock, and we won't leave until we've done it.' He watched Brody closely. The young man didn't seem concerned at what Dave was saying so he continued on. 'We'll need to talk to you and your mother about this at some point. But everything has been overshadowed by the discovery of the body. Once Mac and Shannon leave, we'll be focusing back on our investigation.' He changed his tone to one not to be argued with. 'So, if you know of anything, it would be a good time to tell us.'

CHAPTER 13

Mac clicked on his mic and Dave adjusted his headphones as he looked out of the plane's front window.

'Corbett Station traffic, November Foxtrot Mike departed Corbett Station at three zero. Tracking zero niner zero, climbing to fifteen hundred feet. Corbett Station,' Mac told the traffic control tower and pushed the throttle in. Dave felt himself pressed back in the seat as the plane leaped forward down the runway. About halfway down, it started to lift from the ground, the sound of the engine roaring loudly in his ears.

Taking off was Dave's favourite part of any flight—everything was still close enough to see clearly and yet he was looking down from above. Planes and choppers gave the stock squad a clear advantage point, being able to see an overall view, rather than just the paddock in front of them, and sometimes that was how they managed to apprehend an offender. More than once Dave had been in a car chase where an aircraft had been giving him instructions from the air. It took a little to get used to instructions coming through the radio, but rarely did they have problems in a chase like that. Obstacles were avoided and if the car made a sharp turn down a hidden track, they could follow.

Today, as they took off, the body on the beach was a distant memory. Bob had taken statements about it last night and now Dave couldn't wait to get started on the sheep investigation. It was the first time in months he'd looked forward to something and he guessed last night with Shannon was responsible for that.

Still, he couldn't help the self-condemnation that knocked into him every time he thought of their love-making. *It wasn't warranted*, he reminded himself. He needed to get over it. For all he knew, Mel might have a new bloke anyway. When she'd left him the first time, they'd still been stationed at Barrabine. It hadn't taken long for a man's name to start to filter through their conversations and Dave had never been sure whether there was something going on between them, or if they really were 'just friends' like she'd told him.

Today the sky was a vivid clear blue and the colours of the wildflowers stretched out like a patchwork quilt across the red soil. From his viewpoint in the sky, Dave saw the beauty in the heavily stoned country; olive-coloured trees and bushes dotting the landscape and white-trunked gums lining the river.

As the plane banked and started to fly east, Dave caught sight of the beach he and Shannon had been on last night.

Today there were a few people walking along it and a couple more swimming.

Good thing they hadn't been there last night, he thought, with a secret smile. He remembered the feeling of the water caressing them and their bodies moving together. He kept his face turned towards the window so no one could see his grin.

In the distance, the continuous calm of the ocean stretched out until the blues merged together to become one.

He depressed the button and spoke into the mic. 'How far as the crow flies to DoubleM Station from here?'

Mac showed him the map which was sitting on his lap and traced the flight line with his finger. 'Only about eighty k,' he said.

Bob leaned through the seats and pointed to the north. 'Can we fly along the edge of that bushland?' he asked. 'Bit lower than we are. Is that the crown land or station lease country?'

Mac fiddled with a couple of the controls and the plane dipped slightly. 'Fifteen hundred feet okay?' he asked.

'Lower if you can,' Bob said.

'I'm not a bloody crop-dusting pilot,' Mac retorted, but reduced the power and angled the nose slightly towards the ground. 'One thousand feet,' he told them. 'No lower.' Once the plane was cruising, he looked down at the map. 'Right, crown land starts here.' He pointed to a spot on the map.

'And we are?' Bob asked.

'Here. Just about to overfly the boundary. This is Corbett Station Stay.' Mac outlined the station, then circled the spot where they were flying.

The country drained towards a waterhole in the middle of the scrubland, which doubled as crown land, and there was a clearing where drovers and Indigenous people would have camped in times gone by. It looked to Dave as if there had been a trough made out of stones, so it was easier for the stock to get water.

'Circle back over the waterhole, please, Mac,' Dave said, still peering out. 'Bob, did you bring the glasses?'

Bob handed him the binoculars and Dave put them to his eyes, hoping to see something of use, but the landscape seemed empty, save for a few roos leaning over the water, having a drink.

'Too high to see any vehicle traces,' he said to Bob.

'No, I can't,' Mac said, pre-empting Bob's request to descend further again. 'I haven't flown in a muster, I'm just a vanilla pilot.'

Dave laughed.

'Come on, son,' Bob said. 'Where's your sense of adventure?'

'It's in not dying!' Mac swung the controls back to the west and they started towards DoubleM Station. 'The crown land stretches in between Corbett Station Stay and DoubleM. There's about twenty thousand acres, all bushland. Look up there.' Mac pointed into the distance, where the country broke out from bushland into sweeping, wide plains, devoid of bush and trees. The rangelands were covered in grasses. 'That's where the boundary starts.' They followed along the fence line while both Bob and Dave looked out either side.

'Can see sheep here,' Bob called out.

'I've got a mob this side,' Dave said. He grabbed the binoculars and zoomed in. The sheep had heard the noise of the plane and started at the loud, droning sound.

Instead of grazing quietly, they were now streaming across the paddock, stretched out in a long line. They knew the country well, as they ducked and dived around bushes and rocks. Up the hills and into the deep gullies. Trying to get away from the noise they couldn't see. Long dark shadows from the hills made them impossible to keep in sight until they came out the other side.

Even from the air, Dave could see the sheep pads, the paths that the mob would use daily, winding through the scrub down to the river where they could drink. They were only about thirty centimetres wide, but carved deeply into the dirt from the constant use. Sheep rarely took another path once they had a track sorted.

The sun was reflecting off a windmill further to the south, where another trough and tank stood. The outline of the fences was clear, too, graded wide tracts of land, running in a straight line with droppers and steel posts appearing like dots against the red soil. They were still too high in the air to see any light tracks made from vehicles or sheep that had only passed that way once.

One thing was clear—Mick was right. The only way off his station was through the front gate, which went right past his house. From the air there weren't any hidden or less used tracks that led off through the bush or boundary. The river system had sheer cliffs and the hills that surrounded the places were too stony and upright at the top to be able to get over. If those sheep had been stolen on a truck, or even walked out by people on horseback, they'd gone out the front gate.

'Mate, I think we'd better head back,' Mac's voice came through the headphones and Dave turned around to ask why. They were getting some good info from above!

Mac was pointing to a large bank of cloud to the west, coming in over the sea. 'Don't like the look of that.' He put a call in to the traffic control tower and asked for a weather update. 'Squally storms forecast to hit in two hours,' he relayed to them. 'Bugger, it was clear when I got the forecast last night. It's so bloody unpredictable up here. Should've trusted my gut and got off the ground early with Shannon rather than doing this.'

'Seen it happen before,' Bob said. 'Clear skies one hour and then we're swimming for our lives the next. Go on with you then, son. Head for home.'

Mac flashed him the thumbs up and turned the controls back towards where they'd come from. Dave checked his watch and saw they'd been airborne for forty-five minutes—and seen a lot of country in that time.

He had a better sense of the topography now, and of what roads were there and not there on the map. And if he ever had to set up road blocks, he'd know where to go.

⌒

Back on the ground, Bob and Dave compared their notes, while Mac refilled the plane.

'I reckon we should go for a look around Corbett Station,' Dave said. 'Head out for a drive and see what we can see. This place has three tracks that people can come in and out of, without going through the station area here. I saw them from the air, but they're marked here, too.' He tapped on the map they had open between them, lying on the bonnet of the troopy.

'I'd like to chat to Brody first,' Bob said, 'then we can do what you're suggesting. But let's get Shannon and Mac off the ground first.'

As he spoke a lightning flash opened the sky to the west of where they were standing. In the distance the ominous sound of rumbling started.

'Ah, shit,' said Mac as he pulled the fuel nozzle out of the fuel tank on the wing and looked up at the sky. 'Surely not.'

Furious black clouds stood out against the blue sky, and they were moving quickly. They all watched as the clouds continued to roll in and then Dave felt a large plop of rain on his head. He could hear heavier rain drumming on the earth, in the distance as the storm made its way towards them. A deep hollow sound.

Shannon walked around the plane, with a bag in her hand. 'Guys, I don't think we're going anywhere,' she said, her voice strained. Dave knew she really wanted to get the body back to Perth and start work on it as soon as she could. 'I'm going to leave the body in the coolroom for the time being,' she said. 'Mac, we won't get off the ground in this will—'

The last of her words were drowned out by another thunder roll and the sound of rain pelting to the ground a distance from them; the storm was moving closer by the second.

The pummelling rain looked like it was coming down from the sky in a grey sheet of water, even blocking out their view of the homestead. The trees started to bend in the wind.

'Run!' yelled Bob. 'Under cover! Now.'

Shannon and Bob took off at breakneck speed, while Dave helped Mac drag the Avgas drum back into the shed; when the water hit them it felt to Dave like someone was throwing small rocks at him.

'Holy hell,' Mac yelled, staring in amazement at the water sheeting across the land. 'Where did that come from?'

'What?'

The sound of the rain on the shed's tin roof was deafening. Dave hadn't seen anything like this before—oh, he'd heard about these freak storms that blew up out of nowhere in the north of the state, but he'd never experienced one.

What was clear to him was that the power of nature was enormous and not to be messed with. He moved a little closer to Shannon and sought her eyes, but they were glued to the outside, in awe of the force of the rain.

Outside, the gutters on the shed overflowed, the water heaving onto the ground and running inside the shed in deep rivers.

'I reckon we're stuck,' Shannon said to Dave.

'For a while,' he agreed.

Out of the grey shroud of rain, Brody appeared on his motorbike, soaked to the skin. He roared inside the shed, trying to wipe the water streaming down his face away. The action was futile because his hands and clothes were as wet as his face was.

Kicking the stand down, he got off and ran his fingers through his hair, trying to get rid of the excess water before heading over to a cupboard, where he pulled out a couple of rags and wiped them across his face, then rubbed them through his hair.

'Well, then, that should put a stop to any more campers coming or going,' he said as he took off his shirt and hung it over the handles of the bike. 'And hopefully any rumours about finding bodies out here. No one will be able to get in or out for a while.'

The warmth of the air was surprising because the rain had been freezing against Dave's skin when he'd been out in it.

'River will come up?' Bob asked.

'Yeah, depending on how long this goes on for, might take a few days before anyone can get across it.' He walked to the entrance and looked out. 'Even then you'll need a four-wheel drive. The water will lay there for a bit.'

'How long could this rain go on?' Shannon asked, following him.

'Couple hours, maybe. When storms hit so strongly like this, there's usually a shitload of water but it doesn't last for long. This country is pretty well drained and the water runs off into the river system.'

A strong gust of wind rattled the shed and the plane's wings wobbled.

'I need to tie the plane down,' Mac said.

'Wouldn't be going out there, mate,' Brody advised. 'There's lightning around. Saw a tree split in two during the last storm we had like this. And it killed a few cows back when we had them. I found them afterwards. These types of weather systems are bloody dangerous.'

Mac stared at him. 'Lightning hit some cows? How did you know?'

'I don't think it hit 'em, because there weren't any burn marks on the carcasses, but there were three all touching each other, right near a fence. I reckon the electricity came out from the fence and got them that way. One of them had a burn on the hoof, but that was all. Nothing else would have killed them like that.'

Mac's eyes were wide. There was no way the pilot was from farming stock.

Dave took note that Brody was solid in his knowledge of the land. He might be young, but he knew and understood what was going on.

Which could put him in the prime position to steal stock.

Or not.

He knew Mick had stopped short of accusing Brody, but he'd also said he wasn't a patch on his father. Didn't seem that way to Dave.

Dave glanced over at Bob and saw he'd noted the same thing.

Filing the piece of knowledge away, he remembered Mick's comments about tourism. Maybe he was more than annoyed that Corbett's were running a station stay.

'But the plane,' Mac said, standing like a runner at the start of a race. 'It needs to be safe.'

Bob moved to stop him. 'You can't mate. It's too dangerous. We can replace a plane, but we can't replace you.'

Again, the wind swept around the shed, sounding like a train, and the rain continued to fall. The road was now underwater and rivulets were forming across the yard. Visibility was down to about ten metres.

Brody let out a heavy sigh. 'Bloody hell, love the rain but the worst thing about this is that I'm going to have to pump out the mongrel septic tanks again.' He looked over at Dave. 'The joys of being a station stay.'

Shannon raised her eyebrows as if she hadn't thought about that before. 'What happens if there is an emergency?' she asked. 'If someone needs medical attention or the like?'

Brody shrugged, reaching for a new rag, trying to stem the dripping coming from his hair. 'We gotta try to make sure that doesn't happen. The strip will be too slippery for a day or two, so no one will be able to get in or out that way. Same with the road. I guess if it was imperative we needed help, one of us would take a bike and try to get through, but the river will be running a banker by now, I reckon.' He turned to Mac. 'That means,' he translated, 'that the water will be at the top of the river bank and could overflow out onto the flood plains. And the current is really strong when it's like that. Bloody dangerous. Wouldn't take too much to get swept away.' He looked up at the sky. 'The phone might be working, but probably not. And the internet most likely will have been knocked out. The satellites don't seem to like any sort of weather! If it's cloudy it runs slow; if it's hot, it drops out; if it's raining, well, it's pot luck then!'

'So, we're completely cut off from the rest of the world?'

'I guess, if you put it like that, we are,' Brody said.

CHAPTER 14

The storm blew itself out three hours later, and by then, all of them had risked running back to their rooms. Brody had headed to the homestead to check on his mum.

Dave had wanted to question Brody, but Bob told him to leave it. They were going to have plenty of time now.

Bob, Dave and Shannon were sitting in the camp kitchen, steaming cups of tea at their side, watching the clouds blow across the sky. What had been black clouds were now a dirty grey but they were lit with brilliance by a rainbow that seemed to come from one low cloud and stretch across the sky until it hit the beach in the other direction.

In his mind, Dave sung the song about the colours of the rainbow that he used to sing to Bec whenever he saw one and she was with him. He tapped his fingers on the table in time to the tune in his head. Bec would have loved seeing this rainbow; she'd been fascinated by them from a very young age, pointing to them every time she saw one.

Dave didn't know how Alice would react; he'd never been with her when there was a rainbow around.

Swallowing hard, Dave tried to forget about Mel and his kids and looked out of the door, wanting to find something else to focus on.

Sunlight lit the land and the wind dropped until there was no evidence there had even been a storm, except for deep puddles. Deep gouges crossed the roads and camp sites, and heavily laden leaves drooped with the weight of the water.

'How does it even do that?' Shannon asked in wonder. 'So full on and then nothing.'

'Madness, isn't it?' Dave's voice was soft. 'But wonderful.'

'Geez, you two have gone soft in the head,' Bob said with a snort. 'Going to make our life a pain in the arse now. We've got a body in the coolroom in case you'd forgotten. We won't be able to get back to DoubleM Station to do a check around now, or any of the other neighbours. Won't be able to have a look around here either. We're going to be stuck here, twiddling our thumbs for more than a couple of days, mark my words.'

'I wasn't forgetting the body, Bob,' Shannon said softly. 'Getting him to Perth ASAP would be my preference. And a storm like that? Well, I've just never seen anything so intense.'

'Is your hangover still bothering you?' Dave asked.

Bob shot him a frustrated stare, so Dave changed the subject.

'Hopefully, this won't hold us up too much. I reckon we should be able to get up to the northern part of this station for a look around. It appeared a lot sandier up there than around here. I'll check with Brody. I can take a motorbike if you don't want to.'

Bob seemed to relax and leaned forward. 'Son, I for one will not be digging any vehicle out of a bog. If it means we spend a few extra days up here, then so be it.' He nodded as if he'd put a full stop on his sentence and there was to be no argument. 'Like I said earlier, we're going to have plenty of time.'

'Well, obvious I know, but I'm stuck here, too,' Shannon said. 'God knows what amount of work I'll find when I get back.' She jiggled her knee up and down. 'Still, the boss will be filling in for me so,' shrugging, she smiled at Bob, 'what can you do?'

'Absolutely nothing, love,' Bob said to her. 'This is one of those times you just have to go with the flow. Anyhow, think of the overtime you might have when you get back.'

Shannon stood up and stretched her arms above her head. 'Overtime? Guess that goes for you two as well. I'm going for a walk down to the beach,' she said. 'I usually run every day and go to the gym when I can, and I'm feeling like I'm tightening up.'

'That's bad for your health, you know,' Bob said. 'The number of fellas I know who have been out for a run and dropped dead of a heart attack . . .'

Dave scoffed. 'You're a freaking ray of sunshine today,' he said.

'I think I'll risk it,' Shannon said. 'I need to check the coolroom, too, and make sure it's still freezing. I don't want to have those remains any more decomposed than they already are if I can help it.'

Dave stood, too. 'I'll check that if you like. Shouldn't be a problem because they're on generators here. If mains power was the source, then I reckon it would have been knocked out in the storm.' He turned to Bob. 'Do you want to talk to Brody yet?'

'What's with the impatience? I don't think there's any rush. We can do it later today when you've finished your jobs.' Bob took a sip of his tea and opened the file sitting in front of him. It was marked *Corbett Station* in bold black texta. 'Don't forget you've got those invoices and sales records from DoubleM Station to work through, and I've got enough reading to do here for a while.'

'Right, catch you a bit later on then,' Dave said, indicating Shannon should go in front of him.

Bob didn't answer, already engrossed in his reading. Dave looked over his shoulder as they left and saw his partner scratching notes into his book. Hopefully, that would keep him busy and away from the scotch bottle for a little while longer.

'I'll meet you at the beach if you like,' Dave said, putting his hand in the middle of Shannon's back. Their footsteps were heavy as the mud collected on their shoes. Then Shannon's feet slipped out from under her and she fell onto her knees.

'Bugger!' She laughed as Dave offered his hand.

'It's the red dirt. Slippery as hell.' He indicated the lawned area. 'Should walk on that.'

'Embarrassing,' she said, wiping her hands on her shorts, leaving finger marks of red across her bum.

'No, it's not. The dirt doesn't look slippery until you step on it.' He wanted to take her hand as they walked, but wasn't sure if that was the done thing, so he kept his own hands in his pockets.

'I'll come and check the fridge with you,' she said and this time tested the ground she put her foot on before taking a step.

'Have you ever had a body in a coolroom like this before?' he asked as they walked carefully across the ground towards the homestead.

Shannon gave a laugh. 'Can't say I have, but I'm grateful they've got one. And that Bob suggested it. I probably wouldn't have thought to ask. I've heard of other people, not only pathologists, having to do it, though. Not for murder, but if people have died unexpectedly and they can't get to town quickly.' She laughed. 'I'm probably not telling you anything you don't know. You guys have a lot more experience of outback life than I do.' She gestured to the land around them. 'Right from when we first met, you said that you wanted to work your way up to the stock squad and you did. You've achieved what you set out to do, which is a credit to your determination and tenacity.' She looked over at him. 'Why do you love the country so much?'

Dave took his time in answering. He mostly kept the real story for his need to be involved with the stock squad to himself—only a few select people knew his father had kicked him off the family farm when he was twenty-three, and that he hadn't spoken to any of his family since.

'My dad was a tyrant,' he said. 'And for some reason, he and I never saw eye to eye.' He paused finding the right words. 'My older brothers, Dean and Adam, were already entrenched on the farm when I came home from ag college. Dad didn't give a lot of credence to what he called "book learning" and neither of my brothers had gone away to school, so when I turned back up with some new ideas and different approaches to the way we did things, he wasn't that impressed. It was a case of never try to teach an old dog new tricks.'

Dave was quiet for a moment, the only noise the squelching of water under their shoes and some birds' loud and enthusiastic song as they darted in and out of the trees, showering their feathers in the droplets, or sat in the puddles, fluffing their feathers up, giving themselves a bath.

'It was the day of Dean's buck's party.' Dave took a deep breath as he relived the discovery that he wasn't going to be part of the farm the next year. 'Something that the bank manager said to me at the party. He was drunk and never should have said anything, but I was pleased he did. "Dave, I'm telling you," he said, "you need to think about what you're going to do next year because Wind Valley Farm isn't going to be your future."' Silence.

'I remember those words like they had been said to me this morning. I knew Dad got the shits when I tried to change something or had a suggestion, but I didn't think it was enough to turf me out.' He swallowed and Shannon reached out and took his hand from his pocket, holding it tightly.

Feeling comforted, he continued on.

'Anyhow, it was. I found the budget for the next year in the cashbook ledger. It didn't include me in the wages. I couldn't believe it at first and Mum didn't know either—she turned up as I was looking at the budget. Then Dad came in and said they couldn't afford me. That it was a simple economic decision.' He shrugged as they came to a stop in front of the coolroom. The yelling and arguing, the pure disbelief and anger he'd felt towards his dad were still fresh. The loathing that was oozing towards him from his father.

'I don't know when he'd planned to tell me if I hadn't found out. Whether he was going to let everything go along as it had been and just not pay me, I don't know.' Dave ran his thumb along the back of Shannon's hand. 'I'd always wanted to farm. The stock squad is the next best thing. I still get to hang out with farmers, talk shop, muster, you know, all that sort of stuff, and I don't have the responsibility of overdrafts and farm repayments. Perfect compromise really.'

'You don't mean that, do you?' Shannon asked, looking up at him.

'I do,' Dave answered honestly. 'Dad did me a favour—that doesn't mean I'm not angry with him anymore or want anything to do with him. I don't. I haven't spoken to him or any of the family since that day. Mum and I write occasionally, but not too often in case Dad sees the letters. I have nothing to do with the rest of them. Couldn't even tell you if Dad, Dean and Adam are still alive. And I'm not interested.' He took a glance at her to see if she was shocked at his words, but her face was impassive.

'I love what I do now.' He let go of her hand and fished around in his pocket for his pocket knife. 'And I don't want to change anything.'

Shannon didn't say a word.

He cut the tape and opened the door. A blast of freezing air hit him. 'Reckon everything should be okay by the feel of that.' He went inside and poked the body bag. The flesh under his finger didn't yield.

'Yep, all good,' he said.

Shannon was checking the temperature gauge just inside the door. 'Minus seven. That's good enough for a while. Hopefully, not more than a day or two though.' She scratched at her arms and Dave wondered if she was agitated about something. 'Especially in this humidity. The freezers always struggle to work when the air temp is hot and humid. I'd rather see it at minus fifteen or so.' Shannon turned away as she spoke.

'You okay?' he asked as he shut the door and replaced the crime-scene tape. The humidity was beginning to rise, and Dave had to wipe the sweat away from his forehead. 'I didn't say anything that upset you, did I?'

'No, not at all.' She took his hand and smiled up at him. 'Why?'

'You seem a little . . . quiet.'

They walked down the road, towards the beach, staying clear of any obvious slippery patches.

'You've been through a fair bit in your life, Dave,' she said. 'I think it's interesting you still love what you do. I imagine there would be other people who hated a job that had caused the breakdown of their marriage and the deaths of people they loved.'

Dave raised his eyebrows. Shannon had summed everything up succinctly, plain as you like. He'd never thought about it in such a clinical way. He'd kept all the emotions and wounds of the last couple of years close as if they were a badge of honour. 'I guess so,' he said slowly.

'I'm not saying that's a bad thing. Not at all. I wonder how you'll think about it in ten years' time, though.'

Dave, not sure he was ready to have this conversation, didn't say anything. He looked across the water. 'What about your family?' It was time to change the subject. He had no idea how he'd feel in ten years' time because he didn't know what the next ten years held. All he knew was, although he missed his kids intensely, he wouldn't have changed his job. And even though Ellen and Spencer had been killed at the hands of Bulldust and his brother Scotty, he was glad he had at least had Bulldust sent to jail. All of the trauma that had happened still could have occurred, even if he'd made the decision to leave the force like Mel had wanted him to.

Shannon bent down to take her shoes off and Dave did the same. They shoved them off the pathway and headed towards the water's edge.

'Not much to tell,' she said. 'Mum is in a nursing home and I wish there was a way to contact her. She'll be worried that I haven't called her. My sister is a teacher and my dad, a lawyer. But he's retired. Mum has motor neuron disease and Dad gave up practising when she got really sick. Then he couldn't look after her anymore, so we made the call to put her in a home.' Shannon stopped and stood still, looking out to sea as she spoke, her arms crossed over her chest as if she were protecting herself.

'Mum asked us to. It was as if she knew looking after her was going to be too hard on Dad and she didn't want to be a burden, so she took the decision-making away from us. I don't think I've ever known anyone like my mum. That was a pretty brave decision.'

'It was,' Dave said. 'Do they look after her well?'

'Oh yeah, she chose what home she wanted to go into and everything.'

The waves lapped at their feet and the silence stretched out between them.

'It's weird being locked in here without any communication or way to get out,' she said. 'If I wanted to be here and stay, it wouldn't be a problem, but I don't like it when my choice is taken away. I ring Mum every day and . . .' She started to walk again, gently kicking the water as she went. 'That's why I was a bit funny when I first realised we wouldn't be able to have any outside communication. She'll be wondering where I am.'

Dave nodded. He understood. 'Choice is a very important option, and I think when it's taken away, we fight against ourselves.' He paused. 'You can use the sat phone to call her. It's in the front of the troopy.'

Shannon smiled her thanks then seemed to shake off the sombre mood that had settled between the two of them. 'Come on, race you to the end of the beach,' she said, taking off at a jog. By the time Dave realised what was going on, she had a thirty-metre head start on him.

'Oi, that's not fair,' he called, walking out of the water and watching her run. He didn't really want to chase her, he wanted to stay behind her and watch.

Shannon looked over her shoulder and yelled something, but the words were taken away from him. Then she slowed and looked around, her nose in the air. Her arms waved at him frantically.

'What?' he called. Now he did break into a jog. 'What's wrong?'

'Can you smell that?' she yelled.

Stopping, he sniffed. Nothing but salt.

Shannon walked towards the red hills where the beach became scrubland.

Dave caught up to her. 'Smell what?' he asked again. 'Oh.' He stopped as he got a whiff.

Shannon turned to him; the joy in her eyes had left. 'I'd know that smell anywhere.'

CHAPTER 15

At the base of the sand dunes and in among the bushes, Shannon dropped to her knees and scraped around in the sand.

Dave couldn't see what it was, but he could smell it. He'd only smelled something like this once before, and the odour hadn't been as strong as on the case he and Shannon had first worked together, with him as a senior detective. The body down the mine shaft.

'There's a body here; another body!' She got up and carefully backed away, looking at Dave, her eyes slightly wild. 'What the hell is going on?' she asked.

'Good question,' was all Dave could manage. He was doing his best not to gag as Shannon moved back into the scrub and uncovered more of what was buried. The air filled with the putrid smell and, from nowhere, blowflies appeared. He had to keep batting them away, fearful they had touched the body and were now landing on his face.

They looked at each other in shock, until Dave gathered himself and walked away a bit. 'I'd better get Bob,' he said, breathing through his mouth. 'Reckon we'll have to handle this because the locals won't be able to get access. We were told that they didn't have the resources to send anyone out for the first body. Plus, that rain will have stopped any type of transport getting in here, and last I heard they haven't got a chopper out this way.' He looked at Shannon, who had also recovered from her shock and pulled on her professional face. 'Have you got stuff with you to dig the body out and collect all the evidence you find?'

Shannon took a breath. 'I'd like a forensic team up here, but from what you're saying I don't suppose that's possible. I don't have another body bag. We'll have to find something else to wrap this one in. I think it's been here for a while by the smell.' She got out a hankie from her pocket and put it over her face then went back over to the grave, looking carefully in the bushes as she moved.

'A while?' Dave asked.

'Judging by the smell. Don't know until I look at it, but maybe a week. I'll have to find out what the temperatures have been like over the last fortnight anyway.' She stared at the ground and bent over as if to see something more clearly. 'Do you have any gloves?'

'What? No. Not on me. I thought we were going for a walk, not recovering a body!'

'We've got to preserve this site ASAP. Obviously, this is a suspicious death—this person didn't bury themself.

Someone has done it for them. And the sand, god knows what we've missed here already. The storm—'

Shannon's voice broke off and Dave knew exactly what she was thinking. The storm would have washed every ounce of evidence away.

Being at a crime scene and knowing it was going to offer up very little made everything feel futile.

Getting up closer to the bush, she pointed. 'Wisps of what looks like padding from a puffer jacket. Strange, considering the weather's so warm at the moment. Wish I had an evidence bag.' Shannon looked around as if one was going to miraculously appear.

'Do you . . .' Dave had never been at the discovery of such a decomposed human body before. Nothing had prepared him for the stench. Even dead cattle and sheep didn't smell that bad. 'Do you want to stay here?'

'Yep,' she said. 'And keep everyone away from the area. If you can bring Bob back . . . I hope like hell your sat phone is working because we need to get this body back to Perth ASAP. Wonder if they can send a chopper up from there? I don't want these remains to decompose any more than they already have.' She paused. 'I seem to keep saying that.'

'There's the coolroom.' He didn't comment on the prospect of a helicopter arriving because Shannon knew as well as he did that wouldn't be their call. It would depend on what was happening elsewhere and if there was one available.

'Yeah, but I'd rather that this poor soul is in my freezer in Perth, where I know the temps and everything I need is at my fingertips.'

'Right-oh, I'll head back and get Bob, get the camera and tent so we can preserve the site.' He looked around, checking where they were in relation to the track down to the beach.

The grave was in between two sand dunes and behind some scrubby bush, which blocked the view of the beach. 'Not easy to see,' he commented. 'But easy enough to find if you were following the smell. I guess whoever did the burying wouldn't have factored in a heavy storm that washed away the sand, exposing the grave. Looks like that's what's happened.'

Shannon stood up and looked around. The grave was as Dave had said. Swathes of what looked like rivers of sand running out of it and deep lines from where the sand had come from. 'Yep, you're right.' She frowned as she slowly turned in a circle taking the whole scene in. 'But why would they bury a body so close to a camp site? Unless whoever did it wanted it to be found. As the crow flies it's what? Couple of ks?'

'It's two to walk down here, so it'll be closer in a straight line over the sand dunes.' He held his arm out in the direction of the camp. 'Or maybe they didn't know the camp site was there,' Dave countered. 'I'll be back shortly.' He turned to leave, then looked around as Shannon started to speak again.

'Find someone who has a jar of Vicks and bring it back with you.'

Dave opened his mouth to ask why, then realised. When they brought the remains out of the ground, the smell was going to be even worse.

~

'You are fucking kidding me?' Bob looked at Dave over the rims of his glasses, his mouth hanging open slightly.

'I wish I was. Shannon's still down there. She doesn't have another body bag and I don't think we've got one, have we?'

'Nope.' Bob stood up and started to pack his paperwork away. 'Right-oh, we'd better get down there and do something with it.'

'She'd like a forensic team up here.'

'Good luck with that. Especially with the weather that's just been through. Still, I'll ask. They might be able to get a chopper out here.'

'You'll call it in?' Dave was turning away.

'Yeah. We'll have to go and see if Brody has any heavy plastic we can use. Just give him the bare minimum details. Only if you have to.'

'I know,' snapped Dave, frowning. 'Shannon's gear is still in the shed near the plane from this morning. We need to grab that on the way past.'

Bob nodded. 'Don't get testy, son. What's the problem?'

'Sorry, nothing.' Dave looked down. 'I can't say I was expecting another body.'

'Don't suppose any of us were. Still, you know in this job, expect the—' Realisation spread across Bob's face. 'Jesus, you've never seen a ripe one before, have you? You okay?'

'Yeah, yeah, it's nothing I can't handle. The one at Barrabine, I never saw it. Smelled it, but never saw it.

Shannon went down the shaft and dealt with the whole thing. Spencer and I were on the surface. I didn't see it brought up; I was off looking for evidence.' He took a breath and ran his fingers through his hair. 'She's amazing to be able to do that sort of thing every day.'

Bob regarded him for a second. 'Well, son, there's a first time for everything. Better here where it's just you, me and your girlfriend than in front of a whole squad. You're up to it, I know you are.'

'Bugger off, Bob. She's not my girlfriend.'

'Whatever you say, Romeo. And, anyway, it's not like she deals with this type of scene every day. Periodically, sure, but most of her bodies will have come from the hospital morgues, not ones like this. Her stomach might be turning, too. Come on, let's get moving.'

'Um, have you got any . . . You got any Vicks?'

'For you, I do. Good piece of equipment to always have with you. Never know when you're going to need it in our line of work.'

Dave yanked open the troopy door and got into the driver's seat while Bob collected his things and got into the car, with a groan.

Reaching for the satellite phone, Bob dialled HQ as Dave put the vehicle into four-wheel drive and started off slowly to the hangar to grab Shannon's gear and then head to the house.

Bob was still talking when Dave jumped out and knocked on the homestead door. The two dogs were lying in the sun at the door and Oreo looked up and growled as if to say, 'Careful, buddy. Not another step.' He didn't move, though.

'Come in,' Jane called. 'Ignore the dogs, they won't hurt you.'

Dave eyed them both, still wary, as he pulled open the door and soon found Jane in the kitchen, having a cup of tea, alone.

'Brody around?' he asked.

'No, he's gone out on the bike to check a couple of fences he thinks will have come down in the flood. There's a part of the river system that only runs when we have rains like this and we've got flood gates in the bottom of the river so we only lose a small amount when it floods, rather than kilometres. Doesn't take too much to string together another gate, thank goodness. This type of rain does good, but also causes a lot of damage we could do without.' She paused and put her hands on the wheels of her chair as if she was ready to move. 'Did you need him urgently? I should be able to get him on the radio if you do.'

'Well, we were wondering if you had any heavy-duty plastic we could use?'

Jane raised her eyebrows in surprise at the question but answered without asking why. 'Belle brought me some out earlier this year to line the veggie patch. It'll be at the side of the house, I think.' She pointed to the back door, where Dave hadn't been.

'Would you mind if we took it?'

'Go your hardest,' she said; the query was on her face, rather than her lips.

Dave nodded. 'Thanks.'

He made a quick retreat, found the roll of plastic and threw it on board, just as Bob put the phone back in the case.

'Fuck it,' he said as Dave got in and started to head towards the beach. 'HQ can't do much for us at the moment. A forensics team is too difficult to get up here. Sounds like they're fully stretched. There've been multiple deaths down south; looks like a murder–suicide with a heap of bodies, so they're under the pump.

'Perth said they'd try to arrange another plane, but like I said to them, bloody idiots, there's nothing wrong with the one we've got here; it just can't get off the ground because the strip is too slippery. Some of those young comms guys and gals wouldn't know if their arses were on fire when it comes to things in the bush.'

'Chopper?'

Bob's face was grim when he answered. 'No can do either.'

Dave didn't bother to ask why. If the commanders up the tree had said no, then that was the answer.

The troopy's wheels grabbed at the beach sand, which was now very soft since the rain, and Dave quickly pulled the vehicle into low range four-wheel drive. He pointed out to Bob where the grave and body was and Bob looked behind him, getting his bearings.

'Don't think that's too far from where we found the other one, is it?'

'Nah, but they're completely different. This one had been buried here; who knows where the other one came from, since it had been out at sea.'

'Too close not to be related,' Bob cautioned. 'I realise the other one washed up, but to turn up on the same beach as another body? Too coincidental for my liking.'

'Suspicious death was all Shannon would give me, until she looks at it.'

Bob glanced over at Dave, a half smile on his face. 'Surely you're not surprised? You know forensic pathologists never give us anything until they've looked at the evidence and they're positive.'

'I wish they wouldn't be so cautious sometimes. I mean, obviously it's a murder! You can't bury yourself.'

Dave put his foot on the brake and the car brought itself to a stop with a jerk. Shannon was sitting a little away from where Dave had left her and she was fanning the flies from her face.

'You need to get rid of that impulsiveness,' Bob said. 'There're one hundred other reasons this body could be buried where it is. You know as well as I do that a good investigation is a methodical one. Start at the start and finish when you've gathered every piece of evidence and spoken to every person you can.' Bob opened the door and gave a little groan as the smell hit. 'Guess we'd better grab a shovel.' His tone was unenthusiastic. 'Where're we looking at?'

'Behind those bushes.'

'Okay, cordon off the area with the crime-scene tape. I'll start recording.'

Shannon walked over to them.

'What do you think you've got, Shannon?' Bob asked.

'Deceased person. Haven't got much further. You're right to record?' While she was talking she opened her bag and took out white plastic overalls and a face mask.

'Yeah, I'll document everything,' Bob said. He picked up a hand-sized video recorder and switched it on. Panning out across the land, he filmed everything in situ, then followed Shannon in between the bushes.

The soil was disturbed from where Shannon had swiped the dirt away, earlier. There were water rivulets cutting across the mound of the grave, and on the left-hand side there were ghoulish, swollen blue fingers protruding from the sand, covered in ants.

CHAPTER 16

'You'll have to dig gently,' Shannon told Dave. 'I'll record my findings on my dictaphone.' She looked at them both before slipping on a pair of plastic glasses. 'Let's go. Start out here, Dave.' She pointed to a spot about a foot away from the body. 'If you can pile the soil up here, we'll sift through it.'

Dave finished securing the tape and suited up, then grabbed the Vicks that was sitting on the dash of the car. He took a generous amount and ignored the burning on his skin as he pushed it up his nose.

'Want some?' he asked Shannon and Bob. Bob, not taking his eyes away from the camera, held out his hand, and Dave put a dollop on his finger. He held the jar out to Shannon, but she was already completely focused on the body.

He threw the jar onto the front seat, hoping the smell, which was enough to make your eyes water normally, would be strong enough to mask the smell of rotting human flesh.

Shannon had already uncovered a small part of the head and, as the scent wafted closer, he gagged again.

What was his favourite smell? he wondered as he opened his mouth to breathe deeply, wishing he had a clip for his nose. Rain on the dry earth? Mown hay, drying before being rolled into bales? Coffee? Baking bread?

He tried to imagine every single one of these scents, while looking at the corpse being uncovered in a gradual and meticulous way.

Didn't make much difference. He thought he could almost taste the smell of the decomposing body on his tongue. His mask sucked in against his face as he took another deep breath through his mouth.

'Fuck,' he muttered, loud enough for both Bob and Shannon to hear. 'I didn't sign up for this sort of thing.'

Looking up from her assessment of the body, Shannon's bright eyes laughed at him. 'Surely this isn't too difficult for you, Dave? This is what I do all the time!'

'It's got knobs on it, that's what it's got.' He batted more large blowflies away—he felt them hit his hand; they could've been bees they were so large.

He and Shannon stood side by side, him scraping the sand away while she directed his use of the shovel. Bob kept videoing from every angle. Dave held his breath as his work with the shovel started to expose the back of a head.

Sand mixed in with blood, both red, only different shades. The ants were swarming over the area as Dave continued to scrape.

'Do you want to keep any of that dirt as evidence?' he asked.

'Keep it off to the side. We'll look at it when we've finished here.'

Dave got onto his knees and used the smaller trowel to collect the clumped and blood-infused soil, and then gently pushed it out of the way. Shannon spoke again from behind him, her voice was muffled as she was so close to the body and speaking into her mask.

'Subject has long black hair,' she said into the dictaphone as strands of hair were uncovered. Pointing to where they were, in case Bob hadn't see them, she continued on: 'And a large gash to the back of the head. Bob, you'd better zoom in here.'

They were quiet as Shannon showed the camera where the wound was and outlined where it started and finished. The hair was matted with blood.

'Enough to kill?' Dave wanted to know, still breathing through his mouth. He wished his water bottle was close by. The inside of his mouth was almost completely dry and he hoped the water might wash away the foul taste on his tongue. Breathing through just your mouth wasn't easy when it had to be done for long periods of time.

Shannon just looked at him over the top of her plastic glasses then continued to examine the remains.

'Ah, look here.' She got out her tweezers and picked something up from inside the grave. 'Cigarette butt.' She held it aloft and Dave looked for a brand but there was nothing he recognised. He grabbed a wet strength paper bag and held it out to her.

'Exhibit one,' she said. 'You log that, Dave?'

'Yep.' He grabbed a black marker and wrote on the bag a large number one, sealed it and placed it carefully inside his vehicle.

Exhibit One, he wrote in the log, filling in the time, date and place they'd found it.

'DNA?' he asked.

'Hmm.' Shannon was concentrating on teasing something else out of the grave, so she sounded distracted. 'Maybe. Unfortunately, the way it's been buried, any DNA might have deteriorated, but you never know. We'll give it a go. Never knock back anything that might help.' She turned her attention to Bob. 'Can you get in close here, too?' she asked, pointing to the body's neck and shoulders.

They were bruised red and engorged. There was something inside the body making the skin move. Maggots?

'Jesus!' Dave threw down the shovel and took off into the bush above the grave, where he ripped his mask off before heaving the contents of his stomach onto the ground. Bending over, he put his hands on his knees and stayed like that until his stomach was empty.

Behind him he could hear Bob gagging, but still taking video footage, stoically. Shannon seemed unaffected.

'How are you not affected?' he called to Shannon.

'Oh, I am, don't worry. But I'm so used to it that it doesn't bother me. I've seen bodies in worse condition than this one.' She talked into her dictaphone again before returning to the conversation with Dave. 'I had a case where a man had been in a rubbish bin for about two weeks. Flies, maggots, and a pool of fluid. And the stench was about twenty times worse than this poor person.' She glanced up at Dave and he saw the compassion in her eyes. 'I made sure I got every skerrick of evidence off that body so the bastard who murdered him never had a chance to get off. And he didn't.'

Dave knew she was smiling under her mask because her eyes crinkled at the sides. He imagined the deadly, no-nonsense smile he'd seen her use in the morgue before.

Shannon traced her fingers above the body and looked carefully at the shape. 'I believe this body is that of a girl.' Her voice was soft as she said, 'And only very young.'

'Young?' Dave's daughter flashed into his mind.

'Early to mid-teens, I would think.' She bent down and used her gloved hand to brush a sprinkling of sand away then looked up at Dave. His face was pale. 'Again, that's an educated guess. We're going to have to be very careful in getting her into the bag. Decomposition is advanced. And look here . . .' She pointed to the blueish-green exposed skin, and after a moment, Dave realised it was the girl's wrists. They were behind her back.

Bob leaned in and grunted. 'There's your proof it's suspicious,' he said. 'Hands tied behind her back. She didn't go in there willingly. Murder? Probably can't tell that until you examine the wound on the back of her head properly.'

'That's right. But if you're looking for something, these two things together and . . .' She leaned closer to the head.

'If you see how deep it is . . . Mmm, well . . .' She pushed her fingers in around the wound and Dave saw the skull push in, yielding as it shouldn't have done. 'I'd say it was almost enough to kill her, but that's unofficial and not conclusive,' she warned. 'There could be other things I find internally.' She stopped and squinted, thinking. 'You know, there could be water in her lungs if the other body is related to this one.' Shrugging, she went on. 'Anyway, I won't know anything more until I've got her on a slab in the morgue. Let's try to turn her.'

Dave nodded and started to dig around the body again until there was a clear path and they could get the remains onto the sheet of plastic, then together all three of them helped turn the body over.

Fluid spilled from the body, and it took all of Dave's willpower not to drop the side of the plastic he was holding and run to the bush again.

Methodically, Shannon worked her way over the front of the body, documenting the decay and anything else that was obvious. When she spoke next, her voice was soft with curiosity. 'Her facial structure appears to be that of Asian descent.'

Bob stilled. 'Interesting that. Remember we need to get onto Border Force, Dave.' He went back to videoing and Dave made a note.

'Make sure we haven't missed anything there,' Shannon said, pointing to the pile of sand they'd shifted.

Dave picked up the sieve and headed over to sift carefully through the pile. He'd already collected some hair, which he thought was the victim's, from the bush, and the padding Shannon had noticed before, marking them as exhibits two and three. They were a little short on evidence, which was not surprising considering the force of the recent rain. It didn't stop him from wishing he could have found a footprint they could make a cast of though.

At this point, they didn't have any proof to even place another person at the scene. They would be relying on the secrets the body held to give up the person who had inflicted these wounds on her.

Sweat trickled down his back and he itched to head off into the sea to cool down. He glanced back at Bob, whose face was cherry red, but his partner's look of concentration was clear. For someone who enjoyed the heat, Dave was letting the environment get to him. Well, it was the smell more than anything. Somehow, he had to pull himself together.

Dave's stomach started to heave again and he quickly walked away, trying to get some distance from the strong odour. Taking deep breaths, he dragged fresh, clean air into his lungs and looked around. The rain had certainly made its mark on the countryside—there were deep erosion lines through the sand, where the water had cut its way towards the beach, running out into the sea. Trickles of water still ran through some of the gouges.

Seagulls were stalking the crime scene, as if they were hoping for a scrap of food to be thrown to them, and he'd noticed the shadow of a wedge-tailed eagle pass overhead while they were recovering the body.

Dave was surprised there hadn't been any wild animal damage. The smell alone would've brought the foxes or dogs in—even if they'd only been the dogs from the homestead. The ants, well, they'd appear anywhere, quickly. They had nests all over the place and they loved meat, too.

The fact people had been on this beach the day before and no one had noticed the smell was interesting. Still, he supposed that no one had gone up near the dunes. He and Shannon hadn't when they'd walked there last night.

He slumped onto the ground, knowing he needed to return to the grave where Shannon and Bob were still working, but not able to bring himself to do it yet. Digging his fingers into the sand, Dave clenched his fist around a clump of sand, bunching it into mudpie-like cakes. Another and then another, lining them up next to him. His brain racing. Two bodies, one murder. Who knew if Shannon would be able to get any details from the body which had washed up on the beach. What could have happened out here?

The blue waters in front of him were as smooth as glass. So still and serene. And yet, not long ago, there had been violent acts at this piece of paradise.

He pushed into the sand a fourth time and his fingers came up against something hard. Frowning, he looked down and dug in a bit deeper. Not knowing what he was touching, he turned onto his knees and bent over the area.

Flicking out the sand as quickly as he could, he looked down and stared. 'Jesus. Bob, you'd better get over here.'

CHAPTER 17

'We should be getting those drugs out now, Bob,' Dave said loudly. He was pacing the sandy beach, running his fingers through his hair, agitated.

'Son, we need to leave the drugs where they are.' Even though Bob's voice was low, he was not to be argued with. 'The best thing is to cover them back up. Look at what we've got. Two bodies and now a packet load of drugs. Use your noggin for once, Dave! With the drugs included, this isn't about just a washed-up body on the beach.'

Bob had shot footage of the bricks of what they were assuming was heroin, wrapped in black plastic and buried deep in the sand, as soon as he'd reached the spot where Dave had been digging. 'We don't know the size of what we're dealing with here. Could be bigger than Ben Hur and, if that's the case, we need time. Right now, the most important thing is to get the body back and secured. I'll get on the blower once we've done that. Ring the locals and see what they can do to give us a hand.' He spread his hands and gestured around. 'What we do have going for us at the moment is the gift of time. No one is coming in or going out of this station because of the rain and river being high. Whoever is meant to be collecting these drugs isn't going to be able to get in either.'

'What if they're already here? We should seize it, Bob.'

'No, son. We are not going to do that. If they're here, we'll find them. And we'll try to keep an eye on the drugs if we can. Now, this is a murder scene and that's what we need to focus on. Let sleeping dogs lie for the moment, all right?' He stopped and put his hand on Dave's shoulder. 'Don't you think this girl deserves our best? Fuck the drugs, they can wait. Come on, let's get this poor girl up to the coolroom.'

Dave glanced around wildly. Leaving the drugs in the ground and not at least cataloguing what was there went against everything he'd been taught during his detective training, but he had to admit what Bob said made sense.

The law of the land was different out here. In the city they could have called in another team to take charge of the haul. Out here, it was just the two of them and they had to make do the best they could. Prioritise.

And the body of the girl . . . Bob was certainly right there. If it had been his daughter lying there in a body bag, he'd want the copper who was investigating her death to do everything he could for her.

Finally, he nodded. Bob was already using his foot to push the sand back into the hole. Dave waited for a moment then started to help. The two men were silent as they finished covering the drugs back up and then returned to the troopy.

~

Dave pulled off his gloves and threw them into the rubbish bag, then held it out for Shannon to do the same.

They'd just finished manoeuvring the heavily wrapped body into the coolroom and now they stood out the front of the shed.

Brody stood off to the side, looking ill, while Jane had wheeled her chair outside onto the homestead's verandah and was watching from a distance. Dave wasn't sure, but she seemed to be fiddling with something in her hands that could have been rosary beads. Her head was bowed as if in prayer.

Dave found this interesting because there was nothing in the house to indicate that Jane was Catholic. In many houses he'd noticed the cross hanging on the wall, but in all the rooms he'd been in here, he hadn't seen anything like that.

'Right.' Bob turned and beckoned to Brody. 'Time for us to have a chat back at the house,' he said.

'I'm heading for a shower,' Shannon said. 'Then I'm going to find Mac and see when we can get off the ground.'

Dave followed Bob and Brody. He noticed the young man was stooped as he walked, defeated even.

I'd be upset if someone had made this kind of discovery on my station, too, Dave thought.

By the time they reached the homestead, Jane had already turned her wheelchair and headed back inside. Dave could hear the rubbery noise of the tyres on the lino floor as she wheeled herself along.

Inside, they pulled out chairs and sat down.

Bob took the lead. 'Now you both know that we've found another body—'

'Who is it?' Brody interrupted.

'We'll be working on identifying the remains as quickly as we can. Do you think you have any information that could help us?'

Jane spread her hands out. 'This is terrible, but we have nothing to do with it.'

'I'm not accusing you. This is information-gathering. First off, what details do you keep on the campers who come through here?'

Brody and Jane looked at each other.

'Bob,' Jane's voice wobbled a little, 'this is a cash business. All I've got is the car rego and the first name of the person who booked in. Sometimes we get the number of people who are staying. Oh, and the nights they stayed. I don't get surnames or phone numbers or anything.'

'Aren't you required to keep details of the people who stay?' Bob asked.

'Mum told you. It's a cash business,' Brody said quietly. 'Like we've just said, we record the first name of people and rego of car and caravan, or whatever vehicle they're in.'

Jane interrupted. 'Let me explain properly. This business,' she waved her hand towards the camp sites, 'it keeps us afloat.' Her voice dropped. 'We only declare to the tax office enough income to offset our outgoings. The rest is black money.' She paused. 'It's been the only way we've been able to keep our heads above water since my husband died and I had this accident. It means we don't have to take any personal money out of the station.' Frustration crept across her face.

Dave was taking notes, but felt Bob push his foot into his leg under the table and immediately put the notebook down.

'Right-oh, you need to understand we are not the tax department. We are not interested in what you do or don't pay to the ATO, okay? We won't be reporting it unless we find it's imperative to our investigation.' His voice was gentle as he spoke. 'Okay?' he repeated.

'That's, uh, good to know,' Brody said, looking at his mum.

Jane's face had registered relief, but it was quickly replaced with trepidation. 'If this gets out to the campers, we probably won't have anyone come to stay, anyway,' she said, her voice tight. 'It might ruin us.'

Brody reached forward and took his mother's hand. 'It'll be okay, Mum. We'll work something out. You know what people are like. Give them a couple of months and they won't even remember this has happened here.'

'I hope you're right, love, I really do.'

'Can you tell me who has been here with you in the house during the past two weeks?' Bob asked and Dave picked up his notebook again.

'Just me and Brody,' Jane answered. 'Oh, and Belle, my daughter. She came out for a visit this week. She only stayed for one night and left early the next morning.'

Brody nodded in agreement, his face turned towards the table, picking at his fingernails.

'And Belle, where is she based normally?'

'Lives in town with her boyfriend.' Jane gave a wry smile. 'She's a very caring daughter and nurse who continues to impart her great knowledge about what I should and shouldn't be doing.'

'Does that annoy you?'

'Not particularly.' Jane smiled. 'Best interests and all that.'

'Is she coming back out here again?'

'I'd imagine as soon as the river goes down. She doesn't like being away for too long. Or leaving me to my own devices. I'm sure she thinks that I'm incapable a lot of the time.'

'Mum, you know that's not true,' Brody broke in. 'I keep telling you, she just wants to make sure you're okay. It's not like you haven't had any problems since the accident.'

Bob looked over at Jane. 'Problems?'

Fixing Brody with a resigned, if not annoyed look, Jane spread her hands. 'Perhaps I overdid things a little early in the piece. Had a fall out of the chair and couldn't get back in. Belle found me outside near the shearing shed; Brody was out on the bike. She had a lot of trouble getting me back in the chair and I think that upset her . . .'

'Think?' Brody shook his head. 'I know it did.'

Graciously, Jane smiled. 'Yeah, I was a bit of a pain in the arse back then. And of course there's been a few personal, um, body issues, because of the paralysis. Belle likes to make sure we catch them as soon as they appear.'

'I see,' Bob said. 'You've all had a lot of adjustments to make in the last few years.'

'We certainly have.'

'Okay, so no other visitors. Friends? Neighbours from surrounding stations?'

'No, not that I can remember. Brody, do you want to get my diary from the office, please? I'll double-check and make sure I haven't got any of the timeframes wrong.'

Brody got up and did as he was asked.

'Tell me about the routine here at Corbett Station Stay,' Bob said, leaning back in his chair. 'You get people just dropping in, hoping for a site?'

'Yep, that's how most people do it,' Jane said. 'Occasionally, we get a phone call, but they'd have to be in a town to make it, unless they have a sat phone. Anyway, it doesn't matter because we can fit people in, even if we're full—there're thousands of acres out here! Thanks, darling,' she said to Brody who had come back in and put the book in front of her. She flipped through the pages, then shook her head. 'No, no visitors. The last time before Belle was here, Mick Miller and his wife dropped in on their way to town to see if we needed anything. Kind of them, because it's hard for me to get to town. Brody has to do all of that. The bus we have that fits my chair into it isn't four-wheel drive, so it does limit my town visits.' Jane threw Brody a fond glance. 'Mick has been great with Brody since Mal died, hasn't he, darling?'

One of Brody's shoulders rose in a non-committal shrug. 'Not too bad.'

'You don't like him?' Dave asked.

'Find him a bit overbearing, that's all.'

'Ah, Brody, he only does it because he cares.'

'Like Belle does to you,' Brody told her gently.

Jane stilled for a moment. 'Fair enough.'

Dave made a note to have another Mick conversation when Brody's mother wasn't around.

Bob brought the discussion back to the campground. 'Do you have any security cameras around the homestead or camp sites?'

'No. Never had a need for them,' Brody said.

'Okay, down at the communal camp area, it's a shared fire, showers and loos. Do you light that at the same time every day? What's the usual, Brody?'

Dave knew that Bob was keeping Brody involved in the conversation, and he'd also found the interaction between mother and son interesting. They had clear respect and care for each other, but were still able to pull each other, gently, into line.

'Ah, I light it in the morning, I'm up early, you know, four thirty or five-ish. Got to light the hot water system. Or donkey, as it's called up here. It's all wood, you see. I try to keep it going all through the day and into the night, but sometimes I get busy and it goes out. Most people seem to like hot showers in the morning, rather than in the evening. They get on the booze and then fall into bed mostly.'

'And do you often have trouble with people when they've had too much to drink?' Dave asked.

'Nah, not really. Sometimes people get a bit loud, but the other campers tell them to shut up. Very rarely have I had to go out and do something about it.'

'Would you hear a disturbance from up here?' Dave asked. 'The camp's a good few hundred metres away.'

'On still nights we can,' Brody said. 'But if the wind is up a bit, no. But I don't usually leave down there until I turn the generator off, which is about ten. Doesn't mean people have to leave then, as all the solar lamps come on, so there's light for everyone to get back to their camp sites. You've got to do this for the families with young kids, you know.'

'Yep. Good. And the kitchen, do you have to do anything there?'

'If I don't give it a clean, then the girls do. Take the rubbish away. Again, I do that all in the early morning before anyone is around. Gives me a chance to get rid of all the empty bottles and so forth from the night before. Kelsey and Hannah do most of the cleaning, I just fill in when they've got their days off. And I do all the heavy stuff.'

'Do many of the people who stay here go to the beach?'

'It's like Perth's freakin' main street at peak hour, during the winter.' Brody nodded.

'Swimming, that type of thing?'

'Oh yeah, and sunset walks. People take their towels down there and stay for a while. When you get a few families, often the cricket bat comes out and the kids play until they get tired or bored. Take their lunches to the beach.'

'And in the last two weeks, was there anyone down there more than normal?'

Jane and Brody looked at each other. 'Brody will have to answer that. I rarely get down there anymore.'

Brody shrugged. 'What's normal?' he asked. 'One family might spend the whole day down there and another might only go for an hour.' He stood up and got a glass of water. 'That's a really hard question to answer. And I have to say, I wasn't looking for anything suspicious around the place because I didn't know two bloody dead bodies were going to turn up here!' He turned, frowning. 'This is shit!'

'I know, son.' Bob's voice deepened. 'It can be hard when these types of things happen and you're asked to remember something you'd never really taken notice of. But take your time, because I often find that memories pop up out of nowhere,' Bob said. 'And of course, if you remember anything after we've talked, then come and find us.'

Bob seemed to think about his next question for a moment. 'People are allowed to drive on that beach?'

'Yep. Anyone with a four-wheel drive. The beach is twenty-five ks long and most of the sand is usually pretty hard. Driving on the beach is one of the selling points for this place. A secluded, private beach with free access. The campers make the most of it when they're here and, because it's hard, even people who don't have any experience driving on sand can drive on it.' He gave a bit of a laugh. 'But that's not saying I don't have to go and pull people out occasionally. Doesn't have to be wet and boggy to get into trouble out there; in sand, a car can just sink. Just due to deeper, loose sand, or not driving to the conditions. Or not knowing how. I always recommend cars head to the north along the beach because the other way, to the south, it gets pretty sandy and you have to know how to drive on that.'

'Have you had to pull anyone out in the last two weeks?'

'Nup, not for a while. It usually happens after a rain when the sand loosens up a bit and gets soft. You would've seen what it's like out there now. And sometimes heaps of cars churn the sand up leaving it boggy.'

'Ever get anyone caught by the tides?'

Brody raised his eyebrows in surprise. 'Actually, no. Even with the tides being high up here, the beach is so wide, there's rarely a time when you can't get around the water.'

'And can people camp down there?'

'We prefer they don't. And if I find them, I ask them to go back to the camp site. Better to keep everyone in the same spot. Lessens the risks of someone getting in trouble and us not knowing for a while.'

'Has anyone been camping down there in the last two weeks?'

'Nah, there've been people driving along the beach but they've always come back. I check the camp sites at night to make sure people are there, although sometimes it's hard to know where everyone is. They might be at the showers or cooking tea in the kitchen. But I do walk around the sites and talk to the campers. Someone always has a question of some description.'

'And boats, do you get boats mooring in the bay?'

'Very rarely. I haven't seen any for ages.' He turned to Jane. 'When was the last time that happened?'

'I'm not sure I could tell you. It's funny because even though it looks sheltered around the bay, it's actually not. It's open to the west, which is where our weather predominantly comes from, so any boats in the bay are not always as sheltered as they think.' She paused. 'If that's important I can go back through my diaries and find out. Brody or Belle would have had to tell me, of course.'

'Do you think there's been one in the last, say, three months?'

Both Brody and Jane shook their heads. 'Not a chance,' he said.

'It happens so infrequently, we'd both remember,' Jane agreed.

'But would you see?' Dave asked.

There was silence. 'I guess I couldn't say one hundred per cent,' Brody finally said, 'but it's rare I'm not down there every day at some stage.'

Bob tapped his fingers on the table and Dave gave his hand a break from writing.

'I guess the question is, in the last two weeks to a month, have you seen anything out of the ordinary? Anyone acting suspicious or moving around the station at night-time? Being in places they shouldn't? Anything that could be different from what you've seen in the past. Any unusual campers.'

The kitchen was silent, save for the ticking clock. There was a heavy sigh and Dave realised it was one of the dogs that had somehow come inside and was sleeping underneath the table.

'I don't think so,' Brody said. 'There is absolutely nothing that springs to mind.'

'Jane?' Dave asked.

'Well, look, you know I do get around a little bit on the motorbike, but not during early mornings or evenings. Everyone who has come to the house has been courteous and respectful. So, in all of my dealings with the campers, nothing has stuck out to me either. I'm sorry we can't tell you anything more.'

'Okay.' Bob pushed his chair back. 'Thanks for your time. We'll be back to talk to you when we've got more information.' He paused. 'Are the girls cooking dinner again tonight?'

Jane looked relieved to be talking about something normal, rather than the two bodies she had in her coolroom. 'Of course. Life has to go on when you've got visitors. There's not as many in the camp site tonight. Quite a few left for the rodeo, but some got caught with the rain and flooding. I can promise, Bob, there will be a steak or beef burger for you tonight.'

'Thanks. And, look, I know this is disconcerting for you both, but hopefully we'll get this cleared up quick sticks and we'll be able to focus on what we came for.'

'God, I'd almost forgotten that you were here because of some missing sheep,' Jane said. 'I guess you need to get on with investigating that.'

'We've got time to do everything we need to do,' Bob said with a smile at Jane. He turned to leave. 'Oh, Brody, would you mind if I have a word with you outside?'

CHAPTER 18

'I need to speak to all of the campers who are left here,'
Bob said to Brody as they walked a little distance away
from the homestead. 'Could you organise for them to be
in the camp kitchen tonight at about six please?'

Dave waved his hand towards the camp site. 'I've got to—'

'Yeah, no worries, son, I'll be down there in a bit,' Bob
said, eyeing his partner. Dave's face was red and perspir-
ation was beaded across his forehead. The humidity didn't
seem to be suiting him at all.

He turned back to Brody. 'We need to catch up with
everyone and let them know what's going on.'

'Do we?'

'We sure do. We don't want unsubstantiated rumours
flying around.'

'Sure, okay. I can do that.' He scratched his neck and
batted a few flies away. 'Can you tell me anything about
who it is?' Brody repeated his earlier question.

'We don't know anything like that right now, mate. Lot of work to do before we get to that point. Not often our bodies come with identification, although we wish they did. It'd make our job a lot easier.'

'But how—' Brody's voice broke off and he blinked a couple of times as if trying to understand. 'Mum's right, you know,' he said softly. 'I said this to you before. If this gets out, no one will come here anymore. We'll go under. I won't be able to pay for her care.' There was panic in his voice. 'It's the only way we're staying afloat right now.'

'I don't think we'll be able to keep this under wraps. I'm sorry, Brody,' Bob said. 'Once the media gets wind of it and the roads open up, I suspect you'll have a few visitors you don't want. But we'll try to keep it as quiet as we can for the time being. Now, could I ask you about your mother and sister's relationship? Seems like they might come to loggerheads at times?'

'Mum and Belle? I guess, but not really. Belle likes to throw her weight around sometimes. Nothing weird, just caring.' He stopped and looked Bob in the face. 'Both of us are pretty scared of losing her, you know. We've had a couple of goes at losing people we love and neither of us like it much.' He stopped as a young woman clutching a small boy to her hip walked up to them.

'Excuse me,' she said. 'I've heard that you found a—' she dropped her voice to a whisper '—a body. Are we . . . are we safe? I mean I've got little kids and—'

Bob put his hand up to stop her panicked questions. 'I'm Detective Bob Holden and my partner, Detective Dave

Burrows, and I are going to catch up with you all in a few hours and let you know what's going on.' His tone was calm and full of authority. 'But what I can tell you is there is no reason to believe that you and your family, or anyone else—' he smiled and reached forward to pat the child on the cheek '—are in any danger, whatsoever. None.'

'Are you sure? It's just that . . .' She looked around fearfully.

'Yes, I am.'

'Oh, that's really good to know.' There was relief in her voice. 'People have been talking and, since you wouldn't let us go down onto the beach, we thought it was something really awful, you know.'

'Where have you come from?'

'Us? Oh, we're from down south. Just holidaying for a couple of weeks. My husband, he's got a very high-pressured job and every year we come north, just to get away from his phone.'

'What does he do?'

'He's the CEO for a mining business.'

'Ah well, you'd all need that break, I'd imagine,' Bob said. 'And what's your name, young'un?'

The woman's face broke out in a smile. 'This is Alex. How old are you Alex?' she cooed.

The little boy held up three fingers.

'Three?' Bob leaned backwards, rocking on his heels. 'Well, now aren't you a big lad? I bet you love it up here. All that big beach to play on. Do you go to the beach often?'

The little boy nodded his head, his thick brown hair falling over his eyes as he did. 'I like to play cwicket.'

'Ah yes, great game! And when was the last time you went down there?'

'Yesterday.' His voice was high pitched and soft; it reminded Bob of Dave's little girl, Bec. When she'd climbed on his lap so he could read her a story, her voice had always been soft. It had been a long time since Bob had had anything much to do with littlies.

'What did you do while you were down there yesterday, hmm? Play cricket? Swim?'

Alex moved his arms over his head in a swimming motion.

'I bet you're a good swimmer. Check out those arm muscles!' Bob looked at the woman. 'I'd better get on, but pop over to the camp kitchen tonight and we'll all have a chat, yeah? Please don't be concerned.' He smiled reassuringly at her and ushered Brody away. Bob indicated they should walk towards the machinery shed, so they wouldn't be interrupted.

'How did you do that?' Brody asked.

'Do what?'

'Reassure her the way you did. She was so agitated at first but by the time you finished with her she was relaxed. Like she didn't have a care.'

'Son, we are going to have to keep the whole camp like that. We do not want anyone being silly. Or trying to leave because they're concerned. We're responsible for everyone's well-being here, and if some decide they're going to be dickheads and try to get out, well . . .' Bob spread his hands. 'We'll be pulling cars out of washouts left, right and centre. That river will be running pretty strongly about now. We don't want anyone getting washed away. We have to handle this carefully.'

Realisation spread over Brody's face. 'Shit, I hadn't thought of that.'

'Bob!' Mac appeared from around the side of the shed. 'I think we're here until at least tomorrow,' he said, stopping in front of them. He had mud over his hands and legs and a swipe of dirt across his face. 'The plane wheel has sunk into the ground and I need it to dry out a bit before we even try to take off. Probably need a few able-bodied people to give us a lift and see if we can get the old bird out of the pothole.'

'Sure, we'll give you a hand with that.'

'Still a heap of casual water around, so don't reckon it will be until mid-morning at the earliest.'

They rounded the edge of the shed and saw the plane sitting outside, leaning to one side.

Brody sized it up. 'How do you fit the bodies in the plane? What happens if they defrost before you get back to Perth?' he asked.

Mac gave a grin. 'They won't be doing that on my watch. Only a few hours to get back there, anyhow. And I'll fit 'em in, but they'll be in the main cabin. Good thing I'm not scared of the dead, huh?' He laughed, his eyes flashing. 'I love my job. No one day the same.'

Brody was silent for a moment. 'Lucky you.'

Bob clapped Brody on the shoulder. 'It'll be fine. I'm sure your coolroom will be all right, too. They're wrapped up pretty good. Smile, okay?'

Brody looked as if he were about to vomit.

'Anyway, I'll be off,' said Mac. 'Looks like you two have a few more things to talk about.' He gave a wave and headed off down the track.

'Where are you going?' Bob called out.

'For a walk!'

Bob shook his head. 'These young ones,' he said to Brody. 'Always trying to do what's good for them. In my day, we would've been holding up the bar by now.'

'Did you want me to open it for you?' Brody asked.

Bob huffed. 'I do, but you can't. Now, son.' Bob anchored his feet to the ground in a wide stance and crossed his arms, staring the younger man straight in the eye. 'Talk to me. Tell me how this camping venture you've got going here is keeping you afloat.'

Brody looked away for a moment, unsmiling. 'It's been hard since Dad died. I told you the other day, there wasn't a will and it took us ages to get everything sorted out, but we did. Then Mum had her accident and the hospital costs mounted up. Added to that, there were a few years where the stock prices were up the creek and so was wool.

'Mum's care isn't as expensive now, but it is ongoing, and we have to get vehicles that can fit her wheelchair in and so on—all of that has an extra cost involved.'

'That's a pretty heavy load for you to carry, son,' Bob said.

Brody gave the half shrug that Bob was becoming accustomed to. 'It's just the way it is. Belle and I, we'd do anything to make Mum comfortable.'

There was something heavy about the way Brody spoke, and Bob thought back to his comment earlier about Mac being lucky to love his work.

'Yeah, sometimes life throws curve balls at us, for sure. It must have been a pretty traumatic time for you—losing your dad, then your mum's accident on top of everything. Were you close to your father?'

Brody leaned against the side of the shed and put his hand down to pat Booster the border collie, who had come to sit at his feet.

'Sort of. As close as you can be when you're a young bloke wanting to have a crack at doing things yourself and not have your parents interfering.'

Bob gave a bark of laughter. 'Mate, that's what parents are there for, to tell you how to run your life.'

'Yep, too right.' There was no humour in his tone.

'Where were you when you learned about your dad's accident?'

'Still at boarding school in Perth. Halfway through year twelve.'

'Ah.' Bob let the silence string out, knowing Brody wouldn't stop there.

'Yeah. I managed to finish the year, but I had to come home as quickly as I could. Mum could handle things, but it was always going to be easier with someone else here to help her. And all the neighbours pitched in and helped, too. You know, Mick from over at DoubleM Station, and then there's Sandy and his wife, who have the station next door. All our three properties adjoin with the crown land in between. Mick and Sandy are all part of the Wild Dog Advisory Board that Dad was on.'

'Ah, your dad was on that board?'

'Yeah. Did six years, I think. Mum knows more about his involvement there than I do. Most of those years I was away at school.'

'You liked boarding school?'

It was the first time Bob had seen a proper smile on Brody's face.

'Yeah, I really did. I know there're heaps of people who hate it. Say that they miss the wide open spaces and such, but I liked it. Liked the people, the opportunities to play sport and go to concerts. And I really loved being challenged at school, you know. Maths and physics and stuff. Good fun.'

'Were you always going to come back here and work on the family station?'

Brody paused for a moment. 'Yep, that was the plan.'

'Yours or your parents' plan?' Bob asked quietly.

There was that half shrug again. 'Probably both.'

Noting that there seemed to be nothing truthful in that answer, Bob decided to leave it for a moment.

'A lot of responsibility running a station at such a young age. Bet there're plenty of old fellas who tell you that you're still wet behind the ears.'

'Every chance they get.' Brody finally looked at Bob. 'How'd you know that?'

'Ah well, son, I've been around a bit. Just a wild guess. Must be a bit infuriating.'

'Hopefully, when I make forty, they'll stop.'

Bob laughed again. 'Bit like moving to a country town. You're never local until you're there fifty years.'

'Oh, is it that short? Thought the family had to be there for at least five generations.' There was a bit of a sparkle in Brody's eye.

'True enough, son, true enough.' Bob gave a sigh and cast his eye around the land. 'Now, how about these sheep that are missing from DoubleM Station. You haven't done your shearing yet, have you? So, we wouldn't have your up-to-date figures?'

'Nah, Mum's only just organising the shearers now. When Belle was here. With these bodies and everything, we haven't talked about it again, but I know she's been trying because I saw her notes in the diary.'

'Brody, this will probably be a hard question because you have so many people moving around here, but have you seen any tracks in places they shouldn't be? Truck tracks, car tracks, even horse tracks. Campers in spots that aren't designated areas. You know, that type of thing.'

Brody continued to pat Booster quietly. The animal sat there with his mouth open, his tongue lolling out as if he were the happiest and most content dog in the world.

'Look, I can't think of anything that would be useful to you, and I'll just say again, I haven't been looking. And before you ask—' he turned to look at Bob '—I've been wracking my brains for anything since we've started having these conversations. But there's nothing.' Frustration crept in. 'Yet there must be because of what's happened.'

'The tiniest thing.'

'No, there's nothing. My life consists of dealing with tourists and Mum. The time I get to go out around the stock, I'm usually enjoying the freedom of being by myself rather than looking out for anything suspicious.'

'What about your sheep? Have you noticed whether there looks to be any less in a mob when you've been out around them? Or more, as the case may be?'

Brody's head snapped up. 'You accusing me of stock theft? You go to jail for that sort of shit!'

'Ha, believe me, I know that, Brody. I'm usually the fella that puts people there.' Bob's tone was serious. 'I'm not accusing you of anything. There could be a busted boundary fence the sheep have wandered through and ended up some-where on your place. Dogs might've chased 'em through a fence.'

'Well, I haven't noticed them if they're here, and I'm sure I'd know.'

'Steady on, fella,' Bob said, his hand raised and pumping the air in a calm down gesture. 'I have to ask these questions but I'm not throwing accusations around. This is how we gather information, okay?'

Half shrug.

Bob changed tack. 'Got any wild dogs around?'

'Belle said that when she was talking to Mick the other day, he'd mentioned there were a couple. And, because of that, I have been looking for dog tracks. Haven't seen any, though. As far as I know, when Sally rang to book your accommodation, she spoke to Mum about it briefly. Again, I've been busy with these bodies and tourists and I only saw the notes in the diary. Some days the only way Mum and I get to catch up is through notes.'

'Where had he seen them?'

'I'm not sure. Belle didn't say, and Mum didn't write it down. When she was talking about it, Belle said it was more on the sheep theft angle.'

'Ah, so others know about it?'

'Guess so. That sort of news would travel pretty quickly. Let the neighbours know, so they can look out. Mick would've told everyone, not just us.'

'Yep, the old bush telegraph.'

'Look, I'd better get on,' Brody said. 'If you want me to round everyone up, I'd better start knocking on doors.'

'Just a couple more questions,' Bob said good-naturedly. 'I know I'm holding you up, but they won't take long. Do you get on with all of your neighbours?'

'Course. Except for the comment here and there that I don't know enough to be doing what I'm doing. Everyone gets on well. Like I said, everyone pitched in to help us when Dad died.'

'What about when your mum had her accident?'

'Same thing. I was here then, though. Everyone from miles around came to help. Sandy kept an eye on the sheep

210

while I was in Perth when Mum was in hospital. She had a good eight or nine months down there, what with rehab and stuff. And Mick, he came over, too. Offered all sorts of advice. Aggie Dorrell cooked up a heap of meals. We were lucky to have so much support.'

'All of the people around here would know your station pretty well, then? Where the waters are, paddocks, fence lines. That sort of thing?'

'Yeah, well, I guess they would. We were all up and down from Perth so much for a while, we had to rely on the neighbours to check everything for us.'

'And who's your stock agent?'

'Tingles Grey. Office in Carnarvon but covers a fairly big area.'

'Now going back to Mick . . .' Bob paused, trying to find the wording. 'I'm really getting the impression there's some problem between the two of you.'

'Nope. No problem,' Brody answered.

Bob noticed his eyes flicked away for only a moment, but long enough for him to know that Brody wasn't telling the truth. He waited.

'I heard him talking to Mum once,' Brody relented. 'He didn't know I was there. Not long after Dad died. He wanted to take over the management of Corbett Station Stay. Said I was too young.'

'You wouldn't have liked that.'

'You bet I didn't. And I've always thought he's had the hots for Mum, but I wasn't sure if he was nice to her because he actually liked her or because he liked the idea of getting hold of the station.'

'He's a fair bit older than Jane,' Bob countered. 'And married.'

'Like that's ever stopped anyone before.'

Bob thought back to Ivan Pyke's comment that there was more to Mick than other people knew. His comment had been that the station owner had a wandering eye, so what Brody said made sense.

'Right-oh. Thanks for that, Brody.' Bob made to walk off. This time Brody stopped him.

'Just in case you're wondering. I know we're short on coin at the moment. I've been very open and honest with you about that.' He walked up to Bob and looked him straight in the eye. 'I'm not desperate enough to have to steal sheep to pay my bills, Detective Holden.'

CHAPTER 19

Dave threw down the satellite phone and slammed his fist into the verandah post next to where he was standing.

Not successful.

Two words that had not only ruined his day, but they had the potential to ruin his life.

His lawyer's message hadn't sugar-coated anything. They had been negotiating with Melinda's lawyers so Dave could see his girls again, but HQ had just relayed a message from his lawyer: the idea had been rejected.

He wanted to scream a long and very loud *Fuuuuccccckkkk* across the landscape, but there were too many people close by who needed to know that the police were trustworthy and dependable, in what was a frightening situation for them all.

Instead, Dave thumped the pillar again and again and again.

'Bad news, son?' Bob asked, appearing at his shoulder. He was tucking his notebook into his pocket and watching Dave, concerned.

'Yeah, no good.' Dave straightened. He knew his face was set in an angry expression. 'Bastards! What gives them the right—'

'Son,' Bob interrupted, 'we've been through this before. There is nothing you can—'

'Yeah, there is! I'll take them to court, I'll get full custody . . .'

'Ah,' Bob said mildly. 'There's a good plan. You've got the little ones and you get called out in the middle of the night to a scene and you have to leave them, or call in a babysitter.' He rounded on Dave. 'There's no way that would work unless you gave up being a detective.' Bob took a breath. 'Is that what you want?'

Shades of conversations he'd had with Spencer in the past filtered back to him: 'You can change yourself all you want but it might not be enough.' And: 'Sometimes they're not angry at the job. It's their husbands. And you won't ever be able to change that.'

'Surely,' Dave said tightly, 'surely I have the right to be present in my own girls' lives?'

Bob stared at his partner intently. 'Of course, you do! Don't ever question that. But at what cost?'

'Money isn't everything.' The words came from the depth of Dave's belly. 'I love them, Bob. All I want to do is keep them safe.'

'I'm not questioning that. But if you bankrupt yourself in fighting for them, what sort of a life would you have with them? Lawyers and court dates aren't cheap. And let's not forget what happens to the kids when they see their parents fighting and being revolting to each other.' He paused and let go of Dave. 'In time, things will change. You know why, son? Because your kids will grow and be able to make their own decisions. Not take any notice of Mel or Mark. Wouldn't that be the better way?'

Dave thought back over his father-in-law's hatred of him. It was without reason; except for the small fact that his daughter had chosen a copper as a husband, and he hadn't approved. Mark had done everything in his power to corrupt Mel's thinking and turn her against Dave. He had been on his way to success when Ellen had been shot by Bulldust. Well, the game had been over then.

There was no going back.

～

Sparks shot up into the sky as Brody threw another log on the communal fire.

Dave, dressed in a fresh stock squad uniform of pale blue shirt and jeans, stood close to Bob, watching the group of about twenty campers slowly emerge from their caravans and campervans to take seats around the fire. They were subdued and clearly anxious, waiting for an explanation as to what was going on.

Most were dressed in shorts and thongs, while a few had stocky, hard-wearing boots on. Shannon stood next to Bob, and Dave caught sight of the fire reflecting in her eyes.

He wanted her. There was no question.

But the message from his lawyer was sitting heavily in his stomach, while the anger churned around in every other part of him.

Maybe he should just pretend he didn't have two children and get on with life. Maybe Shannon would be part of that, maybe she wouldn't.

But he knew walking away wasn't a possibility. How could he forget he had two children? Two little girls he loved so much that he thought his heart might burst when he thought about them. When he saw them.

He stared into the fire, his thoughts as red as the flames that were burning around the logs.

How dare Mel treat him like a second-class citizen.

'Oi,' Bob nudged him with his elbow.

Dave shook himself. 'Sorry. What?'

'Stop stewing. There's nothing you can do right now.'

'I know.' Dave's voice was low and the words short.

Bob turned back to the people who were gathered together and clapped his hands, asking for everyone's attention.

'How's everyone tonight?' he asked. 'We are,' he indicated to Dave, 'Detectives Holden and Burrows. Thanks everyone for coming out. We know there've been a few rumours floating around the place and we wanted to put your minds at ease.'

Dave saw a movement to his left and turned. Kelsey and Hannah had arrived and were standing behind the circle.

Brody moved towards them and stood alongside Hannah. They looked at each other and Kelsey kicked the ground with her foot.

Mac was sitting with his legs outstretched, a guitar across his lap, and Dave briefly wondered where he'd snavelled that from.

The lone light from the house glowed. Jane would be at the kitchen table, looking out of the window and wondering what they were saying, Dave was sure.

'I can't go into the details of what has happened here, other than to say we have recovered two bodies from the main beach area, which is why it's been closed.'

A collective gasp went up from the circle of campers.

Dave watched them all closely, the flicker of flames lighting their faces, to see if there was any other kind of reaction, but all he saw was fear and shock.

'What are bodies, Mummy?' a small child asked loudly. She was quickly hushed by her mother, while her father indicated that they should go back to the caravan. The woman shook her head violently.

Dave's heart gave a thud and he turned to look at the little girl. She sounded just like Bec did when she was curious about something.

Her large eyes were watching Bob intently as if she knew it was a serious moment.

'We're sorry for the inconvenience to your holiday. We know most of you would like to spend time down there.'

'Are we in danger?' a man close to Dave asked.

'No, that's what I'm here to talk to you about,' Bob continued. 'We don't believe there to be any kind of threat to you.' He paused. 'Unfortunately, we won't be able to open the beach tomorrow. We're hoping we'll be able to the next day, but that will depend on a few things. We can update you on that tomorrow night.'

'How do you know we're not going to be hurt in any way?'

'I'm certain because of the evidence we have.'

There was a general murmuring as the campers looked at each other and tried to process what they'd just been told.

'Now, on another note, the rain we have had today has caused the river to rise and the road is cut off, so you'll be enjoying a few more days of Brody and his family's hospitality at Corbett Station Stay, and I have to say, Kelsey . . . Where are you?' Bob swung around looking for the young backpacker. 'Your burgers are bloody marvellous, so everyone should try one.'

Kelsey held up her hand and waved. 'Thank you,' she called out.

'Any other questions, come and see me or Dave privately. We're happy to allay any of your concerns.' He paused. 'Or, if you have any information, we would like to speak to you, too.' He stepped away from the fire. Quietly he said to Dave, 'Let's see what comes of that.'

The sound of guitar chords floated across the general shuffle as people got up and moved away, or stayed, talking to each other in low tones, their heads bent towards each other.

Mac called out, 'Who likes Slim?' He strummed the chords to 'A Pub with No Beer'. 'Come on, everyone. Who knows the words to this?' He started to sing the first verse with gusto, but no one joined in.

A man got up and walked over to Dave and Bob. 'I don't understand how you know nothing can happen to any of us here,' he said.

Dave held out his hand. 'I'm Dave. And you are?'

'Jim. Jim Craven.' They shook hands.

'Well, Jim, there's a lot we can't tell you,' Dave said and Bob, next to him, nodded. 'It's all part of our investigation, you see, but we're very sure that no one is at risk here.'

Jim didn't seem happy with that.

'Look, I've got a young family. I feel like I should be able to leave and move on. It's obviously not safe.'

'Normally, that wouldn't be a problem,' Bob said. 'But as you can see, there's been a lot of rain and you just can't get out at the moment. We're not holding you here, it's the way the weather has played out, unfortunately.'

Jim leaned forward and poked his finger in Bob's face. 'I'm going to hold you to this, mate. If anything happens to my family, you'll wish you'd let us leave when we wanted to.'

Bob raised his eyebrows and gently pushed the finger away. 'I'd rather you didn't take that tone, sir. We understand your concern and we're doing our best to keep everyone safe.' Bob took a couple of steps towards the bar. 'I'm off to grab some tea.'

Dave moved with him.

Mac had been able to get some enthusiasts to sit with him and join in the country music he was playing on the guitar.

Shannon fell into step with Dave. 'Didn't know he played.'

'He's not too bad. Hopefully, distracting the likes of Jim,' Bob said.

'Bit angry. Perhaps we should have more of a chat to him.'

'Yeah, but not when he's ready to explode. Tomorrow will do.'

Dave was quiet, feeling the heat from Shannon's arm as she walked alongside him. He wanted to move away from her, because this afternoon, when that message had come through, he'd had a stupid thought that perhaps he should try again with Mel. Even though he knew there was really no going back. Even after everything Bob had said, the thought still lingered. Because maybe that was the only way he was ever going to see his kids again. To go to her and beg her to take him back.

But that would mean giving up his job and, really, the woman he'd fallen in love with wasn't there anymore. She'd been hidden by a curtain he couldn't open.

The familiar tear in his heart was there again. He tried to push all of the crazy thoughts and feelings aside and concentrate on what Bob was saying.

'I think your talk went across really well,' Shannon said, glancing back at the campers. 'Well, maybe not with that one guy . . .' She smiled. 'Everyone is still worried obviously, but they're calmer now that they've got a bit of an explanation of what's happened.'

'Yeah, I agree,' Dave said, more to drown the voices in his head than anything else.

The dogs at the house let off a round of barking which rose above the sing-along but died off quickly.

'Reckon I should check that?' he asked Bob. Dave had observed the dogs only seemed to bark when people were at the house.

Bob had also stopped and was staring back at the house. 'Hmm, probably wouldn't hurt. Got your radio?' Bob's hand slid to his waist where he felt for his and Dave did the same. They were both back in the rooms.

'I'll be right. You stay here in case.'

Dave looked at Shannon, whose face was hidden by her hair as she bent forward to tie up her shoelace. 'Be back shortly,' he said.

Slipping around the side of the shed where the bar was, he made his way quietly towards the house. The puddles had started to seep into the ground and the soil wasn't as slippery as it had been earlier in the day.

As he followed the solar lights along the pathway, he concentrated on where he put his feet, so he didn't slip and draw attention to himself. Alert to the dogs and his surroundings, he was glad for this distraction.

The light from the kitchen spilled across the verandah, but as Dave circumnavigated his way around the house, he saw the rest of it was in darkness. Everything inside was quiet and unmoving. The generator was growling quietly in the background. Set well away from the house, it was only a hum in the distance.

Stopping to listen for any strange sounds or disturbances, he heard a muffled noise. He listened hard.

A voice. Coming from the shed that held the coolroom.

Dave couldn't make out the words, but he knew someone was there.

But there was only one voice . . .

He felt for his torch, at the same time as he looked to the sky. The light of the moon would be handy tonight, but it hadn't risen yet and the stars didn't throw enough brightness for him to be able to see where he was putting his feet. He'd have to risk heading over to the coolroom without any light.

Step. Step. Step.

Dave's heart thudded in his chest as he went towards the shed, wondering if someone was trying to get into the coolroom. The door had been chained and padlocked. No one could get in, but it was odd that someone would be over here without a light on.

He held his torch up, ready to shine it in the offender's face if needs be.

'Hey, don't throw that shit on me.'

The voice floated across and Dave stopped to listen. It wasn't one he recognised.

'Nah, that's not what we agreed on. Don't you—' The voice broke off and was silent.

Dave frowned. It sounded like a phone call, but all the lines were down because of the storm. Unless . . .

'Look, it's bad enough that—'

Dave realised whoever was talking was on a satellite phone. He crept closer, wanting to see who the speaker was.

'There's a saying, love. When you lie down with dogs, you get up with fleas. You've got a bad case of fleas and you're trying to infect me. Get your shit together and leave me out of all this.'

CHAPTER 20

Dave melted into the bush as a male figure came out of the shed and jogged past where he was standing, then headed towards the house.

Whoever it was, he was wearing a black hoodie, heavy jacket and baggy jeans. The darkness hid his face.

The night was a balmy mid-twenty degrees and certainly didn't call for a heavy jacket. The mozzies were bad, so Dave could understand that perhaps long sleeves could be helpful, but not the get-up this bloke was wearing. He was either trying to hide who he was or . . . well, Dave couldn't think of another reason. And after the last couple of days' discoveries, nothing would surprise him.

A beam of light lit up the darkness as the man turned on a torch and stood in front of the house for a moment as if he couldn't decide what to do.

Dave watched, wondering if the man was going to step onto the verandah.

Jane was in there by herself!

He tensed, took a step forward and opened his mouth to tell the man to stop.

No sound came out and then the man started to move; a walk to a slow jog. Down the road and away from the camp site and house.

Dave frowned. Where was he going?

Before he could react, the light disappeared.

Dave followed again, stepping carefully, stopping to listen occasionally.

The heavy steps were still close by.

A branch caught Dave on his face and he stopped. His hand flying to his cheek to stop the stinging, teeth gritted so as not to make a noise.

Then there was silence.

Had the mystery speaker heard him and stopped? Melted away so he couldn't be found?

Dave had no way of knowing. He took a few more tentative steps down the track, but he had nothing to follow this time, so he turned around and headed back towards the homestead.

Playing the conversation he'd heard over in his mind, he wasn't really sure what it meant. There wasn't anything in the words that made Dave think that it could be related to the two bodies. Except that last sentence about fleas and, really, that could be anyone saying don't involve them in something they didn't want to be part of. Still, the fact that the man had just disappeared into the dark was more than a bit suspicious.

Dave stopped in front of the house for a few minutes, making sure that no one was going to appear from the bush and that Jane was safe, then he started the five-minute walk back to the camp, intending to go to the bar.

Coming to the units first, he was overcome with a deep exhaustion. Not the kind of tiredness that sleep could fix, but one from having to fight all the time. Fight to see his kids, fight against his own thoughts and emotions.

Laughter reached him as he opened the door and he ducked into his unit. Glad of the night, he sat down and, breathing deeply, he put his head in his hands, closed his eyes and let his thoughts run wild. He guessed Shannon would be expecting to spend the night with him again—he would if he was her—but Dave couldn't face her tonight. He wanted to forget the bodies and Bob and Shannon, and feel everything that was hurting him . . . then let it go.

Letting out a groan, he put his hand over his chest, where his heart was. The girls. What could he do to see his girls? If the lawyer's negotiations hadn't worked, where did that leave him? Court. Did he have it in him to drag the girls through that? Did he have the money?

'I think you'll find a magistrate will be really sympathetic,' his lawyer had said. 'I'm sure that every magistrate on the bench wouldn't look badly on what you've done because you were in a job where you looked after the community.'

'What if it doesn't work?' Dave had asked.

There had been a pause. 'Then there won't be any other options other than to accept the finding of the court.'

The words had punched the air from his lungs.

No other options. That meant no hope, and when hope was lost there was nothing.

If he didn't go to court maybe there would still be hope because they could find another way around Mel and Mark's lawyers.

He switched his torch on and took out his wallet. Opening it, he looked at the photo which was behind the plastic pocket inside. Bec was on the swing in their back-yard. Her mouth was open in a silent scream of delight, while Alice sat in the pram next to the swing set.

This photo had always been his favourite. Alice, although tiny, was watching Bec with wide, curious eyes.

When it had been taken, Mel had been in the house, dressing for her mother's funeral. Dave had known this might be one of the last times he saw his daughters, while he was still married, and he'd spent many long minutes avoiding going inside to get dressed in his suit. He knew he'd be walking towards the end of their time as a family.

Instead, he'd pushed Bec, taken photos of both his daughters and cuddled Alice. He'd breathed in her baby smell and blown raspberries on her cheek. She'd laughed, her little arms flailing around as the giggles had burst from her.

Dave breathed in again, hearing Bec call to him, 'Push me, Daddy! Push me higher!'

Then the harsh shout from the house that had followed. 'Are you coming or are you going to do what you always do and avoid your responsibility?' His father-in-law, Mark, had been standing at the door, his face a mask of hatred.

Sadness welled in Dave now. He really wanted to see his kids. Mel, well, yes, her too, but it was complicated. Shannon . . .

He shifted the torchlight and looked at the satellite phone case sitting on the bed. He'd lent it to Shannon to ring her mum earlier in the evening.

Should he?

Without waiting for an answer, he opened the hard, plastic case and dialled Mel's number. The dial tone seemed to take an age to connect and Dave imagined the signal bouncing around space, off stars and comets until it hit the right satellite and the phone started to ring.

He held his breath.

'Hello?'

Mel's voice echoed down the line, with a pause in between the answering and when Dave heard her.

'It's me.'

Silence.

Dave thought she'd hung up, but then he heard Alice crying in the background.

'Mel, please. Can I say hello to the girls?'

More silence. Then a sob. 'How can you even think that is okay?'

'I'm not a danger to them by talking to them over the phone.'

The voice changed and now Mark was speaking. He must have taken the phone out of his daughter's hand. 'You're a danger to everyone. The sooner you understand that the better off we'll be. If you ring again, I'll get a restraining order taken out against you. How would that look against a detective?'

The phone went dead.

'Bastard,' Dave hissed through clenched teeth. 'Bastard.'

His chest felt so tight he could hardly breath. Getting up he paced the room, slamming his fist into his hand.

Slap. Slap. Slap.

'Bastard.'

Shannon's face slid into his thoughts. Her smiling, understanding face and guilt hit him again.

His mind argued otherwise. *She's done with you.*

'Am I done with her?' he whispered.

Doesn't matter, she's done with you, the voice argued. *You know there is no going back.*

How could he put all the years they'd been married aside? The memories, laughs and private jokes. Admittedly there hadn't been much laughter or joking around in recent years, but the early days had been different.

Squirming, Dave thought about how good it had felt to be with Shannon; how great it was when they talked about work. The way they could communicate without shutting each other down; their mutual respect. In the short time they had been together there was an intimacy with Shannon that he had never had with Mel.

Did that push everything he'd had with Mel aside?

'You all right in there?'

The voice that came out of the darkness made him jump.

'How'd you get on?'

'There was someone up there.' Dave put the phone back in the holder and snapped the lid shut. He let Bob in, telling him what he'd seen. 'Pretty sure he's gone for now.'

Bob handed Dave a beer. 'Right, we'll follow up in the morning. It'll still be damp so there might be tracks.' He looked at Dave. 'Why are you even wrestling with this?'

'What do you mean?'

'Why are you even wrestling with this?' Bob repeated as he sat down on the bed.

Dave felt the mattress sag underneath Bob's weight.

He looked down at his hands. 'How did you know I was?'

'Not very bloody hard, son. You've had a marriage bust-up that you blame yourself for, you shag one of the prettiest girls on the force and yet you're feeling guilty.' He leaned forward. 'Even. Though. You. Are. Separated.'

'Well, fuck,' Dave said, running his hand through his hair. 'You can't throw away a marriage.'

'You didn't. She did.'

'Stop making so much sense.'

Bob didn't laugh. 'When you have a break-up, the first time you get into another relationship with someone it's gonna feel weird . . .'

'I'm not in a relationship!'

'Right, I'll be as blunt as a dull axe. First time you sleep with someone afterwards, it's gonna be weird. I know, I've had to do it, too. All those years you've been with one person and then suddenly you're with someone else. It doesn't feel right. But you need to do it. It will help you move on.

'A very wise mate told me once that as soon as I split up with my ex-missus, I needed to go and shag someone else. And she was right. It helped me let go.

'And trust me, Mel isn't having you back, no matter what idiotic thoughts you're having right now.' He indicated the phone. 'Trying to call her isn't going to help. Just because you're experiencing regret at the loss of your family doesn't mean she will be feeling the same. You're just setting yourself up to fail.

'I'm not saying you have to marry Shannon. I'm not saying she's just a means to moving on either. I'm saying, stop feeling guilty. You haven't done anything wrong. For all you know, your ex-missus is out there shagging half of Bunbury. Who knows? Who cares?

'You are allowed to be happy, son.' Bob paused. 'And you need to get your head back into this case.'

Dave was silent. He took a swig of the beer Bob had given him and thought about what his partner had just said.

Bob crossed his legs and let out a sigh. 'Right, I'm going to tell you a story. Ever played the game Stingers?'

'Stingers?'

'When you play tennis and you lose a point, you've got to take your shirt off and the fella at the other end of the court fires the ball at your chest. It stings when it hits you, yeah?'

Dave looked at Bob, his eyebrows raised. 'What the fuck? Who plays that?'

'Drunk idiots. But you get my meaning, don't you? The ball stings when it hits. If you keep going back and back and back—by picking up the phone, wallowing in guilt and sadness—it keeps on stinging.

'Don't go back. Put it to one side. You and Mel are done.'

'The girls . . .'

'Are a completely different issue.'

After another swig of beer, Dave realised Bob was right. There wasn't any point in thinking about a reconciliation with Mel. Neither of them wanted that.

Dave was happy without her constant ridicule and blaming. He was sad that they hadn't been able to sort their differences and that Mel had constantly asked him to give up the force. He could never have done that. There were people relying on him.

'How do I show these dickheads that I'm not a risk to my kids?'

'Son, that bit I don't know. I think you need to rely on the lawyer.'

'I don't think we're getting anywhere. And I don't think I can afford to go to court.'

Bob screwed up his face in frustration. 'Son, I understand. I really do. I see your pain every day. I see you missing them. But I don't know how to help you with that side of things. The law doesn't always favour the father. We see that every day in our job, don't we? And we see the consequences.' He stood up and put his hands on Dave's shoulder. 'Son, I'd be happy if I never went to another suicide that's happened during a marriage breakdown and I certainly don't want to be going to yours. So, just promise me you'll keep talking about how you're fairing. If not to me, then to Shannon. To whoever you're comfortable with.'

Dave shook his head and drained the last of his beer. 'Not sure how we got from feeling guilty to suicide, but I take your point.'

Bob let out a breath. 'Good.'

'I was feeling guilty about Shannon. And it fucks with your head.' Dave banged his fist gently on the wall. 'I know that it's okay to get involved with someone else, but there's this hangover feeling in here.' This time he tapped his chest.

'Son, going through a divorce is about grief, too. You're losing something you always thought you were going to have. It's like a death. You have to give it time.'

Dave looked at the ground. 'I don't want to hurt anyone,' he said softly. 'I think I've done enough of that.'

Bob took a breath. 'Bulldust was the one who hurt Ellen and Spencer. Not you.'

'Stupid, isn't it? I know that. Just like I know that Mel and I are over. But there is this piece of me that always says: *what if?* What if I hadn't gone undercover? What if I had done what Mel wanted me to and resigned from the force? What—'

'You cannot deal in "what ifs",' Bob interrupted. 'They're a farce; they're not true. I know it's what we do in detecting, but you can't do it in life. You know why? Because you didn't make the decisions you're wanting to change now. What's done is done and we have to accept that and move on.'

'Yeah,' Dave said in low voice. 'I'm still not sure how to do that.'

The silence stretched out between the two men.

Dave shifted his thoughts from himself to Bob. 'Jane's an interesting woman, isn't she?'

Bob gave a small humph. 'Tenacious, I think the word would be.'

'You're impressed.'

'Aren't you?'

'She's been through a lot and still smiles. That's always impressive.'

Dave sat back and watched his partner. It was the first time since they'd started working together that Bob had showed any interest in a woman.

CHAPTER 21

'Right, let's try to lift on three,' Mac called.

The plane's left wheel had sunk into the mud on the edge of the airstrip and they needed to lift it out and try to get Shannon and her cargo back to Perth.

'One, two . . . three!'

All five men—Bob, Dave, Mac, Brody and a man from the camp they'd asked to help—heaved.

The mud sucked at the wheel, like a suction cap not wanting to come off.

'And again,' Mac shouted. 'On three. One, two, *threeee*.'

This time the plane lifted from the muddy slop.

'Hold it there,' Mac called excitedly. 'Try to swing the whole aircraft around so it's facing the strip.'

The men shuffled around and Dave felt the aluminium wing pushing into his shoulder. Sweat poured down his cheeks as they pushed and pulled to try to line the aircraft up, without damaging the undercarriage.

After what felt like an age, Mac called out, 'Right-oh, stop there.'

The men gently let the aircraft sink back onto the ground and took a breath.

'Bugger me, dead,' Bob huffed as he wiped his brow. 'How do those things even get off the ground? It's as heavy as all get-out.'

'In short, it's airspeed,' Mac said as he came around the wing, testing the flaps. 'Taking off into a headwind helps lift the plane from the ground when it gets fast enough.'

'I know,' Bob said. 'It's still amazing, though. This thing must weigh about a tonne.'

'Just under, actually. And fully loaded this baby would be one point six three two tonnes.'

'Incredible,' Bob muttered. 'I wonder why someone looked at a piece of tin and thought they could create an aircraft that might fly.'

'Do you need me for anything else?' the man asked.

'Nah, mate, thanks for your help,' Mac said, his face alight. 'We're going to get her onto the strip and then load her.' He glanced up. The sun was shining in a vivid blue sky and there wasn't a cloud anywhere to be seen. 'It's gonna be a good day for flying!'

'Shannon's up at the coolroom,' Dave said. 'I'll go and help her bring everything down here.'

'You want to check out if there're any footprints while you're there?' Bob asked in a low voice.

'Was planning to.'

'Good job.'

Dave looked across the land, wondering where the man from last night had disappeared to when, in the distance, he saw the land quivering and shaking.

A mirage.

Surprised, he commented to Bob. 'Didn't think it was hot enough for one of those.'

'They seem to come up after rain.'

The sound of engines reached him and they turned to see two four-wheel drives, caravans hooked on, heading towards the track out of the camp.

'Oh no,' Brody said. 'I'll be back.' He jogged towards the cars, waving his arms.

'Wouldn't be him for quids,' Bob said. 'Dealing with inexperienced campers would have to be like herding cats, I'd reckon.' He indicated with an arm to the water still lying around. 'Who in their right mind would think they'd be able to get somewhere today without getting bogged?'

'Not even that,' Dave said. 'I can hear the roar of the river from here. There's no way they'll be getting over it.'

'Even more reason to get off the ground,' Mac said. 'Come on, let's get cracking. I'm going to the house to put my flight plan in, if you guys can make sure that the cargo is ready.'

'Dave's onto that,' Bob said. 'I'm going to get some paperwork sorted for you to take back since I can't fax or email HQ.'

Mac tested the flap. 'When Brody gets back, we'll refuel and be ready when you guys are.'

Dave started the troopy and drove carefully towards the shed. Off the road, the mud was still slippery, so he drove in the middle of the gravel, taking care to keep all wheels away from the sticky mud.

He reversed into the shed and opened the door, hearing heavy tape tearing as Shannon ripped it from a roll and wrapped it around the plastic. There would be no seepage here.

Instead of going straight to her, he ducked outside, shading his eyes against the glare of the sun and checked the ground for prints.

Nothing.

Walking to the house, he kept his eyes on the ground, searching.

Still nothing.

It was as if the man had disappeared into thin air, or Dave had imagined him.

'Hello, Dave,' Jane called from the verandah.

'Morning.' He walked towards the house. 'Beautiful day.'

Jane smiled and cast her eyes around, looking content. 'They're all beautiful up here.'

'Wouldn't be dead for quids,' he said, then cursed himself as he thought about her husband. He wanted to say sorry, but instead he posed a question. 'Did you hear anything unusual last night?'

'Uh, no . . .' She drew the word out as she thought. 'No, nothing. The dogs barked, but that's not unusual. Why?'

'I thought I heard the dogs. Didn't think they barked unless someone they didn't know was around.'

Giving him an inquisitive smile, Jane said, 'Well, then, that would be most of the time, wouldn't it?' She gestured towards the camp. 'No one over there they've met before.'

'Right, so not unusual for them to bark at nothing?'

'Not nothing—they will have thought there was a reason to bark, Dave!'

He laughed. 'Good point. So, you didn't hear anything?'

'No. I had tea about seven o'clock and watched the ABC news, then read for a while, before going to bed. Brody came in about ten, I suppose, and him coming into the house was the only thing I heard other than the generator.'

'Thanks. The plane's ready to go, so your coolroom will be free very soon.'

'That will be a relief.'

Giving her a wave, Dave headed back to the shed.

Inside, he blinked a couple of times to adjust his eyes to the dimness. 'Plane's out,' he said, spotting Shannon still inside the coolroom.

She looked up, unsmiling. 'Good. We should be able to head off then?'

'That's what Mac's working on. He's just gone to put the flight plan in.' He paused. 'I'm sorry about last night.'

Shannon shrugged and went back to fastening the tape. 'You don't have to explain anything to me.'

Dave touched her gently on the arm to get her attention, then waited until she stood and looked at him. 'I do. It wasn't that I didn't want you with me last night. I needed to think through some things.'

'We're not in a relationship, Dave.' She avoided his eyes. 'We talked about this. I know you're not ready for anything serious and I won't be forcing the issue.'

'And I told you that I'm interested but, yes, I have something to work through and last night was one of those times. You understand enough of what's happened to me to know this divorce isn't straightforward and that how it's all come about is pretty awful. Sometimes the thoughts take over and I need to be by myself.' He paused. 'Especially when the lawyers have just told me that my last-ditch attempt to see the girls was rejected by Melinda's lawyers, so court is the next option.'

Sympathy flashed in her eyes as she brought her head up and looked at him. 'That's horrible, Dave. And last night is completely understandable.'

Dave wasn't sure but he thought her tone told him otherwise. He stepped away and gave her a smile. 'Good. I'm glad we've sorted that.' He was going to take her on face value because he didn't have the energy for anything else. 'We'll have another drink when I get back then.'

'Sure.' Grabbing the plastic, Shannon unrolled a long strip and nodded to one of the bodies. 'Can you help me place them on here and then roll them up.' She handed him a pair of gloves. 'Put these on.'

Glad to be doing something other than talking about feelings, he grasped one end and did as she instructed. Within a few minutes they had both bodies safely secured in the extra plastic.

'Right, in the troopy with these two,' she said.

The bodies were unyielding as they carried them one by one to the troopy. Dave had thought they would be easy to manage but he was wrong. They were cold, which froze his fingers, and heavy. He put his end into the back of the troopy and said, 'Are you right to hold them there? I'll get into the front and help pull them through so we can shut the door.'

Shannon nodded and he eased his way past her. He could sense a change in her behaviour. He was sure her hurt went deeper than she was showing. Why did things have to be so complicated?

Still, he couldn't think about that now. Something in his mind had flipped last night; after what Bob had said to him, he knew he needed to focus on the job and let everybody else do theirs. Perhaps he was destined to be the lone detective who sat at the dark end of the bar most nights.

Perhaps relationships were distractions that detectives didn't need. He'd thought about all the coppers he'd worked with and, within the stock squad, there was only one who had been in a happy relationship. That had been Spencer, until he was murdered.

The rest were busy solving crimes.

The drive to the plane was quiet, and just before they arrived, Dave put his hand on her knee. 'I'm sorry,' he repeated.

This time she smiled a sad smile. 'Don't be. We did talk about this. You took me by surprise, that's all. I thought we'd get another night together.'

'And if I hadn't heard from the lawyers, we would have. Now, about that drink when I get back . . .'

Shannon looked at him. 'I would really like that but see how you feel,' she said. 'Don't commit to something you find you don't want to do.'

Dave nodded. She was making it easy for him to opt out if he wanted. He pulled to a stop close to the strip and wound down his window.

'Where do you want me?' he asked Mac.

Shannon opened the door and got out, leaving Dave alone. He glanced at her retreating body and wanted to call out to her, to ask her to stop. To say he'd made a mistake and he knew he wanted to see her when he got back, but he couldn't do it.

Instead, he listened as Mac gave him instructions and then guided him in, with hand signals.

They both tried to manoeuvre the first body through the small plane doorway. Mac got into the aircraft and crouched down, helping guide the rigid package through. He gave a hard yank and Dave felt the body slip out of his grasp.

His hands grappled at thin air as his end of the body hit the steps of the plane.

'Shit.' Dave glanced over his shoulder hoping that Shannon hadn't seen. These remains should be treated with respect—he would want his loved ones treated as such. 'Sorry, Mac,' he said in a low voice, as he grasped hold again.

'You're good mate. Tricky.' Mac's voice was low, too, both knowing Shannon wouldn't have liked what had happened.

Finally, both bodies were in the plane and strapped down to the floor.

Shannon was standing alongside the plane with her bag and an envelope Bob had given her. She smiled. 'Well, we'd better go,' she said and held out her hand to Bob. 'Thanks for your help. I'll be in contact once the autopsies are done.'

'No worries. If it's been passed on to another team, I'll let you know.'

Dave wasn't sure how she was going to say goodbye to him, and was surprised when she kissed his cheek. 'See you round,' she said and climbed aboard before he could answer her.

Mac shut the door and made sure it was fastened, before shaking the men's hands. 'Real good to meet you fellas in person,' he said.

'Nice to meet you, too,' Bob said. 'Hey, keep up that guitar. You're real good at that, son. I enjoyed your performance last night.'

Mac nodded and touched his finger to his forehead in his trademark salute. 'Catch you boys later.' He looked out at the strip. 'Right-oh, let's see how this goes. I'm not one hundred per cent sure we'll get off the ground, but I'll be doing my best.'

'Be safe,' Dave said.

Bob and Dave backed away as Mac fired up the engine. They watched the propellor spin to life and, after a few false starts where the wheels spun, they finally got traction and the plane lurched onto the strip.

Mac revved the engine a few times, then jerked forward. Mud flew up behind them, pinging off the body of the plane, as they raced down the strip.

The wings took on a strange angle.

'Shit,' Dave said, half moving forward as if he wanted to stop the plane. 'Is he . . .'

'Fuck. Yeah, it's going . . .' Bob screwed up his face and stood waiting and watching.

They watched in horror as the plane started to slide towards the edge of the strip, towards the gutters where deep water was lying. They heard a loud rev as Mac gave the shuddering plane full throttle and managed to get the front wheel off the ground as the plane was sliding sideways.

The front wheel then the back lifted and they were off the ground, only inches from the water.

Dave hadn't realised he'd been holding his breath until he took in a deep one, trying to catch up on the few he'd missed.

'Holy hell, that looked hairy,' he said.

'Better them than me, for sure.' Bob continued to watch until the plane circled back over them and Mac waggled the wings, saying all was okay.

Bob turned back to the troopy. 'Right, well, we'd better do some of *our* work now,' he said as he pulled the door open and went to climb in. 'Let's hope all of the excitement has gone from here for a while,' he said as Dave started the engine.

'What's the plan then?'

'Well, I've been through the Corbett Station paper-work and there hasn't been any influx or decrease in stock numbers over the past three years. They've held pretty steady. When the sheep come in for shearing, there should be about six thousand, give or take, allowing for deaths and so on.' Bob indicated towards the shearing shed. 'Let's swing over there and have a look in the shed. I think Jane told me it was a five stand.'

Dave turned the wheel and drove towards the shearing shed and yards, which were made out of wood and tin. A steep set of stairs on the outside of the shed led up into it and the sliding tin door was wide open.

Bob went to open the troopy's door just as the radio crackled to life and they heard Mac's voice.

Bob snatched up the receiver of the police radio. 'Got you loud and clear, Mac. All okay?'

'Affirmative,' he replied. 'Listen, I wouldn't be trying to land anything on that strip for another two or three days. It's too wet. Slippage is gonna be a real problem there for a while. Landing is different from take-off and I'd be concerned that the undercarriage might collapse under the nose if the aircraft slipped off the runway when they came in to land. That'd be a real possibility if you tried too soon.'

'Understood. Thanks for the advice,' Bob answered.

'I can also see two vehicles that are bogged. They're due east from the homestead. Not on the main driveway. Looks like they've gone exploring and come off second best.

Might need to send a recovery party to them. I've circled them and can see four men. They're about ten kilometres from the homestead.'

'Roger that. They're on a road, though?'

'Affirmative. A track that heads towards the beach.'

'Roger. We'll sort it. Can you see much water around?'

'Yeah, there's a bit laying on the surface of the land, but heading towards the crown land we saw yesterday, I think you'll be okay to try that sandy part of the property. Only on bikes, though, if you're going to be off-road.'

'Cheers for that.' Bob hung up the mic. 'Talk about no rest for the wicked. Come on, we need to go and find these cowboys. Better get Brody to bring his tractor just in case.'

CHAPTER 22

The road was slippery as they drove towards the bogged vehicles Mac had directed them to. Water ran in the drains along the side of the road, in a rush to get to the river, while the sun shone.

It seemed to Dave that this country was a land of contradictions. The water and rain should indicate cold, but it wasn't. The atmosphere was humid and hot.

The stock they saw as they drove were full wool ewes and they were happily out grazing across the grasslands. Although they looked healthy and in good nick, Dave knew they were a time bomb waiting to happen.

The little bush flies were everywhere, buzzing at the crevices of their bodies. It wouldn't take long for the blow-flies to turn up and make their home in the wet, warmth of the wool.

'They'll want to get on to the shearers pretty quickly now,' Dave said as he turned the steering wheel gently following the curve of the road. To the north of them, hills rose into the sky, trees covering the rocky ground to about three-quarters of the way up where the rocks took over and not even the hardiest of plants could force their roots through the stone. 'Must ask Jane where she got to with that because Brody didn't seem to know.'

'Flies will eat 'em for sure,' Bob agreed. 'Must be hard when you know you've gotta do a job and yet you can't get the people in to do it. The shearers won't just be sitting around waiting for them to call.'

'Take a week or so for the yards to dry out properly and get them all mustered up.'

'Yeah, anyway, this is a good opportunity for us to do a muster and get a count of what's on this place.' Grabbing the file from the dash, Bob flicked through a couple of pages and tapped some of his notes. 'Okay, like I said before, there should be about six thou' sheep running over Corbett Station Stay. They buy their rams in, but breed their own ewes, so they're a closed flock. Only sheep that go off here are the wethers for export. Muster twice a year.' Bob shrugged. 'There's always opportunity for stock to get stolen when you're only getting them in the yards twice a year. Some mongrel could come along a day after you put them back out in the paddock and you wouldn't know for six months.'

'That's the trouble up here, isn't it? The huge distances and timeframes. Pretty easy to get onto a place without anyone knowing you're there. Bit like these clowns who have got themselves bogged. Brody said he didn't know anyone was out here.'

Bob shook his head. 'Hope they've had the nous to stay with the vehicle. I don't really fancy having to launch a search party when I've just recovered two bodies and found a shitload of drugs all in the space of three days. There's no ability for us to get another team in here to help out. What I wouldn't give for a chopper.'

'Surely we'd be able to get a fixed wing up to search though, even if they can't land.'

'Of course, there're options, son. I just feel we've got a bit on our plate. We need to get on with our own investigation. I'd feel better if we could get another crew in to recover those drugs, too.'

'I still think we should have brought them in.'

'I know you do, son, but what would we do with them? Where can we keep them under lock and key and—' Bob pointed his finger at him as they rattled over a rough patch of road '—if we recover them, we can't use them to lure in the dealers. I'd like to have a go at that, wouldn't you?'

'Yeah, I understand why we haven't, but I'll be bloody annoyed if the dealers get to them before we do.'

'So will I, son, so will I.'

As Bob's voice trailed off, the two bogged utes came into sight and Dave let out a whistle.

'Done a good job there.' From a distance, it looked like the Hilux was on a strange angle, indicating it had sunk to the axles and its nose was on the edge of the river, not far from the water. The roar of the water was constant, and he could see leaves and debris caught in the exposed roots of the trees.

The second ute was parked behind the first one and that was bogged, too, but not as badly. From what Dave could see the wheels just couldn't get traction. That should be an easy fix. There were footprints around the utes where the men had tried to push it out. There was a frayed and snapped rope still attached to the deeply bogged vehicle.

Dave surmised he'd be able to pull the second one out with the troopy and a couple of snatch straps, but the other one . . . He picked up the mic.

'Got a copy, Brody?'

'Yeah?'

'You're going to need to bring the tractor.'

There was a silence and Dave imagined him swearing a little. With every reason. These were cowboys who were being a nuisance.

'Roger, on my way,' Brody answered finally.

As they pulled up, the four men, who were sitting around a fire, jumped up and came towards them.

'Not gonna get too much out of that with wet wood,' Bob said, seeing the fire was more smoke than flames or heat.

Bob wound down the window and one of the men leaned in. He was in his early twenties with dirty brown hair and a beard, thin and wiry with a tattoo of an eye on his forearm. The cap he was wearing was on back to front.

'Mate, we're pretty pleased to see you,' he said. His clothes were muddy and wet and he had mud caked onto his beard. The others looked just as shabby as the man who had his head stuck through the troopy window.

'You fellas need a hand?' Bob asked. 'You're looking a bit stuck.'

'Got anything to eat first? And, yeah, we could do with some help.'

'Eat? Sure.' Bob got out and went to the back seat, then opened the fridge. 'Run out of tucker? How long have you been here for?'

'Ah, couple of days. Since that first big rain came through. I'm Rory O'Brien.' He put out his hand and Bob shook it.

'G'day, Rory. I'm Bob and this here is Dave. You other blokes want something to eat?' He held out some bananas and there were murmurs of thanks as they took the offerings.

'Any of you blokes hurt or need medical attention?' Dave asked.

'Only our pride, I reckon,' Rory said. He gave a bit of a laugh. 'Stupid, huh, come out here for a week or two of fishing and camping and we get in up to the axles. Not our finest hour.'

'And who might you other fellas be?' Bob asked.

Rory pointed to each man, who in turn raised their hand and gave embarrassed grins. 'Harry Wilson, Sam Watson and Nick Austen. All out here reliving our youth.'

'Badly by the looks,' Bob quipped.

'Yeah, we weren't sure what we were going to do, to be honest,' Nick said as he came over to stand next to the vehicles.

'Good thing PolAir saw you.'

'For sure, for sure,' Rory said. 'We heard the plane.'

Dave inspected the utes and noted the numberplates down. He hadn't noticed any fishing rods, only swags and a barbecue plate, piled haphazardly into the tray. As he walked around the utes, putting together a plan on how to pull them out, he listened to the conversations.

'Looks like you boys have taken the wrong track,' Bob said. 'How'd you all get here? Did you come in past the house and camping ground?'

'Yeah, mate, we did.'

Dave peered into one of the windows and checked out the contents. A car chock-a-block full of mess. Takeaway cardboard containers, empty energy drink and beer bottles littered the floor and back seat of the dual cab. Screwing up his nose, he assessed the men.

All four had beards and were dressed in jeans and checked shirts. Their rolled-up sleeves exposed defined arms, like they worked out at the gym. He wondered if they were city boys on a trip, and out of their depth. Was certainly looking that way. There wasn't even a tyre repair kit in among their gear, and that was a necessity when you headed out bush.

'So, why are you here and not camped at the grounds?' Bob asked.

'Look, we're all fine and we're sorry to cause any trouble,' Rory said. 'If you could help us get out, we'll be on our way in no time. Think we've had our adventures for these holidays, don't you, boys?' He looked at his mates and they all nodded.

'Glad you've come to that conclusion. But that doesn't explain why you're not at the dedicated camping area.'

Rory shrugged. 'Thought we might get a bit too rowdy for there,' he said. 'We're here for a good time, not a long time.'

Dave wanted to roll his eyes.

Bob indicated the swollen river. 'Don't you know not to camp in or on the edge of a creek?'

'Didn't know it was going to rain,' another one said.

'Always expect the unexpected when you're out here, son. Listening to a weather forecast is also a good idea.'

'You own this place?' one of them asked.

'Me? Ha! Nope. I'm a detective. So is Dave here.'

'Detective? As in a copper?' Rory's voice rose in surprise. 'What are you doing out here?'

'My job. We're with the stock squad. Anyhow, we'll be able to pull you out. Especially this one here.' He indicated the less-bogged ute. 'We can do that now, but for this old girl, you'll be waiting for the owner. He's bringing his tractor to give you a hand.'

'Appreciate that. Thanks a lot,' Rory said. He finished his banana then threw the skin into the bush and Dave did a double take. As an experienced camper he wouldn't have done that; he would've put the skin in the rubbish bag in the back of the troopy and got rid of it when they'd gone through a town and could use a rubbish bin.

Always leave the bush as close to the way you found it as you can. His grandfather's words came to him.

'Right-oh, let's have a crack at getting this ute out before Brody gets here,' Bob said. 'Dave, you do the honours?'

Getting back into the troopy, he started the engine and made sure four-wheel drive was in low gear before he reversed towards the ute. Bob hooked up the snatch strap and held it as Dave inched forward and it tightened. He called out, indicating for Dave to stop.

'You right in there, Rory?' Dave heard him ask. Not hearing the reply, Dave searched the side mirrors to get Rory in his line of sight. 'You'll be right, son. Put the ute in neutral and keep your foot away from the brake until it's needed. Your job is to make sure you don't hit Dave there in our vehicle, okay?'

Rory's head bobbed up and down in the rear-vision mirror and Bob caught Dave's eye, indicating he should move forward with his hand.

'Slowly, son,' Bob instructed. 'Slack has been taken up.'

Dave let out the clutch and felt the wheel slip a little. He gave the accelerator a few more revs and held his breath, hoping the wheels would get a grip on the ground. It wouldn't be great if he got stuck as well.

'Stop!' Bob yelled. He came around to Dave's window. 'You're gonna have to go a bit harder, mate. Those back tyres are going to dig in if you're not careful.' He stepped away and called to Rory. 'Ready?'

'You want us to push at the front?' one of the other men called out.

'Nah, you stay where you are,' Bob instructed.

Dave let the clutch out and pushed down on the accelerator. With a roar, his troopy lurched forward and he felt the bogged ute give way behind him. In the mirror he saw it was moving behind him. Dave breathed a sigh of relief and towed the vehicle further up the road until he was sure it was in a safe spot.

'Good job,' Bob called out.

Dave reversed back slightly to take the pressure off the strap and then turned the vehicle off.

One of the other blokes ran in to disconnect the two vehicles and gave Dave the thumbs up.

'Cheers, mate.'

In the distance they heard the drone of the tractor engine.

'Ah, here comes Brody,' Dave said. 'We'll get this one out now, too.'

Rory got out of the vehicle and tried to brush the mud off his jeans. All he did was smear more over them. 'Tell you what,' he said to his mates, 'how about I take off in this ute and see if I can get out and you blokes can follow?'

'There'll be none of that going on,' Bob said with a shake of his head. 'You'll have to camp back at the station stay for a couple of days. You won't get across the river at the moment. You can see that it's high. You're going to be here for a while.'

Rory's face fell. 'Shit, I really need to get back to work.'

Bob shrugged. 'Can't be helped, son. Mother Nature's had different ideas.'

'Right, well, I'll go and see if I can get us a camp site then,' Rory said. 'Nick, how about you come with me, then we'll be ready when you other blokes get there.'

'You don't want to make sure your mates get out?' Dave asked.

'They'll be okay with you. No worries. We'll see you at the camp.' Rory and Nick got into the ute and drove off, leaving Bob and Dave staring at their tail-lights.

'Nice mates,' Dave muttered to Bob.

'I wouldn't want them.'

Dave sauntered over to the still-stuck ute. 'Lucky you fellas didn't do a nose dive into the river,' he said. 'Looks like you came to an abrupt stop.'

'Yeah, it was. Spilled my beer,' Sam said. Harry was quiet, not contributing to the conversation at all.

'Go camping often?'

'Often as we can. Like it out here in the wilderness, don't we?'

Harry nodded his agreement.

Dave silently repeated the word 'wilderness' to himself. They didn't even sound like blokes who knew the bush.

'Here comes the tractor,' Bob said.

Dave turned in time to see the brake lights come on at the back of the disappearing ute as they slowed, going past the tractor. Rory hung an arm out of the window and gave a wave, before disappearing around the corner.

Bob and Dave looked at each other. Their spider senses were going off. There was more to these four men than met the eye.

CHAPTER 23

Dave was shaking his head as they got into the troopy and headed back towards the camp site. 'So, these guys have almost no camping gear, hardly any food and no fishing rods,' he said, looking across at Bob. 'That's a bit strange, don't you think?'

'Not a lot of experience when it comes to camping out, that's for sure,' Bob said.

'Why are they out here?'

'Let's ask them.' Bob fiddled with the satellite phone. 'I'm going to call HQ,' he said. 'I want to know if they've got any active drug-running investigations in the area. And if any of these boys are known to them.' Dialling the number, he swore as the troopy hit a deep rut and lurched him forward in his seat, hitting his head. 'Bloody hell, son. Careful. You'll give me concussion driving like that.'

'Sorry, couldn't see it.'

'Drug squad, please,' Bob said as the phone line connected. 'Yeah, g'day, Colin. Bob Holden here from the stock squad. Look, mate, we're north of Carnarvon out on Corbett Station Stay and we've discovered a load of heroin . . . What's that?'

Pause.

'Yeah, buried in the sand in Turquoise Bay.'

Pause.

'Mmm, wrapped in blocks and black plastic. Interestingly, we've also recovered two bodies. One from the sea—on first glance a male. Bit hard to tell too much more because he'd been in the water a while. The other a young girl of Asian origin. Just wondering if you fellas might have an active investigation up here?'

Dave couldn't hear the reply, so he concentrated on the ute in front of them. Brody had managed to pull the second ute out without too much fuss and now Sam and Harry were driving it back to the camp site.

Dave and Bob had given them a lecture on how lucky they'd been because, the way the river was running, they could have been swept away.

'Really?' Sam had looked ill.

'Yeah, mate. Sure, it could have,' Dave answered. 'Fast-flowing rivers and creeks are not the sort of thing that should be mucked around with. People die out here, you know.'

Sam and Harry had looked at each other, then back at the ute as the squelching mud had let go and the ute came back onto dry land.

'Are there . . . are there crocs in there?' Harry asked.

'Not this far down, mate, but don't try this if you ever get to Broome or Kununurra,' Bob said, just to get the message across that being in the outback wasn't to be taken lightly.

Now, Bob asked Colin his last question: 'Can you run a check on these names for me? Just get back to me on that when you can.' He gave the names of the men, thanked Colin then pressed the disconnect button. 'Interesting,' he said. 'They don't have anything active.'

'They want to know more?'

'Of course, but again, they can't get anyone out here. They've instructed us to recover the drugs, document everything and lock them up. We should be able to lock that coolroom if we get a chain and a padlock. Just means one of us needs to be close by all the time, which is a pain in the arse, because I want to get out and start doing a muster. Those ewes we saw on the way out here, I reckon we could get around them and bring them in. The ground is a bit higher there and better drained. We'll have to ask Brody to give us a hand. And we've got the motorbikes in the trailer, too, so I think we'll be okay. I might get you to do that once we've got the drugs locked away.'

'No worries, I'd be keen to get out there.'

'Okay, so the plan of attack is that we need to catch up with Jane and Brody and tell them what we've found and get the use of the coolroom again—it'll need to be turned off this time because the moisture in the air in the fridge will bugger up any chance of finding any fingerprints. Though I don't know how we'll go at getting any, because the packages have been buried and the sand has been wet, too.

'So, let's tell Brody and Jane what's going on, get the drugs out and locked away, then you can do a muster and I'll hang around and keep an eye on things. I want to talk to those young lads, too.'

Dave brought the troopy to a standstill in front of the homestead, just behind the ute Sam and Harry were in. Nick was walking towards them, with keys in his hand.

'Got some units,' he told the others. 'Come over this way and you can have a shower and get a feed.'

Sam and Harry gave Dave and Bob a wave as they followed Nick down the road.

'Wonder where Rory's got to,' Dave said.

'They all looked like they needed a bloody good shower to me,' Bob said as he pushed the door open. 'Ah, hello there, old dawg.' Slamming the car door, he bent down to pat the border collie, who had sidled up next to him and stood there waiting for a pat.

Jane was on the verandah, waiting for them. 'Hello,' she called. 'Got them all out?'

Bob grinned and walked up the path. 'Sure did. They certainly were in a sticky situation. Once they've had a shower and a feed, I'm sure they'll be much happier.'

Bob held onto the door, so Jane could swing her chair around.

'Cuppa?' she asked, smiling up at Bob.

Dave noticed a softening in his partner's face as he looked at her.

'Love one, thanks. Dave and I have something we need to talk to you and Brody about.'

Jane's expression changed from happiness to trepidation. 'Surely there can't be anything else wrong now, can there? I mean, two bodies . . . Anyone would think we're cursed!'

Dave found himself agreeing with her. Sometimes families just seemed to have an awful run of bad luck.

'Cursed? Ah, come on now, Jane,' Bob said with a laugh in his voice. 'I'm sure you're much more practical than that. But, yes, we've got a bit more news.'

The door banged shut again and they heard Brody's footsteps before he appeared in the kitchen doorway.

'That's a good job done,' he said. 'Some people are so bloody stupid, though. I mean, why would you try to drive through a flowing creek? No brains about that lot.' He stomped over to the stove and turned on the gas so he could boil the kettle.

'Did you know any of those men?' Dave asked.

'What? Nope. Never seen any of them before. Why do you ask?'

'Well, they said they headed out into the "wilderness" at any chance they got, so I was wondering if they'd camped here before.'

Brody shook his head as he got the cups out. 'Never seen them before, and I'd be surprised if they camped out much at all. They were so disorganised.'

Dave wanted to agree but he held back.

Jane pushed herself towards the table. 'What did you want to talk to us about, Bob? Sit down and tell us.'

'Well, when we were recovering the last body, Dave here made another discovery. Some drugs buried on the beach.'

Brody swung around, a look of horror on his face. 'What? Drugs?'

'Yeah. We need to retrieve them today, so—and I'm really sorry about this—we need to close off access to the beach again.'

'Jesus!' The word was low and angry. 'Again?'

'I'm sorry,' Bob said.

'Drugs?' Brody repeated. 'This is getting beyond a joke. What the fuck is going on here? I wish to Christ I'd never seen you two.'

'Brody!' Jane snapped. 'Enough. They're here to help, not hinder us.' She turned to Bob and Dave, taking a couple of deep breaths. 'Although, I have to agree with part of what Brody said, this is getting beyond a joke. How would they have got there?' Jane asked, her hands twitching with anxiety. 'I just don't understand what is going on here. Brody, do you? Are the two bodies and the drugs connected?'

'I have no idea, Mum.' This time he sounded defeated. 'It's almost like someone has it in for us. I mean, Dad, then you, now this.'

Dave's head snapped up at those words. He made a note to check the accident records for Mal. He knew Bob had brought that file with him, but neither of them had looked at it. Maybe it wasn't an accident.

Something Mick Miller had said niggled him, but he couldn't quite remember what it was.

'We're not sure how they've got here either, but I suspect they've come in on a boat and been buried, just waiting for someone to come and collect them.'

'But why our place? I've heard of drug smuggling up further north, but not down this low before.'

'I can't answer that,' Bob said. 'All I know is that they're here.'

Dave was watching Brody, who had sat down heavily at the kitchen table, his head in his hands.

'Brody, you got any idea about this?' he asked.

'What? No, of course not.' He was angry now. 'What is seriously pissing me off is all the work I've done to get this station stay up and running to ensure we've got the money to keep operating, and now I can see it going down the shithouse. No one is going to want to come and stay where there are bodies and drugs galore.'

Jane reached out and put her hand on his arm. 'Hopefully, no one will find out about it.'

Dave leaned back in his chair and surveyed both Jane and Brody, before asking, 'Do either of you have any enemies? People who have got a grudge against you? With Mal even?'

Silence stretched out across the table.

'Um . . .' Jane's hands twitched again, agitated. 'No. Not that I know about.'

The phone rang, startling them all.

'Looks like we're back online,' Jane said, her voice subdued.

'I'll get it.' Brody got up.

'You never really know when it's going to start working again,' Jane continued. 'It just does. I sometimes think it's when the line dries out.' She looked at Bob, seeking reassurance. 'You think someone is doing this to us purposely?'

Dave answered, because the question had been his and he and Bob hadn't discussed this. 'I think we should leave all lines of inquiry open at this stage.'

Tears welled in Jane's eyes but were gone as quickly as they'd appeared. She seemed to gather herself and find the stoic station woman she was. 'I see. What will happen once you've recovered the drugs?'

'Like I said, we'll need to keep them under lock and key until another team is able to get in here and either fly or drive them out. I'm not sure which it will be because I don't know how much is there.'

Dave heard Brody answer, 'Corbett Station Stay,' and turned back to Jane, taking up from Bob.

'Another unit of guys will get here as soon as everything has dried out or the river has gone down. And let's hope none of the previous guests talk about this business, when they leave here,' he said. 'We'll be as discreet as we can be, but I guess closing the beach will get everyone's tongues wagging again.'

'Mum.' Brody stood in the doorway. 'That was Belle. She wanted to know if we were okay because a journalist stopped her in the street asking about a body.'

Even from where he sat, Dave could feel the young man's anger and noticed a tic pulsing in his forehead.

'Newspaper?' Jane asked.

'They wanted to know if we could comment on the body found on the beach. How the hell . . .'

The phone rang again.

'Leave it,' advised Bob. 'You'll have to screen your calls if this is out. The people who've already left must've talked. The ones that got out before the big rain,' Bob said. He frowned. 'I'm so sorry about this.'

They were silent, listening to the message being left on the answering machine.

'Hello, this is Ali Teague from the Carnarvon *Courier Mail*. I'd like to interview you about the happenings on the beach at Corbett Station Stay. Would you return my call . . .' She left a phone number.

Jane took a breath. 'Ah, well,' she said with the matter-of-factness of an outback grazier. 'Nothing can be done about it now. We'll just have to live with whatever comes our way. What did you say to Belle?'

'That I'd ring her back with more details, but yes, that it was true a body had been found on the beach. She wants to come out but I told her she wouldn't get through.' Brody pounded his fist on the doorframe. 'This is shit!'

'You don't have to talk to the journos, Brody,' Dave said. He was sure the angry young man didn't hear.

'Everything I've done . . .' He turned and stormed down the hallway. The door slammed behind him and Dave heard the motorbike fire to life and head towards the camp site.

Dave got up and went to stand at the window, while Bob turned off the now boiling kettle and poured the water into the cups that Brody had already set up on the bench.

'Jane, did you recognise any of the men who came into the camp just now? The ones who were bogged?'

She shook her head. 'I only saw the one called Nick. He came and booked into the units. I haven't seen him before.'

'Okay.'

'I'd better ring Belle back. I don't want her hearing anything more on the grapevine, and if the media has got hold of this already, then . . .' Her voice trailed off.

'Sure, no worries,' Bob replied.

Dave sat back down at the table across from Jane. 'Before you do, Jane, let's just go back to the question of grudges. There's no one you can think of? Maybe an upset camper or someone you've sold stock to who doesn't think they got a good deal? Anything.'

Jane wrinkled her brow. 'Honestly, no. I think we have a great relationship with everyone: neighbours, stock agents. Of course, you get the one-off camper who gets annoyed because of something minor, but I don't remember an incident that would have caused a grudge. But that's only from my point of view. If someone was capable of doing this as a grudge, then clearly they're annoyed with us.' She held out her hands. 'I don't know what else to tell you.'

'Did any of the neighbours ask to buy you out after Mal died? Perhaps they thought you couldn't cope?'

Jane gave a hard laugh. 'Yeah, there were lots who thought we couldn't cope, more so after my accident than after Mal's death. But I wouldn't have ever left here. I mean, where would I go, this is my home. Any interest that we got, I put to bed very quickly.' She paused. 'Although Mick

Miller was reasonably persistent. Still, I made our position clear. This is Brody's heritage!'

'Brody told us he went to boarding school when he was younger.'

'Both Belle and Brody went away. You don't have a choice up here—well, you can see what the telecommunications system is like and it was worse back then. They spent their primary school years doing school of the air, but secondary school, well, no choice.'

'Did they both enjoy it? Some kids get really homesick, don't they?'

'Oh sure, some do, but neither of mine did. Brody revelled in everything down there. He made so many friends and always got involved in everything that was going on.

'Belle, she was a little more reserved once she got down there, but she still took part in all the extracurricular activities. I think she missed home more than Brody did.'

'And when did Brody come to be back on the station?'

'After his dad died. He was about due to head home anyway, but Mal dying sped everything up.'

'And Brody was happy to come back here to work?'

'Of course. It's what all sons do, come back to work on the station and take over. I can't imagine Brody wanting to do anything else, actually.'

'Right. Oh and what boarding school did they both go to? Are there better ones than others?'

Jane nodded and drained the last of her tea. She named the two different schools. 'Mal's family had long relationships with each school, and they are both top-notch schools education-wise.'

'And the boarding side of things?'

'Just all the normal complaints of bad food and horrible, grumpy house masters and mistresses. Let me tell you, every child talks about those things.'

Bob laughed. 'Yeah, I've heard that.'

Dave had made a couple of notes in his book and got up to look out the window again. He couldn't see Brody or the motorbike, but he thought back to what Bob had told him. That Brody wasn't happy here. That didn't compute with what he was hearing now.

Did Jane really believe what she was saying, he wondered, or did she just want it to be true?

CHAPTER 24

Dave wandered across the yard, looking for Brody. He needed the front-end loader and for the beach to be closed off. His initial digging around the packages to ascertain what could be there had showed they had been buried deeply. He'd dug in a two by two metre square area and hit packages every time the shovel had gone into the sand. The machine would make digging these out much quicker and easier than doing it by hand, especially now that it was so hot and humid.

He saw the motorbike parked in front of the camp kitchen and headed towards it, just as Brody came out. His steps indicated he was angry and he looked like he wanted to smash something.

'Hey, Brody!' Dave waved his hand.

He looked over, trying hard to disguise the annoyance that came over his face. 'How can I help?' he asked when Dave got close enough.

'Going to need your front-end loader down at the beach to help us out, please. And we also need to close the beach. Could you give us a hand?'

'Who's going to pay for the fuel?' Brody asked, crossing his arms.

'The coppers. You'll get reimbursed, I'll make sure of it.'

'Right. I need to light the hot water system before I can go anywhere. That thing doesn't wait for anyone.'

'No worries, just so long as we're done before dark, but it's not going to be a hard recovery, I wouldn't have thought.' Dave stopped. 'Mate, what's really going on here? You're acting very strange and I don't think the fact that you might see a dip in clientele is the main reason. Did my question about people holding grudges stir something up? Want to talk to me?' He paused. 'Believe it or not, we're here to help and if I can, I will.' Dave didn't think he needed to mention that he'd also arrest someone as quick as look at them, if they were a prime suspect.

Brody threw a couple of stumps into the hearth of the hot water system and tossed a bit of kerosene in before lighting a match.

Dave heard the *whoomph* as the kero took hold and flames closed in around the wood.

'My parents had one of these on the farm when I was growing up,' he said, hoping to establish a rapport. 'They're mongrel things, aren't they? Gotta keep them lit all the time, or the water gets cold and takes ages to heat up. Poor Mum, she spent most of her life either lighting it or cleaning up around it!'

'They're hard work,' Brody said shortly.

Dave waited. Staying silent was sometimes the best strategy because people always felt the need to fill the silence. Spencer had used this strategy well; so well that Dave had called him Peter Pause at times.

He'd learned a lot from Spencer and Bob; a good mentor was one who listened, guided and let the mentee still be themselves, without imparting their own beliefs. Both men were that kind of mentor. They'd taught Dave the importance of never assuming and methodical detecting; and Spencer, in particular, had shown Dave how community policing was as important as investigative work.

Spencer had saved the life of one man, Jeff. He'd walked out on his family and gone bush for a few days because he couldn't cope with the constant pressures of new fatherhood, marriage and his depression. Spencer had talked to Jeff man to man, but with compassion. Made him feel that getting some help was okay. He even gave him the name of a counsellor.

Brody needed some of that type of community policing now.

Dave hoisted himself onto the steel table close by and waited while Brody fiddled with the wood and made sure the fire was going to light. Finally, the young man stood up and looked at Dave.

Brody went to say something, but it seemed like the words wouldn't come out. Then he closed his eyes and let out a heavy sigh. 'I don't know how much longer I can do this for. Especially if we lose clients.'

'Do what? The station stay?'

Brody opened his eyes. 'Why did you become a copper?'

'That's a long story, but I got kicked off the family farm, basically. I was the youngest son. I have two older brothers who were already home, and by the time I got back from ag college, there wasn't room for me.' He gave a shrug. 'I thought getting into the stock squad would be a good way to still have contact with agriculture and I'd be able to do what I loved.'

'Different from me,' Brody said.

'It is if you didn't want to come home from boarding school. Look, I have to say, I wanted to be a farmer. That's all I ever wanted, then when all of the shit happened at home, I had to find something else. I didn't think about being a copper until someone mentioned this job to me. Now, here I am and I love it.'

'Yeah, totally the opposite to me. I never wanted to come back home. It's slow, hard work for not much reward. Hot and dusty. People say this type of country gets under your skin and stays. Well, all it does is annoy me, like an itch I can't get rid of.' He gave a bit of a harsh laugh. 'I'd be the only son from around here who didn't want to come home. Odd one out. Black sheep of the family. That's me.' He took a deep breath. 'Never told anyone that before. Those words, I couldn't let them pass my lips. Anyway, I've said it now.' He continued to talk. Ramble even. 'I think Belle knows, but she's never asked me. It would upset the family dynamics if I wasn't here, looking after Mum and running everything.'

'How so?'

'Mum wants to be here. She'll never sell the station—it's been in Dad's family for generations. She loves it, and if I wasn't here, someone else would have to be.' He shrugged. 'This is where the expectation is really high.' He made quotation marks with his fingers. '"It's been in our family for generations." One person from every generation has come back, lived here and worked the station. Can you imagine bucking a system and an expectation like that? That I'd be the one who broke the generations of compliance?'

Dave nodded his understanding. A long line of family pride and tradition.

Brody continued. 'Mum's okay by herself, but she can't drive too much; the country, as you can see, is pretty rocky and she had a fall off the motorbike a while back, knocked her confidence. So, if I wasn't here, Belle would have to come out and stay. That couldn't happen because she's a nurse and we're too far from the town for her to commute. And we'd have to employ a stockman.' He paused. 'The trouble with that is no one looks after your station and stock the way that the owners do.'

'I hear what you're saying, Brody, I really do. Life has thrown some tough curve balls at you for sure. And if you don't want to be here, then that's doubly hard.'

'Just the way it is.' His tone held the resignation of someone who knew their circumstances weren't about to change any time soon.

'You didn't feel you could have a discussion with your parents? Tell them what you wanted to do?'

Brody shook his head. 'I thought—actually I hoped—Mum would sell after Dad died, and she could have. Mick Miller offered to buy us out and so did a couple of others, but she didn't. In fact, she was even more dogged that this is where she wanted to be, but all she's doing is hanging on to Dad's dream.'

'Not your mum's dream, too?'

Brody stopped. 'Yeah, well, it must be hers as well, I guess. After all, she's not wanting to sell or go anywhere else.' His voice rose in frustration. 'Every bloody school holidays I was pulled back here to help with stock work or fencing or something. Every school holidays I wanted to stay in Perth. Hang out with my mates and go to the movies, or swim at the beach.

'You know they never asked me what I wanted. They told me what I was going to do. I got angrier and angrier . . . Then Dad died and I sort of believed there could be a bit of hope. In the end, there wasn't.' The heat seemed to leave his words and his shoulders sagged a little. Bending down, he pulled open the door into the donkey and checked the fire. Another couple of small pieces of wood in there and then Dave could feel the heat coming through the wall.

'Yesterday, I was so bloody jealous of Mac when he said how much he loved his job, and then I realised that once the word gets out about everything here, well, there won't be any point in us trying.' Brody stood up and took a breath. 'And then we won't be viable. I might not want to be here, but I don't want it to go under. I will not be the generation that loses the station. That's not the way us

Corbetts work. I don't want Mick Miller to get this place either. I told Bob earlier, I always thought he had the hots for mum, so I've never trusted his intentions. I know she isn't interested, but that's not the point. I don't see why he thinks he could waltz in here and just take over.'

'What would you have liked to do? Work-wise, I mean.'

'Teach. Teach high school kids. In the city. Not out bush. I don't like the isolation. In a way, this job with the campers suits me because I'm meeting new people, but I don't enjoy it.' His voice was wistful. 'I'm not who I used to be.'

'In what way?'

He shrugged. 'I just know I'm not.'

'I feel for you, mate, I really do. It's hard when you're stuck in a situation that you can't get out of. Why don't you just tell your mum? You might be surprised at her reaction.'

'No chance. She wants to die here. She's already told me that.' He spread his arms wide, indicating the vast area. 'Imagine. Another twenty or thirty years out here. No life, no wife, no change. Just me and the campers. And the sheep.' He gave a harsh laugh. 'Now, isn't that something to look forward to?'

Dave rolled this information around in his head. Certainly, it stacked up with what Jane had said about Brody; he got involved with everything at school and loved it. Had friends galore.

'You still see any of your mates from school?'

'I rarely get away from here. They're all down south anyway.'

'Talk to them much?'

275

Brody looked out across the camp grounds. 'Mate, I don't even have a girlfriend. It's hard when you're out here. Just picking up the phone isn't the easiest thing to do. Hell, it's not that long ago we were all still on a party phone line. You couldn't talk to anyone without your neighbours listening in. I go into town about once a month, and Hannah and Kelsey look after everything for the weekend, but . . . It is what it is.'

'No one comes up here to visit you? Would've thought this was a great place for them to get out of the rat race.'

'I don't want them here.' His voice rose as he said the words. 'They wouldn't understand. I'm a glorified gardener, yardman and general dogsbody. Don't you know there's this romantic view of what a station owner is? Someone like Mick over at DoubleM Station, getting around in R.M. boots and moleskins.'

Dave wished he knew what to say to make this young man feel better, or at least give him some hope, but he didn't believe there were any words that could do that. Only actions. Big ones that would take courage and determination. 'I think you're being pretty hard on your assessment of what you do. Sure, you have to keep the place tidy, but you also run the stock side of things, and that takes ability. Otherwise, you end up with a lot of dead sheep.'

Brody didn't answer.

'Have you thought about leaving? I mean really thought about it? Because that's the only option I'm seeing which is going to make you happy. Everyone deserves to be content with their life.'

'No. Short answer. Not until Mum's not around anyway, and that'll be years away.' He gave a wobbly smile. 'Well, I hope it's years away.'

'I reckon you're a brave man, Brody, and a loyal one. Those qualities will take you places.' Dave turned and looked towards the beach. 'Guess we'd better get down there and sort these drugs. Mate, I know I've asked you this before, but you haven't remembered anything that would help us find out who might have buried these drugs here?'

Brody shook his head. 'I wish I could help, 'cause I'm not liking it myself.'

'It's an interesting situation we've got here, for sure. You know, the bodies and the drugs. We're reasonably sure the two—or rather, the three—are connected, but we need more information. If you had something, even the tiniest of snippets . . .'

'I know nothing about them. Nothing about the bodies either.' The words came out fast and louder than before. 'I don't want to know anything about them.'

'Haven't heard any funny conversations or—'

'Nope. Nada. How about this? If I'd known the drugs were there I might've taken them and sold them. A few extra thousand in the bank wouldn't go astray. Bit of a buffer, you know.'

'I don't know that that'd be helpful.' Dave looked around. There was something itching at the back of his mind, like he knew there was a question he needed to ask, but he couldn't find it.

There were too many coincidences and not enough answers.

Dave switched topics. 'How about those stolen sheep?'

Without warning, Brody erupted. 'I've told you before, if you think I'm stealing sheep to pay the bills, I don't need to. Yeah, we're short on cashflow, but we've got investment properties in Perth. If worst came to the worst, I've got no doubt Mum would sell them to keep Corbett Station intact and in the family. Haven't I just made it clear to you about the expectation of keeping the property? Go and check that out. The only thing we've done that isn't legal is to take cash and not declare it. You can put that in a statement, and I'll sign it.'

'Whoa.' Dave held up his hands in a calming gesture. 'Steady on, Brody, I wasn't implying that at all. I was wanting—'

'G'day, fellas.' Rory appeared from around the side of the bathrooms. He'd showered and was wearing cleaner clothes than when Dave had seen him last. He did a double take, recognising the anger coming from Brody. 'There a problem here?'

'No, there's bloody not,' Brody said. The rage was still radiating from him, and Dave knew he'd stuffed up big time. Gone in too hard. Bob would have something to say about this when he told him. He'd been trying to get Dave to understand that his slow and steady way of policing was better than going in boots and all, Dave just didn't quite have it down pat yet.

Bob would have said something ridiculous like, 'Slowly, slowly catches the monkey', which would have made no sense until Dave had stopped and thought about it.

That would have been the point. To stop and think.

Now, still cursing himself, Dave tried to defuse the situation. 'G'day, Rory. All settled in? Notice that you're in a unit, not camping?'

'More comfortable that way.' Rory's stare slid across to Brody. 'Although,' he looked around, 'everything's pretty primitive. I notice you haven't got beer on tap even. And the camp sites . . . I've seen better.'

Brody seemed to struggle with himself before he tried to smile. 'Hard to transport it out here. Is there anything I can help you with? If not, I've got a few jobs to do.'

'I'm all good. Thanks for pulling the utes out. We'll have to reimburse you.'

'It's all part of the service out here.' The words were short and clipped. 'Glad we could be of help.'

'Didn't catch your name,' Brody said suddenly to Rory.

'Rory.' He held out his hand, but Brody ignored it.

'Well, Rory, sorry the camp sites aren't up to your standard. Hopefully, the river will go down real quick and you'll be able to get out of here.'

Dave knew he needed to change the subject. 'Look, I've got to get on, too. We've got a job to do.'

'Oh yeah, what's that?' Rory asked. 'Anything we can give you a hand with to say thanks for helping us out?'

'Thanks, but it's police business.'

'What time does the bar open?'

'Four thirty. Kelsey and Hannah will be there, so if you need a feed, just let them know. It's cash though. We don't have EFTPOS.'

'Cool, cool, sounds good to me.' Rory smiled. 'Well, I guess I'll let you all be. Go find something else to do.' He looked around. 'Turns out this isn't quite how I'd imagined this trip. Bogged and rain and mud. Still, what can you do?'

'Have you seen the shearing shed that's here?' Brody asked, pointing towards the shed. 'There's a heap of history in it and we've got it all written up in there if you're interested in a squiz. That should fill in a bit of time for you.'

'Not really my thing, but thanks for the heads-up.'

'What were your plans for when you got up here, Rory?' Dave asked.

'Oh, you know, like I already told you. Bit of fishing. Swimming. Beer drinking with the boys. That sort of shit.'

'Is that right? You been camping much before?'

'Yeah, mate, us four blokes, we love camping. Always heading out bush somewhere. Our favourite pastime.'

'Dave, you ready?' Bob called from across the yard and indicated he should head back and get into the troopy with him.

Dave raised his hand in acknowledgement and turned back to Rory. 'Catch up with you at tea. Enjoy your stay.' He turned to Brody. 'You ready?'

'Yeah, I'll just restoke this fire and head over there.'

Dave nodded and walked back towards Bob. Once he got to the other side of the shed, and was hidden from view, he stopped and turned around, peering out from around the corner of the shed, looking at Rory and Brody.

Brody was bent down, throwing more wood into the donkey and Rory was now perched on the table like Dave had been. He could tell they were talking to each other, but it didn't look to be a comfortable conversation.

Frowning, he continued on over to Bob. 'Check those two out. What do you think?'

Bob followed Dave's gaze. Brody was standing now, his body tense, and it seemed that Rory was laughing. 'What are you thinking?'

'I'm not sure.' Dave shook his head. 'Rory was downright rude and Brody fired back. Still high emotion stuff, I guess.'

'Reckon they've come across each other before?'

'Can't say for sure.'

'You know what? Rory's acting suspiciously. I'm not going to wait for the drug squad to get back to me. We're going to run a check on all of those blokes right now.'

CHAPTER 25

While Bob dialled the number, Dave found his notes where he'd written down the rego numbers and the names of the men when they'd first introduced themselves. He held the book out for Bob to see.

'Yeah, g'day. Bob Holden here. Can you run a couple of regos for me, thanks?'

Pause.

'Three Juliet, Papa, November, dash two, eight, six and second plate is eight Foxtrot, Victor, Mike dash three, nine, two.'

Pause.

'Right. First one is owned by Harry Brian Wilson. I asked the druggies to run a check on him, but they haven't got back to me. Can you? Anything outstanding on him? And connections, too, please.' To Dave, he said, 'He's the same age as Brody. Want to jot that down?' He focused back on the voice on the other end of the phone.

Dave did as he was asked and waited for the next piece of information. In his mind he was already visualising a whiteboard with the men's four names on it, their dates of birth and any important information. Photos of the bodies in situ were there with question marks as to their identity. The information they had was written up in dot points.

- *Male body.*
- *Female body.*
- *Drugs.*
- *No suspects.*
- *No evidence. When would Shannon complete the autopsy?*
- *Did these blokes somehow connect to the drugs? Said they were going fishing but didn't have any rods.*

Frustrated, he wished he could put all the information on a whiteboard and look at it, not just see it in his head. There was a connection he knew, but he couldn't piece it together. He flicked back through his notes.

'You're kidding me?' Bob's voice cut through Dave's thoughts. 'Which bikie gang?'

Pause.

'The Insurgents? Really?' He held the phone away from his ear. 'He looks like a baby, not a freakin' bikie, no matter the beard.' To the person on the end of the phone, he said, 'Any priors? No, okay, And the other car?'

Pause.

'Rory O'Brien. And anything on him?'

'Done for drugs? Possession or supplying? Possession, what year? Last year? Right.' Bob scratched the information down. 'And has he got any link to the bikies?'

Pause.

'None known, okay.' He stopped and tapped his fingers against his mouth as he thought. 'Right, I've got three other names I need you to run. Got a pen? Ah-huh, mmm. Right: Brody Corbett, Sam Watson and Nick Austen.' He turned back to Dave. 'Now this could be interesting. Tell me how these young blokes could get mixed up in a bikie gang?'

'Not all of them, just Harry?'

'At this stage.'

Dave tapped the name Harry Wilson. 'Isn't there a Wilson who's involved with the bikies? What was his name. Old codger. Jack? Nah. James? James Wilson. Maybe a family connection?'

Bob put the phone back to his ear as Dave heard the voice coming from the earpiece. 'Who are the leaders of the Insurgents?' He pointed at Dave and nodded, smiling. 'You're onto it. James Wilson. President. So, does he have any connections which can link back to these young blokes?'

Pause.

'I see.'

Dave looked at the notes Bob scribbled. Harry Wilson's uncle. Drawing the family in, as all good bikie gangs did.

'Right, well, if the Insurgents are involved in this, it's huge. We're going to need another team up here pretty quickly. You might have to chopper them in.'

Pause.

'Yeah, Dave and I'll get the drugs out, for sure. I'd imagine that's what these guys have come to do, but they got fucked over in the process of looking for them. They're all pretty young so I don't think they'll be too hard to control.'

Pause.

'Can you also do a check on Jane and Belle Corbett, and throw Mick and Sally Miller in for good luck. Any links or family connections. Anything that's going to help us tie all this together.'

Pause.

'Yeah, ring me back when you've got all the intel. Quick as you can, please. Nope, you won't be able to fax or email it, you'll have to ring. Good on you, thanks muchly.' He looked over at Dave. 'They're on to it. Going to have to watch those young fellas a bit closer than I thought. The Insurgents!' He sounded stunned.

'Just got to go and see Jane for a moment,' Dave said, his mind ticking over quickly.

'Yeah, and I'm going back to the units. I need to grab my gun and radio. You want yours?'

'Yeah, my gun, please. Radio is in the glove box.'

Bob nodded and got out. 'Won't be long.'

Dave walked over the verandah, and stood at the door. He could hear Jane talking and he assumed she was on the phone because he could only hear one side of the conversation. He tapped gently and heard her call out, 'Come in.'

'Only me,' he called back. 'Take your time.'

Jane continued talking as if she hadn't heard him. 'Yes, love, I'm doing my exercises.'

Pause.

'I know, I know, it's a pretty rotten thing to have happened, but the police are here and they'll get it sorted.'

Pause.

'Is it?' Her voice dropped a little. 'Well, be careful telling your brother that. He's really worried we'll lose customers over this.'

Pause.

'The front page? Not ideal. Not ideal at all.'

Pause.

'Well, it can't be helped. Now, are you planning on going to Perth when the new tenant moves into the Cottesloe house?'

Dave heard her hmm-ing.

'Belle, those investment properties are your responsibility so if you feel you need to go, then do. I'll trust your judgement on that.'

Dave wandered over to the fridge and looked at the photos on it. There were numerous pictures of Belle on a horse, on her graduation day and standing next to a tall, lanky young man who he assumed was her boyfriend. It wasn't Brody anyway.

Brody's photos consisted of him in a footy jumper, covered in mud, holding up a gold medal, giving the photographer a large grin and the thumbs up. A grand final win, presumably. Another one with him holding a horse, while Jane sat astride, and the third one seemed recent; taken from behind as Brody looked out over the sea. It must have been windy because his hair was standing up and the shirt he was wearing blew against his thin frame.

'If you want my advice I'd go down and get a feel for the new tenants. Sometimes it's better to look people in the eye.'

Pause.

'I know it's expensive, but it will be worth it, if they don't present nicely, or their car's a mess. You can tell a lot by talking face to face ... Oh, I know, love, it's hard when you can't get out here, but we're fine. Honest. And we really are pleased the police are here.'

Dave took the footy photo off the fridge and looked closely at it. The camera was focused in on Brody, but he could see other blurry figures in the background. He heard her say goodbye and put the phone down.

'That was Belle.' Jane wheeled her chair towards the table. 'Poor thing, she really doesn't like it when we're cut off. She's desperate to get back out and make sure I'm doing all the right things.' She gave a rueful half smile.

'Only because she cares,' Dave said.

'Yes.' Jane nodded. 'I put her in charge of the investment houses we have in Perth, when I had this accident. I can't get down there without a lot of effort, and she's never been quite confident enough to make decisions about them by herself ... Oh, you've seen that photo, isn't it a ripper?' A grin split her face. 'That was just before Mal died. Brody played in the grand final and won best and fairest. We were both so proud of him that day.'

'Nothing like a grand final win,' Dave said. 'I've never had the honour but I wasn't as good at sports as what Brody was, or is, by the sounds of it.'

'Mal and I flew to Perth for the game. Came right down to the wire and one of his teammates kicked a goal about a minute before the siren.'

'Got any more photos of the game? Anything of the action?' Brody looked so happy in the photos, maybe if Dave could talk to him about this footy final, it would help build some rapport.

A thoughtful frown crossed her face. 'I think . . .' she said slowly. 'I think there's some in the yearbook. Hold on.'

Jane wheeled herself away and he heard her talking from the far end of the house. 'I always thought Brody had the ability to be a league footballer but he wanted to be back here, as we all do . . . Ah, here it is!'

She reappeared, the yearbook in her lap. 'Here you are. Take it and have a look when you've got time. Just make sure you bring it back.'

She held the book out and Dave took it.

'But I'm sure you didn't come here to hear me gush over Brody's short-lived footy career,' she said.

'Actually,' Dave said, 'I just came to put our tea order in for tonight. But mostly to see how Kelsey and Hannah are going.'

Jane's face sobered. 'They're actually getting on better than I thought they would. Sometimes those girls can be a little, um, sensitive. But they seem okay. They told me they slept better last night and without nightmares. Thanks for checking on them.'

'Hopefully, I'll get to ask them face to face tonight. They'll be at the bar?'

'Sure will. So, I'll put you both down for a burger?'

'Reckon we could get a steak tonight?'

'Consider it done.'

'Great, see you later, Jane. And don't worry, I'll get this back to you.' He held up the book.

Bob was waiting in the troopy when Dave got back. He tossed the yearbook onto the back seat and climbed into the driver's seat.

'All good?' he asked.

'Yeah, just done a bit of research on James Wilson. He's a nasty bit of work. Former security guard, got charges for grievous bodily harm on a fellow bikie member, couple of DUIs and a few assaults. Got four firearms registered to him. No drugs charges, though. And there's nothing on Harry.

'Still bikies and drugs go hand in hand,' Bob continued. 'Got a nephew here that isn't all he seems. Pretty clear, huh?'

'You'd normally tell me that was a coincidence.'

'Yep, I would, but this isn't. I also know Harry is young, inexperienced and not really sure what he's doing. Not being convincing on the camping front isn't the only problem that's got my antenna up. Rule number one is to persuade anyone you're doing what you say you're doing. Whether the other boys are involved . . .' Bob shrugged. 'We need to find out their histories. What I do know is I'm glad we're only dealing with these boys and not any of James Wilson's heavy-handed goons.'

~

Brody stood up from the hot water system and looked at Rory. 'Mate, what the fuck are you doing here? You weren't supposed to come anywhere near the joint,' he snarled.

'Course I had to come. I've got to make sure they picked up everything properly. Obviously things have gone a little awry.'

'A little awry?' Brody's voice was low and furious. 'I thought you were my mate and suddenly in the last few days I've had two bodies and a stash of drugs turn up here. What the hell is that all about?' Brody got into Rory's face and glared at him. He wanted to punch him, but he couldn't risk Dave or Bob asking what had happened, or them even seeing they were speaking to each other. He hoped Dave had gone down to the beach already, but he hadn't heard the vehicle yet. The front-end loader was waiting at the shed and, if he wasn't careful, Dave would come looking for him.

'I could ask you the same thing. What the hell are the coppers doing here?'

'I didn't know they were turning up. Some fuckwit reported his sheep stolen and they just arrived.'

'Ah.' Rory crossed his arms, with a cocky smile. 'And what's that got to do with you?'

'Nothing,' Brody snapped. 'This isn't about me, it's about you leaving dead bodies and drugs behind.'

'Really? Nothing at all? Are you sure? What I'm hearing behind all that huff and puff is that you know something. Wouldn't that be a laugh, Mr Pure as the Driven Snow arrested for stock theft.'

'What's got into you?' Brody asked, leaning in closer. 'We're mates, we're not supposed to be at each other's throats.' He could hear the desperation in his voice and hated himself for it. The last thing he wanted was for Rory to see any of his weaknesses. That's how he'd managed through boarding school; never showing anyone that he was upset or sad. That was him—Brody, the life of the party. The one touted most likely to succeed. He'd had to act the same out here. Maintaining that game-day face so no one would ever know he didn't want to be on Corbett Station Stay.

'There are no mates in this type of business and you need to remember that's exactly what this is. A business transaction. You've been paid a tidy amount and now you turn a blind eye to everything else that's going on here. Those two bodies should be warning enough that the people we are doing business with don't play nice when they get upset.' He paused. 'This is a cut-throat business, Brody. Literally. If you can't handle the heat, get out of the kitchen.' Rory smiled a slow, mean smile. 'Oh, that's right. You can't now.'

'Look,' Brody tried the tone of steel that his dad used to use when Brody and Belle had said they didn't want to do something, 'I told you I don't care what you bring through my place, but bodies were not part of the deal. And whoever has dropped them off has got the wrong bloody bay. You were supposed to be a couple over; nowhere near the camp grounds. You've mucked it all up. Put us all at risk.' He crossed his arms and lowered his voice. 'Anyway, they already know the drugs are there. They found them yesterday when they were removing the other body.'

Rory stilled. 'What?' His voice was low and ferocious.

'I've got to go and help recover them.'

'You can't. You'll have to get them to us somehow.' His tone made it clear he'd accept no argument.

Brody swung around and stared at Rory. 'And how the hell am I supposed to do that? I told you early on, I want nothing to do with any of what you're doing. I said you could use this as a depot, or pick-up place or something like that, but I didn't want to know about it. Instead . . . well, it's pretty clear what I've ended up in. A shit fight. So, don't you go around telling me what to do, when it's your crew who've stuffed it up.'

'We need those drugs. Have you got any idea what will happen to us if we don't take them back?'

There was desperation now in Rory's voice, and Brody shrugged as he sensed a shift in the power. 'I've got an idea. And if you're so eager, why don't you go and ask Dave if you can have them. You never know, they might help you. Some sort of plea bargain.' He turned away and started to walk towards the shed. Rory ran after him.

'If you hadn't had the cops here none of this would have happened.'

'I didn't bring the cops here. They came. I told you that. And they would have turned up anyway, because I would have had to report the first body on the beach. My staff found that body! Two young girls possibly scarred for life.'

'You're as weak as piss, Brody. Always were. You're the one who's fucked it up, so you need to fix it.'

'I don't know how you work that out.' Despite his words, Brody experienced a familiar surge of helpless anger flow through him. He turned away and felt a stab of terror as he saw his mum slowly riding towards them. 'Get out of here now. If Mum sees you . . .'

Rory's hand flew to block his face and he left. Quietly he said, 'This will be on your head.'

Jane bumped over the gravel tracks and came to a stop next to Brody. She put the motorbike into neutral and smiled.

'Hello, love,' Jane said, looking at the retreating figure. 'Everything all right?'

'Yep, just getting organised to head down to the beach.'

She reached out and put her hand on his arm. 'I just want you to know, it will be all right. I don't know how, but we're bred tough out here. We'll be okay. It's worrying, for sure.' Her glance swung around to Rory's retreating figure then back to Brody. 'We've been through worse, Brodes.'

'I don't know if we have, Mum. But I guess it's too early to tell yet.' He looked around.

'I've spoken to Belle and filled her in properly. She said she'd let us know if she heard anything, but the newspaper has run a story. And she also said that Mick and Sally have been caught in town with the rain. They won't be back for a few days.' Her fingers danced on the handles of her bike and Brody knew she was more distressed than she was letting on.

'I can't get over to their place to do anything for them,' he said, 'so I guess everything will just have to look after itself. Where are their dogs?'

'They're fine. Apparently they left them heaps of food and water in their cages.' She paused. 'Brody, that young bloke you were just talking to, who is he?' Her voice rose as she asked the question.

'What?' Brody looked over his shoulder and saw that Rory had disappeared. 'Oh, I don't know. He turned up with the crew that were bogged over by the eastern creek. Just wanted to know when the water was going to be hot. He wasn't happy when I said it would be about half an hour because I'd only just lit the donkey.'

'He looked so much like that young O'Brien boy you used to go to school with.' She shrugged. 'I don't know, sometimes you young fellas all look the same to oldies like me.'

'You're not that old, Mum,' Brody said. 'I'd better go and help Dave and Bob. Are you okay to get home?'

'Yep, I'm going to go over to the camp kitchen first, though. It's been a while since I've been there and I want to have a look around. Make sure the girls are doing a good job of cleaning.'

'They've been a bit flat since they found that body. I know they're trying hard not to be, but they are.'

'Oh, those poor girls. Such a horrible fright for them.' Jane stopped, and let out a little groan. 'And the poor person, whoever the body is. Or people.' She put her hand to her chest in distress and was quiet for a moment. Then she swallowed and, when she spoke next, her voice was stronger. 'You know, it's all feeling like these incidents are connected, don't you think? It's so strange that first there was one, then two bodies, and now these drugs. I'm wondering if the people who put the drugs there are involved with the deaths. Seems like something off the nightly news.'

'Well, it would make sense, but I think the cops are all over it, Mum. Nothing we can do but help them when they need it.'

'Yeah, I know you're right. But still . . .' She brightened. 'Anyway, if you're talking to your sister, you can tell her I've done my exercises for today! She was at me about them when I talked to her earlier.' Jane started the bike and turned towards the kitchen.

Brody laughed. 'I'm not sure she'll believe me.' He watched his mum go, hoping she would be okay. The terrain was rough and she could get bogged, but Brody knew better than to offer help.

'Oh, by the way,' Jane stopped and manoeuvred around to face Brody. 'I think Belle is going to go to Perth to make sure the tenants get settled into the Cottesloe house okay.'

'Fine, I'll talk to her before she goes.' A little feeling of resentment pierced his chest. How easy was it for Belle to get away, down to Perth, whenever she wanted?

Belle was lucky, but he had never been able to hold anything against her. She was his sister and, even with her bossy ways, he loved her and she loved them. Being overbearing was the way she showed she cared. Station life didn't suit Belle and, yet, it was supposed to suit him.

Putting the destructive thoughts aside, Brody went to the shed and started the front-end loader.

It took fifteen minutes to get to the beach, and when he did, he saw that Dave and Bob had already put up a sign saying the beach was closed today. A few kids were standing at the rope with cricket bats and balls in their hands. One adult was with them and he looked annoyed.

Brody slowed down and opened the door. 'Sorry, guys. You can't be out here today. The police are doing some tidy-up work.'

The kids groaned and one threw his bat to the ground, while the man came and stood near the door.

'Is everything okay down there?' he asked. 'Not another, um—' he glanced over his shoulder at the kids '—you know what?'

'Nope, nothing like that. Collecting a few things they left down there.'

'Right. So we're still safe?'

'Safe as houses here.' Brody grinned at him, trying to use Bob's tactic of calmness to relieve any fears.

'No worries, I'll take the kids back up to the grassed area.'

Brody waved him goodbye and continued on to the beach until he saw Dave and Bob. He took in a deep breath as he wondered why he'd ever agreed to let Rory bring drugs in through his station.

CHAPTER 26

The drugs were lined up on the beach in bricks of about ten kilos each, Dave had surmised. Thirty of them. Brody had carefully dug deeply around where Dave had marked, then they had sent him back to the camp. Neither of them wanted him around while they brought the drugs out.

Dave had got down into the hole, with a shovel, then tossed the packages up onto the beach, with Bob videoing everything.

'We're going to have to get a ute in here to take this stash away. I think there's too much for a fixed-wing aircraft, don't you?' Dave asked Bob.

'No, I don't think so. Just so long as they send the right type of plane.' He paused. 'And that will depend on the strip and what type of aircraft can land.'

They were both bent over the bricks, which were wrapped tightly in black plastic, dusting them for fingerprints. Bob hadn't been convinced they'd get any, but they had to try.

'If these have been offloaded from a boat, then they would have had to carry them to shore. We might be lucky,' he said.

'We don't know they came in a boat,' Dave said.

'I can't see any other way of them getting in here, can you? Even if they'd come through the camping ground, they would've had to dig a hole the size of a small car and then unload them into it.'

'Same if they'd come in through the bay.'

'Yep, but cars on the beach during the night would raise some eyebrows, wouldn't they? Brody's already told us he doesn't allow people to camp on the beach and if he finds them he moves them on. A car moving around the camp site late at night would draw attention. Or even coming in past the house; someone would hear it. Too risky. A boat, not so much. They can moor out there until everyone had left the beach and come in after dark. Few hands make light work. Beach sand is soft. Would have taken three or four people to dig a hole this big.' Bob shook his head. 'Nah, they've come in from the ocean for sure.'

'Yeah, I see what you're saying.'

'Have you taken photos of them spread out like this?' Bob indicated the thirty parcels that were lined up neatly next to each other.

'Yeah. All done.'

'And I got the video when you were getting them out of the hole, so that's taken care of.'

'Yep.'

'This all has to be documented properly. If these drugs are linked back to the Insurgents and there's any thought even an ounce has gone missing, we do not want to be the ones held responsible. Even if some of them are locked up, there will be other members who could come gunning for us.'

Dave frowned. 'Excellent. Just what I need. Some other toe rag having it in for me.'

'All I'm saying, son, is we need to document everything and leave nothing to chance.'

Dave took a few more photos and then packed the first lot of bricks into the troopy. He looked around to make sure there was no one watching and then checked the bay.

The water was a deep blue, as was the sky, and the water lapped gently at the beach. The shadows were stretching out longer as the sun crossed the sky towards the western horizon. Dave estimated they had about an hour left of daylight.

'We've forgotten to get in contact with Border Force,' he said.

'I asked the drug squad to do that when I spoke to them the first time. Haven't heard anything back. Here, take this. I've fingerprinted.' Bob stood up and stretched his back. 'I don't think there is a single usable print.'

'How much do you think is here?'

'Oh, hard to estimate, but if each brick is ten kilos, and we've got what? Thirty bricks? Is that what we counted?'

'Yeah.' Dave lugged a second brick into the troopy and did the maths in his head. 'Must be around three hundred kilos then.'

'Three hundred kilos of heroin. Depending on the quality that could be worth fifty to eighty mill!' Bob said. 'The drug squad boys are going to love us. What a freakin' haul.' He looked pleased. 'Wonder how many lives we've saved by you finding this.'

'I'm as nervous as,' Dave said, looking around again. 'These guys won't think twice about killing us, you know.'

'Yeah, I'll be happier when the drug squad is on the ground, no two ways about it. They'll need to put the case together, not us.'

The satellite phone rang, so Dave snapped off his gloves and went to answer it.

'It's Shannon,' the voice on the other end said.

'How're you getting on?'

'I've got both autopsies done, still waiting for toxicology results and so on, but I thought you'd want to know the initial findings.'

'Please.' Dave fished around in his pocket for his pen and laid his notebook on the bonnet of the troopy, ready to write down the important bits of information.

'Okay, neither body had any type of ID and no features I can use to circulate among the media to help identify them.

'First body was a male, Anglo-Saxon descent. He had water in his lungs, so cause of death is drowning. My guess is that when I get the toxicology results back, he's going to be full of heroin. Giving someone a blast is a great way to have control over them. Toss them over the edge of the boat and there's no struggle. This bloke has no injuries that I can find—no little knife nicks in the bones or anything.'

Dave underlined the words 'male' and 'drowned'. 'How old?'

'Between twenty and thirty.'

'And no way of IDing him?'

'No fingertips left, so no prints. I've taken samples for DNA but we can really only use that if we find his family. And teeth . . . I'm going to try but I'm not sure if we have enough. When bodies have been in the water, there is so little left of the features and soft tissue that I usually need to help me piece everything together.'

'Right-oh. And the second one?'

'You'll need to hang on to your hat for this one. Girl aged between fifteen and twenty-five, Middle Eastern or Asian descent as we talked about before. Now the gash on the back of her head, which I thought may have killed her, didn't. It wasn't deep enough.'

'What did?'

'I found sand in her nostrils and lungs.'

Dave turned and looked out across the sea again as he rolled the words around in his head. 'Did you?' he finally said.

'They buried her alive.'

'Bastards.'

'Again, I'm guessing, and I won't be able to tell you conclusively because of the decomposition of the body, but I think she's been sexually assaulted.'

'What makes you say that?'

'This girl has died violently. Horrifically. She's from another country and you have a large haul of drugs there. I don't like conjecture, but I've heard of this type of thing before. Drug runners snatch a girl from the streets and take her with them as a sex slave.' She let the words hang in the air and Dave felt a prickle of horror slide over him.

'Do you think the two of them are tied together?'

'The two bodies? If they both come back with heroin in their system, then it seems so. Especially with the find you've made. The other thing that I found on both bodies was a minute piece of blue canvas. The girl had it in her hair and the man inside his mouth.'

Dave held his breath.

'I've run a few tests on both pieces and I'd conclude they are from a piece of canvas tarp. Like you'd use to keep the rain off goods.'

'Like drugs.'

'Yeah, like drugs, or food or something, you know. Could have been used as a shelter.'

'So they are connected?'

'I believe so. But I want the tox results back before I say with certainty.'

Letting his breath out in a loud whoosh, Dave walked over to Bob. 'Shannon is waiting on one last test result, but she is fairly sure they're connected,' he said.

'Thought so.' Bob didn't look up, just continued fingerprinting.

'Thanks, Shannon,' Dave said into the phone.

Bob yelled out the same words and Shannon laughed.

'Tell him, you're welcome,' she said. 'I'll let you know when the tox report comes back in, and anything else I get, but I knew you'd want to know what I got ASAP.'

'You're a legend.'

'Good. Catch you later.'

'Shannon?' the word was out of his mouth before he could stop it, but she had already hung up.

He sighed and put the phone down. He didn't even know what he was going to say to her, all he knew was he wanted to hear her voice for a little longer.

'Come and give me a hand here,' Bob called. He'd stacked four bricks together ready to go into the vehicle.

Dave carted the four back, feeling the weight in his hands. The plastic was beginning to cool. When they'd first laid the haul out, every brick had been hot to touch, as they'd dusted and photographed.

'Those bastards buried that young girl alive,' he said. 'No ID on either of the bodies.'

'I wouldn't put anything past drug dealers, son,' Bob said wearily. 'They're nearly the lowest of the low. Alongside paedophiles. No regard for human life. The best we can do is find them and lock 'em away for as long as the law will allow.'

The satellite phone rang again and Dave ran for the front of the car, where he'd left it sitting on the driver's seat.

'Burrows,' he said.

'Looking for Bob Holden.'

'I'll get him,' Dave said and started to hand the phone over.

'You take it,' Bob called. 'I'm just about finished here.'

'He's asked me to take the information,' Dave said, introducing himself properly.

'Right, Jackson here from the drug squad. You asked for checks from HQ on all the boys you picked up today. Samuel Watson has three guns registered to him. Handguns.'

'Any priors to go along with that?'

'No, nothing. But a search of their car wouldn't go astray.'

'Will do. Anything else?'

'Yeah. Two of these lads have got sealed records, from when they were in high school. Not sure what's in them. But . . .' He let the word hang there. 'Interestingly, the arresting officer is a mate of mine, so I gave him a call. Remembered the case. Six young lads; he couldn't remember all their names, but the ones who have the record are Harry Wilson and Rory O'Brien. They were picked up in Northbridge with heroin on their person. They'd nicked off from two different boarding schools. They were also in the company of a bloke named James Wilson, and we all know who he is.'

Dave stilled as realisation dropped in. *Those boys all went to high school together. They've been mates for a long time.* He reached into the back of the troopy for the yearbook.

'What happened to the others?' he asked as he flicked over some pages.

'Had to let them go. There was no reason to hold them.'

'What were they doing out when they should have been at school?'

'Come on, Burrows! We all wagged school at some stage! My mate remembered the others were shit scared. The two who were arrested gave false names, but the others were smart enough to say who they were and where they were from. When they did that, there was nothing to keep them on. Gave 'em a fair talking to, though. That's about as much as my mate could remember.'

'Hold on, you said six?'

'Yeah, six in total.'

'And you can't find out their names?'

'Only those two were charged, and they didn't arrest the others, so no.'

'Six? We've only got five up here. Brody, Rory, Nick, Sam and Harry. Any idea about the other one? Where is he now?'

'Could be anywhere. Maybe they fell out and aren't even mates anymore.'

'This gets more interesting by the hour,' Dave said.

'I'll keep working on this line of inquiry.'

'Thanks, let me know when you've got something more. Now, for your information, we've got about three hundred kilos of heroin here. We've got it out and fingerprinted it. Taking it back to the homestead now to lock it in the coolroom.'

'Doc'ed it all?' Jackson asked after letting out a long breath.

'Yeah, photos, video and exhibit log. Not that there was much to log; it's all pretty clean.'

'As you'd expect. Ring in with an airstrip report tomorrow. Hopefully, we can get there. I've sent a team to Carnarvon to help you out; they're sitting, waiting, ready to go as soon as you're clear.'

'Great to know. Thanks. Did your fellas get in contact with Border Force?'

Dave heard the flicking of pages as Jackson looked for more information. 'Yep, nothing out of the ordinary in the last five days. They offered to help, but they're well and truly out to sea on patrol. It'll be quicker to get a plane to you ASAP.'

'Right-oh, and did they have any other ships before this timeframe?'

'They intercepted a small boat on the way to Indonesia, but not coming in. Fishing boat, they'd strayed over the border by the sounds of it. Searched the vessel and didn't find anything incriminating. Sent them on their way. We've got the information and IDs of those blokes, so we can find them again if we need to.'

Dave wasn't so sure. If those blokes were part of what was going on here, he assumed they'd head back to their port and disappear into the depths of the jungles where they'd never be seen again. Still, he didn't work in the drug squad and those blokes would know a lot more than he did about drug runners.

'Okay, maybe they didn't come in a boat. Or they came up instead of down.'

'We'll look into it all, don't worry. I'm keen to get these bastards. You know how much that amount of heroin is worth on the streets?'

'Yeah. A shitload.'

'Right, stay safe.'

'Cheers, buddy.' He put the phone back in its holder and went to report to Bob. The rest of the drugs were already loaded into the troopy and Bob was tidying up the last of the hole so none of the kids would fall into it if they came this way. He scraped the shovel across the top and leaned on it, wiping his brow with his hankie.

'Well, glad that's done. Must be time for a drink?'

'I think we've got two more jobs we should do before that.'

Bob looked at him.

'Sam Watson. Got three handguns registered to him. Should do a search and secure them, just in case.'

'Little fucker. Is he dangerous?'

'No priors with the guns, but there is for drugs.' He repeated what Jackson had told him. 'But then there's this . . .' He held up the yearbook. 'Jackson said that there were six boys pulled up when they were in high school for heroin. Rory and Harry were charged. There are four blokes here. And Brody's acting strange. What's the possibility that these blokes all went to school together? Brody's school? They're all the same age, dress the same . . .'

'Good thinking,' Bob said. 'But where did you get—'

Dave flicked through the magazine until he found the Year 12 photos. 'I asked Jane for some footy photos so I could try to connect to Brody better. She gave me this.'

Brody's picture was on the first page. A young, smiling man with a look of expectation in his eyes. Happy. With hope.

'Good thinking, Ninety-nine. We'll make a detective out of you yet!' Bob leaned over to look at the photos with Dave.

Next page and then the next. Dave stopped at one photo and tapped on it.

'This could be Sam ... It's hard to tell when they all have beards and are wearing sunglasses.' He paused. 'Nah, that's not Sam. Different name.'

Dave turned back to the yearbook and looked for Rory's name.

There he was. On the second to last page, in alphabetical order. Dave checked for the other two names, but they weren't there.

Then he found the grand final footy picture. Two teams from opposing schools staring each other down. He nodded.

'There's the link,' he said, turning the book so Bob could read the names: Nick Austen, Harry Wilson and Sam Watson. 'Different schools, but they all know each other.'

'Come on.' Bob indicated for Dave to get into the troopy. 'Let's do it.'

CHAPTER 27

The bar was loud when Bob and Dave arrived. They were thirsty after securing the drugs and taking more photos of them in situ in the coolroom.

Now, there was a heavy chain and large padlock locking the door with yellow and black crime-scene tape crisscrossing not only the door but the entrance to the shed, so they would know if anyone had entered.

Kelsey and Hannah were busy handing out stubbies and drinks, while small groups of people sat at tables with burgers and steak sandwiches in front of them. Everyone seemed a lot more relaxed than they had been the previous evening, and Dave was glad. Relaxed people were happy people.

Rory, Nick, Sam and Harry were sitting down, leaning against the back wall, each holding a beer and also looking much more comfortable than they had that morning when

Dave and Bob had first found them. Brody was nowhere to be seen.

Dave sat down next to them, while Bob went to get the drinks.

'How you boys getting on tonight?' he asked.

'Better than being wet and cold,' Sam said, holding up his beer. 'We need to buy you a couple.'

'No need for that,' Dave said. 'Happy to do it.'

Bob came back and handed Dave a lemon squash.

'What's this? Not drinking tonight, lads?' Rory asked. 'Thought you'd be on the gas for sure. That's what you coppers do when you're out on a case, isn't it? Get on the beers and play nookie with the local girls.'

Bob smiled blandly. 'Not all the time. Settled in okay?'

'Bloody better than being stuck out in the bush. Units are pretty comfortable considering what they are. Primitive but comfortable.'

'When do you need to be back at work, all of you?'

'We'd only planned about five days away, hadn't we, lads?' Rory said. 'Still hoping we can get back in time. Boss'll crack the shits otherwise.'

'You seem pretty familiar with each other. Known each other long, have you?'

'Oh shit, I dunno,' Nick said. 'Must be eight or ten years, I guess.'

'How'd you meet?'

A questioning look came over Harry's face. He took a swig of his beer, while Dave watched him carefully.

'Boarding school. Us three,' Nick waved his finger around at Sam and Harry. 'Rory went to a different one, but we got to know each other through footy.'

'And girls—don't forget the girls.'

The young men laughed. 'That's right. Rory was going out with this chick and her best friend was going out with Sam. That's how it went, wasn't it?' Nick asked. He took a sip of his beer and let out a burp. 'We all ended up at the same movies and stuff while we were trying to get the girls to go out with us.'

'That's how it was, my friend,' Rory said and held his hand up in a high five. They slapped around, although Harry was looking decidedly uncomfortable.

'Let's keep it down a bit,' he suggested, glaring at his mates. 'There're kids here.'

'You fellas know Brody then? I'm told he went to boarding school, too.'

'Brody?' Rory spoke quickly. 'The camp owner? Nah, we never knew him, did we, boys?'

There was a murmur around the table as they all agreed.

'Oh. Are you sure you don't know him? Because see, boys, I've got a yearbook here that shows me that you, Rory, went to the same school as Brody, in the same class even. And you've also said that all of you guys have been mates for a while, so I'm guessing if Rory knew Brody, you others would, too. That be right?'

The smiles dropped from their faces and Harry stood up. 'That's enough chat tonight. We're done.'

'Sit down, Harry,' Bob commanded.

Harry stayed standing for a few short moments, then sat, putting his beer on the table.

'See now, it bothers me that you might be lying to me,' Dave said. 'And if you can lie about something so simple, what else might you lie about? Now, let's start again. Do you know Brody?'

'Yeah, I went to school with him,' Rory said finally. He glanced at the others as he spoke. 'Don't know if you others remember him or not?' He looked at his mates, whose faces had all changed to more serious expressions.

No one said anything. The noise of the bar rose around them and Dave heard a young voice in among the crowd. 'Mummy, can I have some more chips?'

Trying to block her out, so he could stay focused on the conversation, he spoke, 'See, we've got a bit of a predicament here. We know two of you have been arrested and charged with drug possession in an earlier life and, Harry, we also know your uncle is involved in the Insurgents. Bikie gangs like drugs. And now you guys are up here without enough camping gear to convince us that's what you were coming for. So, we're wondering why you're here and why you're pretending not to know our host.' Dave held his hands out in a 'can you please explain' gesture. 'All of this causes us some concern, as I'm sure you understand.'

It was Bob's turn. 'And, Sam, today I get a call telling me that you're the proud owner of three guns. Handguns of all things. A specialised type of weapon. Have you got them here with you?'

'What? Nah, they're locked up at home.'

'Are you sure? Because I have the authority to search your car and I'd really like to do that.'

'Hey, you need a warrant for that,' Sam said, jumping out of his chair.

Harry grabbed his arm and pulled him back down. 'Sit the fuck down and keep your voice low,' he said, looking around the room. So far nobody had noticed their conversation had got a little heated.

'Should we go and have a look now?' Bob asked.

All four men stayed seated and looked at each other.

They look worried, Dave thought. *And they certainly aren't as clever as they think they are.* It made him relax slightly.

'Come on.' Bob's tone held no argument. 'Let's go and have a look. All of you.'

Bob stood up and indicated for all of them to do the same. Realising there wasn't a choice, all four men stood and filed out, Bob and Dave behind them. Dave noticed they copped a few stares when they all left together, but he smiled and gave a wave to a couple of people and stopped to pick up a toy dog that a baby in a pram had dropped on the floor. Community policing.

The laughter and chatting kept going as they left.

Outside the only lights were the solar ones lining the path back to the cabins, and one spotlight on the camp kitchen.

'You need a warrant,' Sam spat out again, as they walked towards the utes.

'I don't,' Dave said. 'If I think you're a danger to the people in this camp site, I can do what I like. Now, the easiest thing would be if you go and get the guns and give them to me to secure. You do that, I won't give a fuck what else is in those two vehicles. Weed, heroin, whatever, I won't care. But if you don't, then I will go through that car with a fine-tooth comb and charge you for every tiny thing we find in there. How does that sound for a deal?'

'Come on, man,' Rory said. 'This is all a bit over the top. We're just some guys out for a camping trip. You both are coming on all hot and heavy like we're going to massacre everyone here.'

'Well,' Bob said with a slight smile, 'I'd rather know where those guns are, if you don't mind. So, which way are we going to play it?'

'Just give them to the filth,' Harry said. He turned to Dave and Bob. 'We want them back before we leave.'

Bob and Dave looked at each other. 'Always the quiet ones who cause the most trouble, isn't it, Dave?' Bob said. He took a step closer to Harry. 'Watch your mouth, son.' He turned to Sam. 'Sam, how about you get your gun licence out for me to have a squiz at. Then I'll know whether or not you can have them back. Can't be carrying guns in your vehicle if you haven't got a licence to do that.'

'Jesus,' Nick said. 'Does Brody know how you're treating his guests? He won't get anyone coming to stay here again.'

'That's the least of my concerns right now,' Dave snapped. He made for the two utes and put his hand on one of the doors.

'For fuck's sake, Sam, give him the bloody guns,' Harry shouted.

Dave slowly turned around. 'Maybe,' he said, 'maybe we should just search these vehicles. What do you think, Bob?'

Bob came to stand alongside him and leaned his elbow on the side mirror. 'Certainly some angst here around us having a look in there. You know, boys, you'd get a better hearing if you just tell us what's going on.'

'There's nothing to tell,' said Sam as he yanked open the back door and lifted up the back seat of the Hilux.

Dave's hand strayed to his belt and he realised he didn't have his gun. Shit! They were still locked in the gun cabinet in the vehicle from when they had been recovering the drugs. Both he and Bob had put themselves in a position where Sam could bring the guns out loaded and cocked and ready to shoot.

'Stop,' he said. 'Back out of the ute, Sam. Back away from the ute.'

Sam froze and put his hands up in the air, showing Dave he wasn't holding anything.

Dave grabbed him by the collar and pulled him back, nodding to Bob, who took Sam's place. He snapped on a pair of gloves then got out his flashlight and looked into the compartment under the seat. He pulled out the first gun. A black steel Beretta with a wooden handle. Dave had to hand it to Sam; he had good taste when it came to guns. It was a beautiful piece and he knew it would be worth about six grand.

The next one was a silver steel Beretta; not worth as much, but still on the upper side of two gees. The third was the same as the first.

Bob laid them on the tray of the ute while the others watched on without saying anything. Dave could feel Sam was fighting within himself not to go and pick up the guns, so he turned and gave him a warning stare. 'Stay where you are.' Harry shifted and Dave's hand automatically went out and grabbed him. 'You, too.'

'There's more here,' Bob said.

'Ah, interesting,' Dave said as Bob brought out three extra magazines, packets of bullets and a black and gold Bul Armory pistol.

All six men looked at the haul on the tray of the ute.

'Lot of money for these guns,' Bob observed as he made sure the chambers were empty and the safety switches on. 'What do you think, Dave, about fifteen grand here?'

'Might be more. Big investment for a young bloke not that long out of school. What do you do for a crust, Sam?'

'Diesel mechanic. Nearly qualified.'

'So still on an apprenticeship. Don't pay much, do they? How did you fund these?'

'Savings. What does it matter anyway? They're registered. I'm allowed to have them. My grandad was in the Pistol Club in Perth and I grew up around them. I've always had guns.'

'Sure, all except this one?' Bob waved the Bul Armory Trophy pistol. 'Is it registered to someone else?'

A look of annoyance crossed Sam's face. 'That's my grandad's. He died last year and I haven't had time to transfer it across to me.'

'Who was your grandad?'

'What the . . . Geez, does it matter?' Harry asked. 'You've already got the guns.'

'It matters,' Bob said. 'Who was your grandfather, Sam?'

'Robbie Buckman.' He seemed to drag the name out and Dave felt a flicker of recognition but couldn't place the name. Wishing they were closer to their computers, where they could access the system to run checks on people, he felt a surge of frustration again. Everything took time when you had to phone in looking for information. If they had internet access, they'd be able to use the large, heavy laptop they had in the troopy.

Dave nodded and wrote the name down. It would have been great if he could have linked the name straightaway— given the men something to worry about—but he couldn't.

'Really?' he bluffed. 'Robbie Buckman?' He locked eyes with Bob, who gave a slight shake of his head and grunted.

'What do you need these types of guns for out here, Sam? Not like you can shoot a kangaroo from a distance with them. These are up close and personal weapons.' It was Bob who asked the question this time.

'Protection. Haven't you heard of *Wolf Creek* and Peter Falconio?'

Dave wanted to laugh. *Good answer*, he thought. *But we've heard it all before.*

'You know what I think?' Bob continued. 'I think you guys are up to your neck in something horribly illegal, and I have an interest in that. So, here's what we're going to do. We're going to fingerprint you all and send the prints back to the lab to see if any of you have any dirty little secrets we should know about.' Bob smiled at them, but it wasn't genuine. 'And you guys won't be going anywhere until we have heard back from the lab. I'll have the keys to the utes, please.' He held out his hand, while Dave moved to package up the guns into evidence bags.

'Sorry to take the shine off the night, boys.'

'You've got nothing on us,' Nick burst out. 'Nothing at all. You can't fingerprint us without reason.'

'I'm the one with the badge, Nick,' Bob said. 'I can.'

'Spider senses,' Dave said.

All four men turned to him, confusion on their face.

'You blokes are setting off our spider senses. See, a lot of policing is about gut reactions as well as evidence. We've got a bit of both with you lot.'

Dave went around to the front of the vehicle and looked in through the driver's window. 'Hey, Bob,' he called. 'We've got a sat phone in here, too. You boys been making any late-night phone calls from the sheds up near the homestead?'

'What?' Rory asked.

'You heard,' Bob said. 'We know there was someone making a phone call a couple of nights ago. Before you boys were around. Perhaps that was as you snuck through the campground on your way out into the "wilderness" as you called it.' He raised his eyebrows as he spoke.

'Don't know what you're talking about.'

'Ah well, don't concern yourselves, lads. We'll just pull your phone records.'

Rory was fidgeting alongside Harry and he made to swing around and leave in disgust. 'You're both going to lose your badges when I get back home and can get to my lawyers. You've got nothing.'

Dave opened his mouth to spew out something about entitled, privileged private school boys, but didn't. Instead, he said, 'I'm wondering, you five were obviously all mates together. You four and Brody. Anyone else in your group?'

The four looked straight ahead, not saying anything, but Dave picked up a flicker on Nick's face.

CHAPTER 28

Dave locked the guns and vehicle keys in the gun cabinet hidden in the rear of the troopy and pocketed the key.

'Not sure where I sit with Brody's involvement in this,' Dave said to Bob as he holstered his gun. 'What do you think?'

'We certainly need to ask him some questions, and we know he lied about knowing Rory, so that's put a dent in his credibility.' Bob paused and ran his hand through his hair, thinking. 'I'm still of the opinion he's not involved. His reactions have been too real to be staged. Anyway, we need him to help out here. There're two of us and four of them. He also knows the station like the back of his hand, so we need him.'

'I think you're right,' Dave said. 'He's certainly genuine in the conversations I've had with him. And if there is a problem, we've got him close so we can control what he does.'

'Yeah. In light of that, can you get Brody to take all the keys out of the station vehicles, too, please,' Bob asked. 'Lock them away as well. I'm going to have a chat with Jane and see what I can learn about these blokes. Surely she should have some idea about her son's school friends.'

'No worries, I'll go and find him.' Dave stopped and looked at Bob. 'Did you hear the bikie reference from Harry?' he asked quietly.

Bob nodded. 'The filth. He's in among them for sure. Interesting what you can learn from people's language.' He stretched. 'Right, you'd better check the coolroom, make sure it's locked up as tight as it can be. Perhaps you'd better check with Brody, too, and see if he's got boltcutters or large pliers, or angle grinders that need to be put out of sight. Anything that could be used to force the padlock or chain.' He looked up at the night sky, tapping his foot on the ground. 'I wish the bloody drug squad was here. I feel like I'm flying blind without all the information on these fellas.' He scratched his cheek tiredly. 'Good bluff with Robbie Buckman's name. I know it, too, but I can't think who it is.'

'Whoever it is, Sam didn't want to give us his name so there must be something in it.' He leaned against the side of the ute and tapped his fingers on the bonnet, something he always seemed to do when he was thinking. 'I agree with your earlier comments,' Dave finally said. 'I don't think these fellas are dangerous. They're not seasoned or smart enough.'

'Well, I'm not so sure now. They may not have the smarts they need, but when someone is backed into a corner, you can never predict how they're going to react. These guys might come out swinging if they've got a lot to lose. Rory has a temper and Harry . . . well, he's too quiet for my liking. Probably got a few more street smarts than the others.' He started to head off towards the house. 'You good, son?'

'Yep. I'll go and find Brody. He might be over at the camp kitchen and communal fire by now.'

'Keep your guard up.'

Dave nodded as he headed off. He recognised his feelings now; they were the same ones he'd felt when Spencer died last year. A copper in the middle of nowhere with hardly any comms and no back-up but plenty of the general public around. Just as they were here.

⌒

Bob watched Dave leave and tried to push down the concern he was feeling. The drug squad would certainly be more than useful here.

He felt like he was in a Slim Dusty song, 'Only the Two of Us Here'.

Light spilled across the verandah from the kitchen and Bob followed the path across to where he knew Jane would be at the table, reading a book or looking at the accounts ledger. Every time he'd been in to see her, she'd greeted him warmly and he liked the way she made him feel when he sat with her talking. Like he was important and what he had to say was interesting and meaningful.

It had been a while since he'd really looked at a woman, he'd been burned too many times before. Women saying they'd stay forever, then realising what his job was and shooting through. See, he understood Dave's situation more than Dave would realise.

Jane was different. A salt of the earth type woman, who had awakened something in him. Her warmth and genuineness, her ability not to feel sorry for herself with everything that had happened. She loved life and still had so much love to give and that had been an eye-opener to Bob. There was no way he could see a future with her, but he'd decided to enjoy her company while he was here and not let any of his feelings get out.

Never again, he'd sworn, after his last girlfriend had left. Nora had hurt him more than the others, because she'd taken his dog, too. Every night, when he sat down with a whiskey, he'd think about her. Only for a second, but she had left her mark and he couldn't risk putting himself through the ups and downs of a copper's relationship again.

Tapping on the door, he called out to her. 'You here, Jane?'

He heard the squeak of the rubber wheels on the floor as she moved her chair. 'Yep, sure am. Come on in.' She appeared at the doorway. 'Everything okay?'

Bob laughed. 'For once I'm not coming to tell you we've found another body or more drugs.'

'Well, I've got to be happy with that, don't I? I was beginning to think we were getting a reputation.' She gave a laugh and pushed her hair back from her face. 'To what do I owe the pleasure? Did you want a drink?'

Bob's hands itched to hold a whiskey. It had been two days since he'd had one, but he didn't think he could risk dulling his senses right now. 'A cup of tea would be nice,' he said. 'I can put the kettle on.'

'So can I,' Jane said with a smile.

Bob held up his hands and nodded. 'Sorry.'

'Don't be. Everyone offers to do things, but I have to be able to live here by myself and handle all the little things. You never know when Brody is going to be caught out mustering or so forth. I need to be self-sufficient.' She wheeled herself around to the stove and put the kettle on. 'After the accident, Brody and Mick changed so many things for me. Well, all the neighbours came and helped, but mostly Mick. Right down to the clothesline so I can hang the clothes out. All their hard work has certainly made life a lot easier than it could have been.' She got out the cups, and the milk from the fridge, expertly wheeling her chair around. 'Have you had something to eat?'

'I'm fine, thanks.' Bob leaned back in his chair and watched Jane. Her permanent smile and long hair framed what he realised now was a very thin face. 'Do you get much pain still?'

'I'm one of the lucky ones. When you read about what can happen to paraplegics, I have very few symptoms. Well, I guess I should add "yet" to that statement. I haven't been in a chair that long.

'But I do get neuropathic pain, which is because the spinal cord has been injured. My legs often feel like I've got pins and needles or a burning sensation. Nothing that a few drugs don't help.'

She said the words with the pragmatic tone of someone who had accepted her lot in life and was content where she was. There was nothing bitter about her and it made Bob wonder if he could ever be like that about the car accident that had scarred him. Could he accept the part he'd played in two people's death, knowing he didn't actually cause them? Thoughts like this gave him pause.

'Your outlook on life is amazing,' Bob said as he took the cup she offered. 'I don't think I could be quite as happy. More like bitter and twisted, I think!'

Jane grinned. 'What's there not to be happy about? I'm living in the best place in the world, I've got my family, everything is great.' She set her cup down on the table and looked at him. 'No point in being bitter and twisted. You have to roll with what life throws at you. I'm glad I'm alive. The other option is much worse. What about you?'

'Ah, not much to tell about me,' he said, fiddling with the cup. 'Been a copper for so long, I've forgotten there's anything else out there. But I love it. Get to be on the road a lot and see places like you've got here. I don't think I could do anything else. I don't want to do anything else.' He glanced over at the photo of Brody, Belle and Jane. 'You must enjoy having Brody here. Do you miss Belle?'

'Oh, she comes out often enough. And to be perfectly frank, she's always getting on my case about exercising and making sure I'm taking my meds. Belle has always had grand ideas. She was desperate to put a pool in so I could get out of the chair and do more exercises.'

'You didn't?'

She smiled. 'I did actually. I have a small pool under-cover, so the visitors don't know it's here. Otherwise, I'd be inundated with people wanting to use it, even when there's a beach on their doorstep. Brody rigged up a swing for me to get in and out, and I use it most days, although Belle doesn't need to know that. Her being a nurse has been a blessing and curse all in one. I like stringing her along sometimes. She does take herself very seriously at times.'

Bob laughed. 'I can only imagine. And Brody, what does he manage to do in his spare time—does he get any?'

Jane raised her eyebrows. 'Now come on, Bob. I'm sure you've been around farms and stations enough to know there's always something going on.'

'Of course, you're right.'

'It's good having Kelsey and Hannah here, they take a bit of the pressure off him, but not all of it. And they can't do the musters. They haven't had any experience with stock.'

'Big job for him. Do you ever get anyone in to help?'

'Just the contractors. Shearers, and so on. Actually, I managed to get the shearers for next week, which I think will work well because the river should be down by then and I reckon that's enough time for the sheep to dry out. I guess you know they can't be shorn when the wool's wet? Can't bale the wool?'

'Yeah, and that doesn't do the shearers much good either.'

'I love shearing time. Before I had my accident, I used to work in the shed as the roust-about. The smell of the wool and seeing it come off the sheep and going into the wool packs . . .' She traced an outline on the table and looked down, hair falling in front of her face.

'I used to work in a shearing team,' Bob offered. 'Back when Adam was a boy. Don't think I liked it quite as much as you did, by the sounds of it, but the job was a means to buying beer at the end of the week.'

Laughing again, Jane leaned forward, interested. 'What job did you do on the team?'

'Penner-upper. Is that even a word?' he wondered.

''Tis in the shearing industry.'

'What does Brody do during shearing? Follow in his mum's footsteps and work in the shed and yards?'

'He's got to do all the legwork, unfortunately. Mustering and everything outside. He'll have a busy few weeks coming up. Kelsey and Hannah will have to grow another leg and take on some of his jobs while he's tied up with shearing.'

'We'll be able to help with the mustering, you know. That's why Dave and I were here in the first place: to do a muster of your place and others and see where everyone was at for numbers. We still need to look into the sheep stealing report.'

'Really? That would certainly make things easier for Brody.' She gave a sigh.

Through the darkness, Bob heard the generator thumping quietly away like an old friend. The grumble of the engine drowned out any other noise.

'And Brody is happy here?' Bob asked.

A smile split her face. 'Of course. Running Corbett Station—that's what we called the place before the station stay began—was all he ever wanted to do.'

'But he loved boarding school?'

'Oh yeah, he really did. Had such a lovely group of friends. Never seemed to be home when I rang. Especially on weekends. He was always off at the movies or playing sport. Was a real champion at footy.' She stopped and swallowed. 'The carefree days before all the responsibility he had to take on.'

'Who were his mates?'

Jane's brow crinkled. 'Gosh, I'm not sure I could remember all their names. He doesn't keep in contact with too many now, I don't think.' She stopped. 'I gave Dave the yearbook actually, but I might have another photo. Hang on a second.' She wheeled herself out of the kitchen and down the hallway, talking as she did. 'It's hard for him to keep in contact with anyone; our phone lines are so dodgy. I do feel for him. I'm sure he's lonely and would love to meet someone. I've often thought about introducing him to some of my friends' girls, but they're all down south and probably wouldn't fit in up here. Got to be of a certain constitution to make it in this country. All I can do is hope he'll meet someone from around here, or even further north.'

There was a silence as Bob heard her rustle through papers and books. 'Ah, here it is. This was taken on the last day of school. The boys went to different schools but they all got together right at the end. Actually, I reckon they headed off to the pub after this was taken. Underage of course, but that never seemed to worry anyone! Here.' Jane held out the photo to Bob and he took it, slipping his glasses on.

The boys were on the bow of a yacht, all wearing reflector sunglasses and wide smiles. Their arms were around each other. Brody was in the middle, wearing a T-shirt that said, *Like a boss.* Bob recognised Rory; he was wearing one that said: *I'm already the best, so why try harder?*

Bob nodded his head slightly. That was the impression Rory gave, for sure.

Flipping the photo over he was rewarded with the hand-written names of all the boys.

Rory O'Brien, Nick Austen, Brody Corbett, Sam Watson, Harry Wilson, Shane Fletcher.

Shane Fletcher. Now that wasn't a name he'd heard.

'Who's this bloke?' he asked Jane, tapping on the boy at the end. He had fair hair and freckles and wasn't as tall as the others.

'Oh, that's Shane. He came here a couple of times and spent some time with us during the school holidays. Nice kid. Pretty quiet. I've got no idea where he is these days.'

'And any of the others?'

'I remember Rory quite well. He used to come out to dinner when we went down to the city and took Brody out. His parents were in Queensland and he didn't get home very much. Always felt a bit sorry for him.' Jane took a breath. 'Funny he should come up now,' she said reflectively. 'I actually thought I saw him in the camp yesterday, but Brody said it wasn't him. They change so much as they get older, don't they? I'd probably not recognise any of them now.'

'Yeah, I wouldn't know any of the kids my daughter went to school with now.' He didn't add he probably never knew them in the first place because he was always off solving some type of crime.

Bob examined the photo again, wondering about Shane. *Was there any chance*, he wondered, *that this was the bloke Dave saw talking on the phone at the shed the other night?*

'Can I take this with me?' Bob asked, holding up the photo.

Jane threw him a curious look. He recognised it now. It meant she wanted to ask why, but she was too well mannered and respectful of the work they did.

'If you need it.'

CHAPTER 29

Dave could hear the bleating of sheep. He checked his pack for the day: lunch, binoculars, water, notebook. He had his gun with him, but only as a precaution. Bob and he thought they'd scared the four men enough to stay out of trouble for a while. They were still concerned about Shane. If he was out on the station somewhere, he could cause them some problems when they were least expecting it. They'd both have to stay on high alert.

The other blokes hadn't come out of their units that Dave had seen, and he'd made sure that Brody had been busy getting ready for the muster, so he wouldn't have any time to see them.

In further conversation with Bob last night, they had decided against talking to Brody yet. Do a muster, let the drug squad get here and then talk to them all. That was their plan. The motorbike he'd unloaded from his trailer was parked near the fuel bowser and it took a few minutes to check the oil and refuel the bike. Even though it was warm, Dave knew that once they got out into the bush, it might be cold, so he'd borrowed another jacket from Bob.

'Ready?'

Dave turned at Brody's voice. He was dressed in a heavy jacket, waterproof pants and a beanie.

'Sure am. You look like you're dressed for Tasmania!'

'Surprising how cold the chill factor gets when you're on a bike.' He spread out a map on the seat of his bike and indicated for Dave to come closer. 'If you head up this fence line, I'll go in the other direction and we can meet in the middle here.' Brody pointed to an X on the map.

'Watering point?'

'Yeah, there's a mill and trough system there. If we hadn't had the rain it would be easy to think that's where all the ewes would be, but with all the puddles around and the good feed, they'll be spread across the whole paddock.'

Dave nodded.

'If we push them down this way . . .' Dave followed Brody's finger along the western fence line. 'The holding paddock is here and, once they're in, we can guide them to the yards. We mightn't get them into the yards today, but there's no reason we can't make it to the holding paddock.'

'Right-oh.' Dave committed the map to memory and looked for some landmarks. 'There's a range to our left?'

'Yep, those hills aren't in this paddock, but if you keep them on your left all the time, you're headed in the right direction.'

'Great. That I can do.'

'And you're fine with the bike?'

'I grew up on one.'

'Good.' Brody passed a handheld two-way radio over. 'There's not a lot of reach with these things, but they can be helpful. And watch the rocks. They're mongrel things for tipping you off.'

Dave laughed. 'I'll have to hold on with my knees.'

Brody smiled and nodded. 'You're not on a horse. That won't stop the bike from tipping over.'

His lame joke had fallen flat.

Brody turned the handle of his bike and looked over his shoulder. 'See you out there,' he said.

Dave straddled his bike and turned the key, before kicking the engine over with the kick-starter. The engine roared to life underneath his hands, and he smiled. This is what his job was about. He quickly fastened the helmet and gave the hand accelerator a rev before following Brody out onto the road.

The wind made his eyes tear up and his nose run. He wished he'd remembered to bring his sunglasses, but the freshness brought his mind to life. Every way he looked he could see something new: a shoot on a bush, a flower, a puddle. Red earth squelching under the wheel of the bike.

Feeling the bumps in the road and the mud kick up onto his jeans, Dave searched the landscape for signs of sheep he'd heard earlier: fresh tracks and shit. They'd be easy to see because the tracks would be deep in the mud.

A little further on, Brody pulled up and flicked the stand down, before opening the gate. He pointed. 'Holding paddock,' he called.

Giving the thumbs up, Dave angled the bike to the right. 'This way for me?' he asked, pointing along the fence.

Brody nodded and kicked off, heading in the opposite direction.

Slowly Dave rode down the fence line, stopping occasionally to look at a set of tracks or some shit. The ewes were getting some green pick because their shit wasn't pebble-like. His grandfather had always told him you could tell a lot about the health of an animal by looking at its shit. Pebble-like faeces were normal for sheep. These girls, well, their tummies were getting used to rich, green feed which they probably hadn't seen in a while.

Dave wound his way through the small sheep pads, the ones they travelled every day and where they left deep grooves in the soil. Water lay in some areas and flew up spraying him, but he didn't care. The sense of freedom he had was incredible.

The two-way crackled to life and he heard Brody calling him. Pulling up, he unclipped the mic and held it to his mouth. 'Yeah, gotcha, Brody.'

'Large mob of about two hundred on the southern boundary fence. I'm pushing them downwards. You keep heading your way. There's about eight hundred in this paddock.'

'Roger that,' Dave said and clipped the mic back on then rubbed his hands together, blowing on them. He wished he had some gloves, but it wouldn't be long before the sun rose and the heat would filter through. Later, he wouldn't be riding all the time, there would be the stops and starts of pushing gently behind the mob, and he would heat up quick enough.

He rode on, keeping the fence on his left. Out of the corner of his eye, he saw movement and, as soon as he found an open space, he wheeled the bike around and went back for another look.

The ewe was down, under a tree, blood covering her wool. Her insides were trailing out from her stomach as she tried to get up.

Dave froze and looked around. He knew it would be hard to spot a dog in the bush that was covering the landscape. Their colour would camouflage them and dogs were devious and sneaky. Quiet.

Dogs on the move also covered ground quickly. There was nothing to say the bloody thing was nearby at all now.

He got off the bike and went over to the ewe. Her throat had been torn, but not opened entirely, and her hind leg had a large bite mark. Full wool ewes wouldn't be that hard to pull down, but to bite through the wool would take a bit more effort.

Dave followed the tracks to where she'd been attacked; he could follow the trail of wool wisps on the sharp sticks of the bushes and across the spinifex. Drag marks and one set of dog prints, gouged deep in the mud, as the dog had run her around and around and around, until she'd tired and it had gone in for the kill.

Dave could see the dirt had been kicked out from under her legs where she'd tried to get up time and time again, while the wild dog had torn at her throat and her stomach.

He could see it all playing out in his head.

'Mongrel,' he said, getting the camera out of his backpack. He snapped some photos and then found his gun. Checking the chamber, he slid a bullet into it. 'Sorry, old girl, but I think this is best for you.'

He put the gun to her head and pulled the trigger. The ewe gave a couple more kicks as the bullet drove into her brain, and then stilled as the glaze of death fell over her eyes.

Turning back to the bike, he shut off the engine and listened. The burblers were singing loudly, flitting through the grey-coloured bush, and the small bush flies buzzed as the sun continued to rise.

The bike engine ticked as it cooled. There was nothing to indicate there was a dog close by. No howling, no puffing from exertion, no barking.

Dave went back to the ewe and bent down close. The blood on the wool was fresh, so that bastard wasn't far away. Even if the attack had happened a few hours before, the blood would have started to dry.

He cocked the gun again and did another sweep around, then got out his binoculars.

Nothing.

Putting the gun away, he went back to the bike. If he didn't keep going, he'd miss Brody at the watering point. He'd have some news for Brody and Bob when he got back.

There *was* a dog around.

⁓

The sun was beginning to sink as Dave, feeling weary from his day on the bike, brought the stragglers to the gate of the holding paddock. He was on the left flank, while Brody was on the right.

The station dogs ran from side to side, their tongues hanging out of their mouths, tired but never giving up.

Dave could see Booster was footsore, yet he still stood eye to eye with a ewe when she turned and tried to run from the mob. In every mob there was one, Dave knew. One that wouldn't conform.

This one had broken away many times and the collie had headed her off and turned her back in. A couple of times she'd stopped and stamped her foot at the dog. He'd done nothing but drop to the ground and stare at her, then slowly, slowly lifted himself to a crouch position and taken one step forward. Then another. And another, until the ewe and dog were inches from each other's noses.

Brody had yelled out, 'Get up her!' and he'd barked, turning the ewe around and forcing her back with her mates.

Dave grinned. The smell of lanoline, shit and fresh air washed over him. He felt a bit for Bob, who loved mustering just as much as he did. But Bob had phone calls to make and drugs to guard. And hopefully a lot more of the puzzle pieces to tell Dave about tonight.

Brody rode up next to Dave and whistled to his dog, who flew across the ground and onto the back of the bike. He switched off the engine. 'Good job,' he said. 'Much easier having another person to help.'

'They were good to get in, weren't they? And you, my friend,' he leaned over to stroke the collie's ears, 'are impressive to watch.'

'Yeah, he's good, isn't he? I trained him from a pup.'

'Well, you've done an excellent job with him. I've seen a lot of dogs work and there's not many like him.'

'Love the collies. Most people up here have kelpies. These guys with their long fur need to be shorn when the prickles come out, but they're just as good as kelpies. If not better. Oreo is Mum's dog and won't leave her side. Loyalty is another kelpie trait, but Booster has that in spades.'

'You reckon we got them all? Normally, what we'd do is put a plane up after this muster and see if there were any stragglers left behind,' Dave said. 'But that's a stock squad muster, not a shearing muster.'

'Do you want to run the gate over them now and give a count? My records say eight hundred and twenty-nine for here.'

'You're going to have eight hundred and twenty-eight,' Dave said. 'I found a ewe about five ks in, dead. Dog attack.'

'Dog attack?' Brody asked, his voice rising. 'You're kidding?'

'Nope. I've got photos.' He indicated his pack.

'Shit.' Brody seemed dazed at the thought. 'Okay, didn't expect that. Still, I guess Mick and Sandy have been talking about them, but I haven't seen any sign here at all.'

'You have now.' Dave kicked the stand down and got off, stretching his arms high above his head. 'But, yeah, let's run the gate over them now. I can count if you want to keep them bunched up so they don't get too far out back in the paddock.'

'Easy as.'

Dave walked over to swing one gate closed and the other the way the ewes were going to be running.

Brody gave two short, sharp whistles and threw his hand out in the direction of the back of the mob and Booster took off, stretching out like an athlete as he ran.

The ewes stopped and turned for the gate, then ran at it, fast.

Another whistle and the collie dropped to the ground, watching. Dave held his hand out and slowed them down as they ran, letting only four or five through at a time.

Out in the paddock, he could hear the chug, chug of the motorbike as Brody slowed them down and held them there until the last one had run through, then Dave switched the gates around and grabbed his bike to help push them back into the holding paddock.

The ewes made no noise, except for their hooves on the stones as they ran. Normally, with lambs on them, the sound would be deafening, each mother calling for her lamb, but without them, the girls moved in silence.

'Seven hundred and twenty-two,' Dave said, when Brody pulled up next to him.

'Shit. Down a few. What's that? Hundred and five. We work on a natural loss percentage of two to three per cent, which is about sixteen or seventeen sheep. That's too big a loss to be natural.'

'When you've done your water runs did you notice the tanks weren't emptying quite as quick? Or perhaps the area around the watering point wasn't being eaten out in the timeframe you would have expected?' Dave asked.

Brody scratched his head. 'I'd probably have to look in my diary, but I don't know if I would have even noticed.'

'Well, we've got something to look into here, without a doubt. When did you have these in last?'

'Weaning. And I double-counted them out.'

Dave wrote that down. 'Let's go and have a look at your records in the office.'

'I've got to check the camp first. Make sure everything is okay.'

'No problems, I'll follow you there.'

CHAPTER 30

Dave stopped the bike at the shed and turned it off, before stretching again. After a day like that he knew he'd be sore tomorrow; it had been a long time since he'd spent a whole day on a bike and he'd forgotten how much energy it took to bear the brunt of the rough ground and hold the bike steady.

As he'd come to discover more of Western Australia, travelling to stations in different areas, and camping out bush, he'd realised there was much more to the country than what could be seen from the long, straight bitumen highways.

He'd been surprised at the continual rockiness of the land. There were patches, but in the paddock he'd been in today, the ground was littered with stones the size of cricket balls, causing the bike to slide out from underneath him more than once. His jeans were ripped in a couple of spots and both his knees had come in contact with the ground and were grazed.

Wobbling his head from side to side to try to loosen the tight muscles, he gave a sigh, hoisted himself off the bike and grabbed his backpack.

Under the inky sky, the stars shone brightly, reminding him of the night he'd spent with Shannon on the beach. He imagined her skin under his hands again and felt himself harden. Oh, she was something special, he knew, but the surge of desire was quickly saturated by thoughts of his girls.

Bec would have loved seeing Booster work today. She would have pointed and asked to pat him. Then giggled wildly as the dog had stared down the ewe who was being difficult.

He noticed the lights were on at the homestead and the spotlight they'd rigged up earlier shone brightly on the coolroom. Even from where he was, he could see the chain still wrapped tightly around the handles. It didn't look like anything had changed.

Good.

Following the solar lights on the path, he went to his unit and unpacked his backpack, clipping his gun on his waist and tucking his notebook into his pocket. He needed a shower, but he was going to find Bob first and see what he'd found out during the day.

There were no prizes for guessing where Bob would be so he wandered towards the bar, past the communal campfire, which was burning brightly. He'd taken about five steps past it when he realised, even though the fire was shooting sparks and flames into the sky, there was no one sitting around it.

He stopped and took stock of where he was.

The generator hummed in the distance, but there wasn't any laughing or talking or noise. This type of silence was unnerving.

Dave backtracked a couple of steps and melted into the shadows of the buildings, trying to work out where everyone was. Doubling back, he checked Bob's unit, finding it empty. He knocked softly on a couple of caravan doors, but there were no answers.

Back at the troopy, he tried the door but it was locked and he didn't have a key. Shining his torch in to where the satellite phone usually sat, he saw nothing but an empty case. Dave wanted to yell and slam his fist into the side of the car, but he couldn't. He couldn't make a sound.

Where was Brody? Had he been caught up in this, too? More than likely, Dave surmised, because he'd gone straight to the camp kitchen . . .

'Fuck,' he whispered, his eyes swinging around, because then there was the issue of Shane Fletcher. Bob had filled him in on the name of the sixth young man the night before, after he'd come back from seeing Jane.

Where was he? Would he be watching Dave right now? He must be because the other blokes would have left a lookout, he was certain.

What about the camp kitchen? It was a contained room with one door in and out. Easy to herd all the campers in there.

What to do? He was the only one who was obviously on the right side of the law still free, if that was the correct word. And where were the rest of the campers? Bob? Jane?

Dave's eyes shot straight to the homestead. He should check on Jane and make sure she was okay.

Keeping in the shadows, he jogged towards the homestead and quietly crept up onto the verandah. Peeking in the windows, he saw Jane sitting at the table, reading a book with a cup of tea to the side. She looked as she always did—calm and peaceful.

Gently, so as not to startle her, he knocked on the door, his gun in his hand.

'Hello?' she called straightaway. 'Who's there?'

'Jane? It's Detective Dave Burrows.'

'Oh, how nice. Come in, Dave. Can I get you a drink?'

Letting himself inside, he quickly made his way to the kitchen before she could come out.

'Are you okay, Jane?' he asked quietly from the doorway.

Her eyes flicked to his gun and he saw her start. Then wrinkles lined her forehead and she put her hands on the wheels of her chair and moved towards him. 'Yes,' she answered, slowly. 'Why wouldn't I be? What's going on?' Her voice held a small shake of fear, the first he'd ever seen in her.

'Look, I'm not one hundred per cent sure what is going on here, but I think all the campers have been taken hostage, Bob included. There's no one around at the camp site. Not at the fire and no one answered when I knocked on a few of the caravans. Did Brody come here?'

Jane looked around, frantically. 'Well, I don't . . . I can't . . . Yes, I'm fine, I don't know what you're talking about.'

She took a deep shuddery breath. 'What are you saying, Dave?'

'When did you see Bob last?'

She looked around wildly. 'Um, maybe a couple of hours ago. He came to check the coolroom, then popped in here for a chat.'

'And have you seen anyone from the camp since then?'

'No, no, I haven't, but that's not unusual.' Her hands fluttered around her face. 'What are you telling me?'

'Brody, have you seen him?'

'He was with you!' Her voice was low and frightened. She looked around as if someone was going to come rushing into the kitchen.

'Jane, I need you to get on the phone and ring triple zero. You tell them we're going to need the tactical response team and as many coppers as they can send. Tell them they'll have to be choppered in and not to stuff around. We have an emergency here. Do you understand?' Dave hoped he spoke calmly enough not to scare her anymore.

Jane's hands found their way to the wheels of her chair and she nodded, finding a coolness in the face of an emergency.

'Yes. Tactical response team and other coppers. Emergency. I'll call now.'

'Good,' Dave said. 'When I leave, I want you to lock the doors and don't let anyone in—and, Jane, I mean anyone, Brody included. Not until either Bob or I come back.'

'What's Brody done?'

'I have no idea,' Dave answered honestly. 'Just lock the doors.'

'They don't lock.'

'Fuck, of course they don't.' Cursing country houses and the lack of security, he thought quickly. 'Have you got a room that is lockable?'

'Ah, I can't think . . . Um, yes, the toilet.'

'Get in there and stay there until either myself or another copper tells you it's okay to come out, okay? And ask them to send ambulances, too.' He stopped. 'I don't want to frighten you any more than you are, Jane, but you have to make sure you're safe, okay? We don't know the where-abouts of Shane Fletcher. If he's here on the station or not. He is an unknown, so please follow my instructions.'

'Jesus, Dave, what—'

'Do it!'

Jane nodded, and Dave let himself out then headed back to the camp kitchen.

Brody's collie, Booster, attached himself to Dave's leg and walked with him as Dave's unease grew. Brody was either involved or being held captive with the rest of the campers.

Taking a breath, Dave watched the lights in the camp kitchen for a minute, but there was no change—no calling out, no crying, no nothing.

Maybe they weren't there. Maybe they were somewhere else. Wishing he had back-up, he crept towards the kitchen window and flattened himself against the wall, inching along until he could peek through.

What he saw, made him draw in a breath.

The campers were huddled in a corner together, Rory standing over them with a rifle. The parents had their hands over the children's mouths so they didn't make a noise. Others were crying silently. Some of the men were just staring ahead, with terrified looks on their faces.

The other three young men were sitting on the kitchen table. Sam had a beer and Nick and Harry were both smoking cigarettes. Neither had guns.

And Brody, he was leaning against the wall, away from the other men, his arms crossed and eyes cast downwards at the floor.

Where was Bob? Dave's eyes swept the room, knowing there was no way that Bob would have let everyone be taken hostage without a fight. His heart beat faster when he realised he couldn't see Bob anywhere.

Nick got up from the table and came towards the window. Dave slid down and took a few calming breaths. Wherever Bob was, Dave knew he'd be okay because Bob always was! He was like Spencer, a wily old detective with loads of experience.

And Spencer's dead! Dave's brain screamed at him.

Blood rushed through Dave's head, blurring out any noise. He needed to find Bob, make sure he was okay. He had to be okay.

Forcing himself upright and telling himself to breathe slowly, he looked in the window again. Nick had moved away and the four men were in deep discussion.

'Where is he?' Nick asked.

Silence. Nick walked over to Brody and got in his face. 'Where is he, motherfucker?' His voice was low and angry.

'I. Don't. Know,' Brody answered, pushing himself off the wall and glaring at Nick.

'He should be here by now.'

'Dave'll come. Don't forget, he's a hero. He'll want to make another name for himself,' Harry spoke, and as he did, he slid a small pistol from behind his back. 'He'll come.'

Dave realised that they must have had other guns hidden elsewhere. He tried to think what the best way to handle this was. Did he wait for back-up, not knowing how long it would take, or did he try to talk them down? Back-up could be at least a couple of hours away. Did he have that long?

What he really wanted to do was find Bob.

As the four men moved apart, Dave caught a glimpse of a body lying on the floor. Bob.

'Fuck,' he whispered, his heart hammering in his chest.

From where he was, he couldn't tell if Bob was breathing, but there was a lady sitting next to him, holding a cloth to his head. It was stained red.

He took a step towards the doorway. Booster, who had been at his heels the whole time, whined and padded into the kitchen, obviously looking for Brody.

'What the—' A gunshot ricocheted around and there were loud screams and cries.

'Don't! That's my dog!'

Dave knew he had no choice.

Moving quickly, he flattened himself against the doorframe and peered into the room. Gun in his hand, he came around quickly and pointed it towards the men.

'Drop the weapon,' he yelled.

A woman from the campers screamed above the cacophony, 'Help us!'

The four men turned and Rory turned the rifle towards where Dave's voice had come from.

'Drop yours,' he snarled.

Dave took a breath. 'Put your weapon down,' he commanded.

'No one lives unless you do exactly that.'

Dave swallowed, but held steady. There were close to twenty people in that room, and their lives depended on him. Ellen's screams cut through his mind and he shook his head.

'Don't,' he muttered to himself. 'Breathe.'

'Come on, Burrows. All we want is the key to the coolroom and a ute. Nothing too difficult. Who's wearing the boots now?'

That was Harry.

Fucking little bastard.

'Couldn't get in?' he asked pleasantly.

'We just need the drugs. That's all. Everyone can go free once we're out of here.'

Suddenly, Dave launched himself further into the room, taking everyone by surprise. There was screaming and yelling, while Dave kept down and made a beeline for

Rory, hitting his knees and bringing him down. The rifle skittered across the floor and Dave launched himself after it, sweeping it up into his arms.

Harry tried for his gun but someone else bolted towards him and flattened him, taking his pistol.

The kids were crying and Dave had to hold his nerve. *Do not think about the girls*, he told himself.

Focusing, he glanced at the man who held Harry's gun and motioned for him to bring it to him. Taking it, he held the gun up, pointing it only at the four men. 'Don't move,' he said calmly, never taking his eyes off them as he walked backwards to Bob. 'You too, Brody. Over there with your mates.'

'Me?'

'Don't bloody argue,' Dave yelled. He waved the gun at Brody who put his hands up and gingerly covered the small distance to the other men.

Dave kept them covered with the gun and leaned down, feeling for his partner's pulse. 'Anyone here have any medical training?' he asked.

A woman put her hand up. 'I'm a nurse.'

'Can you help him, please. The rest of you, can—'

'Dave?'

His head swung around and he saw Jane in her wheelchair in the doorway with a .303 rifle across her lap.

'We're good, Jane. Just leave, please.'

'Oh no, oh, Brody. No!'

Dave followed her stare to where Brody was beside Rory and Harry.

'What have you done?' Jane screamed at him. 'Why are you with them?'

'Nothing!' Brody screamed back as he looked wildly around. 'I've done nothing!'

Jane's shaking hand covered her mouth.

'Stop!' Dave's voice roared over them all. 'Stop. Right, all of you, on the ground.' He glanced around. 'Someone give me a hand to cover them,' he said to the crowd.

No one, including the five men, moved.

'Get on the floor, you fucks,' Dave yelled, taking a step towards them and cocking the gun. 'That includes you, Brody.'

Brody and Nick dropped first, then Sam and Rory. Only Harry still stood.

Dave waved the gun.

Harry dropped, his head up in defiance, still staring at Dave.

Three of the campers came forward.

'Hold these,' Dave instructed them, passing them each a gun.

He took four cable ties from his pocket and, working quickly, fastened each one around the wrists of the men, leaving them unable to move freely.

'Oh, Dave,' Jane's wavering voice from across the room filtered through to him. 'What's going on?'

'Not now. Go back to the house. I need to get these fellas away from the campers. I'll bring them one by one to your house and lock them in the toilet.' He knew it would be large because the wheelchair would have to get in there. Large enough to fit four criminals.

'Brody . . .'

'Do as he says, Mum. I haven't done anything.'

Jane turned her chair and headed out into the night.

~

With the help of another man, Dave pulled Brody to his feet and walked him up the path and into the house. There wasn't any fight left in Brody, he let himself be pulled along to where Dave wanted to take him.

And that was the kitchen. Dave pushed him down into a chair then got out a few more cable ties and fastened his ankles to the chair.

'I don't know how or if you're involved in this, Brody, but you lied about knowing all these men. We know you went to school or played footy together, and I need to get to the bottom of that. I'll be back.'

It took half an hour to trudge the other four up the path and across the lawn to the house. Jane was sitting on the verandah with the gun across her lap, watching every move.

To Dave's knowledge she hadn't once looked or spoken to Brody since he'd placed him in the kitchen in the house.

Each time he was in the camp kitchen he looked over at Bob. And each time the nurse said there was no change.

No change was better than nothing, Dave supposed, feeling a trickle of fear for his friend.

Finally, he could be sure that all the campers were out of danger, with all four men locked in the toilet.

'What did triple zero say?' he spoke quietly to Jane.

'ASAP,' she answered.

'Can you ring again and get an ETA.'

She nodded. 'Where are you going?'

'To check on the campers and Bob. You okay?'

'Of course.'

Dave went back down to the camp kitchen, taking in the dazed and frightened faces that looked at him. 'You're all safe,' he said. 'I need you to go back to your caravans or campers and stay there. More police and some ambos are on their way. We'll get you all checked out and get these men off Corbett Station Stay.' He took a breath and strode over to where Bob was still lying on the floor. 'What's your verdict?' he asked the nurse.

'He's unconscious and he's had a serious head injury, so we need to get him to hospital to make sure there's no bleeding on the brain.'

Dave nodded. 'Can you keep looking after him, please?' Then he took a deep breath and headed back to the house.

Brody was still looking down at the floor when Dave pulled a chair out and sat opposite him. His gun was still in his hand, and with the other one he got out his notebook and pen.

'Now, we're going to have a decent conversation and you're going to tell me the truth. What the fuck is going on here?'

'Nothing,' Brody said. 'I haven't done—'

From behind him, Dave heard a gun cock and he stilled.

'Shut up, Brody.'

The voice came from behind him, and Dave turned and looked into the face of Jane.

'Jane,' Dave's voice cut across the room. 'Jane. Stop. Pass me the gun.'

A look Dave couldn't decipher crossed Jane's face and, as if in slow motion, she brought the gun up and aimed it at Dave.

'No. You stop.' Behind her appeared Rory and the other three men. They were unarmed, except for their arrogant smirks.

The room went still and Dave blinked. 'Jane.'

'Give me the gun, Dave.'

Keeping his eyes on her, he squatted down and put his pistol on the ground, before holding his hands up.

'Good. Now over there against the wall.'

Shuffling backwards, Dave followed her instructions, his heart beating fast and his eyes looking for an escape.

There was none as the four men moved towards him.

'Jane, what's going on? The tactical response team is coming! What's going on here?'

'You think I really called them?' She gave a bark of laughter. 'As if. One thing you need to know about me is I always deal with any problems that arise myself. And here we are. You're a problem and I'm going to deal with you.'

Jane wheeled herself over to where Dave leaned against the wall.

'You blokes fucked everything up,' Jane said, staring at Dave. 'Turning up here on the off-chance we had some stolen sheep or we'd had some stolen. You had no idea what you were walking into.'

'Why?' Dave asked.

'Ha! You reckon it's cheap looking after someone in my position? You think it's easy? How would we ever have afforded the pool if I hadn't organised something like this? Huh? No way I was selling the investment proper-ties—they're my superannuation. No, I had to think of another idea.'

'You?'

'Well, of course. You don't think Brody could have organised it, do you? He couldn't organise himself to breathe in an iron lung.'

Dave's eyes slid across to Brody whose face had flushed red.

Tethered to the chair, the young man sat up. 'What the hell have I been doing for you these last few years? I've got you everything you've wanted.' Tears sprung to his eyes. 'You've never understood, Mum. I hate this joint, always have. If you hadn't insisted—'

'Enough,' Jane barked. 'Enough from you.'

'So, you did all of this—organised the drugs, the murders—just so you could get money to keep living here?' Dave asked, incredulous. 'How—'

'Oh no, you're not going to pin those murders on me. I know nothing about that. But these blokes do. I think you'll also find they know something about your mystery man, Shane Fletcher.' She swung the gun towards the four friends. 'You lot can get over there with the detective, thanks, boys.'

The smirks that had been on their faces suddenly fell away. None of them were armed so they didn't have a choice.

A wild look came into Jane's eyes. 'Have you got any idea what it's like to have your independence taken away? To have people looking over your shoulder the whole time? Belle is a classic for that. *You shouldn't be doing that, have you done your exercises? Don't go outside, Mum, you'll get hurt.*' She shook her head. 'One good thing about Brody is he knew not to offer to help me too much.

'But this . . .' Her eyes gleamed. 'The secrecy, the organ-ising, the fact I was making money for the station, keeping everything afloat, *from my chair.*'

'What?' Brody croaked.

Dave kept looking for a way to get out, but there was no way he could see. He was trapped deep inside the kitchen, with a table and a woman with a gun in his way. If more coppers weren't coming, he needed another plan.

'You don't really think that camping ground made enough money to keep our heads above water, do you? I know you don't understand figures much, Brodes, but really? Of course it's doing well and helping to contribute, but it's me who's done this. I've kept this place going the whole time I've been in this mongrel chair. Harry had the contacts. Such a great help when I rang. Needed a place they could use as a depot. And I was happy with that. Until bodies started to show up. Not a good look for our other business, was it?' Jane waved the gun around again.

'But I said that Rory could come to the station with no questions asked. I never knew what he was doing. I never asked,' Brody said. 'He paid me not to.'

'Yeah, that's right,' Rory said. 'Your mum's organised everything else.'

'Rory, shut your mouth,' Jane commanded. 'Now, where is the key for the coolroom?' she asked. 'Like the boys said, that's all we need. No one will get hurt if—'

Without warning, Brody launched himself at Jane with a scream. How he got the ties undone, Dave didn't know, but he was grateful.

Brody fell just short of her chair and tried to crawl across the floor to her feet.

Jane didn't move, only continued to hold the gun steady, aimed at her son. 'Please don't do that, Brody. I don't want to have to hurt you.'

Her calmness unsettled Dave.

'Can't you see you already have?' Brody cried.

From outside there was a noise, something Dave couldn't understand.

'Police! Freeze! No one move!'

Jane swung the gun around. 'What?' the surprise on her face cut through her poise and for a split-second Dave thought he could reach her.

'Oh no, you don't,' Jane said. This time she clicked the safety off and put the gun to her shoulder. 'Stay where you are!'

'Put the gun down,' screamed the cop at the door.

Dave inched his way towards her, hoping she wouldn't turn around, as heavily armed police officers stormed through.

Jane took aim and a loud crack reverberated around the kitchen, deafening Dave, who had managed to kick the wheelchair over as the gun had gone off. Before he'd lost his hearing, he'd heard the thud of the bullet embedding itself in the wall.

The room was in chaos, but Dave couldn't hear a word. He saw a police officer taking the gun from Jane and pulling her hands behind her back. Another cop was hand-cuffing the men, and Brody was still curled up on the floor sobbing.

There should have been so much noise, yelling.

The scene played out in front of Dave's eyes in silence, bar the ringing in his ears.

Out of the corner of his eye, Dave saw Hannah and Kelsey, ashen-faced, and suddenly he understood how help had arrived so quickly.

EPILOGUE

Dave looked into the hospital room and knocked gently when he realised Bob was awake.

He was carrying a bunch of flowers, but they were only a cover for the few nips of whiskey he'd smuggled in.

'Ah, you're a sight for sore eyes,' Bob said groggily. 'How're you going?'

'More to the point, how are you?' Dave asked, putting the flowers next to the bed. 'Sorry, I know they're not your colour, but they'll have to do.'

Bob grinned and gave a wink. 'They're lovely.'

Pulling up a chair, Dave sat down and looked at his partner. 'So?' he prompted.

'What, son? Don't act like I'm dead. I'm fine, just a bit beaten up.'

'What are the doctors saying?'

'Gah, I don't care what they're saying. Tell me what you found out at DoubleM Station? Where's the investigation got to?' Bob fell back into the pillow as if he were exhausted.

Knowing there was no point in not answering the questions, no matter how crook Bob was, Dave crossed his legs, leaned back in the chair and said, 'Well, Lorri came up to give me a hand when they put you out of action.'

'Ah, good. Get her out of the city a bit. How'd she go?'

'She solved it, Bob. I didn't.' Dave nodded, feeling the embarrassment wash over him again.

Bob pushed himself up in the bed and stared hard at Dave. 'What do you mean?'

'We searched those properties high and low and, yes, there were sheep missing. From three adjoining places. I put out all the usual alerts and talked to the guys from the abattoirs and so on and so forth.' Dave rubbed his hands together, nervously.

'And? Come on, spit it out, son.'

'Lorri took a bike out on the crown land that borders all three properties. There's ten eighty bushes out there.'

'There's what?'

Dave nodded. 'I'm serious. There's ten eighty poison out there. And carcasses galore. All hidden because of the bush.'

Dave could see Bob could barely believe it; he still couldn't believe it himself. He thought about what he knew of ten eighty poison. *A bush that's poisonous to sheep, cattle and rabbits if they ate it. Native animals weren't bothered by it, or at least they knew not to eat it.*

'Prolifically growing out there in the crown land,' he continued. 'I've seen it before, but not like this. And what's even more interesting is the secondary poisoning.'

Bob did a double take. 'Dogs?'

'Yeah, the few dogs I saw were dead, because they've eaten the sheep that have been poisoned. The meat has been contaminated and they've got a dose through what they've eaten.'

'Well, I'll be buggered,' Bob said, leaning back into his pillows. 'Never heard of that before. I knew about there being a bush that naturally produces the poison but never had a case where that was the crim! Fucking weird, that!' He gave a laugh and his monitor started to beep.

A nurse came rushing in. 'What are you doing working yourself up, Bob Holden?' she scolded.

Bob grabbed her hand. 'Betty, meet Dave. He's my partner.'

'Oh, you're Dave,' Betty said, extracting her hand from Bob's large ones and holding hers out. 'I'm Bob's nurse, Betty.'

Bob put his hand on her arm. 'Hoping she'll be more than that when I come out,' he said. He winked at Dave. 'She's got very soft hands.'

'Jesus, Bob!' Dave said, but Betty laughed.

'Such a wicked one, this one.' She turned back and gave Bob the evil eye. 'Behave yourself or I'll have to ask Dave to leave.'

'Sorry, love,' Bob said with a grin.

Dave noticed he didn't take his eyes off her as she left the room. 'What's going on there?' he asked.

Giving a little shrug, Bob grinned again. 'Don't know, but it's nice for the moment. Have you spoken to Shannon?'

'Yeah. Yeah, I have. The body we found on the beach? He was the one of the six we were missing. Shane Fletcher. Went to school with Sam, Nick and Harry.'

Bob's eyebrows hit his hairline. 'Shane Fletcher? They got rid of one of their own? Still,' he sounded resigned when he spoke next, 'that's what the bikies and drug dealers do. I thought it was him on the phone.'

'No, that was someone completely unrelated. Remember Jim? The angry guy? After asking around a bit, he came forward and said he'd been talking to a completely different person. Read into that what you will.' Dave cocked his eyebrows. 'Anyway, Rory rolled on them all. Told how Jane had got in contact with Harry. Brody had let it slip one night that Harry was mixed up with importing drugs. Jane made the call and offered up Corbett Station Stay as a depot, like she said on the night it all went down.

'Brody didn't know to begin with, and he certainly didn't agree with it. He'd worked hard to make enough money to keep everyone afloat just with the station stay.

'Rory said they gave Shane a blast of heroin and tossed him off the boat when he'd insisted they didn't kill the girl we dug up. Shannon told me what she suspected. Dealers nabbed her from the street and used her in a—' he swallowed '—very undesirable way. When they were moored on the beach, Shane tried really hard to save her life, but he lost his own in the process.'

'Unbelievable.' Bob shifted in his bed. 'And the girl?'

'Major crime have taken over that investigation. They put in a request for DNA samples that they've traced through to Java, but they don't hold out too much hope of finding her family. I reckon she'll end up in a pauper's grave in Karrakatta Cemetery pretty soon.'

'See, son, this is what I was talking about when we started this case. We get rid of one and someone else comes along to take their place. What a thankless bloody job we do.'

'But that's not right, Bob. We make a difference to all the people we help. Brody is going to be able to go and study to be a teacher, just like he wanted, because we solved that crime.

'Jane will be in jail, but Brody'll be free. And all those other buggers, the court will throw the book at them.

'Corbett Station Stay, as a pastoral lease, will be up for grabs in the next few months. Mick is going to have a crack at taking it on, but the government will have to approve him, of course. Be interesting to see if he keeps the camping grounds open or not.'

Bob snorted. 'I suspect he won't.' He looked down at the bed sheets and traced the red stamp on the corner. 'I liked Jane. She never entered my mind as the mastermind. I don't usually read people so wrong. I must be losing my touch.'

'We all read her wrong,' Dave said. 'Geez, talk about being shocked when I heard her cock the gun behind my ear. Not something I want to hear again.' He gave a sigh. 'I guess I've buggered up my chance of proving to Mel that I'm not a danger to the kids, huh?'

'What do you mean?'

Dave shrugged. 'Guns and gunfights seems to be where I hang out.' He looked down. 'The girls are better off without me, I think.'

Bob reached out and grabbed Dave's hand. 'Any regrets?' he asked, looking his partner straight in the eye.

This time Dave could answer without hesitation. 'No. No regrets.'

ACKNOWLEDGEMENTS

Firstly, I'd like to point out I have taken some liberties with the dog fence part of this story. In 2002, when the book was set, there wasn't a dog fence. However, funding has been received to construct a 362 kilometre fence to protect 800,000 hectares in the West Gascoyne region.

I'm often asked what it takes to write a book. After finishing *Rising Dust*, I reflected on the question, while sitting on the patio with a wine, screaming, 'Thank god that's done!'

So, I compiled a list:

- A workable laptop. Not one that dies with the only copy of your manuscript on it, two weeks out from deadline.
- A godson who doubles as a tech guru and saves you on that horrible Sunday afternoon and gets your manuscript back. (Bloody good thing that happened because I was on my way to Lucky Bay Brewing to drown my

sorrows and work out what the hell I was going to tell my publisher, when he talked me through how to get the computer working again, not once, but TWICE!) Alex, I think you worked out how grateful I was when I burst into tears after you finally found the edits saved in the temporary file. I owe you big time.

- An unexpected new laptop, worth a small fortune, when you don't trust your old laptop.

- Six bottles of gas. They kept me warm while I sat under my gas heater on the patio, during wind, rain and sun.

- Two dogs. One inside and one outside (they don't get along).

- Numerous bottles of wine. I'm not telling how many.

- Several cups of coffee. If you're ever in Esperance the place to go is Downtown Espresso Bar. My daughter works there and leaves me all sorts of funny messages on my coffee cups. Usually, rude ones but she won't do that to you. And it's the best coffee.

- Text messages from my closest friend. *Is your arse on the chair in front of the computer? Have you typed 'the end' yet? We've got a pinky promise . . .*

- Two angels watching from above: Sarah, my previous editor, and Amy, my previous publicist. They were in the forefront of my mind when I finished and I wished I could tell them. The next morning, I walked out and saw a beautiful rainbow. I'm sure they sent it.

- And lastly, an understanding publisher who offers me a two-week extension on my deadline when, really, she wants to throw something at me for being late, yet again. Many thanks, Annette.

Now, of course there are the usual suspects . . . DB for starts. I've said before, this would be a lot harder without you. Thank you for not only being my go-to informant but also my mate.

Gaby from the Left Bank Literary. Agent and friend.

Annette, Tom, Christa, Sarah, Matt, Andrew and all others from Allen & Unwin who work on any aspect of these books. Deonie Fiford for the edit—thanks for leaving me little messages all over the manuscript and making me laugh.

Rochelle and Hayden. (Hey, Rochelle, you've moved out now. Are you missing the manic me?)

Again, love to all this crew: Cal and Aaron, Heather, Kelly, Lee and Paul, Robyn, Jan and Pete, Lauren and Graham, Kay, Donna and Mike, Chrissy, Shelley and Dave, Lachie, Bev.

The Parnell and Heaslip families.

To all you readers, gift givers, librarians and booksellers, it's a privilege to be able to entertain you in these times when a break from the real world is so important. Thank you for choosing this book among all the other wonderful stories out there. Your support is appreciated and loved by this little writer.

With love,
Fleur x

COMING IN APRIL 2023

Into the Night

FLEUR McDONALD

A fire, a missing man and his dog send Dave and his partner Bob Holden south of Perth, to investigate. Leo Perry has been missing for two days when they realise he's probably not dead. In fact he's more likely to have left his life in exchange for a new one. But why?

They find CCTV footage showing them that Leo is alive, only two days earlier, but then disaster strikes. A phone call from the Meekatharra Police station changes everything that Dave and Bob already know about the case.

'Fleur McDonald is a master of the rural suspense novel, her characters and storyline crackle with authenticity.' *Family Circle*

ISBN 978 1 76106 647 4

PROLOGUE

2002

'Why do you have to be so bloody difficult?' Leo's hands shook as he tried to start the engine of the water pump. Pull out, yank, flick back in. It wound over once but didn't fire.

'Come on, you mongrel of a thing.'

This time the compression was built up inside the engine and the cord was tight. The starting rope was yanked from his hands as he pulled and the wooden handle rapped him on the knuckles as it flew back inside the guard.

Leo wanted to swear, but instead, he stood up, wiped his brow and looked outside.

The pumphouse was set on the edge of a creek. White-painted corrugated iron for the sides and green for the roof, all dirty and peeling. A mirage shimmered across the hilly landscape, golden grass bent over in the heat, the air hot and oppressive, but still. Eerily still.

To the north, there was the normal build-up of huge white thunder clouds, accompanied by crickets chirping in anticipation of a cooler night.

Leo scoffed at the insects' hopefulness. The temperature hadn't dipped below twenty-five degrees at night in nearly two weeks and there was no reason why it would today.

Coffee, his kelpie, was laid out flat on the back of the ute, puffing under the sun. Coffee in colour, coffee in nature. Calming and enjoyable. When Leo let her off the chain in the morning, her large welcoming grin—the sort where her tongue lolled out the side of her mouth—always made the start of his day a good one.

The power was out for the third time this week. The energy company was all talk and no action! They promised to upgrade the lines, to stop pole-top fires by putting in underground cabling or perhaps generators on every farm. But as yet, zilch. Nothing ever seemed to change—the summer outages just kept on keeping on.

Leo's family farm was on the end of a spur line, sixty kilometres from Yorkenup township. There were many days the electricity seemed to forget to run down those wires to spark up his house and sheds, as well as everything else that needed power to work.

On those days, the electric pump was as useless as tits on a bull. No power, no pump, and then the tanks that watered his sheep wouldn't keep filling.

Now, here he was, trying to make sure his stock had the essentials on a day that was forecast to reach thirty-five degrees.

Sighing, Leo thought about the brochures lying on the office desk. A solar pump would solve a lot of problems; the main one being he couldn't leave the farm for a moment during summer. If he wasn't checking the tanks, he was inspecting the troughs or flicking a light switch inside the house to make sure the electricity was still on.

Still, a solar pump was modern, and his father would have to approve the purchase, as he did with any decision Leo tried to make on the farm.

Grunting against the hushed landscape again, he saw himself on an endless treadmill of frustration and sheer hard work. There didn't seem to be any places where he could get off and take a breath.

Just a short while ago, Jill had snapped out that well-worn argument again.

'It's Saturday,' she told him, as if he had no idea of what day it was. 'Are you coming to tennis?'

The children's backpacks were on the bench, filled with toys, snacks and all the other paraphernalia young kids seemed to need.

Charlotte, the older of the two, ran into the kitchen tugging on her mother's short tennis skirt. 'Time to go?' she asked.

Jill put her hand on Charlotte's head and shushed her. Her eyes flicked over to Noah and back to Leo.

Noah was sitting on the carpet, staring bug-eyed at the TV, a piece of toast in his mouth.

'Carmel and Bruce are going to be there.' As she spoke, the lights flickered, before dying. His wife's mouth had formed a thin line. 'Guess that answers that question, doesn't it?'

'I don't do this on purpose,' Leo retorted.

'Sometimes I wonder.' Jill had grabbed her tennis bag and taken Charlotte's hand.

Leo had found his hat, jammed it on his head and stalked out of the house without saying goodbye.

With a heavy sigh, he had stared at the back of the LandCruiser wagon disappearing into town, his family on board, until it wasn't there anymore.

Leo took the fuel cap off the pump and checked inside the tank. Close enough to empty. Well, that would be why it wouldn't start.

Idiot, he thought. *Who forgets to put fuel in the tank? You've got too much on your mind.*

A sigh and a short walk to the back of the ute, where there were three plastic containers filled with petrol. Leo knew how dangerous it was to carry a flammable liquid, especially when one of the containers leaked a little from the plastic join. But other than putting a fuel tank next to the pumphouse, there was no other way of getting petrol to the water pump. His father wouldn't approve such luxuries.

'Take care of the pennies and the pounds will take care of themselves,' his dad always said.

Leo grunted again, his fist curled tight around the handle of the jerry can, the other resting on Coffee's head for a fleeting moment.

Within minutes the pump was full of petrol, and he pulled a rag out of his back pocket, swiping at the spill on the motor. He could see the vapour shimmering in the air as he did.

This time when he yanked the starter cord the engine kicked over. It almost died away but then chugged back to life. By the time it had hit full revs, the loud rumble reverberated around the shed, pushing out petrol fumes.

Leo heard the whoosh and gurgle of water through the pipe and reached out to touch it. The poly was cold and pulsing under his hand; there was water.

Good.

He turned back to the engine and frowned, not understanding what he was seeing. Blue and orange flames, licking around the fuel tank.

Leo stood transfixed for far too long, then sprinted to his ute and his firefighting gear, pulling out his phone as he ran. He had to let someone know. Call for help!

Seeing that there was a line of flames following him outside sent shockwaves rolling over his body. The leaking jerry can that had been on the tray of the ute had left behind a trail of petrol and now the flames were skipping along the line and leaping back towards him. While the fire-fighting tank, full of water, was pushed up against the back window of the ute. Leo flicked the switch on, before starting the pump and dragging the thick hose back to the shed.

'Come on, come on, answer,' he muttered into the phone, while with his other hand he took aim at the flames, which had doubled in size in the matter of minutes. 'John? Fire, my place. Pump shed on the creek!' he yelled into the phone as the fire captain finally answered.

He didn't have time to hear what John said, before a loud whoomph and then a shattering explosion came from the shed.

The jerry can! He'd left it half full inside.

Leo was thrown backwards, screaming at Coffee to 'Come behind!' The dog had jumped from the tray and was running at full tilt down towards the creek.

The roar almost deafened Leo and he threw his arm up in a futile attempt to block the heat that was thrown his way.

Heavy, hot air landed on his body and his skin seemed to shrivel and shrink, even though the flames didn't touch him. It was as if all the moisture inside him had been sucked out. He smelt his own singed hair and he looked around again for Coffee, only to see flames quivering as they wrapped around the wooden beams and threw sparks into the dry grass. Spot fires flared, small at first, then galloping across the grass to meet as one, the ute in their path.

'No!' Leo scrambled back, watching in horror. He upended the hose over his head and let the water cascade over him.

Suddenly, Coffee was next to him, teeth nipping at his shirt. Leo pushed her away, trying to get to his feet.

Another explosion as the blaze found the second jerry can. More flames, touching the sky, the surrounding area a matt of orange, blue and white flames, black burning grass and fierce heat.

So big and hot now, the fire was creating its own wind, jumping across the paddock with a mind of its own.

Coffee: more pulling at his shorts and shirt, and this time Leo stood up and ran, his dog at his heels.

CHAPTER 1

'I've organised for you to see Bec and Alice at a secure location,' Dave's lawyer, Grace, told him. 'The other party are requesting you take precautions to ensure that you aren't followed.'

'You're kidding?' Dave stood and started to pace the yard of the stock squad headquarters. He had been sitting astride his motorbike, ready to ride it onto the trailer when his phone had rung. Grace's name had caused a chain reaction of guilt, regret, sadness, resentment and anger, all in the same measure. 'Do I get to see my kids by myself, or do I have to be supervised?'

'Supervised.' The regret in Grace's voice was surprising. Dave was the emotional one when it came to his kids, while Grace usually kept a professional coolness, despite knowing her client was getting shafted.

Now, with one hand in his pocket and a scowl on his face, irritation was winning out. 'Guess Mark has got something to do with that?'

'I would imagine,' Grace said. 'There will be a car picking you up at one to drive you. The other party do not want you to know where the meeting place in advance, in case your phone is bugged, okay? Any part of this you're not clear on?'

'I'm good.'

'Okay, let me know how it goes. Neither Melinda nor Mark should be present. If one of them is, leave straightaway. Even if you haven't seen the girls. You are not to speak nor get into an argument with either of them.'

'Got it.'

'The car will take you back to the stock squad office once you've finished. Talk to you later.'

The phone went dead.

This was Dave's third pass around the yard; he halted near the door into the shed, then started to walk again, almost before he'd stopped. The bubbling in his stomach made him want to move or jiggle in one spot or knock someone out. Mark preferably.

He should've been feeling excitement at the thought of seeing his girls in an hour's time, but instead he was edgy and annoyed. His former father-in-law always did this just before a visit: changed the rules, caught Dave off-guard. And he was always able to get away with it.

Apparently, the courts didn't like fathers who might be a risk to their children, even if said father is a cop. Mark had played that card throughout the whole custody proceeding, finally wining sole custody for Melinda, Dave's ex-wife. The woman who had wanted him to give up his career because it put those he loved and who loved him in danger.

Jamming his phone back into his shirt pocket, he threw a leg over the motorbike and turned the key. High-pitched revs sounded longer and louder than they needed to be as he drove up the ramp and onto the trailer. All the bikes had just been serviced, and Dave was repacking the trailer for whenever he and his partner, Detective Bob Holden, were called out for their next case.

Detective Sergeant Spencer Brown, Dave's previous partner in Barrabine, had always said: prior preparation prevents piss-poor performance.

After his phone call with Grace, Dave would have preferred to take the bike out onto some bush track, where it was just him and the wind, and let her rip so he could remember what freedom tasted like. Not this boxed-up, being-told-what-to-do-and-when feeling.

If you want to see your children, you *will* do as I say.

If you want to see your children, you *will* conform.

If you want to see your children, you *will* roll over and kiss my arse. Every time.

Fuck off.

Dave imagined Mark's smug face so close to his own that he could reach out and hit him with a closed fist. What pleasure that would bring!

Dave had done it once. Way back when he and Melinda lived in Barrabine, at his first posting as a detective. Mark had taunted him one too many times, and although Dave would never say that punching someone was a good idea, when his fist collided with Mark's chin, he'd known it had been the best idea he'd had that particular day.

Flicking down the motorbike's stand, Dave took the rough rope and quickly tied it to the rail of the trailer and tossed it over the seat, walking around to repeat the process, making sure the bike was bolted down safe.

The swag, tuckerbox and camp kitchen were already packed in the trailer, so Dave secured them as well, then walked around, checking nothing could fall off.

'Dave! Hurry!' Lorri, another detective, stood at the top of the office stairs and motioned to him urgently. 'Come here. Quick!' Then she disappeared back inside.

Dave raised his eyebrows, then, with one final wobble of the rope over the bike, he jogged up the steps and into the station.

'What's up?' he asked to no one in particular. Lorri's office was empty.

'Quick, Dave! Get the defib machine!' Lorri shouted from further inside.

Dave's head snapped around to the sound of her voice. Lorri was bent over a man on the floor in Bob's office. His legs were protruding from the side of the desk and Dave couldn't see his face, only his shoes.

'Call the ambos then get in here and help me.'

For a moment too long, Dave was frozen while Lorri's ponytail swung in time to the compressions she was counting out.

'Twenty, twenty-one, twenty-two . . .'

'Shit!' Dave ran back to the entrance and snatched the defib machine off the front wall. Moments later, he was inside's Bob's office assessing the collapsed man, while talking into his phone.

'Police, fire or ambulance?'

'Ambulance.' The word came out of him like a bullet, as he opened the cover of the defib machine and pressed the 'on' button, listening to the voice prompts take him through what he had to do.

Lorri was breathing into the man's mouth now.

'Need to undo the shirt,' Dave told her.

With her fingers on the man's wrist, Lorri searched for a pulse. Her face held the trained professionalism of a copper, but her breathing was staccato-like, her hands shaking.

Dave knelt now, grabbing either side of the man's shirt and giving one quick tug. Buttons skittered across the floor.

'Got a pulse,' gasped Lorri. She sagged slightly, her adrenalin released.

Dave heard the sirens wailing in the background.

The man groaned, then gave a hacking cough, before his eyes flicked open and his mouth formed an 'o'.

'Don't talk,' Dave instructed him. 'Stay still.'

Lorri kept her fingertips on his pulse and her eyes on her watch as Dave gave the man's leg a firm pat and went out to meet the ambulance crew.

'She got him back,' he said to the first paramedic who was jogging up the steps, gloves on and bag in hand.

The red-haired man nodded and kept going, while his partner, a small thin woman, also wearing gloves, ran up and followed him in.

Dave put his hands to his knees and took some deep breaths, listening to Lorri fill in the ambos.

For a stupid moment, when he'd seen the legs on the floor, he'd thought the man had been Bob, even though he knew his partner was away on holidays until tomorrow. His heart had doubled its rate in a split second. Surely, he wasn't going to lose another partner so soon after Spencer?

Instead, the man on the office floor was Parksey. Detective Senior Sergeant Parks, Lorri's partner. Another integral member of the stock squad. Dave knew he should still be upset, but all he felt was relief that it wasn't Bob.

He took a few shaky breaths and looked at the sky. Everything was the same as it had been half an hour before Parksey collapsed. But it didn't feel as if it should be. Something monumental should be happening outside to show that Parksey had nearly died. If Lorri hadn't got him back, a family's world would have been turned upside down. Dave swallowed hard and went back inside.

The ambos had now fixed the oxygen mask over Parksey's nose and mouth and were about to carry him down the steps on the stretcher.

Lorri was on the phone. 'What hospital?' she asked, holding the phone away from her ear. 'His wife wants to meet him there.'

The ginger-haired paramedic named the closest one, fifteen minutes away.

'What's the go?' Dave asked the female paramedic quietly.

'See what the doc says when he has all the scans, but you guys did good. He was in the right place, could have been much worse.'

Dave nodded. If Lorri hadn't been there when Parksey had collapsed, maybe he would have had to call the funeral directors rather than the ambulance service.

He walked to the head of the stretcher and leaned down to talk to his colleague. 'Mate, if we'd known you were going to lie down on the job, we wouldn't have given you the job as boss while Bob was away!'

From under the mask, Parksey gave a weak smile and held his hand out. Dave gripped it, gave a small shake then let him go. 'Be in to see you soon,' he said.

Back in the office, Lorri collapsed into a chair, her hand over her mouth.

Dave put his hand on her shoulder. 'He was lucky you were here,' he said.

Lorri didn't answer. Her face was pale and covered in beads of sweat that she brushed away unconsciously. 'God,' slipped out in a whisper.

Dave squatted down and looked her in the face. 'You were great. Did exactly as you were supposed to do.'

'This is Parksey,' Lorri gulped out. 'He's fit and skinny. What the hell?'

'The doc will be able to tell us more. I'm not going to promise everything will be okay, because we don't know. But he's going to the right place now and that was because you were here and knew what to do.' Dave stood up, patting her knee this time. 'Tell you what, why don't I lock up and you head over to the hospital. There's no point in you being here. Are you okay to drive or do you want me to call you a cab?'

He went to the water cooler and poured her a glass, then handed it to her.

'I . . . ah . . .' Lorri looked around as if she were seeing the office for the first time. She took a sip. 'Ah, no, I'm fine. Thanks. I'll head over there now.' She didn't move, just kept staring at the ground.

Dave pulled out his phone again and dialled, ordering her a taxi.

'No, no, it's okay,' she told him, as his words filtered through to her, but he held up his hand until he'd finished.

'You've had a huge shock,' he said. 'And we can't afford for you to have an accident on the way to the hospital, then we'd have two of you out of action.' He knew his tone was gruff but there was a bit of a lump in his throat, so taking a practical approach was better. Lorri would probably be fine driving the short way down the highway from the hills of Perth, where the headquarters of the stock squad spread out over ten hectares, but he couldn't risk her or any of the public being injured. The hospital was on the outskirts of Perth and it was peak hour. 'I'd take you but I'm going to see my kids . . .' He glanced at his watch.

The whole medical emergency had taken less than three quarters of an hour. The car Grace had organised would be there to pick him up in about twenty minutes.

Lorri stood up and went to her desk, searching for something. She tore a piece of paper from her notebook. Reaching under the desk, she grabbed her handbag. 'This came through this morning, from Arson. Parksey and I were going to . . .' Her voice trailed off, then she shook the paper at him. 'There was a fire about an hour and a half out of Perth, heading east. Near Yorkenup. The house and some sheds, plus about fifteen hundred hectares of land destroyed. Started by a petrol pump, but they don't think the fire was deliberately lit. More that Leo Perry, the owner, spilt the fuel when he was filling up the tank.' Her voice became steadier as she talked—work was a safe topic right now.

Dave took the page and started to read. 'But . . . ?'

'But they can't find the manager or his dog. Perry called the blaze in. Spoke to the fire control officer and requested help, and that's the last time anyone has spoken to him. There wasn't a body in the burnt-out wreckage of the ute, which was found near the pumphouse, nothing near or in the house or other sheds.' Lorri went back into Bob's office and came out with another file. 'SES are still searching. The area has been advised as safe in the last few hours.

'Locals have done a preliminary interview with the wife. Everything was fine between them, no money troubles, couple of young kids. No action on any of the bank accounts, phone, et cetera. I'm sorry, Dave, but there's a bit of urgency to get out there and find this bloke.'

'Right.' He flipped through the pages, only giving them a cursory glance.

In ten minutes he was due to leave to see his kids, and he needed to let Bob know what was going on.

'He was a manager for his own family farm,' Lorri said as she put her hand on the door. 'It's a weird set-up and Arson is recommending we take over from the locals.'

'Sure. You were headed up there today?'

There was a slight pause before she nodded. All the plans they'd made were now in disarray.

'Leave it with Bob and me, we'll sort it.' He tapped the file to his forehead in a salute.

A horn blasted from outside.

'That'll be you,' Dave said. 'Go on. Ring me if you need anything.'

Lorri nodded and turned to go. 'Thanks,' she said softly.